THE TICKET

KAREN SCHUTTE

THE
TICKET

LANGDON STREET PRESS
MINNEAPOLIS, MN

Langdon Street Press
212 3rd Avenue North, Suite 290
Minneapolis, MN 55401
612.455.2293
www.langdonstreetpress.com

ISBN - 978-1-936183-73-9
ISBN - 1-936183-73-0
LCCN - 2010933628

Cover Design by Jenni Wheeler
Typeset by Melanie Shellito

Printed in the United States of America

TABLE OF CONTENTS

PREFACE

★ ★ ★ ★ ★

In the early part of the eighteenth century, Maria Theresa, empress of Austria/Hungary, offered prime farmland along the Danube, near Belgrade, Yugoslavia, to destitute and war-ravaged German tenant farmers. Many "Danube Swabian" Germans left the Swabian valley and Black Forest area near Frankfurt, Germany. Known to be frugal, enterprising, and devout, they took with them their Lutheran religion and appreciation of classical music.

As custom in Germany and most of Europe, tradition and overcrowding dictated that only the first son inherited the family farm or business. The remaining male siblings were thrust into a life of servitude. There was endless economic depression and constant threat of war. When war was declared, men were forced to leave home to fight, perhaps in a war that either made no difference to them or that they did not believe in.

In Yugoslavia there were frequent bloody raids by cruel Slovak armies, which left German farms burning, the women raped, and men slaughtered. The whole of these circumstances, coupled with Karl Kessels' enduring dream of owning his own farm, drove him to make a life-altering decision when the moment presented itself. This is Karl and Katja's story. I know of it because their son Jakob was my grandfather.

Various names, dates, and events have been changed to protect the privacy of those involved.

CHAPTER 1

Decisions, 1906

★ ★ ★ ★ ★

"Tell me not in mournful numbers, Life is but an empty dream! For the soul is dead that slumbers, and things are not what they seem."
~A Psalm of Life, Henry W. Longfellow

A lone passenger stood at the rail, watching intently as a ragged, middle-aged woman savagely pushed her way through the crowd of anxious passengers. Reaching a disheveled young man waiting to board the S.S. Main, she desperately grabbed and pulled at his threadbare coat. Tears flowed freely from her swollen eyes, screaming and pleading with him not to go, not to leave on the ship. Shouting with vehement irritation, he roughly pushed her backward, away from him and his future.

Herr Kessels face was stoic, showing no emotion as he stood on the main deck of the KronPrinz Wilheim, one of the fastest passenger ships sailing the North Atlantic. Silently, he felt his belly convulse and his head throb in time with the rapid beat of his heart. Concealing his clenched fists deep in the pockets of his new blue jacket, he squeezed a fist and felt the presence of his ticket to America.

Darting from one face to the next, his eyes scanned the crowd of emigrants who stood in lines waiting to board. Karl knew that each person in line carried his own mixed bag of emotion—resignation, panic, elation, anxiety, depression, franticness—but most of all, hope. He noticed only a few emigrants who seemed jubilant; most faces appeared stoic, with tightly pursed lips. Many women expressed anxious tears as they walked slowly and hesitantly up the gangplank into the belly of the KronPrinz Wilhelm. They were walking away from a life of no tomorrows onto the boat, and toward a new life of opportunity and hope.

Cold, gray waves slapped the black steel hull of the great ship as three beefy tugboats shoved the KronPrinz Wilhelm out into open water, away from the safety of the preferred German harbor of Bremerhaven. The ship was filled to the brim with dreams of freedom, second chances—new beginnings. The late-day sun slid behind threatening skies as icy drops of wind-driven rain set the stage for the scheduled departure. Lingering on the Bremerhaven dock, a few persistent souls stood watching as the formidable black hull of the ship slipped into oblivion through persistent rain and thickening fog.

The rear deck was host to a mere handful of passengers yearning for a final glimpse of the land of their birth, the genesis of their frustration and disenchantment. Each was consumed with private thoughts and nagging trepidations. Karl couldn't help but think of his own wife as he observed the frightened and innocent faces of several younger women. Men appeared to be more in control, greeting each other with guarded smiles and respectful nods. Karl knew that underneath their exterior façade, they each harbored their own particular doubts and fears, just as he did.

Most passengers were already below in third class/steerage, getting acquainted with each other and settling in. Deep in the unitary, dank areas of the ship they would call home for the next week or more, men stood near their wives who were busy unpacking and arranging their assigned quarters. Nervous laughter rose now and then above the monotonous din of voices. Initial shyness and cautious fear began to wear off as passengers in third class met new neighbors. Each man's story was unique but they all had one thing in common: the dream of a new life ripe with opportunity, something they had all been denied in their former lives.

Many of the men in steerage were escaping the threat of forced service in some war they did not believe in. Most privileged second- and first-class passengers were seeking a change of lifestyle, adventure, and perhaps even opportunity. All had eagerly embraced the pregnant promises of free land and jobs that garish posters and overbearing salesmen from America guaranteed.

---

[1] *Thanks to Marita Karliisch at the American Swedish Institute for the proper spelling of this Swedish phrase.*

They believed it all, because they needed to believe—it was all they had.

Privileged passengers on the first- and second-class decks were relaxing in lavish salons and luxury dining rooms, oblivious to those less-rewarded souls down in the bowels of the ship. Regardless of which deck they occupied, the passengers appeared giddy with excitement and individual expectations of what awaited them in America.

No one noticed the solitary form of a lean, slightly built man standing away from the crowd on the rear, upper deck. His tweed newsboy cap was purposely pulled low, concealing his eyes. The man was alone, as he preferred—alone with his thoughts and tormenting questions. His large, work-worn hands gripped the polished deck rail in a subliminal effort to hold on to what he was leaving. Karl Kessel's knuckles were translucent and deathly white. He was oblivious to the numbness in his fingers, as mounting grief and fear devoured his senses and wit. Karl welcomed the cold rain and fading evening light that obscured the hot tears sliding down his ruddy, German cheeks. His anguished cry was lost in the swirling mist, "*Mein Gott*—what am I doing here? Am I a crazy or a greedy man to leave my wife and sons behind while I cross an ocean to find my success? Was it that difficult where we lived that I should come to make this life-changing decision to leave my home and family?"

Reaching deep into a left-front pocket he pulled out a piece of paper. Bringing it close to his face in the dimming light, he stared at the words again. Third-class Passage: to New York City, USA. Below was the name of the passenger, Ralf Nimitz, *not* Karl Kessel. This ticket—this ticket was the reason he was here on this ship without his wife and sons. It was his opportunity to go to America to be free and to be his own man. When that happened, he would send for his family, as promised, to begin their new life faraway in America.

Karl's desperate ice-blue eyes again searched the horizon for the harbor, for land, anything familiar that remained. Nothing but fog and mist swirled contemptuously over his frantic face. He peered down into the inky blackness of the water and saw only the reflection of his fear. Without warning, a sharp shudder traveled through the solid steel structure of the 23,500-ton passenger ship as its great steam engines throbbed with life. Swirling black coal-fed smoke belched from her four enormous funnel stacks, blending with the rain and stiff evening breeze. Surging forward under her own power, the impressive ship headed out into familiar turf, the Atlantic Ocean. Frightened by the sudden and decisive forward motion of the ship, Karl lost his balance as he attempted to run. Slipping on the wet surface of the deck, he scrambled to gain access to the area of deck closest to land. Through the darkness he caught a final glimpse of a dim, twinkling light as it, too, disappeared in the mist and the blackness of the stormy night obliterated its flickering presence.

Overcome with emotion, Karl sank to his knees; his lean work-hardened body shook as he was consumed with growing fear and naked realization. Cradling his anguished face in clenched, chapped hands, he implored his maker, "Please, dear God, give me courage and strength to do this thing!"

Suddenly he became aware of a large, powerful hand gripping his right shoulder. "I was looking all over for you and didn't find you below, my friend; so I decided to come back to the deck, and here I find you, *ja!*"

The man caught a glimpse of Karl's tortured face and was alarmed. "*Herr* Kessel, *Herr* Kessel, are you all right? What is wrong with you? Are you ill?"

Startled, Karl raised his eyes to the familiar face of a fellow passenger he met when first boarding the ship at Bremerhaven. Arnold Reinholt was a beefy, blond German from Hamburg, with a face that radiated his good-hearted personality. Karl remembered how impressed he had been with Reinhold's huge hands—the man's fingers looked like ten bratwursts!

Slipping his large hands under Karl's armpits, Arnold pulled the distraught man to his feet. "Come with me, *Herr* Kessel. Let's go together to find some warm food to soothe our growling stomachs before we face this stormy night."

Dazed, Karl allowed Arnold to pull him along as they descended the iron stairway into the steerage section. They did, in fact, smell it before they saw it. The stench and the closeness of human bodies—of people already sick from the sea, mixed with hardy aromas of simmering ethnic food. Pushing their way through the crowded belly of the ship, the two men made their way down the left-side aisle to their pre-appointed bunks/berths. The faces of fathers, mothers, children, and grandparents exhibited a multitude of emotions. Of course they had heard local scuttlebutt; but, none of the passengers knew for sure what fortunes or misfortunes actually awaited once they landed in New York.

The two men were encouraged by a few smiling faces—faces that were fresh, curious, enthusiastic, and optimistic. They watched for a moment as children did what children do. Karl was amused as he observed them making friends, playing games of tag with new friends—and running up and down the crowded aisles. Karl thought of the two small sons he left behind with his wife in Surtschin, Yugoslavia, only three weeks ago.

Like Karl and Arnold, most of the men proudly wore their only suits for this momentous occasion. Some of their shirts were white, some were chambray gray, and many wore ties. Most had removed their suit coats along with their dark-colored fedoras or newsboy caps. Karl accidentally bumped into a young emigrant mother dressed in a starched, white blouse with puffy sleeves and a pin-tucked bodice. He excused himself as he hurried on down the aisle, turning his head to take a last look at her before she disappeared around a corner. She was pretty with her hair pulled back into a tidy bun just like his wife Katja wore hers. Karl caught just a glimpse of her black stockings and high-top black boots. As he moved on, he politely nodded to three grandmothers as they sat talking, their gray heads covered with black babushkas.

This bustling mass of humanity had come to this place, in the belly of this ship tonight, with similar agendas of hope and survival. The initial test of their journey was to endure crossing the Atlantic Ocean, crammed together in the bowels of a huge ship. They had already undergone the strenuous experience of "passenger clearance" at the Emigrants Building in Bremen, Germany. After successfully passing visual assessment and answering the forty or more questions required to board, they had proudly walked up the gangplank onto the KronPrinz Wilhelm.

They all carried tickets similar to the one Karl kept safe inside his breast pocket:

Name of ship: KronPrinz Wilhelm
Captain: Adolph Wambeke
Port of embarkation: Ellis Island, New York,
New York, U.S.
Departure: June 6, 1906
Port of Debarkation: Bremerhaven, Germany
Age: 37   Sex: Male
Calling/Occupation: Farmer
Marital Status: Married
Condition of health: Good   Disabled: NO
Ability to read and write: YES
Polygamist: NO
Anarchist: NO
Period in prison or almshouse: NO
Nationality; race/people: German

Last residence: Surtschin, Yugoslavia
Last country: Yugoslavia
Final destination: New York, U.S.A.
Ticket to final destination for: RALF NIMITZ
Passage paid by: RALF NIMITZ
Money (more/less than $50): $300
Labor contact: Great Lakes Sugar Company,
Cleveland, Ohio
Earlier stays in U.S.: NO   When: NO   Where: NO
Immigration note: NO
Going to relatives or friends: NO

Relationship of relative: Name, Address, Town, and so on.

Bremerhaven, Germany, was the preferred European port because of numerous protective immigration laws passed in 1832. Ships departing from Bremerhaven had to be seaworthy, have a minimum amount of space available per passenger, and carry provisions on board for at least ninety days at sea. Newly installed toilets and washrooms were regularly inspected and a doctor was required to be on board throughout the voyage. Before the year 1832, each passenger was responsible for his own food and general conditions on the ships were deplorable.

When the passengers of the KronPrinz Wilhelm reached Ellis Island it was anybody's guess what might happen during the immigration process. Most passengers realized the trip was going to be long, but they soon learned just how long and how hard it was. Karl couldn't help but eavesdrop as two men engaged in conversation nearby: "*Ja,* I heard—at the end of the voyage, at Ellis Island in America, we will all be inspected for illness, sanity, and the ability to work. If we don't pass their tests, we will be sent back."

The second man remarked, "But what is there to go back to? Most of us are leaving broken lives in the old country where there is nothing left for us, not even hope!"

Karl realized that at this moment, their next communal "mountain"—was to make it through the voyage and the inspection on Ellis Island. Only then, would the doors to the "promised land" be opened for them, in a wondrous place where they believed the streets were lined with gold.

Speculating to himself, Karl mused. *On this first night, I imagine some are dreaming of freedom and opportunity, while others dream of what they left behind and question if they have made the right decision. What if, the streets aren't lined with gold? So many questions we have for which we have no answers; only time and experience will give us answers.*

The KronPrinz Wilhelm was far offshore now and Karl could feel the great ship rise and fall sharply with the swelling ocean waves. His innate alarm increased when the massive ship creaked and groaned as it rolled and slid into a momentary trough. His nerves were rattled by the foreign sound of building waves as they slapped the sides of the great steel ship. Karl thought to himself, *All these alien sounds, sights, and smells that surround me, they all unsettle me. Make me to worry.*

Without warning, Arnold threw his massive forearm around Karl's narrow sinewy back in an attempt to reassure his new friend. Laughing, he declared, "Karl, my friend, you are looking much too serious. We must relax, for I think we are in for a wild ride on this stormy sea tonight."

Arnold and Karl found their assigned berths in the bowels of the ship. They stowed their belongings; then Karl examined the life preservers. "Do you think these things really work? I hope we don't have to find out."

Laughing, Arnold tried to change the subject. "Karl, are you as hungry as I am? *Ja*, well, wait right here and I will find us some food." Before Karl could agree or protest, Arnold was gone, working his way back through the crowded aisles and back up on deck where the food line formed.

Karl eased his emotionally weary body down on the hard edge of the bunk, feeling the tenseness of the day seep from his body. Without intent, he peered across the aisle in the dim light where a young blonde woman of about thirty was quietly reviewing the rules of the journey with her four children. Their eyes were bright and serious with apprehension as they paid careful attention to their mother's instruction. Her intense brown eyes betrayed only a shadow of her own doubt. Instinctively, the woman realized someone was watching her. In a fluid, self-conscious motion, she straightened her simple, gray woolen dress and smoothed her shiny brown hair back into the tight bun resting in the nap of her long neck; then she nodded and gave him a proper smile.

Remembering his manners, Karl stood and gave a slight nod of his head, "*Mein Name ist Karl Kessel*," he said politely. "I think I will be your neighbor for the voyage."

"*Guten Abend, Herr Kessel, Mein Name ist Sophia Volk*," she replied, "and these are my four children."

Nodding his closely barbered head, Karl looked respectfully at her and hesitantly inquired, "Might I ask if your husband is on the upper deck, getting your evening food?"

Lowering her head she replied in a low voice, "*Nein, Herr* Kessel, we have already taken food this night—you must know now, my husband is—he has died in Stuttgart. My children and I journey alone to America, to live in my father's house in a place called I-o-va, I think—I will try to keep my children from bothering you, but they are much excited for the ride on this large ship."

Karl instantly felt protective toward *Frau* Volk and her four children. "I am sorry. I did not know that you were alone. I have, only days ago, left my wife and two young sons in Surtschin, Yugoslavia. I journey to America to a place called Cleveland, in Ohio, where I hope to find work for a wage and send for my family." Karl nervously ran his fingers through his thinning hair as he continued, "*Frau* Volk, if there is, ahhhh, any way I may be of assistance to you or your children during this voyage, please call upon me. I, I am comforted by the presence of your children; they do not bother me."

"Thank you, *Herr* Kessel, you are so kind. I appreciate very much your offer; it is a comfort." She pulled the makeshift curtain across her bunk, secluding her family as they settled down for their first night at sea.

His eyes scanned the perimeter of his would-be home. Karl thought it looked rather confining but workable. *It might even be comfortable as long as it stays dry.* Karl smiled to himself at his humor. He realized that third class/ steerage was, at best, a makeshift arrangement; but it was his home for now. He was curious how a crude, temporary wall had been built down the middle of the belly of the ocean liner. Four rows of temporary bunks were divided by a narrow aisle. Karl inspected his own bunk and saw that it was nailed together with rough, splintery planks, butt end to end with no space between. He was amazed to discover that each bunk measured about four-by-eight feet, with locking storage built underneath. The belly of the ship was fitted with these temporary partitions on the outward-bound voyage, meant to carry human cargo. He learned later that, after the passengers disembarked in America, the temporary partitions were removed and stacked for the homeward voyage; the entire area was packed to the walls with cargo bound for Europe.

As he settled in, Karl discovered a small cove under the bottom bunk where each passenger's chamber pot was stored. He remembered reading somewhere that the ship's crew made daily rounds to empty the individual chamber pots, a job he was thankful wasn't his to do. Like his own, some of the outer bunks had coveted portholes. He pressed his nose to the cold, round window and peered out at the inky blackness. The endless expanse of pitch-dark water deepened his feeling of solitary anxiety as he thought, *Perhaps in the morning light I will actually be able to see something and that will ease my mind. Now, all I see are the angry waves and so much water.*

Karl remembered there were stern warnings about opening the portholes, especially when the seas were high. There was no doubt that some passengers would learn this fact the hard way, when high seas poured through their opened portholes and soaked their bedding.

Walls of the berths were lined with numerous hooks and pegs to hang clothing, pots, garlands of dried food, or a laundry line. Karl reached in and examined the mattress. Constructed like an envelope of rough, ticked canvas, it was stuffed with clean straw. Most passengers left their bulky feather beds behind, using wool blankets instead.

Karl eased back onto his mattress, relaxing and getting acquainted with his berth while waiting for Arnold to return with their supper. In the dim light, he scanned the advertising brochure included with his boarding papers. He was surprised to learn that the KronPrinz Wilhelm was designed to accommodate 367 persons in first class, 340 passengers in second class, and 1,054 in third class/steerage. Karl thought to himself, *That's amazing—to have all those people and a crew on one boat. I never would have believed it would float!*

Karl heard the rooms for first-class passengers were lavish, including salons of carved mahogany wood, resplendent art, marble bathrooms, and spacious sitting rooms. One of these suites might cost as much as $2,000 for a week's crossing. Second class was comfortable, but not as expensive nor as opulent as first class.

A ticket for steerage cost around ten dollars. Karl remembered the descent into steerage was via an iron-railed utility stairway; there was nothing opulent about this area of the ship. At either side of the base of the stairs were washrooms containing twenty scrub boards and tubs along with twenty sinks and twenty toilets meant to serve more than a thousand people. Karl assumed it was probably going to be crowded, but was still was more convenient than he had imagined. He soon discovered that there was always a waiting line for the toilets. Using an indoor toilet was a new experience for Karl; on the farm in Surtschin, they had only smelly outhouse facilities.

Karl remembered reading that steerage passengers were fed twice a day by the ship's crew. Passengers were allowed to cook their own food down in steerage, but this was not encouraged. His wife Katja had packed dried fruit, several ropes of sausage, pickled meat, homemade *zwieback*, beef jerky, and other simple foods that Karl could eat or cook easily himself.

The overpowering odors of cabbage, turnips, onions, pickles, and rye bread permeated the cramped quarters, melding with the stench of human bodies, sea sickness, and despair. Katja had packed small bags of pungent herbs to help absorb or at least mask offensive odors. Karl reached into his bag and hung several bags on the interior of his bunk. The only escape from the unbearable odors in steerage came when passengers were allowed onto the upper decks during daylight hours.

As Karl continued to wait for Arnold to return with the food, he listened to the soothing, monotonous drone of adults talking softly and preparing their own berths for the night ahead. Karl busied himself, organizing his own single bunk. He knew he was fortunate to have the space to himself. The larger bunks had been reserved for families like that of *Frau* Volk and her four children who all slept in the same bunk.

He stored his two bags under the bunk, along with the food Katja packed for him. Karl closed the berth curtain for privacy as he removed his good suit and carefully folded and packed it away. He dressed quickly in simple, brown, wool pants, a chambray shirt, and a light-blue wool jacket, which would be on his back for the duration of the voyage to America.

On board the ship, most adults slept in what they wore during the day, changing only when the soil or smell became too apparent. Many people only had one change of clothing because space was valuable. Other articles and supplies took precedence.

Katja had carefully sewn Karl's extra savings into the lining of the blue jacket, where it would be safe. He vowed to be frugal with money while on board the ship. Karl had been warned about unscrupulous people on the ship who would try to sell various merchandise to the passengers, some of it legitimate and some of it pure robbery. His good friend in Surtschin, Ralf Nimitz, had warned him not to trust anybody and to be constantly vigilant for thieves.

His new friend Arnold had still not returned with their supper, so Karl busied himself by glancing through the *Guidebook for Emigrants to America*, which was written in 1851 by a German pastor, F. W. Bogen. This book served as the bible of preparation for the journey across the Atlantic for a generation. It told of the great blessings awaiting the German emigrant as soon as he stepped onto the shores of America. Traveling was much faster and easier in 1907 than it had been earlier in 1851; nevertheless, Karl decided this would be a good opportunity to review the suggestions.

Pastor Bogen wrote:

> *Preserve as much woolen clothing as you can. Let the wife take as much worsted as she can get, with knitting needles, and let her make you a cap to wear at sea. Your hat, even if it is an old one, will be valuable and you will pay dear if you need to buy one. Make any old shoes do for the sea voyage. All articles of flannel are valuable and take plenty of soap; and be saving of your water at sea that the wife may have a little now and to wash a little for the children.*
>
> *The emigrant comes into a free country, free from the oppression of despotism, free from constraint in matters of belief and conscience. Everyone can travel, free and untrammeled, whither he will, and settle where he pleases. No passport is demanded; no police mingles in his affairs and hinders his movements. Before him lies the country, exhaustless in its resources with its fruitful soil, its productive mines, its immense products, both vegetable and animal kingdom, a portion of which he has never before seem; its countless cities and villages, where flourish industry, commerce and wealth. The industrious farmer is invited by the Far West even by the whole country, to furrow its bosom and reap its treasures.*

Karl was so excited and encouraged by all these possibilities that he laid the book on the bed; his eyes stared into the dimness as he strained to catch a glimpse of the future—to imagine the magnitude of promised opportunity.

When this guide was first written, the voyage to America took approximately sixty to ninety days. Karl had been surprised and elated to learn that once they left the port of Gibraltar and Spain, the KronPrinz Wilheim was expected to make the crossing in ten to fourteen days.

Karl's mind slipped back to Surtschin and the night he and Katja sat reading Pastor Bogen's guide by candlelight. He thought of how her soft, sweet-smelling body had melted into his as they sat close on the settee. Karl remembered how tears had escaped her ebony eyes and rolled unchecked down over her porcelain face. She had turned to him, burying her face in his chest, as her body shook with sobs and her deep fear poured out of her and onto to him. Karl tried his best to console her and tell her of his love. Finally, when all the talking was done, all he could do was to show her again how much he loved her.

Arnold finally returned with food for Karl and himself, apologizing for taking so long, "The food line was quite crowded and they were also running out of the best food. I hope that what I brought will at least still our hunger for the night."

Trying to appear grateful, Karl choked down the unappetizing portion of the unsavory cabbage, sausage, and dumpling soup. Floating bits of hard, brown bread were expected to soak up the abundant grease. Arnold's appetite wasn't curbed by the sight or taste of the food; he was moving the spoon between the bowl and his mouth in record speed. On the other hand, Karl was used to much better food on the farm, and he struggled to eat.

Between bites of food, Karl mentioned, "*Herr* Reinholt, did you notice the large crates of fresh vegetables, fruit, and meat loaded onto board the ship at Bremerhaven? I sincerely hope that means our food will improve tomorrow. This soup fills my stomach but I do not savor the taste." Forcing down another swallow of the hot soup, he was overcome with a melancholy mood. He thought of Katja, *What is she doing now? Is she thinking of me?*

The two men sat together as they finished their evening meal with a cup of hot, black coffee. They tried to talk of home and about individual dreams for opportunity in America. But it wasn't easy or natural for them to express their inner thoughts. They weren't comfortable discussing the subject of feelings and dreams. However, on this, their first night on board, their conversation helped mask and validate their melancholy thoughts of home and family.

Arnold scooped the final spoon of questionable fare into his mouth. He swallowed, chuckled, and remarked, "I am thinking all the children on board are down here in third class. I am not used to all the noise they make. I think I look forward to when they sleep. When do you think that will be?"

Laughing, Karl replied, "Well, *Herr* Reinholt, perhaps you will be used to it by the time this voyage is ended. Take heart, most will soon be in their beds. It does not bother me because I am used to children. I left behind my two small sons in Surtschin and I can tell you, they can make a lot of noise!"

Running his hand through his thick, blond hair in an effort to smooth it back, Arnold said, "Tell me, if you may, *Herr* Kessel, why your wife and sons do not travel with you to America?" He abruptly realized the personal content of his question and quickly added, "Excuse me, please; I don't mean to ask private questions of you. It is actually none of my business and I apologize!"

Karl smiled widely and, putting his hand on his new friend's shoulder, he said, "*Nein, nein.* I don't mind you asking me questions. My wife stayed behind in Surtschin, while I go to find work and a place for us to live in this new country. We did not know how hard the travel would be and also finding work. So, when I am settled, I will send for her and little boys. I hope it won't be long before she joins me. I already miss her and our sons."

The big German smiled thoughtfully. "I am hopeful, as well, that you will be able to send for them soon."

Karl picked up Pastor Bogen's book. "I was wondering while I waited for you, have you read Pastor Bogen's *Emigrants Handbook to America*? It is quite helpful and if you have not read it, I will be happy to lend my copy for your information. I believe it to be most important news."

Arnold replied, "*Ja*, I have read it probably four times and yet realize there is more for me to learn. "*Danke schön*, my friend, for thinking of me."

After quiet conversation had sufficiently relaxed both men, they bid each other good-night, shook hands, and promised to meet up on deck in the morning to share a smoke. Watching Arnold make his way down the aisle of steerage to his own berth, Karl smiled. It had been a good day and he made a new friend to keep company with on the voyage to America. He pulled the coarse curtain closed, removed his wool jacket, and hung it on a peg. He was thankful Katja had knitted him the gray, wool cap to keep his head warm when he was up on deck. His removed and stored his new black boots. Tomorrow he would put on his worn work boots and wear them while he was on board.

Taking a deep breath, Karl laid back and covered himself with a wool blanket. He could hear the soft croon of someone playing a German lullaby on a harmonica. It felt like a familiar caress in the foreign darkness. Closing his eyes, his mind was immediately filled with visions of Katja: Katja laughing,

Katja crying, Katja's dark eyes, her bright smile and, finally, Katja waving goodbye until he could see her no more.

Sea sickness came on Karl in the darkness of the night as the shipped tossed and dipped into the rolling North Atlantic seas. He sat up quickly and for a moment didn't realize where he was. Feeling the bile rise in his throat, he leaned over the side of his bunk. Groping around under his berth, he found the chamber pot just in the nick of time and puked into it. He liked the cabbage soup even less as it spewed from his stomach. His head spun as his guts continued to roll and release until there was nothing left but a vile taste and odor.

"Oh, why did I eat that disgusting slop, why oh why?" The odor was enough to make Karl sick again if there had been anything left in his belly. The next few hours were filled with disorientation, tossing, turning, and continued dry retching as the ship continued to buck and roll through the high seas.

In his delirium, he had fleeting images of his home in Surtschin, thoughts of Katja and his two sons, of the life he left behind. Tormenting images and thoughts flashed in and out of his mind. He had been only a lad when he realized he wanted to make a better life for himself. Now he was on a quest to fulfill his dream, even if it killed him, as this retching was almost to do. He believed God made it possible for him to be given this ticket to America and he vowed to do whatever it was he had to do, to be successful and use this gift of opportunity to his benefit.

In his seasick misery, Karl was vaguely aware of *Frau* Volk, lifting his head gently. "*Herr* Kessel, here, please drink of this warm tea it will settle your stomach so you may sleep in health. Don't fear; it is a mix of calming herbs—caraway, ginger, sassafras, and peppermint. I know it will help you."

Karl sipped the aromatic liquid. He closed his eyes and relaxed as the warm liquid trickled down his throat into his seething gut. It felt good; it felt so good—and soon the violent spasms began to subside. Weakly, Karl thanked his benefactor, "*Danka schön, Frau Volk, Danka schön.*" After the mixture of herbs quelled his heaving belly, Karl fell back into fitful dreams.

His dreams suddenly turned into a reoccurring nightmare where he was standing in fields, prosperous fields, and everyone he knew was working the land, except him. He was bound in many ropes and allowed only to watch as everybody toiled happily with pride. They paraded past him with money hanging from their pockets, laughing, and making cruel jokes about him.

Waking with a start, Karl sat up inside the berth. He put his face into his open hands for a moment then ran his hands back over his head, wiping the sweat from his face. After shaking off the remnants of the dream, he lay back down on the mattress and gazed up into the darkness as thoughts of home again permeated his mind. It had been years since the day he realized there was nothing left for him in Surtschin. It was this knowledge coupled with raw ambition that motivated him as he set out on this life-changing journey. There was no opportunity, no future as a farmer of his own land. His oldest brother Wilfred had inherited his father's farm. The bitter truth of the matter was, as the second son, he received nothing. There was no inheritance and, worst of all, no help from his family. All he received was the order to leave the farm, to become an apprentice or find farmland he could rent. Bitterness still filled his throat when he thought of spending the last decade doing just that, on his father-in-law's land. It seemed there was no future except hard work, work for another man, and wages from another man's profits.

He remembered drinking beer with his friends in the local beer gardens. They all talked and dreamed of something better than they had. They had agreed that perhaps the only place their dreams had a chance was in the great country across the ocean—in America. Of course they had read the posters about America. It was a huge country, with so much land to be settled. Many posters offered free land for the man who would break the soil and plant it. But most of them could only dream of leaving for America; how could something like that be possible for poor farmers like them? The mere thought of leaving loved ones behind was a deterrent for many.

Karl Kessel opened his eyes at first light to the sounds of families waking, dressing, and preparing for their first full day aboard ship. His mouth tasted sour and vile; that is when it all came back to him—his sickness during the night and the tea *Frau* Volk gave him. Thankfully, the nausea and spasms ceased after he drank the herbal tea. Rummaging through his food pack, he found some baking soda and quickly pulled it from the bag. Dipping his index finger into the fluffy white powder, he put the finger into his mouth and vigorously rubbed his teeth and tongue, spitting the residue into the chamber pot. Just catching a whiff of the contents of the pot almost prompted his stomach to convulse again. He slammed the lid back on the pot. His attention was diverted by a growling belly, which had recovered substantially and now was expecting to be fed.

Hearing noises outside his berth, Karl slid the curtain back as three little girls dashed down between the aisles, pigtails flying behind. In the berth on the other side of the aisle, he saw that *Frau* Volk was busy as well, preparing her children for the coming day. When she noticed Karl, a wide smile crossed her face, "*Guten Morgen*, good morning, *Herr* Kessel, and how are you feeling this morning? Better I hope."

Karl replied, "Oh, *ja*, *Frau* Volk, I am well, *Danka schön*. I appreciate so much the settling tea you gave to me in the night, it worked well! Now I am feeling hungry, so I must ask you to excuse me. I hope you and your children have a good day and, if I may be of assistance at any time, please do not hesitate to ask of me!"

He secured his berth, and made his way to the upper deck where he found the line for the morning meal. The storm had passed and the seas were calm and sparkling as he stood in line taking deep breaths of the cool ocean air, letting it sooth and refresh his body. After he finished a light breakfast of black tea and oatmeal, Karl decided to stay up on deck in the fresh ocean air and take a stroll. Allowing the breakfast time to get acquainted with his recovering stomach, he made his way to a less populated area of the ship. Still weak from the night of sickness, he lowered himself slowly to sit on the deck and leaned back against a cabin wall. Thoughts from the life he had left in Surtschin again filled his mind as he put a match to the bowl of his clay pipe.

It had been a hot day in August as he and his father-in-law, Christian Mehll, were walking home from their work in the fields. That was when Karl broke the news. "I plan to immigrate to America."

Christian had been extremely angry when he heard of Karl's plan to leave the country and the certain eventuality that his daughter and grandsons would leave, too.

Karl still believed that Christian was wrong. His angry accusations and his attitude continued to hurt Karl deeply. He wanted this man, this father figure, to understand, to be sympathetic. Karl had not forgotten how they stopped walking and Christian turned on his son-in-law, completely enraged. The incriminating, harsh words his father-in-law spoke were still raw in Karl's memory. "You are a selfish, greedy man, Karl Kessel. I thought I knew you; I thought you were a good man. *Nein*, KARL, you are a hard man, a man of greed and too much ambition. You care nothing for taking my firstborn daughter, my Katja, and my two grandsons away from their grandmother and me, away from their home and their life here. There is much doubt we will never see them again or hold them in our arms. Karl, have you thought of this thing? Do all these hurtful circumstances not matter to you?" Christian had removed his dusty, sweat-stained hat and slapped it against his thigh in anger.

Karl couldn't help but remember his own angry reply, "*Ja*, I have thought of nothing more, for weeks, even months, even for years. Have you ever considered how it is that I feel, destined my entire life working for another man? Do you deny me the right to farm my own land, to be a man of my own making?"

Christian was not deterred. "That is what this is all about—it is your consuming vindictive vengeance and greed that drives you. All because your own father did not give you land of your own and you are required to farm for me or another man. Because of this, you will take my daughter and grandchildren to another land? You will be missing nothing for yourself and gaining all your dreams. Time will tell, Karl, IF those dreams, your dreams, are worth the price that you and your family will be forced to pay."

Karl responded with eyes blazing as he slammed his rake against the hard-packed road, "It is FOR my sons that I am doing this thing, so they can have opportunity I never had—to someday have land of their own and not have to work for another man for wages. So I may give my wife a fine house of her own, a house that I worked to give her, not that is given to us by you in your generosity. It is the only way. Why don't you understand this?"

His father-in-law's face was flushed with grief and frustration as they faced off on the dusty road. "Does it mean nothing to you that your sons are going to grow up without the love of their grandparents? How can you do this thing to us and to them? For YOU, Karl, it is all for YOU and what you want in this life; is it not? You will have to live with yourself for this terrible thing that you do! I doubt your success will be worth it; maybe to you it will be. I know my daughter, and she will end up resenting and perhaps even hating you for taking her and her sons to the other side of the world. Some day you will know, Karl Kessel; you will know what it is you have done!"

Christian turned and began to walk rapidly toward his house as Karl called after him. "I beg you will try to understand. I am a man of thirty-two years; I do not own my own farm and I never will in Yugoslavia, or in

Germany. There is no opportunity or future for Katja and me here. There is only servitude, war, depression, and no hope for a better life."

In all certainty, Christian did not understand, he only heard certain words as he stopped, whirled to face his son-in-law. "Servitude—is that what I gave to you all of these years? You received generous wages for your work, Karl; and you are an important part of our family. Does this mean nothing to you?"

"I want more than that! I want to feel like a man. I want to know success of my own, to say this house, this land, this farm is mine. This can only happen in America. Your farm will go to your son, not to me. Do you expect me to work for him after the farm passes to him? If you cannot recognize this, there is nothing more that I can do or say to help you understand. We want your prayers and your blessing, Christian; do not send us off with this unforgiving attitude."

Karl had always considered himself to be ambitious and, now that he was married, his ambition was not only for himself alone. He would not allow the biting words of his father-in-law to deter him. He would never believe he was guilty of what he had been accused. Karl resented his father-in-law's indifference and accusations. He chose to put a different face on his aspirations, a face he believed in and could live with. Karl convinced himself he did this thing for the love he had for Katja, for his family—to give them a good life, a safe life in America. But more than anything, he dreamed of holding his head high, of earning the respect of people, of making a success. He was in charge of his dream now and he would paint it as he had always dreamed, in glorious color.

That night, in his narrow bed, in the bowels of the KronPrinz Wilheim, Karl Kessel began to change. His unconscious metamorphous began to uncoil. From that moment, he became intently focused on his future and how to get everything he ever wanted.

A smile pushed across his face as he realized that the years of working for other men was almost over. He was determined that when he landed in America, everything he did would be for HIM and what he dreamed of. When the opportunities came, he would recognize them and be ready to execute his plan of success. No one was going to stop him now, no one!

Karl Kessel slept well that night—the sleep of one who is confident, of a man with a plan.

CHAPTER 2

Katja and Karl

★ ★ ★ ★ ★

"Do not cast away your confidence, which has a great reward. For you have need of endurance." ~Hebrews 10:35

Still tormented by the hateful and final words which passed between his own father and himself such a long time ago, Karl tossed and turned in his bunk the second night at sea as further dreams of his past plagued him. He would never forget what had taken place; his own father's condemning words fueled Karl's determination to succeed on his own accord. Weary of tossing and turning, Karl pushed back the wool blanket, set up inside the berth, and reached for his shoes and jacket. He gently opened the curtains and quietly slid out of the berth. Karl inched his way up the iron staircase; he glanced to the right then left—looking for the night crew who would most certainly send him back down to steerage. The coast was clear as Karl moved quickly up and onto an upper deck into the fresh sea air and solitude of the starry night. He stood alone in a darkened corner of the deck, out of sight of the ship's patrol. Tonight, Karl preferred the forward deck, which faced west; he wanted to see where he was going, not where he had been. His future was there—somewhere out there to the west.

Ja, this ocean breeze feels good to my face, he thought. The light of the full moon reflected off the surface of the water and lit up the ship and ocean like daylight. Karl looked to the south, north, and west. *Acht, so much water, I never did know how much water oceans had, and I cannot even believe what my eyes see at this moment. I wonder how deep all this water is? Probably like the mountains and valleys on the land. Or, is it all smooth underneath like the beach?* Karl shook his head in wonder. There was so much he did not know or understand. He had attended school only until the sixth grade, but he never missed an opportunity to learn all he could.

Up on the deck, in the tranquility of the silvery moonlight, Karl began to feel the tension in his body release. He reached into his left coat pocket and pulled out his pipe. He tapped a fresh tobacco plug into the clay bowl, struck a match, and lit it. Holding the pipe stem between his teeth, he inhaled deeply, drawing the smoke down into his lungs. He held the fragrant smoke there for a moment then, with a long breath, expelled it into the cool night air. Thoughts flooded his mind. *It feels good to relax and have time alone, away from the unceasing activity down in steerage. I am already feeling impatient to be done with this ship and ocean. I am most eager yet anxious for America and my future.*

The night sky was filled with thousands of twinkling stars. Karl did not remember ever seeing so many stars. *I feel like I could reach up and touch them. They seem to be so close. I wonder if my Katja is looking at the night sky, too, and perhaps thinking of me as well.* A sudden chill ran down his back as the evening breeze turned cool. Karl tapped the bowl of his pipe over the rail, watching it drop into the ocean. Putting the pipe back into his pocket, he turned and quietly made his way back down into steerage, taking the less-traveled staircase to avoid detection. He stopped at the washroom, relieved himself, and quickly washed his face and hands. With his toilet finished, he walked soundlessly down the aisle to his berth, climbed in, and drew the curtains shut. Karl took off his worn boots and blue wool jacket. It was quite warm down in the bowels of the ship, so he slipped off his trousers and slid under the blanket. Sleep claimed his body, but his mind swirled with dreams of Surtschin and his past life.

1894

Heinrich Kessel was not a tall man, but his muscular girth made him imposing just the same. He stood with feet apart, blue eyes flashing; authority filled his voice as he addressed his second-born son: "Karl, you are now a man, old enough to earn your own way. You have lived in my house and have eaten my food for long enough. There is no more room for you under this roof, working on my farm. You have known for a long time that your brother Wilfred inherits this farm, this land; yet you stay. Now, I tell you to leave;

now you will go. That is how it is done, that is tradition."

Karl's father narrowed his eyes, his voice increased in volume as he continued, "You are a man, not a small boy, and it is time that you go out and find your fortune. Either become an apprentice or hire on as a farm worker. It is your choice. Do not bring dishonor to this house. When I come back from the fields today, you will be gone!"

Karl's heart pounded inside his chest, his ears rang as the ice-blue eyes he inherited from his father flashed with their own volatile anger. "So, this is how many fathers treat sons who aren't firstborn?—cast them off as though they were smelly garbage?"

Standing quietly, in a far corner of the room, Karl's mother, Tateia, stood unobserved. She had long anticipated and dreaded this moment. She knew if she tried again to intervene on behalf of her son, her husband would strike out at her as he had done so often in the past. Heinrich had never treated the two boys the same; he always favored their oldest son. It was a wonder Karl had not left before this simply as the result of the demeaning and cruel way his father treated him. Tateia drew a deep breath and took a step toward the two men. "Heinrich, please do not be harsh; he is our son. Surely there is some way we can help him find his way?"

Annoyed, Heinrich turned his wrath on his wife. "Woman, do not speak of something that is not your business," he bellowed, "I will take care of this matter and it will be done with. Leave us, go and knead some dough or feed your chickens! Do something useful!"

Karl's anger and betrayal were fierce and his raw emotion consumed him. He struggled to speak, took a deep breath and stood tall with shoulders back. Clenching his jaw, he moved within inches of his father and, locking eyes, he spit his words, "If it is so easy to throw me away, I will learn also from you this day. I will leave your house and your land, Father, I will leave Pancevo, and I will never return. From this day forth you are all dead to me; you mean nothing to me. I WILL go out into the world alone and I WILL become a successful man in spite of you and your tradition."

Taking one step closer to his father, Karl snarled, "HEINRICH, I will never call you 'Father' again! I no longer have respect for you. I have *no* father! I tell you this thing now: if *Gott* in heaven ever gifts me with sons, I will not love one more than the next or favor one more than the next." He turned to leave, but stopped and spun around to again face his father.

"Oh, yes—and how did you get your land, *Herr* Kessel? IT WAS GIVEN TO YOU! You did not *earn* it. You did not *work* for it. You took it as a gift from the hand of Empress Theresia of Austria and called it yours. I know this fact, yet you hold yourself judge over my life and what I will be given or allowed?"

His father reached out to strike the impertinence and disrespect from the mouth of his second-born son, but stopped as his son's hand shot out and closed over his forearm like a steel trap. When Karl felt the intended blow soften, he released his father's arm. "And—you will no longer strike or beat me as you are used to doing."

Startled, Heinrich took a step back as the blood drained from his face. He abruptly turned his back on his son and stomped out of the room. Karl crossed the lower room in three strides and took the stairs two at a time. He entered his sparse room and slammed the door. His heart thumping wildly in his chest, Karl leaned back against the old wood door. Sweat stood out in beads on his forehead and his head throbbed in beat with his heart. He could not believe what had just happened. It hurt so deep inside, like nothing he had ever experienced. He had known for as long as he could remember that he would not inherit this farm. However, he also knew many households arranged for their second and even third sons to share in the land. Some fathers even helped their younger sons find acceptable situations so they might earn an honorable livelihood. Not so here, in his father's house; he was being cast out, like the garbage.

Karl was weak and shaking with anger and fear of the unknown. *Where will I go? Where will I stay this night? I should have expected he would treat me this way after all the years of brutality I have suffered at his hand.* Frantic questions and situations were flying wildly in his mind and the answers were not there.

Karl threw the rest of his belongings into a sack and took one last look at the room he had known all his life. Burdened with the weight of his two sacks, Karl staggered down the wooden stairway.

His mother waited anxiously beside the front door. "Karl, son," she pleaded, "Wait, let us speak, please. Where are you going? How will I know you are well?"

Karl paused and, without putting his bags on the floor, he addressed her, "We all knew this day would come. I realize you have no choice but to stand with your husband in his decisions; we both know he cares no more for your words or well-being than he does for mine. I do now what I am forced to do; I am leaving this life behind me as if it never existed. He awkwardly and briefly embraced his mother then pushed past her and hurried from the house.

Tateia's hands flew to cover the shock and hurt that filled her face. She hid her eyes from her son's anguished expression and the sight of him leaving their home.

Half running, half stumbling, Karl made his way down the cobblestone village road. Blindly he ran down road after road. Rounding a corner, he stood in the middle of the street, without a particular destination. The sun was setting behind the vineyard-covered hills as Karl paused to catch his breath. He realized he was standing in front of *Pfarrer* (pastor) Wundermiere's cottage, next to the large evangelical Lutheran church. This was the same church where he was baptized as an infant. He stood for a moment, looking up at the steep hillside behind the church and the symmetrical rows of grape vines that for decades had covered the mountainside. Having no other choice, Karl took a deep breath and knocked tentatively on the front door. He wasn't sure if the good pastor would remember him. The heavy wooden door opened slowly and the dim interior light haloed around the pastor's robust form.

"Please, *Herr Pfarrer*, may I come in?" Karl implored.

"Dear *Gott* in heaven, Karl Kessel, what has happened to you? Come in, come in!" The pastor led the way into the kitchen. Noticing the young man's bulging sacks, he guessed what might have happened. There was a warm, crackling fire in the hearth. Karl inhaled the aroma of fresh bread that filled the room. Crockery bowls of half-eaten, pungent vegetable soup sat on the well-scrubbed wooden table.

"Please, Karl, break bread with us and share a bowl of this nourishing soup. Here, come in here first and wash. Join us in the kitchen."

Still shaking, Karl placed his sacks of belongings against the carved wooden staircase and moved to the washroom. After cleaning up a bit, he walked shyly into the kitchen.

"Sit down, sit down. Now, Karl, what has happened to you? You do not look good, my son."

Painfully, Karl described the terrible scene that had occurred hours before with his father. He explained he was off to find his fortune, but was in need of a place to sleep for that night only. The pastor took a deep breath and with sorrow-filled, knowing eyes put his large hand on the young man's shoulder. "Of course, Karl, you can sleep here tonight; let me think on what you might do to find work. We can pray this night and talk further of this thing tomorrow. Now, put some of this good hot soup and bread in your belly. If I know a young man's appetite, you are probably quite hungry."

After the hot supper, Karl felt renewed as he and the pastor moved into the parlor. They talked briefly about the day and about possibilities of work. "My heaven, Karl," the pastor observed, "you are about to fall asleep as we speak. Come along and I will show you where you will lay your head this night." Karl didn't object as he followed the pastor up the narrow stairs to where a pallet lay in the loft, under the eaves. "Here is your bed for the night, Karl. Have a good sleep, my son!"

"Thank you, *Herr* Pastor, you are correct; I am suddenly quite tired. I will see you in the morning—and thank you again for your kindness!"

After prayers, Karl slept fitfully that night, tormented by the hateful words which had passed between his family and himself that afternoon.

The next morning over breakfast, Pastor Wundermiere was in an exuberant mood. He told Karl of his plan: "I have a good friend down the road in Surtschin and his name is Christian Mehll. He is a successful man with a large farm and only one young son to help him. Just last week he told me he needs more help with all of the work. If this sounds acceptable to you, I will send you to him today, with a note. He is a good Christian man, Karl, and an even better farmer."

Karl was grateful for the pastor's help and for his good fortune. "*Ja, Danka schön*—thank you, *Herr* Pastor, I will go at once. Surtschin is a distance I should reach by dusk if I leave now. God bless you, and I thank you with a full heart for the night's rest, food, and for your help."

The pastor reached for Karl, grasping him by the shoulder as he instructed, "Karl, remember that this help came from our Lord. Do not forget to give the thanks to him and remember to ask him for his help and protection in all you do and in all you say. He will give answers for your life, Karl. He will guide your way. This day is a new beginning for you. Have faith, Karl—have faith!"

Acknowledging the pastor's words, Karl picked up his bags and eagerly set off for the village of Surtschin and the farm of *Herr* Mehll. It was late afternoon when he reached the outer area of Surtschin, just in time to see a parade of farmers coming in from daily tasks in the fields. Like most other villages, the people lived within the protection of each other, in white frame and stucco farmhouses built close together in small villages. Each morning they harnessed their workhorses, gathered the needed tools for the day, and walked to their respective fields, which surrounded the village. The village collectively owned the nearby pine and oak forests where they cut wood to burn in their ovens. Their livestock grazed in common pastureland.

Along the road, Karl halted a couple of weary farmers and inquired, "Excuse me, could you direct me to the house of *Herr* Christian Mehll?"

A burly, sweaty farmer stepped forward and pointed to the south. "*Ja*, down there, *Herr* Mehll lives in a two-story Dutch-style, white cottage at the corner of *Haupt Strasse* and *Neu Grasse*. You can't miss it. It has four cross-windows on the front side of the house, and with an unusual curved roof peak. There are two small windows that look like eyes with eyebrows. It is a unique house, just like its owner, *Herr* Mehll." After thanking him for the help, Karl hurried on down the dusty village road in the direction indicated.

By the time Karl reached the house of *Herr* Mehll, the sun was setting behind the pine and oak woods, sending long fern-like shadows onto the

narrow village road. Karl was tired and road-dusty, with a persistent hunger gnawing in his belly. The farmers had been right; the house was different than the other village homes. After brushing off his clothes and smoothing his hair, he rapped three times at the large, oak door.

The heavy door opened wide and lamplight from within haloed the head of white hair on a dark, looming form. *Gott in heaven*, Karl thought, *I have come to the house of a giant; dare I speak?* A stocky young lad of about ten or eleven years peered out from behind the door.

Christian Mehll noticed that the dusty young man at the door seemed weary and nervous. He gently inquired, "*Ja*, you knock at my door. You wish to speak to me?"

Stammering, Karl managed to speak, "*Ja*, I...I presume you are *Herr* Mehll? My name is Karl Kessel and I have with me a note from Pastor Wundermiere in Pancevo. I am in need of work and he sent me to you. Here, here is the note, sir."

Christian reached for the note, slipped his eye glasses onto his straight Roman nose, and unfolded the message from the good pastor. Quickly reading the note, Christian Mehll stepped to the side and with a grand sweep of his left hand, invited the young man into his house. "*Herr* Kessel, please come into my home and we can discuss this further."

Karl moved tentatively through the doorway into the hallway. Peering down at Karl, Christian Mehll said, "Well, my young man, you aren't a big fellow but I can see from your hands you are used to hard work. The pastor must think you are worthy and I trust his judgment. I will accept you on trial basis for one month and we will see how we work together. Is that agreeable to you, *Herr* Kessel?"

Karl was forced to look up when he spoke to the six-foot-four Christian Mehll, "*Ja*, *Herr* Mehll that is quite acceptable. I promise I will work hard for you and you will not be sorry for giving me this opportunity."

A wide grin broke over *Herr* Mehll's generous mouth and heart-shaped face. Karl observed his classic, prominent German cheek bones and hooded, soft-blue eyes. *Herr* Mehll spoke to Karl, "It is true I need a good strong back to help my young son Chris and me with the work. I would not be able to pay you a large wage until the harvest, but you will have a roof over your head and good food in your belly. Would that be acceptable to you, as well?"

A pleased, but shy, smile crept into the corners of Karl's mouth as he eagerly accepted the offer, "*Ja, Herr* Mehll, it is; it is most kind of you."

At that, *Herr* Mehll grasped Karl's hand and shook it. Karl unconsciously rubbed his arm after the handshake, glad it wasn't dislocated. "Well, now, come into the kitchen and, if you have not eaten, please sit and have evening supper with my family and me. Come now, I will introduce you to my wife, my son, and two daughters."

He hurried Karl into the large, inviting kitchen. Karl smelled the enticing aroma of chicken and dumplings—and was that apple strudel, too? In sheer delight, he said to himself, *Oh. dear God, thank you, thank you for bringing me to this house and for all your blessings on me this first day of the rest of my life.*

Pushing Karl to the foreground, Christian Mehll introduced the newly hired worker to his family. "*Herr* Kessel, I would like you to meet my wife, *Frau* Mehll, son Chris, my daughter Elizabetha, and our eldest daughter Katharina whom we call Katja."

Karl, with hat in hand, politely said, "I am happy to meet with you and I am even happier that you would ask me to supper with you, for I am most hungry!"

They all smiled and Christian pulled out a chair next to his, so Karl could sit at the table. Karl looked around the table at the family and their smiling faces and felt instantly welcomed. They were so different compared to the family that he came from. He liked it here already.

The head of this house wasn't the only one who was mentally appraising their dinner guest. His diminutive, raven-haired eldest daughter, Katja, couldn't help but evaluate this handsome young man who was eating his food so hungrily. She thought to herself, *I like his hair and he has a straight nose, not to small and not too big, with nostrils that flair. His full mustache makes him look older—I wonder how old he is?* Katja amused herself further with quick, furtive glances and was filled with glee as her eyes fell to his chin. *His chin is so peculiar, strong and with that little dimply dent in the middle.* But it was his eyes that most attracted her. *They appear as if they are smiling, and they twinkle like the stars.* Katja was glad her papa had hired this Karl Kessel.

Karl discreetly looked around at the kitchen, comparing it to the house he had been born in. He had noticed off to the side of the entry, a long hallway constructed of fieldstone that probably led to an attached barn.

Herr Mehll's farmhouse was quite warm, clean, and cheerful; Karl immediately felt at home and welcomed. *Herr* Mehll explained, "Our sleeping rooms are up the stairs. It is a good place to sleep in the winter because we stay warm from the *Kachelofen* (stove) below.

After the evening meal, *Herr* Mehll was in high spirits. "*Herr* Kessel, if you have had enough to eat for this night, Chris and I will take you to where you will sleep."

They left the warmth of the kitchen and made their way through the stone hallway to the barn area. Christian Mehll opened the door, ducking his head as he moved into the interior of the barn. Pointing to a ladder, he instructed, "Up there is where we have a nice warm loft for you to do your sleeping!" Christian led the way up the ladder followed by the two young men.

As soon as his head cleared the opening, Karl scanned the room. He scampered the rest of the way up the ladder and surveyed the room with a smile on his face. "*Ja, Herr* Mehll, this room is quite acceptable for sleeping," and with a twinkle in his blue eyes, he continued, "Perhaps I will also find time to read a book or two after a day of work in the fields."

"For sure, there may be some time for you to read a book, at night only!" Laughing, *Herr* Mehll showed Karl where the wash basin and linens were stored. "There is a lantern on the small table and a goose-down pillow, feather bed, and a wool blanket on the bed. You can hang your clothes on the pegs over there."

"I will be quite comfortable;" Karl declared.

Pleased with the events of the evening, Christian smiled and gave Karl a good solid slap on the back, "Well, now, sleep well, for we rise with the sun for breakfast and then to the fields."

With that, the father and son climbed down the ladder and walked back to the house, pleased that they now had a hardy young man who would help with the harvest.

Karl looked around the room again and began to settle in. He hung his coat on a hook and unpacked his two sacks, poured fresh water in the basin, and attempted to remove the dirt of the road from his face and body. A relaxed smile crossed his tan face as thoughts turned to the events of the day. This day in 1894, marked the beginning of the rest of his life. He vowed to remember to thank the Lord in his evening prayers, for all of his blessings as the good pastor had instructed.

Before he climbed into bed, he went back down the ladder and went into the long narrow barn. He made his way down the main aisle to where he heard the horses feeding. Karl approached a stall, stood watching for a moment, then reached through the gate and ran his hands over the head of a big black stud. The roan in the next stall whinnied for attention, so Karl walked over and stroked her nose, too. Admiring the horses, Karl hoped he would be able to work with them in the fields.

There was something about the power of the Percheron horses that Karl found fascinating. He knew these French draft horses gave as good as they got. He also realized the importance of taking good care of the animals that pulled the plow. Karl turned and climbed back up the ladder to his room. He lay back on the bed with his hands folded behind his head as he thought of *Herr* Mehll and his family.

Chris, the son, is already tall for his age and is a handsome lad, like his father. He has dark hair and piercing black eyes like his mother and oldest sister Katja. He looks like he will be even larger than his father. Karl's thoughts then went to the petite, dark-haired girl he had indeed noticed sitting at her father's table. She appeared to be about fifteen and seemed to inherit her mother's small and sturdy structure. Katja was as beautiful as her sister, but in a dark, more pensive way. He thought about her intense, chocolate-brown eyes that shone with intelligence and innocence. *Her face was perfect, delicate and straight, just right for her small oval face.*

Karl smiled into the dark of his room when his thoughts turned to the girl's wide gentle mouth with lips that were full and soft pink. *When she smiled at me, she had deep dimples in the corners of her mouth and her eyes were bright and inquisitive. I like how she parts her silky hair down the middle and pulls it back severely, into a long, thick, jet-black braid.*

Katja seemed different from other girls he had known. *She might be young for me right now; she is probably about seven years younger than I am.* Karl sat up in bed and shook his head to clear the thoughts of the young girl. He decided that he had better concentrate on working hard for *Herr* Mehll. He had yet to prove himself and he was determined to succeed, to become the man he dreamt of being. In the darkness of that room, Karl knew he would be haunted forever by memories of his father and the injustice of what had happened between them. He vowed to make it a constant motivation, to work as hard as he could and to do whatever it took to be a success!

The next morning, Karl woke before first light. He lay in bed, eyes roaming the strange room until he realized where he was. He heard quick footsteps below, and the excited voice of Chris Mehll. "*Herr* Kessel, *Herr* Kessel, open your eyes, it is time for breakfast. We eat and leave for the fields with first light. Throw some water on your face and come to the kitchen quickly."

Jumping eagerly from his bed, Karl threw the blanket over the narrow cot and pulled on his work clothes. He splashed cold water on his face and ran a comb through his hair. Karl grabbed his hat before climbing down the ladder. He moved quickly through the stone hallway toward the kitchen.

Motivated by the heady aromas drifting from the kitchen, he strode enthusiastically into the brightly lit room. Karl made a beeline toward the finely carved oak table which graced the center of the room. He swung his leg over a side bench, taking a seat while *Frau* Mehll finished with breakfast preparations. Karl watched as Katja walked gracefully to a tall oak cabinet and, standing on her tiptoes, reached up and took down blue-and-white dishes, which she carried to the table. Karl decided that he liked everything about this house and the people who lived in it.

Herr Mehll strode into the kitchen with a sunny smile on his face, his hair still damp from the washstand. He took his place at the head of the table, sitting in a stencil-embellished ladder-back chair while the rest of the family sat on the benches. The food was delivered as the rest of the family took their places for the first meal of the day. They bowed their heads for the morning prayer of thanksgiving.

"*Guten Morgen, Herr* Kessel, I trust you slept comfortable in your loft?"

Karl quickly replied, "*Ja, Danka, Herr* Mehll. I was quite comfortable and slept without waking. Oh—and I hope it is with your approval, but before I slept I introduced myself to your two fine horses!"

"Oh, *ja*, that is good. I may give you the job to see that they are fed and brushed each night. Would you like this job? They are good strong horses. Have you experience working with horses?"

Karl's face opened into a huge smile, "*Ja, ja*, on my fath…" His smiled faded instantly as he recalled his father. He recovered quickly and continued, "On another farm, I worked many years with the horses. Oh, and, I would be pleased if you call me by my given name, Karl, if you please, *Herr* Mehll?"

After a hearty breakfast the three men headed for the fields, with the massive Percheron horses pulling the wagons. As they walked out of the village, Christian Mehll asked some questions. "Karl, tell me something, the farm you worked on, was it your father's farm or another near Pancevo?"

Lowering his head in frustrated embarrassment, Karl explained, "*Ja, Herr* Mehll, you are correct; it was my father's farm I just left. My brother Wilhelm inherits the farm and I am out to earn my own way which I have no doubt, I will do. Our last words were angry, *Herr* Mehll. I now have no family and I do not wish to speak of it again, if that is acceptable to you."

Christian Mehll looked at the young man and saw into a troubled heart, which continued to beat in spite of the hurt and rejection it carried. He understood Karl was struggling to retain his dignity and rise above the humiliation he felt. Christian vowed to help him as much as he could and perhaps be instrumental in changing the course of his life.

Wanting to smooth over the questions, he added, "I understand, Karl; this is the way of things with some people. I believe you are indeed ready to live your life and make your own way. We are glad you knocked on the door of our home last night; it is good to have you with us!"

Keeping his head down, Karl only nodded as the three men made their way toward the fields. There was one more issue which Christian Mehll wanted to know about. "Karl, did your family go to the Lutheran church in Pancevo where Pastor Wundermiere preaches?"

Surprised by this question, Karl's head came up quickly as he replied, "*Ja, Herr* Mehll, we went to the Lutheran church of Pastor Wundermiere in Pancevo. But we did not go to services on a regular basis. If there was work to be done in the fields on Sundays, my father made us work instead of going to worship."

"Well now, Karl, you will find in the house of Mehll, we go to the Lutheran church in our village to thank God in heaven for our blessings each Sunday. That is the day of rest as *He* taught us. You will also discover that, whenever possible, we attend the opera house to hear *wunderbar Deutsche* music and opera. Do you like the music, Karl?"

Karl didn't know what to say. He didn't want to disappoint *Herr* Mehll, but he felt compelled to tell the truth. "I am afraid I know nothing of music, *Herr* Mehll. We were not allowed to be frivolous with our time!"

Shocked, Christian replied, "Karl, Karl, you have new and *wunderbar* things to learn and experience. I can hardly wait to share with you the magic and wonder of the great music. Experiencing the pure joy of the music is not a frivolous manner of spending time. Have you not experienced the music in the *Biergartens,* drinking good beer, taking of a pipe, and talking of *Deutschland* or everyday problems?"

Christian Mehll's voice became excited as he became more animated. "Karl, your heart will be filled! Most times we attend the small concert opera house here in Surtschin. BUT, it is a *wunderbar* occasion when we all take our seats in the wagon and cross the Danube on the great stone bridge into the city of Belgrade, to attend the Grand Opera. You will see for yourself!"

His enthusiasm was infectious as he exclaimed, "Karl, music to our people is the joy of our lives. It is the one thing we must have—like the food, the drink, and the sunshine, to nourish our souls. Life is not truly lived without music."

"Oh, Karl, to experience the sorrow of Mozart, the tenacious style of Bach, and the eternal torment of Beethoven—it takes the breath from one's body. You will discover Karl, that this music is so soothing, it caresses your soul."

Karl had to admit he was curious and rather excited by *Herr* Mehll's beauteous explanation of "the music" and the experience it obviously evoked.

As they continued down the road, *Herr* Mehll went on: "You must understand, Karl; to most *Deutsch*, the music, theater, and opera are an essential element to our civilized people, just as we have a duty to experience learning through books and the masters."

Not to be interrupted, Christian Mehll was unrelenting in his description. "At the same time, Karl, we believe we must express and experience the emotion of life through fine music. This is the manner in which we as a people express our sorrow, anger, love, and joy. It is our reward or—how do we say it? It is the sweet after the meal, the glow of the sunrise, or peace of the sunset, the soft emotion of love, and fearful wrath of anger. It is life, young man, it *is* life! We will speak more of this wonder at a later time, Karl; for now we come near our fields."

Karl had not experienced great music in the manner of which *Herr* Mehll was speaking, and now his curiosity was aroused. He looked forward to learning of the exceptional music.

"Karl, do you have experience with growing wheat, sugar beets, and the grape?" Christian Mehll inquired.

He replied quickly, "*Ja*, I know about wheat and sugar beets, we did not grow the grape, *Herr* Mehll. But I am able to learn much and learn it quickly if you will teach me."

"Of course, Karl, we will teach you about the grapes, it is a good thing and all the family participates in picking and the stomping of the ripe grapes into wine. It is a joyous time for us."

Karl vowed silently that he would watch and learn everything *Herr* Mehll had to offer so, in time, he would be able to make his own appearance of a successful man. He would not only study and learn the ways of *Herr* Mehll, but of other farmers and other men. Karl Kessel's ultimate goal in life was to be respected by his peers, to be revered in his success.

They came upon the fields and vineyards of Christian Mehll and as he opened the gate, Christian declared, "Okay, my boys, let us bend our backs to the work."

Late that afternoon on the way home from the fields, Christian praised Karl, "You are a strong worker today, Karl. You show me good persistence and desire to learn new things."

Karl was pleased at *Herr* Mehll's appraisal of his first day of work—something his own father had never given him.

The weeks passed quickly, days of hard work in the fertile fields, ending with nights of exhausted sleep. Karl enjoyed the opportunity to speak with Christian Mehll, which the walks to and from the fields afforded him.

One morning during their walk, Karl confided in his mentor, "*Herr* Mehll, I am happy I am learning new ways, better ways to farm the land. You are a good and knowledgeable teacher." Karl added with a smile, "But most of all I enjoy working with and caring for your fine horses."

Christian Mehll responded, "I am pleased to hear you are learning new ways to farm the land from us. We are proud to have you working alongside us, Karl. You are a hard worker and learn your lessons quickly."

Karl felt too proud to reveal he was also pleased to learn the ways of a gentle and respected man. Each day as the noon hour approached, they stopped work, hobbled the horses, and ate a cold lunch under the trees. If they were working closeby, they were able to come home for a hot lunch that *Frau* Mehll prepared for them.

When she was free from her own chores, Katja cheerfully skipped down the road to meet them at the end of the day. At every opportunity she fell into step beside Karl, something her father never failed to notice. Katja was usually full of questions. Did you thin the sugar beets today? When are the grapes going to be ready to pick? On occasion she took the liberty of announcing what she and her mother had prepared for the hearty midday dinner or evening supper.

The evening meal was usually smaller with cold cuts, cabbage slaw, pickles, and brown bread, but there was always more than enough to eat. *Frau* Mehll explained the reason behind this division of meals, "It is because eating a large meal in the night is not good for the digestion, Karl. But don't fear; I will not let you go hungry!"

She was true to her word; Karl never went to bed hungry while under the roof of the Mehll family.

The day came when *Herr* Mehll proudly announced, "Tomorrow at sundown, we have the opportunity to attend the opera of Surtschin. They are to play especially, the music of our great German composer, Bach. The announcement says they will perform his 'Concerto Number Five,' and also the amazing 'Jesu, Joy of Man's Desiring.' Of course, Karl, we will dress in our best clothes for it will be a *wunderbar* evening. As I promised, Karl, we wish for you to attend with us."

At first, Karl was excited, but then his face flushed with embarrassment as reality struck him. *I have no best clothes, no best suit—no best anything. What am I to do?* Distressed, Karl hung his head, "I am sorry, *Herr* Mehll, but I cannot go with you and your family. I do not own a suit of clothes that would be appropriate."

Surprised, Christian responded, "Karl, this is not a problem that can't be fixed. I am sure *Frau* Mehll can find some clothing which can be altered to fit you. Would this arrangement be acceptable, Karl?"

A wide smile crossed Karl's anxious face, and his blue eyes twinkled bright with joy. "*Ja, Herr* Mehll, I am grateful. *Danka* for your generosity, I am looking forward to the music. I can't imagine, in my dreams, what it will be like."

Christian Mehll expressed his mirth with a big, deep laugh, "Karl, I guarantee that these songs will not be like merry, boisterous *Trinklieder*, the drinking songs that you and your friends sing at the *Biergarten*. The music will touch your soul, deeply!"

Christian Mehll continued, "I am pleased you are looking forward to the opera. Perhaps I should also explain the rules of the evening to you. We believe when we go to the opera, it is similar to when we are in our holy house of God. When the performance begins, nobody leaves or enters the music hall. Only at the end of the first act, will a tardy person be admitted to his seat. The doors are locked before and during the presentation to prevent rude interruption of the performance and the experience."

At last, the anticipated evening of the opera arrived. The family, including Karl, was dressed in their best garments. The family Mehll was giddy with enthusiasm as they walked the short way to the Village Opera House. Karl found himself next to a radiant Katja as they made their way down *die Strasse*. He felt grand in his new suit of clothes which *Frau* Mehll tailored for him, and Katja was glowing with anticipation. As they neared the concert hall, Karl became fascinated by the elegant attire of the patrons and the infectious exhilaration that filled the air. He could hear a kaleidoscope of melodic notes drifting through the elegant, but simple, hall as musicians tuned their instruments behind the red velvet curtains. There was a subdued buzz of conversation as finely dressed people made their way to assigned seats. No one wished to be the last to take a seat.

Herr Mehll led the way into the concert hall, followed closely by his wife Theresia, Elizabetha, Chris, Katja, and, finally, Karl. Karl was not surprised or disappointed that his seat was beside Katja. Her face was animated as she chatted gaily, consumed with the excitement of the evening. It wasn't long before lanterns were dimmed and the heavy ornate velvet curtain was pulled to the ceiling by beefy stage hands. Karl's breath caught as an anticipating hush fell over the audience and a shiver ran down his spine. His eyes scanned the faces of the audience. Their eyes were wide and their breath came in small inaudible gasps as their attention was riveted to the maestro who held his ceremonial wand high in the air. All at once the wand dropped and rose in fluid motion as the orchestra responded with rehearsed precision.

Karl's eyes widened and his mouth slowly fell open when the first compelling cords of Bach's composition of "Jesu, Joy of Man's Desiring," soared through the austere music hall. Karl felt himself being carried away on the musical interpretation of music. He was disappointed when the composition came to a conclusion; he almost wished it would go on for a lifetime.

"Oh, Karl, wasn't that just marvelous? Did you just love it?" Katja twittered as she reached to squeeze his arm.

"*Ja*, oh, *ja*, it was beyond anything I have ever experienced. It was truly *wunderbar!*" Karl exclaimed. He thought to himself, *I also enjoy having you so close to me.*

The next selection was to become an unexpected, significant moment and Karl would always remember this first time he heard the haunting melody. The elevated maestro raised his wand and as he brought it downward, waves of the exquisite notes from Pachelbel's "Canon Four" drifted out to immerse the audience with rapture. Karl sensed the music was literally caressing him, carrying him away to an encompassing peace he had never known. The lyrical vibrations of the music had the power to consume the constant, suppressed anger, and relax the inner turmoil, which seethed and immersed deep inside of him. It encouraged the man he wanted to embody, yet deeply feared he would never be.

That evening left an indelible mark on the remainder of his life. He discovered the power the music possessed, to take him to another place, to ease his spirit, and release his inner tensions. This music seemed to have the potency to erase the blight his father put on his soul. It birthed emotions that elevated him above the reality of his circumstances. When the music was performed, he felt like he could see colored light exploding around the bodies of the musicians. It affected Karl in this manner whenever he took time to release his mind and soul to it.

By the time Karl Kessel was well into his mid-twenties, he was firmly entrenched into the Mehll household. He had become a valued part of the workforce as well as an esteemed, even loved, member of the Mehll family. During this period, Karl found brief interest in several young women from surrounding farms and villages. He soon discovered none of the girls had the same effect on him as Katja Mehll.

He was becoming comfortable with the thought of taking a wife and having a family of his own. He was twenty-seven, had saved a good sum of money, and believed he could afford a family. However, Karl knew he would never inherit a farm, there were certainly none to buy, and *Herr* Mehll had a son to inherit his farm. Karl would be the first to admit he was happy working for *Herr* Mehll, but that is all he would ever have or be—working another man's farm for another man's pay. It was no secret he wanted his own farm, but each possibility seemed to reach a dead end and, in fact, his life seemed comparable to a water wheel! Karl lay awake nights going over various scenarios of ways to change his life, but always came back to the same dilemma—he was a man without a way to make an independent living in the manner he wanted.

That summer while working in the fields, Karl suddenly realized how often he looked down the road for sight of Katja as she brought the afternoon lunch for the three men. He found a certain enjoyment in seeing her skip across the field with her long, ebony braid flying side to side. Her luminous smile and soulful eyes never failed to touch a place inside of Karl in a way that no other girl had. She always had a bright smile for him and seemed to find her seat beside him as they took their lunch in the shade of a nearby tree. The raven-haired Katja was now eighteen and painfully attractive. Her small delicate body had filled out into that of a woman. She carried herself with dignity, edged with a charming innocence. Katja's quick intelligence and sunny attitude was a good match with Karl's serious, omnipresent ambition. She enjoyed teasing him at every opportunity. Even though Karl often became flustered, he enjoyed her wit.

It seemed to happen so easily, so naturally, as destiny simply took over. They found themselves together, playing in the snow, taking long walks, and picnicking in the shadowy pine and oak woods. They enjoyed each other's company and loved to walk the dusty road to the village and dance the polka to accordion music at village celebrations. There were many opportunities to stroll to church and, of course, attend the opera or concert hall with her family. When they were in a crowd or around the family table, their eyes never failed to search and meet. Their acknowledgment and devotion were obvious to everyone, everyone except Karl and Katja.

After each harvest, Christian Mehll gave Karl a handsome salary and, when possible, a bonus. Karl was grateful and, being extremely frugal, he put the money away in a special box to save for future goals or opportunities. Karl prayed each night to his Lord to show him the way, to help him achieve the life he wanted.

Work in the fields usually went well and Karl enjoyed his labors alongside Chris and *Herr* Mehll. One day, however, the village hooligan Heindrick Moeular decided to provoke Karl. Heindrick was a notorious bully who had huge hands with knuckles that looked like cloves of garlic. Heindrick purposely worked the rows next to Karl, stopping several times that afternoon to taunt him. "Karl, where is it you come from that you know nothing of farming? You can't even make straight the rows?" Moeular viciously kicked the straight lines of cut wheat Karl had just formed. He continued to bait and harass Karl all that day.

Karl's facial expression was stoic, unreadable, until his eyes narrowed to slits and he completely lost his composure. Karl let Moeular have it in the only way he knew, the way his father had unmercifully beat into him throughout his youth. Pent-up vengeance exploded so quickly and violently; Heindrick didn't know what hit him. Karl drove his fist straight into the soft, unsuspecting belly of Heindrick. As he bent over, spilling his lunch onto the damp earth, Karl wasted no time in delivering a vicious upward blow to the prominent jaw of the brute. That was all that it took to silence the beefy bully. Those who witnessed the altercation didn't have a lot of sympathy as Heindrick lay on the ground, whining in pain. By that time, a small crowd had gathered, including *Herr* Mehll and Chris.

"Karl, it is enough; let him be, now. Get your rakes and we will be on our way. This day of work is over," commanded a vexed Christian Mehll.

On the road home, Christian inquired of Karl, "What was that all about, Karl? Why did you attack Heindrick like that?"

Karl was in an embarrassed state of shock and humiliation as he replied, "*Herr* Mehll, I apologize to you and to the other men. Heindrick purposely provoked me all the day long. The final straw came when he disturbed my rows of wheat, which I had worked into straight files. He stood up, looked at me, and made a joke of me. When I asked him why he did that, why he bothered me, he just laughed and said because he wanted to!"

Karl, shaken by the incident, took a deep breath as he continued, "My temper got the best of me, *Herr* Mehll, and I apologize for my actions; it was how I was raised by the man who gave me life. He had big fists and a short temper; I grew up in a world of hurt and constant defense. This day I reacted in the only way I know of and now I sincerely regret it because I have brought dishonor to you and your house."

Silently, Karl chastised himself for letting his inner demons escape for all to see. This explosive part of him was something he had intended to keep hidden. He vowed to be more careful to obscure the inherent nature which lived deep inside him. He realized he had to work harder to channel this violence and anger, using it only to drive and inspire his ambition. As Karl had suspected, such behavior was not acceptable to *Herr* Mehll and his family; violence was not the way they settled problems.

Later that evening after the family ate supper, Christian Mehll approached Karl on the subject again. Shaking his head, Christian Mehll said, "Karl, I understand sometimes a man must make a stand. Truly, there are those who would ridicule until they are taught a lesson, but other methods must be first tried. Physical retaliation does not lead to good things—think on that next time. We will not speak of this again."

Weeks and months went by and, no matter where they were, Karl always seemed to find his way to Katja's side or she to his. She was now nineteen and had matured into a beautiful young woman, a young woman who caused Karl's heart to beat much too fast and who put a lump in his throat whenever she came near. Karl now realized that he had fallen in love with Katja and he believed she also loved him. He could tell in the way she always turned and gave him one last, yearning glance with those wistful, chocolate-colored eyes—eyes that seemed to have no beginning and no end. Karl often found himself wishing he could run his hands through her luxurious, glistening black hair. His ardor and thoughts were fueled by what her shy, intimate smile and the subtle movements her lithe body transmitted, even though her lips had not formed the words he yearned to hear. Sensuous thoughts filled his mind whenever she walked in front of him—the way her tiny hips swayed side to side, slow and rhythmical. Just the sight of her filled his mind, his body, with responsive love.

Karl had little experience with women. Yet he was painfully aware of how his body involuntarily responded when she was near or even when he thought of her. He had not even kissed her, but dreamed often of how it would be, what her soft pink lips would feel like underneath his own. He felt compelled to do something about these feelings of love that obviously were not going away.

One evening after the meal, Christian was sitting in the parlor reading his Bible. Startled, he looked up to see Karl standing in the doorway with his hat in his hand and a nervous expression on his face. He stammered, "*Herr* Mehll, please, may I talk with you?"

"Of course, Karl, please come in, sit down; sit down. What is it you wish to speak of?"

Karl remained standing and took a deep breath. He drew himself up to his full five-feet-seven-inches. He tried in vain to swallow the walnut-sized lump in his throat. With difficulty, he began, "*Herr* Mehll, you know, ummmh, I am grateful for all, for all you have done for me, for my life. You have taught me so much good, shown me this world can be gentle and shown me its wonders, especially the great music. You have become like a father, like the father I wish I had known as a child."

"Young man, I understand all of these things you are saying and of course my family has become fond of you; we all care very much for you. But I have a feeling there is something else you have not yet said. What is on your mind?" A suspicious twinkle filled Christian's Mehll's eyes as he waited for Karl's response.

Karl felt light in his head, beads of sweat rolled down the back of his neck and his tongue seemed to stick to the roof of his mouth. "*Herr* Mehll, it is… it, is…is, I have come to love your daughter Katja and I wish for her to be my wife. I have waited for her until now that she is nineteen, almost twenty years of age, and old enough to be a wife. I am now twenty-eight years old and I think it is time I take a wife and have a family of my own."

Christian Mehll remained motionless as a now-determined Karl continued, "I promise, *Herr* Mehll; I will be good to your daughter and make her happy. I will work hard all my life to give her a good life and to bring honor to her. I ask your permission to be married to Katja. I know that usually I would ask for marriage through a *Kuppler* (coupler), but I have no family who is interested, so I have decided to be direct with you." Karl drew in a huge breath of air and expelled it loudly, as impatient thoughts flew through his mind: *There, I have said it, now I wait for the response from Herr Mehll. Why was he just sitting there, looking—what is taking him so long? Speak now, please!*

The elder man lowered his noble head and looked at his Bible. He had already suspected this thing would happen between his eldest daughter and this fine young man. He knew the torment Karl was experiencing at this moment and he did not wish to prolong it.

"Karl, does Katja feel as you do? Have you and she talked of marriage?" Christian inquired of the nervous young man standing in front of him.

The young man responded quickly, "Sir, *nein, nein*, we have not spoken of this; but I know with my heart she feels the same for me. I believed I should respectfully speak of this matter with you first."

Before more words were spoken, Katja burst into the room, "Excuse me, Papa, I didn't mean to listen, but I have heard what you and Karl were talking about and—and I have something to say, if I may."

Shock filled Karl's flushed face as he saw Katja at the door. He held his breath as Christian reacted calmly, with a knowing smile on his face. "*Ja, ja,* of course, my daughter, I want to hear what you have to say about becoming the wife of this young man. You know it is your choice, and not mine, who will be your husband."

She took a step closer to her father, drawing fresh breath into her tiny four-foot-eleven-inch body, she began, "It is as Karl tells you, Papa. I do feel the same about him and I would want more than anything to be his wife; it is in my dreams."

Karl stepped forward, his twinkling blue eyes flashing with his love and excitement of sharing his life with this lovely young woman. He reached out and took Katja's hand in his. "Katja, you will never be sorry that you agree to be my wife. I will do all that I can to make you happy and to make you proud to be my wife."

She looked into his eyes, her emotion shining from her own deep-chocolate eyes. "Oh, Karl, I believe we shall have a good life together and I promise you, I will be a good wife and I will work most hard to make you happy, too."

1898

After the harvest in the fall, the awaited betrothal bans were posted in the gray-stone Lutheran church on the hill. Karl opened his savings box and took out some of the saved money to buy the engagement ring of gold. Per German custom, the engagement ring and the wedding ring were the same. There were no diamonds, only a gold band, which Katja wore on the ring finger of her left hand, during the engagement. After the wedding, she would move the ring to the same finger of the right hand.

The Mehll house was consumed with a flurry of wedding preparations during the next six months. Karl was more than pleased with this new situation of his life; it was one more step in the direction of becoming a successful and respected man. He knew he must be careful to sustain this image of control and gentleness he had created—he could make no mistakes now. He and Katja decided there would be no "bundling" or all-night courting, which was commonplace for engaged couples. They would simply be as they had been before, sitting at the same table for meals, taking walks, and being together with the family.

Karl chose Chris as his representative, and Katja chose her sister Elizabetha to stand up for her. Many friends, family, and neighbors were invited to the wedding. In fact, everybody from the village was invited by the *Hochzeitslader* (the wedding inviter), except Karl's family in Pancevo. No word was sent to them; it was as Karl wanted it. Receiving the duties of the wedding inviter was a coveted position because at each house he visited, it was customary to present him with a glass of *schnapps* before he left. The *Hockzeitslader* wore a festive long coat with a high hat and white gloves. He often carried a decorated cane, umbrella, or a sword. He was quite conspicuous as he proceeded down *die Strasse*, filled with high spirits from all the *schnapps* he had obviously consumed.

The first Saturday in the month of May 1898 was the day Karl and Katja chose for their wedding. The sun warmed the earth as it awoke from the long winter. New life sprang forth from the animals and from the ground itself. Farmers had begun to plow open the sleeping soil, making it ready to receive the seeds they would sow. The pine and oak woods were bursting with fragrant spring flowers and shiny new buds. It was as though the whole village and Mother Nature herself were preparing for their special day, the day in which their joined lives would burst ripe with purpose. Karl had purchased a new black suit of wool serge and shiny black shoes for his wedding. He looked quite handsome in his new attire, but was impatient to see his bride. Karl would never forget how beautiful his Katja looked on their wedding day.

As Karl and Katja planned, the chamber music began to play the

unforgettable music of Pachelbel's "Canon Four." It had been the second song Karl had heard on his first visit to the opera and it would forever be his favorite. His breath caught in his throat as Katja and her father entered the large Protestant church and walked down the aisle toward him. She looked like a fragile porcelain doll he had once seen in the window of a doll maker in Belgrade. As she walked, her navy-blue and gold wedding gown, embellished with embroidered flowers and ribbon, skimmed the church aisle. The beautiful dress embraced Katja's petite body; it nipped her waist with long darts and fell over the soft curve of her hips as it flowed into a full skirt. The high neckline reached up to encircled her elegant neck with a delicate one-inch ruffle. The fragile, Austrian lace veil fell to her knees from a crown of seed pearls and lily of the valley.

At the altar, Katja held her head high as her father bent forward and lightly kissed his daughter's forehead. Making eye contact with her groom, she took her place beside Karl. The veil that covered her face couldn't hide her radiant, dark beauty. Her hair was no longer in the braid of a child but was pulled back and rolled into a large, ebony bun secured at the nap of her neck. Katja's sister had fashioned the wedding bouquet into a ring of life, with seed pearls, lily of the valley, and apple blossoms.

He struggled to breathe. His palms were moist; his blue eyes twinkled with emotion, and his heart felt as though it would jump out of his chest. Karl could not believe this incredible angel was about to promise to be his wife. He stood as tall as he could, stiff, with shoulders back and chest out. He was anything but relaxed at the altar as he and his bride repeated their vows for a lifetime together.

Karl remembered little of the actual wedding. He remembered the throng of well-wishers and the photographer from Belgrade taking their photo. They had a wonderful time at their *Hockzeit* (reception), where they greeted the entire village and danced the polka for hours. The newlyweds did not go away on a wedding trip but, excusing themselves from the wedding celebration later in the evening, they slipped away to the small *Fachwerkbau*, a half-timber construction house that was owned by Christian Mehll. It was where Katja's parents had also begun their married life.

Karl reached up to lift Katja down from the wagon and together, as husband and wife, they went into the cottage. The door closed behind them. They stood looking at each other, feeling shy as they found it hard to believe they now had permission to be joined as one. Their self-consciousness gradually fell away as Karl reached out and touched her angelic face, stroking her soft skin.

He said, "Oh, my love, my life, I can't believe that you are this day my wife and we are here, finally alone."

Katja boldly slid her arms around his neck and pulled him close to her, as she had so long dreamed. "Oh, Karl, Karl, I have waited so long for you to touch me as my husband. I do not want to wait any longer."

Her husband pulled her into his arms and buried his face in the softness of Katja's fragrant neck. He inhaled deeply, never wanting to forget the feel and smell of her neck. Her skin sparkled as Karl's hands washed possessively over her body and slowly slid up her neck and into her silky hair. Slowly, he pulled the pins from her delicate bun and stood back to watch, as her glistening ebony hair fell in soft black waves over her creamy shoulders. "You are so beautiful, my love. You take the very breath from my body. I want to know every inch of you, forever!"

The newly wedded couple embraced and kissed, gently and shyly at first. As their passion and long-suppressed hunger rose, their wedding clothes began to fall to the floor before they buried themselves in the downy feather bed. Their breathing was ragged as Katja's dark hair spilled over the white bedclothes; her virgin body was like a swirling vortex that Karl was pulled into. His eyes narrowed with desire as the flush of his body heat spread to his face and down his belly. Everything else ceased to exist for the couple as they began the night of consummating their marriage.

He was naturally concerned for his wife's well-being because Katja was fragile and so small. He didn't want to hurt her; he knew the first time they made love, it would hurt and he wanted to get it over as quickly as possible.

"*Nein*, Karl," Katja implored, "be slow, be gentle. I have been told it will not be good for me the first time; it is not your fault, but do not act so harsh. Love me slow, Karl; we have time."

True to the words of advice, her first time was painful but recovery was not long and the night had just begun. It was as though they could not be sated. They had waited so patiently and had loved each other almost at a distance. Now, they were one as God had joined them together that day.

As they lay in their bed taking a brief rest, they agreed that if they had known their life together would be this wonderful, they would have been married much sooner. Katja confessed, "Karl, now that you are my husband, my life is now complete. I am finally the wife of the man I have dreamed of for so long and my life is perfect."

Karl, on the other hand, believed his life had just begun. With Katja at his side he would concentrate on the future and his success he hoped for.

After several days of honeymooning in their cottage, Karl and Katja emerged to rejoin the world. He went back to work in the fields with his father-in-law. Katja began learning how to run her own household, with the aid of her mother.

The months flew by in a flurry of hard work in the fields and wonderful nights attending the concerts and opera. On occasion, Karl enjoyed going to the beer gardens to meet with his married friends. They sat and drank together speaking of how their lives were going and how they wished their labor circumstances were different. The men who were second or third sons like Karl were as frustrated as he was with their plight in life. Karl tried to push the discontent regarding his employment from his mind while he continued to work for his father-in-law, for wages.

Married life was full; but for each, something was lacking. For Katja it was a child and for Karl it was a farm of his own.

Several weeks before Christmas in 1899, Katja and Karl were walking on the snow-covered road on their way to the village. As they strolled past the bare oak trees and the deep-green pine trees in the woods, Karl was feeling playful and began to throw snowballs at Katja. She took his hand and drew him into the edge of the woods, where she motioned for him to sit on a rock by their favorite gurgling, icy spring. Karl remembered how Katja had turned to face him, her face beaming with a radiant smile, and her dark eyes sparkling with a secret. Karl, my husband, there is something I want to tell you this day in this special place. You know I love you; you are my life, *ja*? But now, there is more life," she put his hand lightly on her stomach. "In my belly, Karl, there is going to be a baby, our baby!"

He seemed to be struck dumb as he stood rooted to the spot. He had not expected this news. He knew what they did at night in the featherbed made babies, but they had been hoping to have a child for months and nothing had happened, until now. Instant images came into his mind of hearing the cries and screams of wives of his friends as they gave birth, and the women who didn't live through it all. *Dear Gott in heaven, I am full of fear*, he thought, *don't let her die—please don't let this child take her from me, not now.*

"Karl, speak to me, aren't you happy that you will be a papa soon? Oh, Karl, I can see it in your face, you worry about me. *Nein, liebschen*, do not worry, we will put our trust in our Lord. I am healthy and I am not afraid. Be happy with me, Karl."

Katja soothed his face and kissed him. Karl was about to discover another purpose, another reason to succeed.

CHAPTER 3

Crossing the Atlantic, 1906

★ ★ ★ ★ ★

"I have a plan for your life, it is a plan for your good and not evil; it is a plan to give you a future and a hope." ~Jeremiah: 29:11

Waking from a second restless night filled with haunting dreams of Katja and his life in Surtschin, Karl dressed quickly in the privacy of his berth. He slid the curtain open and made his way down the aisle of steerage. Making a quick stop in the lavatory area, Karl poured fresh water in the bowl and splashed it over his face, driving the final signs of sleep from his blue eyes. He slicked back his unruly hair with water, before he climbed the stairs to the upper deck. There, at the front of the ship, he spotted Arnold sitting on the deck floor, his back resting against the wall of a first-class cabin.

"*Guten Morgen*, my friend," Karl greeted, "The fresh air feels pretty good this day, and I am thinking I will light up my pipe and perhaps sit here and talk with you, if I may?"

"*Ja*, Karl, sit down, sit down," Arnold invited. "You know, *Herr* Kessel, I think it would be a good idea if we tried to speak our feeble English when we are together. It would be good practice. But I have to warn you, I may not know if your English is good or not because mine is so bad!" Arnold was amused by his own joke, laughed heartedly, and then continued, "So, Karl, first I must ask you about this particular kind of German which you speak and which I find rather difficult to understand at all times. Where are you from that you speak German in such a manner?"

Karl smiled as an amused chuckle rolled out of his throat. "*Ja*, I now know that my German is not, what do you say—standard? I am *Danube*

Swabian from the region of Hessen originally, but my ancestors immigrated into Yugoslavia to settle farmland there many years ago. We speak a form of High German which is why you might find it difficult to understand some of what I say. I am sure we can work out a way to understand each other."

Shaking his head with recognition, Arnold replied, "Of course, of course, I have heard Swabian before but it is a different form of German and at times I may ask for interpretation!" He laughed at his own joke and continued with the conversation. "You said yesterday, you have left behind your wife and sons in Yugoslavia. Tell me about your family; how many sons do you have and what are their ages?" Arnold asked.

"*Ja*, Arnold, my wife Katja remained at our home in Surtschin. Her family is near to help with our two sons. It was hard to leave them, but I have plans to send for her and our sons soon after I reach America and earn money for their passage."

The sinewy German drew deeply from his clay pipe and, blowing the smoke out, he said, "Two sons, you are a fortunate man, Karl; what are their names?"

A wide smile crossed Karl's face as he began to talk about his family. "My first son, Jakob, is six years old. He was named after my wife's grandfather and my friend. Three years later we were blessed with a second son whom we named Christian after the father and the brother of my wife. Our friends say that both sons are small images of me, as they have my blue eyes and light-colored hair," Karl reported wistfully. "They have many good times together and they keep my Katja quite busy."

He recalled, "My father-in-law, Christian, enjoys being a grandfather and it will be hard for him when they must leave. At harvest, when it is time to crush the grapes, he first washes the small feet of my sons and lifts them into the wooden vat to stomp the grapes to make the wine. They have a *wunderbar* time—there is much singing, laughing, and loud voices."

Arnold shook his large blond head and said, "Living in the city, I have not been witness to such as you describe; but it sounds like very much fun."

Karl related, "My father-in-law also enjoys to hitch up the pony to the cart and inviting his two grandsons to ride with him across the Danube into Budapest for supplies. He put small bells on the pony's harness, which ring gaily as the pony trots down the road. Of course, after the supplies are purchased, he often buys sweets for the boys and perhaps a small wooden toy if they have behaved themselves. They are happy when they come back to their home."

Taking a deep drag on his clay pipe, Karl continued, "Christian loves our two little boys, but he is also strict with them and demands their respect. I remember one time when he told Jakob to fetch his tobacco and Jakob shouted to him, "*NEIN,*" as he ran away.

Christian had thrown his slipper and as it flew past Jacobs' ear, the boy stopped, turned around and began to cry. His grandfather caught up to him and in a stern voice said, "When I tell you to do a thing, you are to do just that and you are never to say *nein* to me again!"

"*Ja*, that is a gute story, Karl, it reminds me also of my parents who loved me and my brothers, but they were strict. I believe I learned early what I could and could not do." Arnold laughed and continued, "So, Karl, how did you come to get a ticket to travel to America? I think that you worked on your father-in-law's farm did you not? Did he buy the ticket for you?"

A solemn, dark expression crossed Karl's face as he said, "It is true I have worked on my father-in-law's farm for many years, and that is all I would ever do. I had many friends and we would meet at times at the *Biergarten* to drink our beer and talk of our lives. Many friends, many men were like me, second or even third and fourth sons, working for a wage as there was usually no opportunity for something to call their own. Not one of us was happy with our situation so we drank more beer to drown our problems!"

Karl stood up and invited Arnold to walk with him, "Let's get some exercise, my friend, I am getting stiff just sitting around. I think we are allowed to walk around the deck during the day."

As they walked the deck, Karl resumed telling of his life in Yugoslavia, "My best friend, Jakob Schuur, would inherit his father's farm and so he did not have the same problem as I. Another good friend, Ralf Nimitz, was also a second son as me. His older brother was to farm the land after he came back from the war. My friend Ralf Nimitz convinced his father to buy him a ticket to immigrate to America that he might find success of his own. His father was wealthy and wanted his second son to succeed, so he bought the ticket. Soon after, they received word that his brother had been killed in the war. The next day, my friend Ralf came into the *Biergarten* looking for me. I was sitting at a table with another friend, when Ralf walked over to us with a pitcher of beer and a serious expression on his face. He sat down and he said to me, 'Karl, my brother Ernest has been killed—we have received word. You remember the ticket my father bought for me to travel to America. I have no need of the ticket now, because now I will inherit my father's farm.' Ralf reached into his pocket and pulled out a paper. 'Karl—I want *you* to have my ticket, for you to go to America and have an opportunity to buy your own farm.'"

Karl stopped walking and shook his head in disbelief, "Arnold, I could not believe that he would do this thing. I am a lucky man to have such a good friend. It was my dream perhaps to go to America someday, but there was never an easy way to do this, and suddenly one day was this ticket in my hand. I accepted the ticket from my friend and thanked him again and again. I soon excused myself from my friends at the *Biergarten* and hurried to my home. My wife was in the kitchen preparing the evening meal. I walked into the kitchen and, in my joy, picked her up and whirled her around and around. She thought that I had stayed too long at the *Biergarten* and was almost to be angry with me when I showed her the ticket to America. She didn't have words at first, she didn't know what to say, and then she spoke. She said to me, much distressed, 'Karl, what *ist das? Eins?* One ticket to America? You go without me and your sons? Why would you do this thing, go without us?' We had often spoken of our future in Yugoslavia. We only had dreamed perhaps someday an opportunity would come to us to own a farm of our own. We did not think the opportunity would mean for us to leave our home and travel to America. America was only a faraway and hopeless dream we had heard about, while we were trying to live with obvious reality."

Taking another deep draw on his pipe, he continued, "After I explained how I came to possess the ticket to America, Katja and I decided I should go to America to the job that my friend Ralf said was waiting for him (now me) in Cleveland. I would work and finally send for her and our sons to come, also. When we told her parents of our plans, it was not as happy for them. There was much accusation, shouting, and crying. They did not want us to leave, but they could also understand that we wanted more of our own success and there was no way for that to happen in Yugoslavia or even Germany. Everywhere it was the same in Europe with the constant wars and depression."

A serious expression crossed Karl's face, "You know, Arnold, I truly believe no one can change the circumstances of their birth. However, the course of ones life *can* be changed. One only has to be determined to find a way in which to do this thing, and have courage to act on it. This ticket my friend gave to me *was* the way in which the direction of my life was changed, in an instant!"

Arnold nodded his head in agreement, "*Ja*, my friend, I believe in this concept as well, as it was the same with the ticket my grandfather gave to me. It has changed my life, too!"

Recalling his family and their reaction to his leaving, Karl said, "They were excited and also sad when finally I prepared to leave for Bremerhaven. They helped Katja prepare my bags, gave me many embraces, words of good luck, and of course many prayers. They promised to take care of Katja and our sons until I would write for her to come also to America."

He turned his pipe over and tapped the remaining tobacco out of the bowl. "Before I left for America, Katja persuaded me to travel to Belgrade to have my photograph made. She thought it would be good for our sons to have a photograph of their Papa, so not to forget my face. I did not want to spend the florins to do this thing, but finally decided perhaps she was right. So now, they look at a picture of their Papa and they remember me."

Karl turned to Arnold and smiled warmly as he thought of his family. Then he motioned, "Let's take a look at what the front of this main deck looks like. I am curious to see how the bow of the ship cuts through the waters."

The two men changed direction and moved casually toward the front of the KronPrinz Wilheim. They reached the bow of the ship and peered over the railing, down into the glistening water below.

Arnold exclaimed, "*Mein Gott!* Look how the massive hull of the ship cuts through the deep water and creates large, curling turquoise waves. See how they spill to the side to blend into the swirling ocean water. It is quite beautiful and wondrous at the same time. I wonder how fast we are going because it is moving strong through the waters. This ship has so much powers, I am amazed. Look at the four funnel towers throw the smoke. I wonder how much one of those huge things weighs."

Tipping his head back to look up at the four impressive towers, Karl exclaimed, "I also wonder how much coal is fed to the ovens below to make it go this fast. I have heard the crew must shovel load after load into the burners. It must be a hot, dirty job, one I would not like, I am sure!"

They turned back and started walking the other direction. Arnold motioned for Karl to join him as he moved toward an unoccupied deck chair. Karl chose a seat next to him and leaned back in a weathered, wooden chair and looked thoughtfully out to the vast ocean. "The day I left on my journey, I remember seeing Katja standing in the doorway of our cottage with her parents and our sons hiding in her long skirts. She was so small, her black hair pulled back into the bun and many unhappy tears came from her beautiful brown eyes. She waved and waved and finally I could see her no more. My sons waved for a time, then ran off to play. They did not understand I would be gone for a long time."

"I tell you, Arnold, I had to make myself put one foot in front of the other, to keep walking for fear I would turn back to my family. Christian took me and my trunk to Belgrade where I bought passage on a boat to go up the Danube to Budapest. I traveled on to Prague by wagon where I boarded another boat for the trip up the Elbe River to Berlin. From there, I traveled by wagon to Bremen where I was taken by boat to Bremerhaven and the Emigrant's Building. All that time, Arnold," Karl said smiling, "I had the ticket my friend Ralf Nimitz had given to me, inside my coat. I never let it away from my coat pocket, even at night it was a part of me."

Karl was in a pensive mood as he continued, "I think when I left Surtschin and my Katja, I was numb. I did not let myself feel sadness because I was so excited. I knew what I had to do and I was determined to do it. For many days I was busy traveling and finally getting permission to board the ship." Karl paused. "You realize I am going to America as another man. According to my ticket, I am Ralf Nimitz. I was quite relieved as I had no trouble with the immigration authorities or getting permission to board the ship. They only looked at my ticket and the name and, from that moment, I became Ralf Nimitz. They did not ask for any identity papers or anything to prove who I was. I had in my possession all of Ralf Nimitz's travel papers and that was that! I had not thought long on this until I boarded this great ship and was standing at the railing, watching the land disappear. That is when you came to find me Arnold; and I am grateful for your help because I was in panic condition. It was at that moment the reality of it all came crashing into me."

Shaking off the emotion of the moment, Karl asked, "So, my friend, you mentioned that your grandfather gave you a ticket to travel to America?"

"Well, Karl, my ticket story is not as incredible as the way in which you received yours. I also was not to inherit in any manner in which I could make my success. My grandfather is a wealthy man and it was he who bought this ticket to America for me and my future. He was convinced this was the direction of my life after a *Neulander* came to our house in Hamburg, and spoke to us of the rich opportunity in America. He convinced us of his own success with his fine suit of expensive clothes and a gold watch hanging from a fob. It was not until later that we discovered these people are dressed and paid by the shipping companies and merchants in America. They receive anywhere from three to seventy florins for each person they sign up to make passage to America. They dress richly so to make us believe they have achieved vast wealth in the great country, and it merely awaits us, also."

Arnold quickly added, "I am also happy to know your ticket is paid for, Karl, and you don't sail as an indentured servant. Have you heard of this situation?"

"*Nein*, what do you speak of?" asked Karl.

"These are people who want to go to America and cannot afford a ticket. So, there are wealthy Americans who tell the *Neulander* they will pay for the emigrant's ticket and when he/she arrives in America, they discover they have signed a contract to work for a certain man or company for five to seven years in payment for their passage. When that is repaid, the person is free to go where he wants. Sometimes this is good, and sometimes not so good if the person's work is bought by a dishonest individual."

Arnold stopped walking and turned to face his friend. "Also, Karl, this next thing I tell you is quite bad and we both must be vigilant when we arrive in America. Sometimes people on the ship, who have access to the luggage, will say they have misplaced our bags. Actually they put them on another ship and then tell you the luggage was lost! You must pay unmerciful fees to retrieve your bags if they can be found. When these passengers cannot pay, they often become indentured servants or returned to the old country! It is just another way for those who are deceitful to receive free workers."

"*Gott* in heaven," said Karl, "thank you for telling me of these things. In Surtschin, my friend Ralf had told me of watching my luggage closely, but he did not tell me what could happen if they were lost. When it comes time to collect our trunks, we must watch them carefully."

"*Vell*, my friend," Karl exaggerated a German overtone, "I vould say vee are both blessed and that vee are beginning our new life together. Arnold, have you given thought to taking further English instruction? I have heard the ship offers instruction for beginning classes on board and I was thinking of looking for it. Vaht about you, vill you join with me?" Karl laughed, "because, as you can tell, I am having a difficult time remembering to pronounce 'wa' instead of '*va,*' and I vant to do better."

Arnold laughed as he snuffed out his pipe and put it into his pocket. Turning to his new friend, he replied enthusiastically, "That is a good idea, Karl; let us go in search of learning *das* English!"

As they walked along the corridor, Karl inquired, "Arnold, when we arrive in America, I have decided that I am going to become an American citizen. I loved *Deutschland* and the traditions—it will always be a part of me, but America is where I will now live and I wish to be an American citizen, it is my dream, *ja?*"

Arnold replied, "*Ja*, Karl, I will also be an American citizen but, for a time at least, I will want to read the German newspapers to still know of what is happening in *Deutschland.* I have heard also there is the *German Press* in America which helps those of us who immigrate, to learn of the new ways of political, social, and economic life. *Das ist gute, ja?*"

As a ship steward passed, Karl asked, "Excuse me, sir, can you tell us where the English lessons are taught on the ship?"

Thankfully the steward spoke German and replied in the native tongue, "*Ja*, you continue to the end of this deck and it is in the large room on the right. If you hurry, you can begin on the first lesson."

Karl and Arnold thanked the steward in unison and hurried off down the deck. They reached the first lesson in time and spent a good portion of each day thereafter, learning sufficient phrases of English to be able to make their way around in their new country, once they arrived.

Later that evening on the upper deck as they smoked their last pipe of the day, Karl and Arnold discussed the route of their passage. "When we left Bremen, we sailed out of the harbor to the southwest, down the coast past Amsterdam in the Netherlands. Next we passed through the English Channel, and that is where I think we hit the hard seas and I got so sick in the night," said Karl.

Arnold interjected, "*Ja, ja,* that is the route we sailed. Now we are off the coast of France, and soon we sail around the northern tip of Spain and along the coast of Portugal to the port of the Gibraltar, the great rock harbor to take on fresh water and food, before crossing the Atlantic Ocean."

The next morning, the four-funneled steamer indeed made its way to the port of Gibraltar. The huge gray rock loomed in the mist of the morning light as the ship eased into the harbor. Karl could see the Mediterranean Sea on the far side of the port. He spotted a large, white-stucco lighthouse built on a reef to the west side of the inlet, as well as one next to the rock at the Strait of Gibraltar. "Arnold, would you look at that light house? Have you ever laid your eyes on anything so beautiful? It is almost as impressive as the size of that solid rock mountain."

Arnold and Karl were smoking their pipes on deck and watching the frenzied activity of dock men loading fresh water and food, along with more coal to feed the hungry steam boilers of the KronPrinz Wilhelm. Passenger excitement began to rise as the last of the barrels and crates were loaded onto the ship. They could hear the shouts and commands of Spanish workmen on the docks, but Karl and Arnold couldn't understand what they were saying. Soon the loading was completed and the great ship was readied for her final leg of the journey to Ellis Island, in America.

Tapping his pipe over the edge of the railing, Arnold asked, "How long do you think the crossing will take from here to America?"

Karl replied, "I overheard some of the crew talking last night. They said if we had good weather, it should not take longer than one week. On the map, we are directly across the Atlantic Ocean from New York. It is why they sail down the coast to Spain—that, and it is good to replenish our fuel, water, and food at this point."

"*Herr* Kessel, my friend," Arnold said as he lowered his voice, looking cautiously to the left and to the right before he continued, "tonight after lights out, let us creep up to this deck and listen to the musicians play in the grand ballroom. I couldn't help but hear some of it last night as I was returning from my smoke and it was *wunderbar*. They were playing Chopin, Bach, Debussy, and some Rachmaninov, too. Would you want to do this, Karl?"

He didn't have to ask a second time. Karl was more than willing to chance being on the forbidden deck. He would do almost anything in order to have the opportunity to listen to music that could take his mind away from the loneliness he felt for his family. Later that night, after lights out, the two men met at the washroom, both dressed in their good suits so if by chance they might be observed, they would blend in with the first and second class passengers who were allowed on deck at night.

One at a time, they slipped up the stairway onto the lower deck. They passed silently along the cabin walls, moving quickly in and out of the shadows. As they neared the ballroom they could hear the endearing melodies of the classical music drifting out of the open windows, and onto the ocean breezes. Taking a casual glance in one of the windows of the grand ballroom, Karl and Arnold observed the ostentatious gaiety. First- and second-class passengers were dressed in grand fashion in their finest suits and elegant gowns of satin, sequins, silk, dripping with diamonds and sapphires. They were entertaining themselves and each other, drinking champagne, talking audaciously, and laughing in an obnoxious manner, rather than sitting quietly, and respectfully listening to the incredible music.

Karl commented to his friend, "Arnold, it is a sad thing. Those people in the room do not understand that by conducting themselves in this rude manner, they are totally missing the ultimate experience of the *music*." The two neatly dressed men sank back onto adjoining deck chairs in order to absorb the phenomenal music of the world's great composers.

Arnold and Karl drew out their pipes and lit them. They didn't speak; they didn't move. They merely drifted in and out of consciousness with the lilting notes of the compositions. Karl was drawn to his memories of Katja and himself and their shared music experiences. The haunting melodies reminded him of times when he took her hair down from the tight black bun and caressing her face, her neck, of making love to her. It reminded him of all the sweetness and treasures in his life, which were no longer at his side but remained in his heart and mind.

Arnold simultaneously recalled his childhood in Hamburg. *My family, especially my grandfather trusted me to go to this new land and to become a success. I am so grateful that he gave this opportunity to me and I vow to make him proud!* He thought of his former lover Lisolette who was now betrothed to another man, a man whom her family had chosen for her. Arnold remembered with deep melancholy. *I loved her so deeply, the sound of her voice, the tilt of her head, the smell of her hair, the look in her eyes after we kissed. It was beyond my control, why it had all failed. I had to hold my head up and I had to be strong, to move on, to leave it all and to sail away to America—but to what? Only God in heaven knows.*

The exquisite notes of classical chamber music that floated out of the French doors aboard the four-funneled steamer that April night were like balm to those melancholy hearts who took the time to listen to the music. Both Karl and Arnold said a prayer, that God would guide them and give them courage to face whatever awaited them in America. They should have also asked God to keep them safe from unknown elements which lay in wait in *"Amerika"!*

CHAPTER 4

Ellis Island, 1906

★ ★ ★ ★ ★

"Young and old, let us unite for one purpose. Let us be temperate, industrious, and frugal. Let us build up in our hearts a temple, wherein the rational farseeing spirit of American liberty may live and flourish, and thus we may become good, happy, and free American citizens."

~Pastor F. W. Bogen, 1851

"When we write home we can tell them we have seen the famous Rock of Gibraltar. We are world travelers, my friend. This is a big, big world. I could never have imagined all the things we have seen already and we have only just begun." Arnold slapped Karl on the back in friendship as the two men stood on deck, smoking their pipes and watching as the colossal rock disappeared over the horizon.

After leaving the Port of Gibraltar, Karl and Arnold agreed on an early night and headed off to their respective berths. Karl slept well, dreaming again of Katja and especially their last night together. Her face came out of the mist in his dream, calling to him, pleading with him. She was trying to tell him something, but what, he wasn't able to make it out. Karl couldn't touch her; he couldn't reach out to her as she stayed at a distance where he could not be with her. The dream continued until the point when he cried out, "Katja, Katja, stay with me, I need you. Let me show my love to you, come closer so I may touch your soft skin and bury my face in the rose powder scent of your neck." Finally, she was there, embracing him and caressing his face, his back, his hair, until he could not bear it. Without warning she disappeared, as if a puff of smoke!

Listening to the chamber music the night before had evoked his memory of the final night he held his wife in his arms. It all came back to him, floating on the notes of Pachelbel's "Canon Four." Karl and Katja had fed their two sons early and carried them up the stairs, tucking them into bed after evening prayers. Arm in arm they turned and walked slowly back down the narrow stairs, returning to sit and talk at the kitchen table. The fire had burned low in the kitchen hearth. The light was soft and sent subtle shadows of illumination floating across the small room. Both Karl and Katja were tense with aching emotion and a nagging anticipation of what lay ahead. Both realized this would be their last night together for a long time. Katja poured each of them a glass of wine, the new crop from her father's vineyards. She stood and lifted her glass. "Karl, my husband, here, let us toast to our future, which begins tomorrow."

He remembered how he had taken a deep swallow of the wine and felt it run down his throat to settle and relax his belly. He took another and began to feel the tenseness melt from his body as he spoke, "We aren't sure of what will happen tomorrow and the days after that when we are apart. I do not know what I will find when I arrive in America and I have to wait until I have a home ready for your comfort when you and our sons make the crossing."

He took another sip of wine, hoping it would settle his emotions. "I want you to remember, my *Liebschen*, I love you always, and I leave your side only to make a new life for us. I have worries about you and our sons, but I am confident your parents will care for all of you. I know they will see to your every need." A twinkle lit up his blue eyes and, as a sly smile formed on his mouth, Karl suggested, "Except the need only I can fulfill for you."

They sipped their glasses of wine as they spoke to each other in low, intimate voices. Finally, Karl rose from the table and threw another log on the fire. He turned to his wife, "Come, *Leibschen,* no more talk, no more wine. Come up the stairs with me, now."

Karl reached for his wife's hand and they climbed the stairs together to their bedroom, eager to partake of their love. That night almost proved to be a match for their wedding night. After several years of marriage, their love had matured to a place where they both anticipated and knew each other's bodies and needs. The initial gentleness of their lovemaking was breathtaking, as if they needed to make a lasting and beautiful memory of their union. He dreamed of how they held nothing back; they understood this night must last them for a long time. They intended to cherish every moment. They made more than a memory that last night!

Karl woke from his dream suddenly, sweating profusely—his breath came in great gasps. The dream was fresh in his mind; his body quivered with arousal. Karl sat up in bed, fully awake. An involuntary shudder shook his body as he realized it was only a dream. He pulled his clothes on and, slipping out of his berth, quietly made his way down the aisle to the washroom. Karl turned the water on and let it run cold before splashing it onto his face. After attempting to wash the haunting dream from his mind, he exited the washroom and climbed the stairs out of steerage. Up on deck, Karl walked to a concealed area of the ship's railing for a change of scenery and a smoke.

The cool night breeze brushed across his face and tousled his hair as he paused and lit his clay pipe. Karl peered down over the railing and into the inky blackness of the Atlantic Ocean. His head lifted to the night sky where a canopy of twinkling stars was like a balm to his tormented body. He thought of Katja. *Is she also looking at the night sky and thinking of me, too?* Karl's mind wandered down unknown paths of speculation, wondering what tomorrow, and the days after, might bring. He lingered on deck that night until a chill crawled up his back. He shivered as he emptied his pipe, turned and moved unnoticed back down to his berth in third class.

The next morning when Karl awoke, he discovered that *Frau* Volk was ill. It was her worst nightmare: becoming ill and not being able to care for her children. Karl and Arnold were quick to see she needed their help.

"*Frau* Volk," said Karl, "please allow *Herr* Reinholt and me to take your children up on the deck for their breakfast. We will watch them for a few hours so that you may rest. Please do not worry; try to get some sleep."

The widow raised her head from the pillow and responded weakly, "Oh, *Herr* Kessel, I cannot ask you for this kindness. We have a few bites of food and my children can eat here in the berth. I believe we can manage."

"*Nein, Frau* Volk, you are too ill and you need to rest. Please do not dispute our request to help. You will please close your eyes now; we will care for your children with breakfast and a bit of fresh air and exercise, too. We will watch them closely; please do not worry yourself."

Before *Frau* Volk could argue any further, Karl and Arnold whisked the four children up and out of third class, into the fresh ocean air and sunshine. The children were eager to leave behind the smelly depths of steerage and their sick mother. They were sure the day would be an adventure and were quite comfortable with the two fellow countrymen who befriended their mother.

Arnold was obviously nervous with the responsibility, as he admitted, "Karl, you will have to tell me what to do with the children. I do not have the experience as you."

The children were well behaved and minded the men's instructions, which relieved Arnold to no extent.

Experienced as he was, Karl handed the four little ones their tin mess kits, which *Frau* Volk had given to him. "Over here, children, we will go through the food lines. The two boys go with *Herr* Reinholt and the two girls come with me. Let us meet over there at the second table and we will eat our breakfast."

As the children made their way down the food line, the ship's crew filled the four compartments with food. In one the toast was laid, the second was filled with a heaping spoon of steaming oatmeal. A hard-boiled egg was placed in the third, and slices of an orange were placed in the fourth.

Karl instructed, "Now, snap shut the lid so you don't spill your breakfast, and follow *Herr* Reinholt to the table. I will go over there and get the coffee for us and hot milk for you."

Karl returned shortly and they said a prayer of thanksgiving for the food before devouring their breakfast. It felt good to be in the sunny, open air and to have warm oatmeal and toast in their stomachs. After the meal was finished, they rinsed their tin kits. Arnold gathered them up and took them below, to stow them in their berths.

When Arnold returned, he and Karl had a moment to themselves as the children were involved with organized morning exercise on deck. Karl remarked, "Remember when we first boarded the ship in Bremerhaven and were given the tin mess kits? Were you as amazed as I was to discover actual ethnic food lines? There is such an assortment of food, each to make the different peoples feel comfortable. I am most happy without selection of soup, eggs, sliced meat, mashed potatoes, sausage, brown bread, sauerkraut, and pickles."

The big German nodded his head, "*Ja, ja*, for sure most peoples will find something they like to eat and, if not, they can eat some of the foods they brought on board with them."

Laughing, Karl turned to his friend, "*Ja*, but one thing that all the different foods have in common are the garlic and onions. The smell is so strong; my clothes will have the smell, too!"

That afternoon, Karl and Arnold were watching *Frau* Volk's children play organized games on the deck. Arnold took his pipe from this coat pocket and, after he lit it, he grew serious as he reflected, "I have been thinking on the advice from Pastor Bogan's instruction to emigrants. Do you remember the part that read: 'Never pay in advance for your fare from New York to the interior of America?' You can gain nothing by this, but lose much. Pay your passage only to New York and not further. If you wish to go to Missouri or Iowa, go by way of New Orleans. Although there is deception enough committed there, it is not bad and the consequences not as pernicious as in New York City. You have the right to remain with your baggage on board the ship for forty-eight hours after your arrival. Make use of this privilege. Do not be in a hurry. Take time; if you intend to go to the interior, be not detained in other great cities by Germans residing there. They will tell you stories about bears and wolves, and impenetrable forests, and poisonous swamps. They will paint you phantoms of terror of every kind in order to detain you in the cities. Believe them not! If you have relations in the interior who have written to you, travel to them. Never buy land that you have not seen with your own eyes. And, never, under any circumstances, get in debt."

Karl responded, "*Ja*, Arnold, I do remember all that Pastor Bogan recommended. I am hopeful that I have a job in Cleveland waiting for me. Now, about you, my friend, what are your plans when we get to America? Would you consider traveling with me and looking for work in Cleveland?"

"Well, Karl, it is interesting you ask that question. I have been giving that same idea serious thought. I have not yet made the decision what I will do after we are checked through Ellis Island. But, *ja*, I will think about going to Cleveland with you. I will think about it. *Ja*, I will do that."

The two men spent most of the afternoon up on deck, soaking up the warmth of the sunshine and breathing fresh ocean air. *Frau* Volk's children were having a grand time playing rambunctious deck games with other children. Karl laughed as he observed, "It is my thought that *Frau* Volk's children are going to sleep well this night. They are getting good exercise in this clean air."

After they had a light supper up on deck, Karl and Arnold returned the children to *Frau* Volk, along with two slices of toast and black tea. She was in high spirits as the result of the welcomed break from her responsibilities and the opportunity to recuperate in peace. A weak smile broke across her pretty face and her sea-blue eyes lit up as she said, "*Herr* Kessel and *Herr* Reinholt, how can I thank you? You have no idea what a blessing you both were to me this day. I wish there was something I could do for you in return."

Karl replied, "I was honored to help you today. It was the least we could do for you, *Frau* Volk. Didn't you make tea for me the first night on board, when I was so ill with the sea and that cabbage soup? It was nothing to take care of your children; they are good children. We would be happy to take them up on deck for a couple of hours tomorrow if that would also be of help to you."

"Oh my, that would be *wunderbar*. There are so many things I need to do, laundry and mending. I appreciate your offer so much, *Danka schön*."

After spending a frustrating morning in English class, Arnold complained to Karl. "You know, my friend, I am ashamed that I am not learning the English as fast as *Frau* Volk's children. It is amazing the English words they know already. My head must be thicker than I thought it was."

By the end of the week, the passengers were aware they were getting close to shore and their American destination. Karl was up on deck having a smoke when he noticed a flock of noisy seabirds flying alongside the ship. Some of the other passengers saw them as well and were delighted in watching them dive into the ocean. The birds flew low near the water, seeking food that churned up in the wake of the great ship. An older female passenger was ecstatic as she loudly declared, "I can smell the land—I can smell America even before we can see it. I CAN, I CAN!"

Karl smiled as he scanned the horizon for a solid dark line, then remarked to his friend, "If she can smell that well, perhaps it is a good idea we don't stand too close to her!" The two men enjoyed their inside joke, as men will.

As they drew near their destination, passengers in each class were occupied in preparation for the arrival. Hair and beards were trimmed, baths taken, clothes scrubbed, bags organized, and checked again. Their frenzied preparation was pregnant with fearful anticipation of the debarkation process at Ellis Island for landing.

Many of the passengers were up on deck at dawn when a loud cheer went up. What was it? People were running to catch a glimpse for themselves. "KARL, KARL—look. There is America—see that irregular line spreading across the horizon? It's LAND!"

The stately KronPrinz Wilhelm moved easily through the "Narrows" and past Staten Island, as wide-eyed passengers gripped the ship's railings. Arnold and Karl were on deck as well, their freshly scrubbed bodies dressed in their best suits. Their baggage was ready and secured below in their berths. As the two friends stood on the deck of the massive steam ship, they surveyed the tight arrangement of huge buildings which rose from Manhattan Island. Both men were struck dumb at the spectacle. It had not occurred to them that they would experience such a fearful thrill when they laid their eyes on American soil for the first time. The brisk inland breeze caressed their faces and tussled their freshly combed hair. Passengers from steerage were falling down on their knees, crying, and laughing as the Statue of Liberty came into view, silhouetted against the brilliant morning sky. *"Mein Gott*, there she is— the statue. We are now free; we are free!" The frenzied joy and exhilaration was contagious.

Arnold and Karl heard a deep, male voice coming from the upper decks. In broken English he recited the poem written by Emma Lazarus in 1883:

Not like the brazen giant of Greek fame
With conquering limbs astride from land to land;
Here at your sea-washed, sunset gates shall stand,
A mighty woman with a torch, whose flame
Is the imprisoned lighting, and her name
Mother of Exiles. From her beacon-hand
Glows world-wide welcome; her mild eyes command
The air-bridged harbor that twin cities frame.
"Keep, ancient lands, your storied pomp!" cries she
With silent lips. "Give me your tired, your poor,
Your huddled masses yearning to breathe free,
The wretched refuse of your teeming shore,
Send these, the homeless, tempest tossed to me,
I lift my lamp beside the golden door!"

Immigration officers from the Quarantine Station had boarded the ship earlier at the mouth of the Hudson River and preformed their duties on board. By the time the ship eased into the Upper Bay, the privileged first- and second-class passengers had gone through inspection and were cleared to leave the ship once it moored at the Hudson River pier. The steerage passengers were not so fortunate. Once they disembarked on the Hudson River pier, they were herded onto waiting ferries which shuttled them back across the water, to the feared Ellis Island, to experience the dreaded and notorious mass inspection and examinations.

Karl had heard these ferries were not much better than ordinary barges, no frills! In winter, passengers nearly froze as they crossed the icy water. In the sweltering heat and draining humidity of the eastern summer, the crossing could be miserable, to say the least. Furthermore, the ferries did not have toilets or life-saving facilities. There were rumors that many died on this final leg of the journey simply as a result of the appalling conditions. Frequently, passengers were kept waiting on ferry boats until there was room for them in the long lines in Emigration Hall.

Karl and Arnold made sure they stayed together, as passengers jammed onto a waiting ferry. There were five ferries, all manned by impatient captains eager to unload their human cargo.

Karl observed, "Arnold, I think we are lucky it is April and not August or December. It would be quite bad to be on this boat in extreme weather."

"*Ja, ja,* Karl, you are right; but I am becoming nervous to get off and finish with this inspection. The thought of it makes me anxious and I am starting to sweat much in this wool coat. I might not smell so sweet when we go through the lines." Arnold laughed.

Enjoying the light-hearted banter, Karl teased, "Well, Arnold, perhaps the inspectors will usher you through the lines quickly because of your aroma!"

Finally, it was their turn to unload. Karl and Arnold made sure they had their bags in hand and were ready to set foot on something that didn't wasn't in perpetual motion. As they stepped off the boat, the land seemed to shift and tilt.

"Oh, *mein Gott*," laughed Karl. "My legs feel all wobbly, like I had too much beer. I think the pier is moving, as the ship." They noticed other passengers feeling the same thing, as they staggered and lurched ahead. "Arnold, I think this is what some persons were naming sea legs. We just have to keep walking and soon we will be better!"

Arnold surveyed the throng of seething humanity, "Karl, have you seen *Frau* Volk and the children?"

"*Ja*," answered Karl, "she is up ahead of us. I saw her just a short while ago. She seemed fine, but we should watch out for her."

As more than a thousand emigrants disembarked from the ferries, they were crushed into a single line that wound its way back and forth like a serpent, from the dock to the point where debarkation officials waited. While a ship's crew member pinned numbered tags onto each passenger's coat, an embarkation official directed people into specific lines. The numbered tags were an indication of each ship's manifest line and page number where a passenger's individual name appeared. This proved to be an effective way to identify and keep track of people. Wobbly steerage passengers fresh off their ships were obviously confused by uniformed persons shouting commands at them in a language most didn't understand. However, they did understand the pointing fingers and stern body language as they were jostled into the correct lines.

Line after line of wide-eyed, impatient people gradually approached the looming principal building. Karl and Arnold soon found themselves three-abreast in a line that wound its way up a steep flight of stairs and spilled into the cavernous hall of the Registry Room. Vigilant inspectors were carefully watching the immigrants as they climbed the stairs, searching for any signs of illness or weakness. They made notes concerning any passenger who coughed, wheezed, limped, or had a difficult time ascending the stairs.

Frau Volk was visually upset when an inspector roughly lifted her two-year-old daughter from her arms. The frightened mother stood back and watched as other inspectors spoke directly into each ear of the small child, checking her hearing. Satisfied with what they saw, they put her down on the floor and watched as she toddled off to her mother. They checked off the related boxes, testifying that the baby could walk and hear normally. *Frau* Volk breathed an obvious sigh of relief as she scooped her child up into her arms; the inspectors motioned for her and the children to move ahead.

Hundreds of inspectors and doctors had their work cut out for them, checking for fifty to sixty specific symptoms in each passenger. The main symptoms they were looking for were those of cholera, insanity, mental disabilities, epilepsy, tuberculosis, and flavus (a nail and scalp fungus). If a person was physically disabled, they were pulled from the line. Actually, only about two percent of immigrants were denied entry to America based on an unacceptable condition. Those two percent were put on a ship going *back* to their homeland at the cost of the shipping line. Because on some days, more than 5,000 persons went through the gates, this percentage could amount to hundreds of unfortunate immigrants in a month. Being sent back to the old country was the unspeakable horror dreaded the most, and it was *always* a possibility.

The two men heard of the unpopular inspection that the doctors performed to check for a highly contagious eye infection, trachoma. As the line snaked around, they had opportunity to see the inspection first hand.

"Oh, *mein Gott*, look at those doctors. They are using a hairpin or button hook to turn the passenger's eyelid inside out."

Karl and Arnold heard *Frau* Volk's children cry out at the sight. When it was their turn to be examined, she was most distraught, trying her best to sooth and comfort all four of them as their eyes were examined one by one.

"Karl," Arnold confided, "I don't think I am going to like that eye test, either. I don't like it when they pinch, push, and look inside me!" His laugh was anything but light-hearted.

In an attempt to put his friend at ease, Karl teased, "Maybe today is your lucky day. Perhaps now they will take one smell of you and push you on through the line! Be strong like your name, my friend; it will soon be over and we will be on our way to Cleveland!"

Pointing to a group of doctors across the room, Arnold said, "Look over there; see how the doctors are marking some people with blue chalk, and now they are directed into another line for more inspections." They learned later a PG was written, if a woman was pregnant. X was for mental problems. FT was for bad feet. Approximately eight out of every one hundred persons were detained for further medical examination. Most of those passengers were sent to the infirmary and some were even hospitalized until they recovered.

After going through the medical inspection and receiving no blue marks, Arnold and Karl were channeled into the main part of the Registry Hall. They entered a maze-like arrangement of metal aisles snaking back and forth, dividing the huge open room into efficient aisles. These metal passageways herded the immigrants forward in an orderly manner toward the verbal interrogation portion of the inspection.

A strange sound, like a frenzied, multi-level buzzing sound, spilled from the cavernous room. The reverberation was the result of hundreds of excited persons speaking in their own language and dialect. On a good day, it took four to five hours for one person to pass through all of the inspections. During this stressful time there were washrooms available where emigrants could relieve themselves and cleanup as well. There was a huge dining room where hundreds of thousands of meals were served to the hungry and anxious immigrants.

During this part of the process, Arnold and Karl noticed several men going through the lines, offering milk and some long yellow things to the children; they called the curled yellow pieces "bananas." *Frau* Volk's children tried to bite the bananas at the end and, after doing so, made a terrible face until one of the men showed them how to peel the fruit, and then eat only the soft white inside portion. *Frau* Volk's son Helmut enjoyed his snack so much that he ran ahead and wriggled back into the line to receive another. Karl commented, "*Ja*, that Helmut is a smart boy; I wonder if I could do that, too?"

Finally it was Karl's turn to answer questions from the inspectors. He was relieved to see that they had German translators, as his English skills were not yet perfected. He had learned conversational English on the ship, but continued to have difficulty expressing himself, especially when he was nervous. First, the inspectors verified the information as listed on Karl's manifest sheet. During this period of immigration, great care was taken to spell the person's name correctly. Years later, immigrants or overworked, impatient inspectors were allowed to shorten or change the spelling of immigrant's surnames.

The aging inspector peered at Karl over the rimless glasses that rode on the tip of his nose. "Mr. Nimitz, how old are you? What is your occupation? Are you married? Where are you going? Do you have a job? Do you carry money to travel? How much money do you carry?"

So many questions, why do they need to know all of these things? Karl thought.

It was the job of the inspector to determine if the immigrant was strong, intelligent, and resourceful enough to find a job and to work at that job. Even though his guts were churning, Karl remained calm and had no trouble answering the questions.

Further up in the line, Karl noticed that *Frau* Volk was speaking loudly and almost frantically, as she gestured to several inspectors. All four children were crying at full volume as well. *Frau* Volk's face was florid and her blue eyes were enormous with fear and frustration. "Sir, please, sir, you do not understand; I am a widow. My children and I travel to live with my father in his house in I-o-va. I have the train ticket which he sent to me. Here, here is his letter to me, to come to I-O-V-A."

One burley inspector stepped forward, as Karl strained to hear what was happening. "Madam, we must detain you and your children until we are certain the person who wrote the letter is indeed your father and not some unrelated male."

The head inspector interceded, "However, I see you do have a prepaid train ticket paid for and sent by your father. You must understand it is our policy that any unescorted women and/or children must be held, for their safety of course, until we can be sure you will be safe in your travels to a legitimate destination. We cannot merely send you out into the streets, for there are many terrible circumstances that might happen to an unescorted woman."

Frau Volk pointed back to where Karl and Arnold were standing. "My friends could tell you that my story is true. Perhaps they could escort me to the train for which my children and I have tickets to travel on."

The inspector looked back to where Karl and Arnold were standing and said, "Mrs. Volk, I am afraid that would not be acceptable, either. We have another rule which states that an unescorted woman may not leave in the company of any man to whom she is not related. However, one moment and I will speak to my superior on your behalf."

He was gone only a short time, when he returned and announced, "Mrs. Volk, you and your children may continue to the train. Continue to the right, down the stairs, the Stairs of Separation, where you will be able to attain directions to locate your luggage and the correct ferry back to the New York Harbor and the train station. There are more people down on the dock to assist you."

Karl and Arnold watched as a relieved smile broke over *Frau* Volk's face as she turned and waved to them as she and her children disappeared down the stairway. It wasn't long before Karl and Arnold also passed the final station and descended the Stairs of Separation, so named because it was the area where the immigrants separated from the inspection process and were officially permitted entry to the United States of America. At the bottom of the stairs, Arnold and Karl were surprised to see *Frau* Volk and her children standing off to one side, obviously waiting. The children ran up to the two men and hugged them around the legs. *Frau* Volk walked shyly over to Karl and Arnold, extending her hand.

"I could not leave on the train until I tell you both *"Danka schön,* for all you did to help me during the crossing. I will remember you both in my prayers that you arrive safely at your destinations. I will leave you now. God bless you both."

Frau Volk and her children turned and walked toward their ferry. The baby was leaning over her mother's shoulder, waving her pudgy little hand at the two men and drooling down the back of her mother's dress.

Karl and Arnold stood for a moment watching *Frau* Volk and her children leave. "I don't know about you, Karl; but I am sad to see those young ones going. I think I should find a good woman and get married so I can have some childrens, too. I think I now like them around!"

"I am sure that *Frau* Volk and her children will be fine for the rest of their trip," said Karl. Changing the subject, he asked. "So, my friend, have you decided to accompany me to Cleveland where I have a position and perhaps you can secure work at the same company?"

"*Ja,* Karl, I think it is a good idea, for I must make sure you arrive at your destination and do not get lost," Arnold said, laughing. The two men got in a line which formed near the 5,500-square-foot Ferry Building. They had survived the maze of health and legal inspections and received permission to begin their lives in America.

The Ferry Building of Ellis Island was probably one of the happiest buildings on the island. The most impressive feature of the modern brick building was the ornate lead-coated copper cupola. As Karl and Arnold entered the building they walked across dark, marble-like terrazzo tiled floors. The two men were duly impressed by the grandeur of the 180-pound bronze chandelier that hung in the central pavilion.

"Karl, look at the size of that candelabra, *mein Gott,* it is so huge and beautiful. I've never seen anything like it, have you?"

His companion responded in agreement. "*Nein,* Arnold, never did I see such a glorious light. In the opera house in Belgrade there were beautiful lightings, but not so large as this one. When we get across the harbor here, my friend, we will be able to buy our ticket to Cleveland, if I understood correctly."

After crossing and finding the train depot, Arnold and Karl located their baggage, and purchased tickets to Cleveland, Ohio. The two friends boarded the train for the final portion of their journey. After settling in their seats, Karl became thoughtful as he pulled Pastor Bogen's book from his small carpet bag, "Arnold, I have been thinking again on what Pastor Bogen recommended once we arrive in America. Do you remember this part?" Karl began to read.

> *No immigrant ought to hesitate for a moment to become master of the English language. As long as we do not accomplish this, can we neither appreciate nor enjoy the whole freedom and independence which this land has in store for us. As nearly every German immigrant takes lodgings at first in a German boardinghouse, he should choose especially one in which the landlord is familiar with English, and he will doubtless have the kindness to make him acquainted with many English words and phrases, and teach him the right pronunciation of the words, which he will find in his grammar and collection of colloquial phrases. It is true that he understands at first only a small part of what he hears and reads; but he must not, on this account, lose his courage. By and by his ear will become more and more familiar with the sounds of words, and his memory more accustomed to retain them. Remember the adage: Practice makes perfect.*

"*Ja*, Karl, I do remember the words of the good pastor. Perhaps when we arrive in Cleveland we can find information regarding a respectable German boarding house. For now my friend, I am quite tired and think I would like to take a long nap. I think it will be easy, just listening to the clickity-clack of the train wheels running over the rails."

Arnold stretched his muscular arms wide and yawned loudly as he plumped his coat into a pillow and snuggled down in his seat. He was asleep and snoring before Karl took another breath.

Karl sat for awhile, looking at his friend as he slept. A smile broke over his weathered face as he thought to himself, *I am a lucky man to have met such a friend as Arnold. It will be good to have him with me in Cleveland; it will be easier to do what we have to do, when we have each other to talk to.* A shiver of anticipation ran down his back as he thought about what opportunities lay waiting for him. He was confident he carried all the personal tools he needed to succeed: ambition, knowledge, tenacity, determination, and faith that God had brought him to this place.

Soon, Karl followed his friend's lead and plumped his own coat, bunching it into a place to rest his head. He, too, was soon asleep; his dreams were not of the past but of the future that awaited him and Arnold in the American city called Cleveland.

CHAPTER 5

Cleveland

★ ★ ★ ★ ★

"Let there never be an end to your dreams, a road too rough to travel, or a sunset that doesn't hold the promise of a new tomorrow." ~Mary Jane Cook

1906

On a late April evening the smoking iron engine pulled into the train station in Cleveland, Ohio. Karl and Arnold exited the train, claimed their baggage, and paid for a large locker to hold their traveling trunks until they could find a place to live. "Okay, I don't know about you, Arnold, but I need to find something to eat before I fall down."

Getting directions from the porter, they walked up the street, until they came upon a small German restaurant where they settled in for some streusel and coffee.

"*Ja, Karl, das ist gut*, we needed this little time for relaxation and to decide what we will do now," Arnold said as he gobbled down his steamy, fragrant apple strudel covered in thick, fresh cream. "If I wasn't so hungry, I would just sit here and smell this gift from heaven." He lifted the oval bowl of fragrant strudel under his nose, closed his eyes, and inhaled.

Karl sat for a moment thoroughly entertained by the way his friend was gobbling his dessert. A serious expression crossed his face as he replied, "I am thinking to ask the owner of the restaurant to recommend where we might rent a room for the night. Tomorrow we will go to the offices of Great Lakes Sugar Company and inquire if they have jobs for us."

They spent the night in Cleveland at a modest hotel, not far from the train station. The next morning the two woke bright and early, excited and eager to experience their first day in their new country. A young man at the front desk gave them directions to the Great Lakes Sugar Company offices. They left their overnight luggage locked in the hotel baggage room, promising to return later to claim it. Once out in the street, they noticed many push-carts propelled by merchants shouting out their products and the price. As they walked down the street, they saw a trolley car rumbling down the tracks in the same direction. With animated excitement, Karl said, "Arnold, I'm tired of walking. Let's part with a few cents and splurge to take the trolley car; do you agree?"

"*Ja,* Karl, I see a stop up ahead. Come on, let's run and hop in, it will be fun."

Side by side Arnold and Karl sat on an empty bench in the red trolley as it rumbled down the streets of Cleveland. Their eyes were wide with wonder as they feasted on foreign and unexpected sights. Large, modern brick and stone buildings lined the main street; the sidewalks were bustling with busy, industrious, well-dressed men, all hurrying somewhere. Fashionably dressed women strolled past them, down the tree-lined boulevards, with large beautiful hats shading their elegantly styled hair. They noticed an assortment of push carts manned by plainly dressed men, selling their fresh wares.

Karl nudged Arnold. "I think we are coming near where we have to get off the trolley. Our destination is not directly on the trolley route, so we will have to walk a few blocks. Are you ready, my friend, to step into our future?"

A passerby smiled as he noticed the two eager immigrants walking briskly down the sidewalk. Their eyes flashed with excitement and their conversation was animated as they chatted loudly in their native tongue while they hurried to their destination. Arnold pointed to the top of a large building, "Karl, Karl! Look! There is the name of the company, over there on that impressive brick building. That name on the wall says it is the Great Lakes Sugar Company."

Karl and Arnold paused for a moment outside the door, smoothing their hair and re-positioning their hats. They each took a deep breath and with, wide tooth-bearing smiles, pushed open the large double doors. They stopped at the information desk. Karl spoke first, after removing his hat, "Please excuse, we are looking for directions to the office of *Herr* Dieter Mohr." The receptionist smiled at their use of English as she pointed them in the right direction.

When they reached the office of *Herr* Mohr, the two men asked the secretary at the desk if it would be possible to speak with Dieter Mohr, the man who Ralf Nimitz had instructed Karl Kessel to contact. She ushered the men into a starkly furnished office and invited them to take a seat. Mr. Mohr entered the room shortly and after greeting the two men, he moved to his black leather chair behind the large, paper-strewn walnut desk.

Karl took a moment to consider his first impression of *Herr* Mohr. He was a fine example of a modern businessman in his three-piece wool suit. *Herr* Mohr appeared to be around fifty and stood over six-feet tall; he was in good shape and probably limited the number of beers he consumed. His graying handlebar mustache and sideburns affirmed the distinguished and successful businessman image.

He rose from his desk and extended his hand to Karl. *"Guten Morgen,* Mr. Nimitz."

Karl quickly spoke up, *"Herr* Mohr, first, I must explain that I am not Ralf Nimitz; I am his friend Karl Kessel. He generously gave to me his ticket of passage to America, because he now inherits his father's farm. He also gave to me your name that I may take his place to work for you. I know much about farming sugar beets; I have worked with my father-in-law on his farm for many years."

A surprised expression crossed Dieter Mohr's face as he said, "Mr. *Kessel,* I am happy to meet you and also happy for your good fortune in coming to America. I am pleased to know you have knowledge about raising sugar beets. I do indeed have the opportunity of a job for you." He turned his attention to the other young man. Dieter Mohr said, "Now, who is this gentleman who travels with you?"

"Herr Mohr," volunteered Arnold, "my name is Arnold Reinholt and I am from Hamburg. I do not know of sugar beets, but I have apprenticed as a bookkeeper for the last seven years. Would you have a position open for someone of my talents?"

"Well, gentlemen," said Dieter Mohr, fingering his waxed handlebar mustache, "I think you both are fortunate today. Yes, Mr. Reinholt, I do think we have a place where we can use your bookkeeping experience as well. I believe you can both begin your employment on Monday morning. Mr. Reinholt, you will be working in our bookkeeping department; and Mr. Kessel, you will begin to learn about our sugar processing factories. When you have learned what we have to teach you, we will send you to Fremont, Ohio, where our largest processing factory is located on the Sandusky River, close to Lake Erie. There you will learn firsthand how we operate. After that we will talk of your future."

"You will both begin at a base salary of $1.25 per day, and after a few months, we'll see how well you are doing. If you do well, you will receive a raise once a year. Now, I am sure you will need to find rooms in which to live, unless you have already taken care of that. Here is a list of clean, inexpensive rooms for rent, which we call boarding houses. I suggest *Frau* Hesterhoff's boarding house which is only five blocks from the Great Lakes Sugar offices, on Superior Avenue; it is an easy walk. For other means of transportation in Cleveland, we have a good trolley system. On cold and snowy days, you might prefer to take the trolley to work rather than walk."

As Dieter Mohr thanked the two men and wished them good day, he thought about Karl Kessel. If his gut feeling served him well, he had just hired a hard-working, clever man. Mohr came to his assessment from observing the way Karl's eyes were bright with intelligence, filled with wary hunger—always searching. Mr. Mohr also noticed the hard, determined set to the man's jaw. *Yes sir, he is going to be a good one. I am sure of it!*

The two men thanked Dieter Mohr for his kindness and their good fortune and headed back out to the street. They decided to walk the five blocks to the recommended rooming house. Both men were in high spirits when they reached the porch of *Frau* Hesterhoff's boarding house. They knocked at the front door and waited patiently for someone to answer.

A small, stooped-shouldered, elderly woman opened the door. "*Ja, Gute Morgen*, what is it you want?"

Karl quickly replied, "*Gute Morgen* to you as well. I assume you are *Frau* Hesterhoff? I am Karl Kessel and this is my friend Arnold Reinholt. *Herr* Dieter Mohr from Great Lakes Sugar recommended your boarding house. We have soon arrived in Cleveland and have now, today, been told we have jobs at the Great Lakes Sugar Company. Do you have rooms to rent to good, clean, Christian *Deutsch* men, *ja?*"

Frau Hesterhoff swung the screen door open and gestured for the two men to enter. Speaking in broken English, she said, "*Ja, ja*, come in please and I *vill* show you the rooms that I have for rent." Karl and Arnold followed her into the house which smelled of cinnamon and furniture polish. She led them up the dimly lit stairway and stopped at the top of the stairs as she opened the door to a fresh-smelling, sunny room.

"Here is the first room. The second room is right next door. You may each choose which room you like. They are not fancy or how you say 'decorated,' but they are clean and you have what you need. Will this meet with your expectations, *ja*?"

Karl spoke quickly, "*Ja, Frau* Hesterhoff it is *wunderbar*. While we are speaking, we would appreciate you speaking English to us and perhaps helping us with our English in that way. We live in in America now, and we wish to speak English like everybody, *ja?*"

Frau Hesterhoff smiled and eagerly replied, "Mr. Kessel and Mr. Reinholt, I would be honored to help you with your English. It is an important thing and while we are speaking, I would like for you to call me Mrs. Hester, for short—and not because I *am* short," she laughed with great mirth.

The petite German woman suddenly became serious. "I also want to now tell you that this is a Christian house; I do not tolerate any actions that are not decent, and that includes no liquor. I think you men are proper, but I always tell my boarders about the rules, *ja?*"

After Karl and Arnold paid their room rent for the first week, they returned to the train station to retrieve their traveling trunks. They rented a wagon to move their luggage to the boarding house. They spent the next couple of hours unpacking and getting settled in their new rooms. Since they missed the evening meal at the boarding house, they asked their new landlady for directions to the nearest restaurant.

On their way, they came to a small newspaper shop that also sold maps. Karl's eyes opened wide and he exclaimed, "You know, Arnold, I think that it would be a fine idea to buy a good map of this city that will be our new home. It is a big city and we do not want to get lost; a map will help us learn our way around. Let's stop in here and see if they have what we need." Arnold heartily agreed as they entered the little shop.

"How much do you ask for a city map?" Karl inquired of the shopkeeper. Noticing that the two men looked fresh off the boat, the shopkeeper shrewdly replied, "The maps are fifty cents; they are good maps as you can see."

They looked at each other with knowing eyes as Arnold spoke up, "You ask almost half a day's wages for a city map? That is too much for a mere map, sir. I think if that is your final price, we will not buy our map here. I am sure there are many places where we will be able to purchase a good map for a better price." The two men turned and moved toward the front door.

"Oh, oh," stammered the shopkeeper, "I will make you a special price this night only for fifteen cents—the sale price."

"Okay, that is a better price and we will take one map only," replied Karl. Trying to hide a smug grin, Arnold paid for the thick map and stuck it his left-front coat pocket.

Strolling down the streets of Cleveland, Karl and Arnold noticed many different kinds of vehicles including rag carts, men on horseback, fancy carriages, large wooden wagons, busy trolleys, and a new phenomenon, the occasional noisy, sputtering automobile. It was indeed a busy place and the two friends were excited with the promise of something new to discover and experience around every corner.

Giddy with all they had experienced on their first day; they were in high spirits as they arrived at the restaurant Mrs. Hester recommended. Before ordering their meal, the pair went into the adjoining pub and ordered a cold beer. Sipping the cold brew, they chatted eagerly about the events of their first day in Cleveland. When they finished their beer, they moved into the dining room and quickly ordered a hot meal, washing it down with another frosty mug of good German beer.

As they left the restaurant and began to head back to the boarding house, Arnold pulled out his clay pipe, lit it and exclaimed, "*Ja*, Karl, this has been a good day, has it not? I am a happy man with a full belly and a clean place to lay my head this night." Arnold walked confidently down the sidewalk as a contented grin spread across his broad, angular face.

The two men strolled down the tree-lined sidewalk of Cleveland and noticed that the tall gaslights at the street corners were just being lit. Only the main streets had lighting, while the side streets remained dark, except for illumination coming from a few homes which lined the street. Karl paused for a moment as he also lit his pipe. "Smelling the smoke from your pipe has made me want a smoke as well. I always enjoy a pipe after a tasty meal; it is a good finish to the day! Don't you agree, my friend?"

Arnold nodded with agreement as they turned down the darkened side street heading in the direction of Mrs. Hester's boarding house. "*Ja*, my friend, I was thinking that I will have to write a letter to my Katja and tell her that we have arrived in America and in Cleveland, and that both of us now have jobs. Soon I think I will have the money to send for her and my two sons."

They were engrossed in conversation as they walked, not concerned with what was going on around them. Now that darkness had fallen over the city, gangs of raucous young ruffians emerged to roam the streets, looking for trouble and victims. They took pleasure in their boisterous and menacing behavior, threatening and preying on those who were brave or foolish enough to be out on the dimly lit side streets past dark.

Karl was first to notice three men cross the street in front of them and turn abruptly, to walk back toward them. The three men stopped, blocking the way for Karl and Arnold. The short one in front puffed up his chest and inquired, "I be a beggin jur pardon, sirs; would yah now have a wee pennae for a hungree bloke?"

Not quite understanding what was said or wanted by the group, Arnold stood perfectly still and looked at the bunch of hoodlums. It was Karl who volunteered the answer, "Sorry there, but we only arrived on this day and we have no money until we are paid from our jobs."

The smaller man turned and spoke to the burly young hooligan behind him, "I say, Master O'Hara, now do yah believe what yah just heard from this Dutchman? They must be mighty im-par-tant Dutchman to have just landed here and have jobs already; jobs that should be saved for us Americans!" The three thugs laughed and shook their heads in agreement as evil expressions crept over their faces and they moved menacingly closer to their victims.

In that instant, Arnold noticed a couple of thugs pulling clubs and knives from under their coats. He replied in broken English, "Now, you listen here, *ve* are not Dutch, *ve* are German, understand, *NOT* Dutch!"

The third man, obviously an Irishman, responded with a hard shove to Arnold's left shoulder, "Hey there, ya high an mighty Dutchie, don't yah go gettin all in yah beers with us!"

Karl interceded, "Boys, let us pass and you can go on down the street with your fun."

At that moment, two more men appeared from an alley behind Karl and Arnold and moved forward, trapping them. Karl turned and the color drained hard, as reality slapped him in the face. The men who came up from behind were dark as the night, and all Karl could see were their white teeth and their eyes. Karl had never observed a dark-skinned man in the flesh. He was filled with awe and a sickening fear. The streetwise gang took advantage of the momentary shock and quickly moved to close the ring of thievery and debauchery. Fists began to fly.

Arnold whirled and took two of the men with the first thrust of his giant fists. Karl spun around and head-butted another as he was punched in the ribs. He staggered and threw a hard right punch into the jaw of the one called O'Hara. Arnold grabbed two of the thieves around their necks and bashed their heads together. Someone lifted Karl up and slammed him against the wall. All at once Arnold let out a piercing yell, doubled over and fell like a rock to his knees, then crumpled onto the pavement.

One of the men screamed, "Dammit it to hell, Paddy, you stupid idiot, why in blazes did you go and stick the bloke? We better get the hell out of here and fast; come on." The five assailants quickly split up, running in three different directions into the dark alleyways of the city.

Stunned and lying against the brick wall, the air knocked from his body, Karl was finally able to pull himself up on his hands and knees and crawl cross the rough brick sidewalk to where Arnold laid. Karl was acutely aware that his friend was not moving. He reached out to Arnold and gently nudged his shoulder, "Arnold, Arnold, my friend, speak to me, please say something." Painfully, he repositioned himself so he was able to ease his hand around Arnold's shoulders in an effort to lift him up. Instantly, he felt warm, slimy liquid gush over his arm, as Arnold's head rolled back. In the dim evening light, Karl pulled his hand out and saw the blood, so much blood. In fearful panic, Karl cried out, "Oh, dear *Gott* in heaven! Arnold, open your eyes; tell me you are okay, please, Arnold, please."

Arnold responded weakly; he opened his eyes, looking up at his friend as he gasped softly, "Karl, I am done, it hurts bad, ahhh," his breath came in sputtering gulps, "I can't breathe good, I…I am done, my friend; go on, save yourself. Goooooo, before those men come back!" And with those words, his head rolled to the side as his eyes fluttered shut and the final bubbles of air came out of his mouth.

Karl heard the voice before he realized it was his own, "NNNNNOOOOOO, Arrrrnold! NOOO! You cannot leave me now, not now after we have come all this way across the ocean! We just got our jobs today and we are going to be a success in America, together. No, not now, you can't leave now, Arnold, oh *nein, nein!*"

Karl's body was wracked with convulsive sobs of pain and fright; he didn't care who saw him crying, he was beyond caring about what people thought as he was consumed with all-encompassing grief.

People passing on an adjacent lighted street heard the sounds of a fight, followed by the inhuman wails of a man. They turned and rushed down the dark side street to where they saw two men down on the pavement. Someone called the police, someone lifted Arnold into the horse-pulled ambulance and someone asked Karl what had happened, where he lived, who he was.

When Karl came to his senses, he was sitting in the police station. They had given him hot coffee and were asking him questions, and more questions. Karl felt like he was having another dream, he was having a hard time discerning between reality and imaginings. All that Karl was able to tell the officers was that he heard the names O'Hara and Paddy, and two of the men were dark-skinned. The police glanced across the table and their eyes met with obvious recognition of the names. Two other cops stood and left the room to search the streets of Cleveland.

A sergeant named O'Reilly took the stunned immigrant back to his boarding house, leaving him in the care of his landlady. Before the officer left, Mrs. Hester asked him to help Karl move to a spare bed in the room next to hers.

Mrs. Hester hurried into the kitchen and brought back a bowl filled with warm water. The landlady bent over Karl's bed and gently washed the blood off his face. After she finished, she returned to her kitchen to fix hot tea laced with brandy and laudanum. "Here, Mr. Kessel, try to raise your head a bit. You need to drink this tea; it will help the pain and for you to sleep."

Creeping through the haze of horror and pain, reality hit Karl like his father's fist. He eased himself to a sitting position in spite of his sore ribs, "Oh, *mein Gott*, Mrs. Hester, they kilt him—those men kilt my only friend." In spite of himself, salty tears slipped from his blue eyes and rolled down his leathery cheek. "What am I going to do now? He was my friend; we were going to be a success together in this America. Now he is gone from me." Karl hid his face in the refuge of his bruised and swollen hands.

Mrs. Hester talked quietly to him like he was her own son; she tried to sooth his mind and ease his anguish. She did what she could for Karl.

The next morning he woke with the same horrible reality that Arnold *was* dead. He was haunted by flashes of memory. His first attempt to get out of bed was met with a piercing pain in his left rib cage, a souvenir of the brutal attack. The pain in his body was no match for the mental pain of the loss of his friend, a pain that tore the breath from his chest. Karl looked at the box of

Arnold's personal effects the police gave him. On top of the stack, Karl's eyes fell on the bloodstained city map, the map they had bought last night. Slowly, Karl reached for it and picked it up as fresh tears streamed down his face. He held the new map to his chest and released all the pent up emotion of the last twenty-four hours. The reality of the horrible attack and his friend's death had come to stay, and his mind found it nearly unbearable. This was the first time in his life that Karl had lost someone he cared about.

Painfully, Karl dressed himself and made his way down the hallway to where Mrs. Hester had breakfast waiting for her boarders. Karl could eat little; he had no appetite. Mrs. Hester encouraged him to drink more of the laudanum-laced tea and eat a bit of her blueberry strudel. Taking a deep breath in preparation for the pain he knew would assail him, Karl rose slowly from the table, informing Mrs. Hester that he must go to the offices and tell *Herr* Mohr of Arnold's death.

Mrs. Hester spoke softly, "Mr. Kessel, I am sure you do not realize, but today is Saturday and the offices are closed until Monday. Come now into the parlor so I may take care of you; you must now rest and allow your body to heal." Karl suddenly felt light-headed and so did as his landlady requested; he slept and healed until the sun cast long shadows across the street.

Karl woke to find Mrs. Hester nearby, sitting in her rocking chair with her needlework, keeping one eye on him as she worked her needle. She lifted her gray head to find Karl watching her from the sofa; she rose from her chair and hurried to his side. "Oh my, Mr. Kessel, it is good that you have slept and given your body a chance to heal. Is there anything that I can get for you? More tea, perhaps?"

Raising his bruised body up on one elbow, Karl stopped; he took a deep breath and using his German tenacity to ignore the persistent pain; he pushed himself to a sitting position. "No, thank you, Mrs. Hester, I just need to sit for awhile." Karl adjusted his body slowly and taking another deep breath, continued, "I wish I could heal the pain in my mind as it heals in my body. Why? Why did God allow this to happen to Arnold and to our all our plans? We just came to this country where dreams are supposed to come true, not nightmares like this! We had so many hopes and plans for our new life here in America and now I am without him!"

Karl hung his head, heavy with grief; "I just *cannot* understand why God let this tragic thing happen! I thought he had a plan for each of us it was why he brought us together to come to this country as friends. This can not be his plan, it *cannot!*"

Mrs. Hester sat stoically by Karl's side, taking his hand in hers and forgetting formal German custom of addressing another with their surname, she spoke, "Karl, oh, my dear man. Sometimes things happen in our lives that don't make any sense, *ja?* As Christians we expect God to be with us and protect us, bless us, save us from harm every day. But there are times when this is not possible. Sometimes, these things happen to good people because there are bad people in this world as well. We must put our faith in God's character, in his faithfulness; we must be certain of who he He is. We must learn to bend with the wind or we will break. We have to learn how to chart a different course and adjust our lives in spite of the hardships, the injustices, the tragedies; we must continue to have faith because we have God."

He put his face into his hands and his shoulders shook with unexpected sobs. "I am not sure what I am feeling now; I don't understand this kind of God. I am sorry to say this to you. I am a Christian and I know all the good that God has done for me, but this was a mistake. This should not have happened. Arnold was a good man, only wishing to have a better life. We were so excited for our new life in America. We needed each other—he was a brother to me and I to him. What kind of a God lets things like this happen? I will not understand why he did nothing to stop it. I will never forget, *never!*"

The landlady laid her hand on Karl's shoulder, "I will think on this; perhaps God was there to stop those men from killing you, too. Maybe it was meant to be this way—that you go on your own without Arnold."

Later that afternoon, the police came to visit with Karl, asking him more questions about the murder of his friend. Karl told them what he could. The officers assured him they were quite sure they knew who committed this crime, and they might be calling him in to identify the suspects in a lineup.

Monday morning, Karl woke early. It was the first day of his new job. He dressed as quickly as the broken ribs and raw bruises would allow, making his way tentatively down the stairs. Karl didn't have much of an appetite, but ate the hot bowl of oatmeal Mrs. Hester fixed for him. She handed him his packed lunch and wished him well. He decided that walking would probably be good for him. As he walked, he felt his body loosen and move freely, feeling good he decided to continue walking the five blocks to the Great Lakes Sugar Company, avoiding the street where Arnold was killed.

Arriving at the brick building, he entered the same doors that just two days before, he and Arnold had eagerly walked through. Karl's face was a map of grief and physical pain, obvious to all who saw him. Office personnel stepped to the side, giving him room to pass. With his hat in his hand, Karl stumbled painfully into the office of Mr. Mohr who was sitting at his desk, going over the morning accounts. Dieter Mohr raised his head, surprised to see Karl standing before him. Mohr's mouth fell open with shock, not believing what he saw. *Something terrible has happened; the man looks frightful. The two immigrants had been so eager to work and excited about their prospects on Friday when I hired them to work here. And—and, where is the other man, the big blond German, what was his name—Arnold Reinholt?*

CHAPTER 6

West To Wyoming

★ ★ ★ ★ ★

"Your Challenges are not over yet. You must still prepare and grow. Be wise; learn from the experiences and mistakes of others.Take courage, go forth and succeed." ~John William Scott

On the fourth evening after Arnold died, Karl sat at his desk in Mrs. Hester's boarding house and began to write a long-overdue letter to Katja. It was time to tell her of the voyage, of Ellis Island, of Cleveland, and of Arnold.

> June15, 1906
> My Dearest Katja;
> I am sorry it has taken me so long to write to you this letter and I write it in English so I may practice. I hope you write back in English, too. I had no problem during my journey to Bremen and on to Bremerhaven. No one questioned who I was. The officials assumed I was Ralf Nimitz, just as the ticket said, for which I was much relieved. Only now that I am free from Ellis Island do I call myself Karl Kessel.
> The voyage across the Atlantic Ocean was exciting and without dread for the most part. When we boarded the ship and settled in our third-class berths, I was glad to meet a kind German woman traveling alone with her four children, just as you will soon. I must admit on the first night out, as we sailed across the English Channel, we experienced rough seas and I became what they call seasick. When I was ill, I was glad I had made an acquaintance with *Frau* Volk, for she heard my distress in the night and offered me herbal tea to settle my belly. By morning I was well. Be sure to

pack the herbal tea for yourself and our sons when you sail.

Accommodations in third-class passage were not the best, but were bearable. There were about 1,000 people down in the belly of the ship, in steerage. I believe most everybody was quite accepting of each other and did their best to remain calm and agreeable, although at times it was somewhat chaotic. The food the ship's people served was adequate and they even had special foods for all the different peoples, foods they were accustomed to.

I met a good man from Hamburg and we became close friends. I think it made the voyage more enjoyable to have someone to talk to. His name was Arnold Reinholt and he became an esteemed friend. We enjoyed having a pipe in the evenings as we leaned against the ship's railing and watched the sun set into the far horizon. I must advise you to go to the English classes on the ship, as it will help you communicate and make the travel easier.

Ellis Island was a haunting and frightening experience, going through the long lines with peoples from all over the world, wanting entrance to America. Some peoples had to go back on the ships because they were ill, criminal, or not mentally good. It was a sad thing. Arnold and I had no problem passing the exams. When it is your turn, take care to keep our sons clean and well, as you always do. I don't think you will have troubles, either. As we waited in line in the great hall, they gave us bananas and milk for a snack, I am sure our sons and you will like this fruit snack.

We found our jobs in Cleveland and a good boarding house in which to live. Now, *mein Liebschen*, I have some bad news which has almost broken my spirit. My friend Arnold and I were attacked on the second night we were in Cleveland, by a gang of men trying to rob us. My friend was killed, my Katja. He died in my arms in the darkness of the street. I have never been witness to anything so terrible. I was hurt some, am fine now. I hold tight to the knowledge that as soon as I earn enough money to buy passage for you and our sons, we will be together again. That is all which keeps me to breathe.

I like my work, and all of the peoples at the offices are most helpful. I am learning much. *Herr* Mohr asks to speak to me soon and it is my hope he will grant me a higher wage. He was pleased for I knew so much about raising sugar beets. Please thank your father for teaching me so well.

I hope you and our sons are well. Know that each night when I look at the moon, I think perhaps you are also looking at the moon and we are together in thoughts!

Ich liebe dich aus herzensgrund (I love you from the bottom of my heart),

Your loving husband, Karl

Katja wrote back:

June 27, 1906

Leibschen:

I was so happy to receive your letter at last. I am much relieved to hear all went well on your journey. I prayed every night for your safety. I think of you throughout each day and my nights are filled with dreams of you. Our sons Jakob and Christian are growing like the weeds in Papa's fields. They take great pleasure in gazing at your picture and often talk of you and remember to say prayers for you each night.

I am so sorry for the loss of your new friend Arnold. I am glad he was with you during the journey and you were blessed to know him. For sure you both had plans to be together in your new life in America, but more times together was not to be. I thank God above that he saved you from those terrible men that kilt Arnold. Are your ribs healed now? Please be careful and do not go on those black streets anymore.

I have been teaching Jakob some English words as I learn them. My father has already suggested I take English lessons, so I may be prepared for the journey to America and life there with you and our sons. How is your English doing? Do you find it easy or difficult to communicate with the local peoples? It sounds like most of the peoples you have been associated with are English-speaking Germans. That is good because if you lose your way in speaking, they can explain it to you. It sounds as though your job is going well, my Karl. If I know you, you are working day and night to learn the factory and machines. *Herr* Mohr must be a wise man to see all the knowledge in growing the sugar beets you have in your head.

You know, my Karl—I will go to wherever you are and make my life with you there. I believe it will be hard to leave my family when the time comes, as I love them so much. But I said my vows with you, Karl; vows where I promised to follow you and support your judgment for our lives. I will do my best to honor you, my husband.

I must tell you of our sons and some of the mischief they have been doing. Jakob has been going to the fields with Papa and me. I have been helping Papa with the planting and Jakob rides the back of the horse as Papa plows and rakes the earth. Our son is quite proud and thinks he is already a farmer; he follows Papa around like a shadow. Young Christian spends most of the day with Mama at the house. He comes with her to bring the afternoon bite of food and returns for his nap. Last week, Papa took them both to the creek to fish. They had great fun and Jakob got quite wet when he slipped on a rock and tumbled into the creek. Papa was quick to pull him out by the belt. Jakob did catch two fish and I think now he loves fishing, much like his Papa. Christian was busy splashing in the shallow part of the creek and chasing frogs. He brought one home in his pocket, which we thought best to let it go to its home in the evening. I told him it had a family and they were probably missing him.

It is time for me to go to bed and dream again of you, my husband. Take care, my *Leibschen*. Remember, *Ich liebe dich aus herzensgrund*,

Your wife, Katja

Karl Kessel worked at the Great Lakes Sugar Company home offices for two more months, learning the American way to process beets into sugar. He stayed up late into the night, studying books concerning operation of their sugar factory and modern machines. Karl discovered reading the manuals was good practice for his English. Often, he didn't understand a word or phrase and had to ask Mrs. Hester or people at the factory for the meaning.

After a while, Dieter Mohr came to expect that every morning when he saw Karl, there would first be a question or two, which he was happy to answer. He knew he had found a hard-working man in Karl Kessel. He had great plans for this young emigrant; soon he planned to approach Karl with what the company had decided for his future.

Everyday Karl felt the aching loss of his dear friend, and every day he thought of the dreams he and Arnold had spoken of—dreams he would now have to pursue on his own. Karl spent his weekends taking solitary strolls through the immense Slovak Garden Park in Cleveland. He allowed the peacefulness of the towering groves of trees, the shrubs, and flower beds to ease his tormented heart and the nagging loneliness he felt for his family.

He thought to himself, *When I lived in Yugoslavia, I never appreciated the majesty of the mountains or how large and beautiful was the great flowing Danube River. I took it for granted that it was normal for all the lands in the world. I am ignorant, I have never traveled or studied other countries and was unaware all places are so different. Of course, there are beautiful rivers in Ohio, but nothing to compare to the graceful meandering of the mighty blue Danube.* Karl enjoyed going down by the docks on Lake Erie to watch the large ships as roustabouts unloaded and loaded the worldly cargo.

Karl found the intense heat and humidity of Cleveland to be almost unbearable at times. Even though he washed carefully every morning and always wore a fresh shirt, before it was time for the noon meal, sweat soaked his clothing and ran down his back. Karl did not like this feeling. Of course he was used to sweating when working in the fields, but this was different. Everybody had the same experience of never-ending sweat oozing from every pore, even when they did not do work. The nights were no different. It did not cool down nor did the humidity drop when the sun set. Night after night Karl tossed and turned, trying to get comfortable in his damp bed clothes. He heard of other areas of America, areas which were different in climate and elevation, like the states which lay to the west. Karl dreamed that one day soon he would be able to see it for himself. *Patience*, he told himself, *patience—change and opportunity will come with time.*

After speaking with *Herr* Mohr earlier in the week, Karl's dreams were now filled with expectations of what his new home might be like; he prayed the climate at least, would be different than Cleveland, Ohio.

>July 15, 1906
>
>My Dearest Katja:
>
>I have received great fortune since I last wrote to you. Do you remember when I mentioned *Herr* Mohr, the company boss asked to speak to me soon? I received a summons from him on Tuesday and so I went in to see him. He first told me he was pleased with all that I learnt and I learnt quickly. *Herr* Mohr also told me he was impressed with how hard I worked at learning English and learning the factory work. He said he had a plan for my future. He asked me if I would consider moving to another state called Wyoming, to work the sugar beet business. It is far to the west and is one where much farmland can be had as well.
>
>The Great Lakes Sugar Company is considering building several factories in that state, because there are many good German farmers settling the land and growing sugar beets. They have no factory nearby to take the harvested beets to be processed into sugar, and so have a problem. *Herr* Mohr is telling me if I will go there, my wage will be one dollar per day. This is less than I am paid now, but for a while I will be only talking to people and making arrangements for the building of the factory. I will be what they call a company agent, in charge of recruiting workers to build the factory when the time comes, and to help the farmers secure laborers for their fields of sugar beets. The company here will change the name of the western factories to Great Western Sugar Company. I will also have opportunity to find farmland of my own in Wyoming. When it is time to build the factory, *Herr* Mohr will raise my wage to $1.25 or $1.50 a day. The wages in Wyoming are not as much as they are in Ohio, but I am told that expenses are not as high and opportunity is far greater.
>
>*Herr* Mohr tells me because I have learned so much, he trusts me to help the building of the new factory. I have told *Herr* Mohr that I am a farmer first and I much love the land—that I will look for a farm to buy in Wyoming. Also, if I have a farm, I can better learn of the other farmers and establish a good kinship with them.

Oh, Katja, oh, Katja, I cannot believe this good fortune is happening. It is like our dreams. I am praying and thinking serious on this matter. I will let you know what I decide to do. There are no streets made of gold in this country, but there are many streets filled with opportunity for those who are willing to work hard.

There are no castles here, as we have in Germany and Hungary. Yes, there are some grand houses in Cleveland, and I hear talk that in New York City there are some houses large as our castles, but I have not seen any. They have some concert halls here, but I have not attended. I am not willing to part with any money for the price of a ticket. Besides it would not seem the same, to hear the music without you by my side. There are no large mountains as we have surrounding our home. Only rolling hills and some higher that the people call mountains. They would be much surprised to see a real mountain, *ja!*

Cleveland, Ohio, is a large city with wonderful open city parks. I especially like the area called Slovak Gardens. They have amusement parks with many rides which spin around and a giant wheel that goes high in the air. People sit on seats attached to the giant wheel and it turns round and round, taking the people high in the air and back down again. I have yet to become brave to take a ride. There are also large rivers, but not any as beautiful as our Danube. Cleveland is built on the shores of a vast lake called Lake Erie. Big ships sail into Cleveland harbor with much cargo. It is a noisy and busy city.

In the state of Wyoming, I am told, are many large, beautiful mountains like our mountains. Some peoples have told me it is cold in the winter with much wind also. There are no large cities, only villages there. It is a new land and that is why we may have good opportunity to have land of our own. The town we would move to is called Lovell. It has a brick factory, a glass factory, and there are plans to build the sugar factory after I travel there. They are constructing a railroad through the state and it will soon pass through Lovell. This will help the other factories and to the farmers so they may send their beet harvest by rail to Billings, Montana, where the only factory is now. A river called the Shoshone River meanders through the town and supplies water for the farms.

I was happy to hear of our sons and their fishing adventure. I am glad your papa is taking them with him and teaching them to be good boys. I am glad to hear you are helping your papa with the planting. You are a respectable daughter. I will write to you and tell you of my decision, but I am thinking this is where the Lord wants for us to go to have our opportunity. There are many German Lutherans who have settled in the area and so with that we will feel comfortable too.

Ich liebe dich aus herzensgrund!

Your Loving Husband, Karl

August 3, 1906

Dearest *Liebschen,* Karl:

Your letter was good and I am anxious to hear from you if you decide to travel to this state of Wyoming. I am glad you take some time to walk in the park, but am sad you are feeling loneliness as I am for you. Have you gone to church there, Karl? I think they must have Lutheran churches in Cleveland with so many Germans living there.

Last month on the 6th day was our son Jakob's sixth birthday. Mama and I prepared a special dinner in his honor on Sunday. We invited Jakob Schuur and his wife Katharina, also Susanna Schmoll, Filipp Littenberg and his wife Sophia, all of Jakob's godparents. I am amazed our oldest son looks so much like you Karl. He is just your picture in all that he says and does. Soon he will begin school to learn his lessons. I do not doubt he will do well as he learns the English lessons I teach to him. He quickly learns and speaks the words sometimes better than I do.

The fields are growing well and Papa is pleased with the crops. Oh, I must tell you, my brother Christian has taken a wife. He and Katharina Scheuermann were married last month. We are all happy with this union, she is a good Christian woman and a healthy wife for my brother. Papa and Mama hope she gives them many grandchildren.

Papa has told me I do not have to go to the fields now because of the heat. So, I am busy with sewing and helping Mama in the kitchen. Of course, I have to watch carefully over our sons. Write to me when you can Karl and if you are in journey to Wyoming, may it be safe and good. How will you travel to this place, Wyoming?

Ich liebe dich aus herzengrund,
Your wife, Katja

P.S. Papa and Mama gave him a wagon for his birthday—he loves to ride in it and makes my sister pull it like his horse.

In late August 1906, Karl asked to speak to *Herr* Mohr at the factory. He knocked twice on the office door and entered when he heard *Herr* Mohr call, "*Ja*, come in, come in!"

Karl took hold of the brass doorknob, his hand shaking slightly as he twisted. Dieter Mohr lifted his head as Karl entered, "Good morning, Mr. Kessel, have a seat, please. Now, what can I do for you this fine day?"

Sitting straight in a chair, Karl cleared his throat and began, "*Herr* Mohr, I have come to my decision. I have thought about the offer to travel to Wyoming as a representative for Great Lakes Sugar Company and of the great opportunity that is offered to me there. This is a good thing, I believe;

this is what I am supposed to do and where I am to go. I am quite certain of my decision and am ready to begin the journey when you instruct me to leave. I will work hard to accomplish all that you ask of me for the company, and also to work toward my dreams of finding land of my own."

A satisfied smile crossed Dieter Mohr's face as he sat behind his desk and, addressing Karl said, "Fine, that is most fine, Karl. We couldn't be more pleased with your decision to accept our offer. But first, Karl, you must learn not to address me as *Herr* Mohr. It is time you learn the new way of America and refer to me as *Mr.* Mohr. Okay, with that said, I am pleased you have decided to accept our proposition to travel to Wyoming to oversee the building of our new factory, and, of course, to find land of your own. I have great faith in you and believe you are the man to do the job. We will keep in close contact with you, Karl, and send the details of what we expect of you as our representative in Lovell, Wyoming. How soon can you be ready to travel?"

Karl responded quickly, "I can be ready in two days, *Herr*, uhh, Mr. Mohr. How will I be traveling to Wyoming, if I may ask?"

"I will see to your railroad ticket, Karl. I will ask for a ticket that leaves Cleveland on the last Saturday in August, if that is acceptable to you. Oh yes, you can pick up your wages at the front desk, and a bonus for accepting our offer. Congratulations, Mr. Kessel and good luck!"

Dieter Mohr rose from his chair and extended his hand across the desk. Karl rose as well and shook the hand of his employer. "*Ja, ja*—I am most excited for this offer, Mr. Mohr. Thank you, thank you for giving to me this opportunity. I will be ready to leave on Saturday."

Karl didn't remember the walk home that day; his mind was spinning with his good fortune and the trip he was scheduled to take to Wyoming. Every day he came closer to the possibilities of his dreams, and they began to consume him.

> August 20, 1906
>
> *Mein Liebe,*
>
> I have forgotten to tell you I have been attending a nearby Lutheran church here in Cleveland. There are many German people who live here. I read in the Cleveland newspaper, there are three times as many Roman Catholic as Lutherans. In the Fremont

district, there is only one Lutheran church. So I suppose I can say, my dear, we are greatly outnumbered by the Catholics here.

The decision has been made and I will indeed travel to this state called Wyoming to be the company representative and to find land to farm. When I do this and become settled, I will send for you and our sons to travel to America to be with me. I leave tomorrow on the train that will take me across the state of Ohio to Chicago, Illinois. From there I will ride the train to Davenport, Iowa, which is on the great Mississippi River. This river is wider than the Rhine or Danube, but muddy I am told. From there I will travel north to Minneapolis, Minnesota. They tell me also, that the weathers will become cooler as I travel to the north. I do not like the climate here because there is much water in the air and it becomes hard to breathe with the heat, too. They tell me that the air in Wyoming is not with water in it, that it is dry and much easier to live.

From Minnesota the train will take me to Bismarck, North Dakota, and into Montana and to a town called Billings, which lies close to the border of Wyoming. There is a railroad line to Cody, Wyoming, from Toluca, Montana, which is a small town a few miles northwest of Hardin. But I do not wish to ride the train to Wyoming; I plan to buy a couple of horses and a wagonload of supplies when I arrive in Billings. I am thinking it would be wise to make this purchase right away. As far as I can tell, the journey from Billings to Lovell is less than a hundred miles. I am hoping for good weather so I can make a timely travel to our new home. It is told that September is often hot and without rain in Montana and Wyoming, so I am with hope that my travel will be easy.

I do not know what I will do first when I arrive in Lovell. I may try and find land immediately or work in the town to build up my money fund. There will be many supplies I will have to buy for a farm when the time comes. I will have to make the decisions as they come to me. Also it will be harvest time when I arrive so there would be no time to ready land of my own and plant the crops. I trust in *Gott* that he will deliver me and guide me in my decisions.

Do not worry, Liebschen, I will be of a careful nature and will write to you when I can, or after I arrive in Lovell. Give many loves to our sons and remember to look at the moon, *mein liebe.*

Ich liebe aus herzensgrund, ihr gatte,

Your husband, Karl

CHAPTER 7

Carving A New Life

★ ★ ★ ★ ★

*"Those who wait on the Lord shall renew their strength, They shall mount up with wings like eagles." ~*Isaiah 40:31

Karl Kessel said goodbye to the many friends he made in Cleveland and Fremont, Ohio. At the Great Lakes Sugar Company, he thanked Mr. Mohr for his faith, trust, and guidance. He remembered to shake hands with his superior, "I will not let you down, Mr. Mohr. I appreciate the job assignment in Lovell, Wyoming."

As he was about to leave the office, he hesitated and turned to face his mentor. "Also, Mr. Mohr, I will try every day to speak the good English. *Ja,* that is a promise." His smile crinkled up the corners of his blue eyes.

For the last time, Karl climbed up the aging wooden steps of Mrs. Hester's faded white clapboard boarding house. She was settled in a rocking chair, working on a blue crocheted shawl. When the kindhearted widow heard him walk into the sitting room, she raised her head, nodding in recognition, with a smile as her fading blue eyes were bright with tears. She had known this day would come and now that it had, it was bittersweet. She thought to herself, *I am truly glad in my heart Karl has found success and is now starting the rest of his journey, but I have become quite fond of him and will miss his enthusiasm and quick smile.*

Karl walked over to Mrs. Hester. Taking his outstretched hand, she rose to her feet. "Karl, I know why it is you visit me this time of day. I know you are leaving and that I may never see you again. I must say to you now, you are a good man with a great dream. You have many ambitions and much knowledge. I know with the help of God, you will do well and in time send for your family to come to this great country and build a new life together. I am sorrowful to say our goodbyes, but I am happy you have realized good fortune in Cleveland and have promise of even greater success in Wyoming."

Struggling to speak, and embarrassed by an unexpected flare of emotion, Karl's words came slowly at first, "Mrs. Hester, I must, I must thank you for all of your help, your comfort, and your good German foods." A lump the size of a new potato stuck in the middle of his throat as he looked down at the floor and shuffled his feet. "You are," he hesitated to gain control of his emotions as he swallowed hard, "you have become to me more than my landlady; you have become my friend. I am grateful for your generous help with this new country and language. I will try to speak better English and to hopefully write a letter to you some day to tell you of my journey and of my success in Wyoming. I would not be here this moment if it were not for you and your Christian goodness, especially helping me when Arnold was murdered. *Auf Wiedersehen*, Mrs. Hester."

Karl paused, turned, and hurried out of his first home in America. He had wanted to hug this dear woman to his chest, but his conservative German ways stopped him from any further display of emotion.

As the train pulled out of Cleveland, bound for Chicago, Karl put his forehead against the grimy window and closed his eyes. His thoughts were filled with haunting memories of Arnold. Only months earlier, his murdered friend was laid to rest in the cemetery near the Lutheran Church on Superior Avenue. Karl thought to himself, *I know in all that is good, Arnold, you are with me in spirit. That thought helps me to go on. I now do what I have to do, for you, too, my friend.*

Chicago was a large city and Karl realized immediately it was a place he didn't want to live. It was even dirtier, noisier, and more crowded than Cleveland—it reminded him of New York City. Karl knew the big cities were not where he belonged. He was a farmer. All he wanted and needed was land, lots of rich open land for farming. Karl's improved English served him well in transferring from station to station, train to train. From Chicago, he continued westward to Minneapolis, Minnesota. He leaned back against the seat and looked out the windows of the train, as mile after mile of large prosperous farms with huge white barns and statuesque brick silos rolled by. Farmers were out in force in their fields, taking in the long-awaited fall harvest. He wished he was with them. He missed working the land, even more than he realized. From studying the maps, Karl knew that he wasn't yet halfway to Wyoming, but the area of land he had already crossed was larger in size than Germany, maybe even all of Europe.

Crossing the great Mississippi river, he saw that it was muddy, as he had been told. It was full of swirling brown top soil, a gift from the great grass-covered prairies to the west, perhaps even from the land that would soon be his. As the trains carried him farther west and north, he noticed thick groves and forests of pine and hardwood trees. By first light the following day, as the smoking train crawled across the great western prairies, trees were occasional and sparse. In every direction, the horizon was composed of windswept, barren, rolling hill after hill, occasionally interrupted with intermittent clumps of stunted trees. As far as Karl's eye could see, hot August winds whipped the long, butter-colored prairie grass that covered the arid hills. He surmised, from the abundance of grass, that the soil was actually fertile and perhaps only needed water to produce crops.

While the train took on water and passengers at the next stop, Karl was overcome by innate curiosity. He stepped off the train and wandered a short distance. Bending over, he scooped up a handful of soil. Rubbing the dirt between his fingers, he felt the life. *Ja, I am right, it is waiting for the water and then—it will grow plants.*

Karl had wondered what the soil would be like in Lovell. If it was good soil, he was confident he could encourage the growth of plants. He was not lacking in confidence when it came to his farming ability, he understood the land, the soil, and he loved it—he loved every part of it.

The black, belching iron horse rolled across the flat, eastern plains of North Dakota. As soon as the train crossed the muddy Missouri River at Mandan and Bismarck, the flat plains evolved into a series of gently heaving hills. Karl was fascinated as he watched the landscape change dramatically. When the train crossed into the eastern plains of Montana, Karl noticed the rolling hills flatten out even more and become another great expanse of prairie. He no longer saw a sea of waving grass; instead the vast expanse of land was covered with sparse, bleached grass and dotted with clumps of dusty gray-green sage brush.

In no time, the small city of Billings appeared ahead. Karl strained to peer out of the train's grimy windows at the huge sandstone and limestone bluffs to the south that cradled the great Yellowstone River. The day was dreadfully hot and a relentless prairie wind swept up from the south, making it even hotter. Karl found the heat was bearable because there was a noticeable and much-welcomed absence of the debilitating eastern humidity.

Karl stepped off the train only to be blasted in the face by some of the hottest winds he had ever felt. *It is like when my Katja opens the oven to withdraw the baked bread.* He took a deep breath and walked along the wooden platform and into the train station. He located his bags, wiped the beads of sweat from his forehead and asked the station master about affordable rooms for rent in town. After making an arrangement to store his large bags at the station, Karl grabbed a small bag and walked down the dusty streets of Billings. Soon he came to the rooming house the station master had told him about. *Tomorrow, if I am fortunate, I will find horses and a good wagon for sale. I will load it with a few supplies I need for the trip and head south into Wyoming!*

Karl fell asleep that night, thinking about the next day and what it might bring. He decided the first order of business was to find and buy Percheron/Norman workhorses. *I hope to buy two horses to pull the heavy wagon which I will fill with supplies. Ja! First, the horses and wagon will take me to Lovell, and later when I find land, I will use them to work in my fields.* Karl enjoyed dreaming about his future and making plans, but he was also realistic, knowing he would have to work hard. He prayed daily for God's blessing and guidance.

Early the next morning, Karl set off toward the Billings stockyards to take a look at the horses for sale. While he was walking down the aisles between the stalls, he noticed a beleaguered farmer arguing loudly with the stockman. Obviously the farmer wasn't getting the price he wanted for his stock. Karl wandered closer and saw a fine pair of matching, black Percheron horses hooked to a wagon. "Excuse me for interrupting, I couldn't help but overhear your conversation. Are these horses and this wagon for sale?"

Irritated with the progress of his bargaining, the old farmer looked over at Karl and replied, "*Ja*, stranger, they are for sale. Are you interested in giving me a better price than this here robber?"

"Well, that depends on what the price is," said Karl.

"I can sell you this fine team of good, strong thoroughbred Percheron horses AND the wagon AND the harnesses for $800. If that is satisfactory, we have a deal." He quickly added, "They are good, strong workhorses, only three years old, and will serve you well. I am selling the whole kit and caboodle because I am getting out of farmin' and movin' back to Minnesota. And just so you know, these horses are for work and not for riding. It would be a rare saddle that will fit around these beasts and putting your legs over the back of one of these boys—well, you will not be walking so easy the next day," he said, laughing. "It would be sort of like straddling a couch. Their names are Ebony and Pitch—you know, like pitch-black! Pitch is a fertile mare and Ebony a good stallion. If you want to lend 'em out for breeding, it might be a way to earn yourself a few extra dollars."

Stepping forward, Karl looked the horses over carefully; he was well acquainted with this French-bred line of horseflesh. He had worked with Percherons his entire life and was well aware of their many assets. These former warhorses had incredible muscular hindquarters and strong legs that opened into a wide, deep chest.

Karl stood on his tiptoes, reached up and pushed back their lips, checking their teeth. He lifted each leg to inspect their large hoofs. "How old did you say these two are?"

The farmer told Karl that the Percherons were around three years old and had many years left to work for him as life expectancy was about twenty to thirty years.

Karl ran his hand slowly over their backs to feel of their spines. This was no easy task as both stood over sixteen hands at the withers, the highest part of a horse's back. At one point he climbed up on a nearby fence to inspect the highest parts of the horses.

When buying something, Karl knew better than to agree to the initial price. He rather enjoyed bargaining before he finally opened his wallet. After satisfying himself that both horses and the wagon were sound, Karl told the farmer he would pay $740 for the lot.

Karl knew what it would cost to feed two of these colossal animals. They each might weigh over a ton and they had appetites to match their girth. He had briefly considered mules. They were smarter and stronger than horses and it took less to feed them; however, their temperament was so unpredictable that they might kick without a reason, or quit working if it was too hot or too cold. Karl knew his and a mule's temperament were not a workable combination! The Percherons, on the other hand, were known for their docile disposition.

After haggling for a few minutes, an acceptable agreement was finally made, and Karl paid $750 for the Percherons, the rigging, and the wagon. Eager to get going, he jumped up on the seat and, with a flick of the reins, the blacks began to pound their way down the dusty city street, toward his hotel. He picked up his bags and found a general store that specialized in stocking homesteaders and farmers. Karl purchased general food supplies like lard, onions, potatoes, two beef steaks, salt, flour, sugar, salt pork, jerky, coffee, and molasses, along with a couple of cast-iron pans to cook with. He bought only enough to sustain himself while he was on the road to Wyoming. He selected bedding for himself, matches, three lanterns, kerosene, nails, and a few hand tools. Just when he thought he was finished with his purchases, he spotted a galvanized tin tub and scrub board. "I will need a tub to bath in and I suppose I will need to wash my dirty clothes at least once a week! And I suppose I'd better throw in a bar or two of that there soap!"

Karl considered stocking up on a variety of seeds for a garden, but realized, it was late August and there would be no garden until spring. I must wait to see *if* I even have a place to plant a garden when the spring comes. He purchased a few sacks of oats, along with a salt lick for the horses.

With his wagon full and excitement building in his chest, Karl decided to go ahead and start toward the Wyoming border. As the midday sun beat down from the big Montana sky, he headed west out of Billings. The horses were eager to stretch their legs and soon eased into the steady trot they were known for. The heavily loaded wagon rumbled down the dirt road for about ten miles before they came to a good-sized river, just south of the little town of Laurel. Karl had been told to watch for a marked crossing through the broad Yellowstone River at this point, because there were only certain places that were safe to ford in a large wagon. Since it was early September, the normally fast-flowing river was running low. He was able to locate a safe ford and after slipping and sliding across the bed of river rock, he crossed to the opposite bank. He spotted a thick grove of cottonwood trees that looked like a good place to make camp for the night.

After the long, full day, Karl felt the signs of exhaustion creep over his body. He hobbled his sweating horses and gave them a quick rub down as they grazed on tender grass near the river. He gathered a pile of dry wood, built a blazing cook fire, and leaned back against a cottonwood tree, waiting for the fire to peak and smolder. His gaze lifted to the sky as the sun was setting in the West. The huge expanse of blue sky was filled with lavender and mauve shades, shot through with coral and gold rays. Karl took a deep breath and exhaled hard—he was here; he was content. After a hot meal in his belly he'd be ready for a good night's sleep in the unfamiliar turf of his new home. He took out the new cast-iron frying pan, and after seasoning it, threw in some lard, followed by a beef steak and a few sliced potatoes. He tossed a bit of salt and pepper on the mixture and left it to simmer over the glowing coals, turning the steak only once. The enticing aroma that wafted on the evening breeze made his mouth water. After feeding his face and his once-ravenous belly sedated, Karl walked to the river's edge, washed his supper dishes, and packed them back in the wagon.

Throwing a log on the fire, Karl stretched out on the ground beside the campfire and thought about all the money he spent that day. For sure, he had put quite a dent in his savings, but he only purchased the things he needed to survive and to operate a farm, a farm he hoped to find in the next few months. He was glad he had been so frugal during all of the years he had farmed for Christian Mehll. Karl had not told anyone just how much he had saved. He reached down and adjusted the money belt Katja had made for him. He hoped it was enough to outfit a farm and purchase a few animals and equipment he and Katja needed to start their new life in America—in Wyoming. He had been careful, even when he was in Cleveland, with money earned and money spent. Karl Kessel was a frugal man and those habits were serving him well. And now, he was on the last leg of his journey. Exhaling a long, satisfied breath, he fell asleep with more visions and dreams of what lay ahead.

Somewhere around two in the morning, Karl woke with a full bladder. He tossed and turned for a few minutes, wishing the urge away. He hated the thought of crawling out of his warm sleeping bag in his long johns. The night had turned chilly and his campfire had burned down to glowing embers. He lay still in his cozy nest, eyes half open, when suddenly he became aware of movement in the brush. Alarm skittered down his spine and gripped his belly. Alert now, he opened one eye a little more and stared at the brush. There, there it was again. This time he caught the glimpse of a worn boot. Still pretending to be asleep, he scanned the campsite in front of him. That was when he remembered he had left his shotgun in the wagon, parked behind him. *A hell of a lot of good it does me there. I have to get to that gun*, he thought.

Karl threshed around in his bed, hoping to send a message that he wasn't sound asleep. Taking a deep breath he crawled stiffly and slowly out of the bag. Walking gingerly over the rocky ground in his stocking feet, he threw a couple of logs onto the fire as he moved toward the wagon. As he stumbled along, he mumbled loudly about having to get out of that warm bag to take a pee, and disappeared behind the wagon. He reached up under the wagon seat and laid his hands on the shotgun. A shudder of relief flooded through him as he pulled it out and released the lock.

Karl edged around the side of the wagon as he leveled the gun at the brush across camp and called out, "I know you're over there; I can see you. Come out now with your hands up or I'll fill that brush and your butt full of buckshot."

In the darkness, Karl heard boots running through the thick undergrowth as branches snapped. He shot the gun into the air as added incentive for whoever it was, to continue their hasty escape. Karl heard two horses galloping away into the dark night. He shuddered. He had not realized there were two men in the brush! Exhaling loudly, he walked cautiously over to the spot where he'd first noticed movement in the undergrowth. The campfire had built to a brilliant blaze, lighting up he campsite. Firing a torch, Karl edged through the brush and saw where the men had tied their horses. They were long gone now and it was a good thing as Karl was not in a hospitable mood. He really didn't want to have to shoot anyone; but he would have, to protect himself.

Karl dropped his flap and released the building urine, then crawled back into the sleeping bag and only dozed. He was too keyed up to sleep. Before the sun rose, he slapped together a quick breakfast, stowed his gear in the wagon, threw water on the campfire, and hitched up the horses. He pulled the clay pipe from his pocket and lit it. By the time the sun rose brightly in the east, Karl had been on the road for an hour. He took a moment to watch the brilliant red, orange, and yellow rays shoot up through the morning sky. He thought, *Ja, the sunrise is the same no matter where a person is. This same sun will shine on my Katja and my boys on this day.* Those thoughts comforted Karl as he flipped the reins and urged the great Percherons to "giddy up." The horses were as eager as Karl to get on down the road and their long, easy stride soon had the wagon rolling steadily along toward the Wyoming border.

As Karl guided the wagon over the rut-filled dirt road that first morning, he took mental note of the meager Montana farms that dotted the landscape.

Beyond them lay endless, sagebrush-covered hills. Suddenly, he noticed a lone mountain that rose abruptly from the prairie to the east of the road. *That must be Pryor Mountain that the guy at the general store told me about; it is impressive how it seems to come right up out of the flat land.*[1]

Karl compared the untouched virgin land to the farmland in Yugoslavia that had been lived upon for hundreds of years. He missed the thick woods of oak and pine that bordered Surtschin. Here, on this water-starved land there were no trees for miles and miles, except for a few twisted and stunted cottonwoods along with some scrawny but fragrant cedar and juniper bushes. The occasional areas of hardy sagebrush growth indicated good soil; he also noticed the telltale chalky-white alkaline soil that would only grow greasewood and rocks! The lack of water or large rivers had not escaped him, either, and was a concern because he knew soil must have water to grow crops. He hoped there was a large river near Lovell for irrigation.

Karl mused, *So, there will probably be only a few trees I will have to clear from the land. I am glad to only plow out the sagebrush and greasewood. Katja is not going to like this, having no trees. Perhaps I should not tell her too much about no trees. I should only tell her of the good dirt to farm!* A sly smile spread across Karl's face, and he chuckled. *She will like it plenty after I build her a good house with lots of trees around it, someday, ja, someday!*

As Karl rode along, he kept a keen eye out for anybody who might be trailing or scouting him, but he didn't see a soul all day. *It's a good thing I don't see anyone following me, because this time I shoot first and ask questions later!*

Beyond Pryor Mountain, Karl was stunned to see higher and more rugged blue mountain peaks rising to the east and south, for as far as he could see. *They must be the Big Horn Mountains which surround the eastern side of the basin*, he thought.

The second night Karl made camp about twenty miles south of the Montana/Wyoming border. A thrill was building in his chest as he lay down to sleep for the first time on Wyoming soil.

The next morning, as his eager Percherons pulled the heavy wagon over the next sage-covered hill, Karl saw more mountains due west. The famed Rocky Mountain chain joined the Big Horns to the east to form the Big Horn Basin [2] of Wyoming. Karl had not seen many farms or even houses since he crossed the state border. He considered the freedom he experienced as he traveled. *Nobody demands to know where I am going or why. Nobody asks me for my business or for identification, or anything; it is truly wunderbar.*

Karl pulled his team of Percherons to a stop at the crest of a substantial hill. Overcome with emotion at the sight that lay before him, he forgot to set the brake as he dropped the reins to the floor. He stood up in the wagon and briefly rubbed his tired and bruised bottom. Looking east and then west, he was suddenly filled with the simple joy of being alive in a free country.

He stretched his arms out wide, threw back his head, and yelled for all the world to hear, "I am in America! I am free! I am free. Wahoo!"

Before he knew what happened he was thrown back into the seat and bounced side to side, up and down. Holding on for dear life, he managed to reach for the reins. After he and his spooked team covered a speedy half mile, Karl was able to slow them down. He set the brake and wound the reins around it before he jumped down from the seat and walked around in front to calm to his frightened team. "I am sorry, boys, for giving you a fright, but you sure enough gave one right back to me, *ja*, that you did. My butt is going to hurt for a week!"

He walked about fifty yards to the west and paused, remembering what he had read about the Big Horn Basin. Except for a small passage in the northwest corner along a river called the Clark's Fork of the Yellowstone where he had entered, the region was entirely surrounded by high mountains, making it one of the least settled areas in the United States. Walking back to his wagon, Karl leapt up onto the seat and headed due south. As the wagon rumbled along, his thoughts were consumed with the possibility of farming with little or no water.

Karl sorely needed another break and, when he spotted a stagecoach stop, he reined in his team, set the brake, and tied the reins to the post. He hopped down from the wagon and walked to the ramshackle structure. He pushed open the weather-beaten door to the shack, knocking as he went in. "Hello, is there anyone around?"

A grizzled old man pushed aside a tattered calico curtain that separated the back room. "Howdy, partner, and what is it that I can be a helpin ya with this fine day?"

Karl removed his hat and slapped the dust off on his pants. "I'm doing pretty good, but my horses are needing a drink of your water before we head on south."

The old man chuckled. "Well, ya be in some luck this day, friend; the water is free, so help yourself and come on back inside here—I'll have a something wet for you as well!"

Karl laughed. "That sounds like a bargain. I'll just go on out and get my team watered up first. Thank you."

Unhitching his team, Karl led the two over-sized horses over to the water trough, hobbled them and walked back across the dusty road to the shack. The stagecoach attendant motioned for Karl to sit as he put a pitcher and two glasses on a dusty, oil-cloth covered table.

"Well, friend, I see by that loaded wagon that you're on your way somewhere to set up. Am I right about that? And I suppose you have a name? Mine is Frank Waddle!" He extended his right hand in friendship. "Uhhhh, would ya prefer water or beer?"

Karl shook the man's hand and, laughing at his options, replied, "Well, since I have a choice, I do believe I would surely like a beer. Sounds mighty good on a hot day like this!" He poured himself a cold beer and after taking a couple of swallows replied, "Karl Kessel here, you are right as right can be, my man. I am hoping to find some work and some land around the Lovell area."

Frank took a couple of swallows of his beer as well, "Your movin' into this har area at jus the right time. The railroad is coming through and I'll be out of a job sooner than a dog gets fleas! People will be travelin' by train rather than by a dusty and rough-ridin' coach."

Karl learned a lot from the old man as they sat at the table. The railroad was making progress, cutting through the Big Horn Basin. Karl relaxed and cooled off in the dim interior as he savored the cold beer. Frank was all too happy to fill him in on the latest news.

"Ya bet your boots—they're bringin' the railroad through here early this summer. It's gonna pass through Lovell and Basin, and on to Worland. Spose it'll stop just south of Thermopolis. I heard they has plans to cut the line through that blasted rocky gorge of that thar Wind River Canyon. Theys sposed to end the line in Casper City—right in the middle of the dad-gummed state."[3]

Karl knew that until a Great Western Sugar factory could be built in Lovell, a local railroad would make it much easier to take the beet harvest north to the processing factory in Billings, Montana. With a railroad going through Lovell, the sugar beet farmers could stockpile their harvest near the depot and ship their beets by rail to the Billings factory.

The old man was pleased to share his knowledge of the area; he loved having an audience. "Yah, theys also building a big ole dam up thar in a sheer rock canyon, about fifteen miles west of Cody—about fifty miles from har, theys goin' to call it the Buffalo Bill Cody Dam. You ever hear'd of Buffalo Bill Cody? Hell of a guy—a real dandy! Anyways, that dam will hold runoff water from the mountains to the west and let it down the Shoshone River, slow like. You will cross the river just before you gets to Lovell. Word is, the dam will take five year to build and it will provide a hell of a lot of water for ear-gation, and drinkin' for the north Big Horn Basin. They a claim'n that it'll make lectricity! Now ain't that goin' to beat all?"

"*Ja*, that is good news to me as I'm planning on finding a farm hereabouts. By the way, I've wondered where the name 'Wyoming' comes from?"

The old coot smiled as he tipped back in his chair and wiped the back of his hand across his mouth, removing the beer suds. "Well now, that's an interesting story. Been told there was a trapper early on who fell in love with a squaw by the name of *Oming*. She hung with him for a whiles and then up and left him in the night. He wandered the mountains for years, looking for her and calling, 'Why Oming, Why'?"

Karl was intrigued. "You don't say?"

The old trader slapped his leg in raucous laugher as he leaned across the table. "Naw, traveler, I was just pullin' yur leg on that one!" He slapped his leg again and laughed. "The name really came from some Delaware Indian word mean'n 'at the big plains.'"

Suddenly leary, Karl pushed back his chair and replied, "Well, Mr. Waddle, I do appreciate your beer and the talk. I better get my team hitched back up and get on down the road. Let me toss a few coins on the table here for taking care of my thirst."

Karl hitched his team back to the wagon, flicked the reins over the back of the team, and they set off at a trot. He looked down at his leg. *What did he mean, he was pulling my leg? I never felt anything.* He looked over his shoulder thinking, *That old timer was a bit strange—probably doesn't get many chances to talk to folks.* Karl laughed in spite of himself and eased back on the seat of the wagon and put a light to his pipe.

He passed a farm using a windmill to generate electricity. He figured he would need a windmill of his own some day, so that his Katja could have electric lights in her house just like they have in the fine houses in Cleveland. He expected it would take years to build power lines from the Cody dam all over the Big Horn Basin.

As the wagon bounced down the washboard road, Karl thought about the things he learned in his conversation with Frank Waddle. Several hundred Mormons from Utah had settled in around the new town. Karl was glad to know that just this year a large influx of German Lutherans had settled on land just below the Lovell post office, and north toward the river. With railroad service to Billings, more farmers would consider raising sugar beets as a cash crop.

Karl Kessel's fully loaded, iron-wheeled wagon rumbled into Lovell around sundown on the fourth day. A small shiver of fear and doubt crawled up his back and nestled behind his neck. Karl didn't *know* what was going to happen here, but he was going ahead full throttle. He drove the team of matching Percherons into the only obvious stable on Main Street.

A grimy, bushy-bearded fellow strode out to meet the wagon as Karl pulled the team to a stop. "Mighty fine piece of horseflesh you have here my friend—I suppose you might be needin' a place for these big boys to eat and sleep this night?"

"*Ja,* that is just what I am looking for; that and a place to lay my head as well. I have been a week on the train and four days on the road from Billings. I am in sore need of a bath. You might be warned not to get downwind of me or you will be sorry." Karl laughed. "How much are you going to charge me to put up this pair for a couple of days? I need a place to park my wagon as well."

The burly stable keeper took a second look at the beefy horses he was expected to feed and replied, "How about six bits? Those beasts look like they could eat my entire haystack. As for your wagon, I have a good spot at the rear of the barn where you can leave it for a while. Nobody bothers anything round here."

"Done," said Karl, laying the fee on what was supposed to be a desk. "Now, where can I get a bath and a hot meal?"

After Karl helped to take the horses out of their harnesses and put them into stalls, the stable keeper directed him down Main Street to a little rooming house tucked in beside the local pool hall. He knocked on the door and heard a husky, female voice yell, "Come on in; it's open!"

He made arrangements for a good hot bath, and climbed the narrow stairs to a simple, second-floor room. Karl peered out the dirt-smeared rooming house window onto the main thoroughfare of Lovell. Across the street stood a large, white clapboard church with a single, wood steeple topped with what looked like an angel. He was eager to meet some of the farmers who had recently settled in the area. After all, they were all there for the same reason, to carve out a future in this free country.

Karl had done his homework in regard to the area and knew the growing season was short—only about 120 days. Since most areas could only expect less than ten inches of precipitation a year, they had to irrigate. He had noticed area farmers were in the process of building a series of canals which would flow from the river, but they needed feeder dams to hold and release the mountain water.

Stripping his filthy clothes from his lean frame, Karl climbed into a tin tub filled with hot soapy water. He slid down into the tub, closed his eyes, and enjoyed a long soak. As the water began to cool, he briskly scrubbed his hair and rinsed before stepping from the tub. He toweled off, shaved, and dressed in his one change of clean clothes. Karl threw the dusty, dirty clothes he had worn for over a week into the tin tub and scrubbed them on a scrub board the landlady lent him. He wrung out his pants, shirt, and underwear and threw them over the short rope line he erected across one corner of the rented room, where they dripped onto the wooden floor.

Cleaned up and suddenly hungry, Karl stepped out of the rooming house onto the streets of Lovell as the afternoon sun sat low to the west. The hotel clerk had recommended a little restaurant just down the street. Karl walked a short distance to the west until he found the small diner. He opened the door and, as he stepped into the cafe, his nose was greeted with the savory aroma of fresh pot roast and potatoes.

Heads turned to take a look at the stranger who walked into Daisy's Café. The diners observed the middle-aged foreigner who was of medium height and clean-shaven, except for the mustache. He held his old newsboy wool cap in one hand as he pulled a vacant chair from a table in the far corner.

Karl laid his cap on the table and turned to meet the stares of the locals; he nodded his head in silent greeting and proceeded to read the menu. Karl put away a generous serving of pot roast, potatoes, and gravy, and treated himself to a slice of apple pie and a cup of hot black coffee. Finished with his meal, Karl rose from the table and approached the four men who sat at an adjoining table.

"Excuse me, please, I have just arrived in your town and would appreciate information on names of the town fathers. I am a company agent for the Great Western Sugar Company and have been sent here with plans for building a beet-processing factory."

Immediately impressed and intrigued, one of the men pulled out a chair for Karl and invited him to join them. An older unshaven man inquired, "We are glad to have you in our town; what did you say your name is, sir?"

Karl quickly replied, "I am Karl Kessel from Cleveland and before that from the country of Yugoslavia/Germany, where I grew many sugar beets, wheat, and corn. As soon as possible, I am also looking for a good piece of land for myself, so I can bring my family here to live."

The men informed Karl they had heard rumors that someone was coming from the East to build a factory. One of the men spoke up, "I know there are many farmers around who would be interested in hearing what you have to say about this Sugar beet factory. Would you be available to meet with the members of the community soon, perhaps tomorrow, here at the Café, say around two o'clock? We'll get the word out."

Karl agreed to attend the meeting.

He walked a short way and decided to stop in the pool hall for a cold beer before hitting the sack. He settled at the bar and ordered a beer, as an old timer took the stool beside him and struck up a conversation. "New here in town, aren't ya?"

Karl turned to extend his hand, "Sure am, name's Karl—Karl Kessel. What might your name be?"

The old gent shook Karl's hand forcefully and replied, "Well, my ma named me Joseph Harely, but folks round here call me Shorty."

Taking a short sip of his beer, Karl turned back to the man, "Nice to meet you, Shorty. How long have you lived around here?"

Shorty perked up to answer the newcomer's question. "I've been here, nigh on five years; got me a nice little farm west of here." He took a big gulp of his beer and continued to talk. "If you're just new in these parts, ya probably don't know about the big range war they had a couple years ago over the other side of the Big Horns."

Not giving Karl time to respond, and realizing he had a captive audience, Shorty went on. "Well, as the word is, it all happened near Buffalo, Wyoming. To tell, there was several homesteaders who herded sheep into the grasslands that had been used by the cattle ranchers for quite a spell. Those cattle ranchers swore on their mother's graves that the damned sheep grazed the native grass too close to the roots and destroyed the range. Well, both sides argued back 'n forth for months and finally the situation blew sky high. Those cattle ranchers and sheepherders started a shootin' at each other and before ya knowed it they had themselves one hell of a range war."

Karl nodded his head in recognition. "*Ja*, Shorty, I heard something about that. Sure hope there won't be that kind trouble on this side of the mountains."

Karl thought of the shotgun he had purchased in Cleveland and hoped he would never have to use it against another man. He remembered the incident his first night out of Billings, on the banks of the Yellowstone River—when he had almost had to shoot a man to protect himself. Karl had bought the gun for protection, but intended to use it mostly to shoot wild game for meat.

Shorty took a moment to light a fat stogie. "Sure hope you ain't a sheepherder; them ain't real popular fellers round these parts."

Karl smiled as he lit his pipe. Taking a deep draw, he blew the smoke out. "No sirree, I don't plan on running any sheep. I'm a farmer and plan on raising a few head of cattle after I get settled."

Changing the subject, Shorty asked, "Ya got kids, Dutch? Well, if'n ya do, this is the place to get 'em some of that ed-u-cation. Yes, sirree, us taxpayers pay for it all. We was one of the first states in these whole United States that passed laws supportin' our free public schools. Got us one of those universities down in Laramie City; it opened nigh on ten years ago and we're mighty proud of it, darn right!"

Karl was amused with Shorty's enthusiasm as he replied, "I am glad of this free school system, because it means my sons will receive the education I want for them to have." Karl expected his sons would attend school to at least the sixth grade, just as he did.

He paid for his beer and slid off the stool, extending his hand in friendship. "Sure was nice to meet you and talk with you, Shorty. I've had a long day; I'll say goodnight. Be seeing you."

The next morning, Karl found a barber shop and treated himself to a badly needed hair cut and a shave. He walked into Daisy's Café at two sharp and was surprised to see the place filled with farmers and businessmen. He hung his cap and jacket on the coatrack, ordered a cup of coffee, and sat down in a lone chair. It didn't take long before he was recognized and invited to sit at a long table against the wall.

Elated with the attention and acceptance, Karl said, "I am most happy to see there is much interest in building the Great Western Sugar Factory in Lovell. I need to tell you that this factory is not going to be built this year or maybe not even next year. We have to wait for electricity, the railroad, and workmen to finally build the factory. However, the businessmen in Cleveland want me to assure you they believe this area would benefit from its own factory and they are most eager to make this happen."

Most of the men appeared to believe what Karl had said and were excited about the prospect of their own sugar beet factory. A few openly ridiculed the "fresh off the boat, Kraut." One man shouted from the back of the room, "What do you know about our land and how we do things here? We don't need some know-it-all Kraut telling us how to do things in our country, much less in our state. You and your big-city ideas! What do you think you know that we don't already know? You aren't dealing with a bunch of ignorant country bumpkins here, you know!"

Irritated on the inside but keeping his temper, a confident Karl rose to address the accusations and doubts. "First, I am *not* a Kraut. I am of German heritage as I am sure many in this room are. I have many years experience working in the fields of Yugoslavia, which is much like this area. When I arrived in America, I was employed by the Great Lakes Sugar Company in Cleveland and in Fremont, Ohio. While I was there, I studied and learned much of how sugar beets are raised in this country and the latest machines used to process them into sugar. The owners of the company have confidence in me and have sent me here as their agent. I will appreciate all information and cooperation you can give to me. Together, we can improve the growing and, more importantly, the processing of sugar beets, right here in Lovell... which, I might add, will keep the money in Lovell!"

Karl cleared his throat, took a drink of his coffee, and continued, "I also plan to buy a farm where I will raise my family, as well as sugar beets and other crops. If any of you know of land that is for sale in the area I would appreciate speaking to you."

Even though Karl sensed some animosity, he felt the meeting went well and he felt accepted into the community. He was confident that time would prove what he had said, even to the few pessimists.

An older man near the back of the room stood and said, "We appreciate you taking the time to meet with us today, Mr. Kessel. Right off, I don't know of any land for sale, but Homer Runtsch out there in Kane needs some help gettin his crops in. He is gettin on in years and having a hard time of it."

Scraping his chair back from the scarred café table, Karl said, "It was my pleasure to meet with you, gentlemen. I appreciate your help and information and I will continue to stay in touch with you concerning further information I receive from the home office. Good day, and thanks for inviting me to sit at your table." Setting his wool cap firmly on his head, he left the restaurant and headed up the street to see about his horses and wagon. Spotting the owner in front of the stable, he said, "How are you doing, Matt? I was just wondering if I owe you more money for feeding those monsters of mine."

"Naw, Karl, you don't owe me anything right now, but come back to see me around the end of the week," the stableman instructed, "and we can settle up. Do you have any idea how long you're going to leave them here?"

Karl surveyed the clean stalls of the horse barn and replied, "Well, Matt, I don't know yet, but hope by the end of the week I may have a better idea. By the way, do you have any horses for sale? I need a good riding horse—going out to Homer Runtsch's farm tomorrow to see if he needs some help with his crops. And, by the way, can you give me directions to his place?"

"You are a man of luck, Karl Kessel; see that nice bay over there? Just got her in and I would sell her to you for forty dollars, if you agree!"

Next morning, Karl had risen and saddled the bay horse before the sun peeked over the Big Horn Mountains. He was eager to get on the road and make the ride out to Kane. He was several miles out of Lovell as the sun began to rise from behind the majestic Big Horns. With the hypnotic clip-clop of the bay's hoofs, Karl began to nod off. He snapped back to his senses just as he felt himself sliding out of the saddle. He urged the horse into a trot to help jostle him awake. Karl thought about the informal way Americans had of addressing each other by the first name instead of "Mr. Kessel" or "*Herr* Kessel." *Mostly, it feels friendly—but, sometimes it is better to address a person with respect.*

As he was riding, he noticed many small, struggling farms here and there along the roadside. He noted crude canal and arterial ditches from the

Shoshone River, feeding water to the fields. It had been some time since he had ridden horseback and he was enjoying it. *It was good that I haggled a bit with Matt—at $35, this big bay is another good buy. I will have to find work this winter and save all I can. Perhaps by spring I will find a farm to buy.*

The seven-mile trip took longer then he had anticipated, partly because he was eager to investigate this opportunity. Shortly after Karl reached the farm of Homer Runtsch, he was hired on to help bring in the harvest. The old man was ailing. "Ain't what I used to be and I'm mighty glad for the help, young man."

Karl agreed to bring his team of Percherons and his wagon the next day to help with the harvest. He planned on sleeping in the wagon since there probably wasn't room for him in Homer's small house. Riding home after that first day Karl thought, *I cannot believe that Mr. Runtsch calls it a house—it looks more like a shack to me.*

After two weeks of harvest work in the fields, Homer Runtsch made an unexpected offer. "Karl, I know you are looking to buy a farm. This is a small, but good, farm. I have decided to sell it and want to offer it to you first. There are forty acres I will sell to you for $20 an acre making a total of $800. Are you interested in buying this farm?" Homer quickly added, "Oh, and, I don't know if you are aware or not; but, if this land had a canal and was irrigated, it would cost you anywhere from $40-$45 an acre. So, my friend, you could make those improvements and this land will be worth much more money. What do you say to that?"

Karl had already checked on the price of land around the area. He had learned that irrigated land was going for around $45 an acre. He knew that, with a consistent supply of water, the land was capable of producing at least double what it currently did. He was stunned. His mind raced. *I know I don't have enough money to buy a large farm yet...that might take years. But this small bit of ground might be a good place to start. Also, there is a parcel of unbroken ground to the west that might be homesteaded someday.*

After quickly going over the numbers in his head, Karl eagerly responded, "*Ja*, Homer, I am interested in buying your land, but I could not pay for it all in one sum. I can give you a partial payment for the farm, now, and pay the rest after next year's harvest."

Homer replied, "Good, I am glad you are interested in the purchase. I would like to have the full amount so I can go back to Minnesota to live near my family. Let's see if the bank in Lovell can help us out. Stay here tonight, and tomorrow we will ride into town."

The next day Homer Runtsch and Karl Kessel met with the president of the bank in Lovell. After they explained the situation, the bank president adjusted his rimless glasses and responded, "I cannot grant an outright loan to you, Mr. Kessel. You haven't lived in this country long enough, but if you agree to put your team of Percherons down as collateral to guarantee the loan, we might have a deal. I am willing to hold your promissory note for $350. If you expect to make the first payment of $175 after the fall harvest, the final payment would be due on," he bent over his figures and continued, "say around December 15, 1908. If this arrangement is agreeable, sign here. Mr. Kessel."

Karl Kessel and Homer Runtsch rode back out to the farm later that morning. When they arrived two hours later, Karl handed Homer the $500 cash down payment for the farm. "Karl, thank you for buying my farm; I love this land, but its time for me to quit the hard work and find a good rocking chair. Would you mind helping me pack up a few things for my trip back east?"

"It is I who should thank you for giving me the opportunity I have dreamed of...to own a farm in America." Karl slapped Homer on the back and said, "Now, let's get you packed and tomorrow I will take you back into Lovell to meet the train to Billings."

Karl accepted the dishes, furniture, and whatever else Homer didn't want to take with him. "You can also have that old black beast of a cook stove. Don't think it will fit in my bag anyways."

In the morning, they loaded Homer's bags onto the wagon and closed the flimsy door to the cabin. Karl climbed onto the seat of the wagon next to Homer who was anxious to be on his way. A short way up the lane, Homer turned in the seat for a last look at what had been his home for the past five years, and began to reminisce, "You know, Karl, Kane actually got started on the east side of the Big Horn River in 1895. A cattle rancher, Henry Lovell, set up a post office over thar an named it after his old foreman, Riley Kane. Yes sir, when the railroad come through here this year is when they gone and built the depot and rail siding across the river from the old Kane post office. Hear tell the foreman got all mad and named his post office Watson. I don't know what is going to happen. It's a damn mess if'n you ask me!" Homer shook his head and took another pull on his pipe.

Karl chuckled, "*Ja*, Homer, I heard something about that but was confused. Now I know why!"

They arrived in Lovell around five o'clock that afternoon. Karl pulled his team to a stop in front of the livery stable and climbed down from the wagon; he talked to Matt and made arrangements to board his Percherons for the night. As they walked down the street toward the train station, Homer offered, "Karl, I'll buy you dinner if you'll wait a spell with me until the train comes."

Karl turned toward his friend and smiled, "*Ja*, Homer, I will take you up on that offer.' He gave Homer a friendly slap on the back and they walked into Daisy's Café.

Later that evening, Homer Runtsch boarded the northbound train to Billings, Montana. Karl stood on the platform and waved goodbye as the train pulled out of the station. He buttoned his coat against the sudden evening chill, turned, and headed back to the boarding house where he had purchased a room for the night. He thought about the new train station and the railroad from Billings to Lovell. *Now, Katja and our sons will be able to ride in comfort directly into Lovell.*

As Karl lay on his back between the clean bedsheets in the Lovell hotel, he stared at the peeling ceiling, making plans for the following day. He decided to rise early the next morning, pick up a load of supplies, and head east to his farm. The last thought in his mind was how much he had accomplished since hitting town less than three weeks ago. Nobody saw him smile in the dark.

Karl was out of bed before dawn and, after a quick breakfast he walked to the stable on Main Street and paid Matt for the board of his Percherons. After hitching the draft horses to his wagon, he headed to the general store for fresh supplies. Karl nestled the boxes under the tarp, secured the ropes on the wagon, and turned the team and wagon onto the road east out of Lovell, back toward the Big Horn Mountains and *his farm*.

Thought after thought played tag in his mind on the slow journey to the farm. *My farm! My farm! It has a good ring to it*, he thought as a smile crinkled up his blue eyes. True, the house and buildings weren't much to look at, but he had big plans to quickly improve them. Most important, the land was good fertile bottomland, close to the Shoshone River, and irrigation. He was satisfied he had made a good buy—*a good start!* As he neared the little farm, Karl urged the Percherons into a trot, and the heavy wagon rumbled down the rut-filled lane to his own farm in America.

Karl pulled the team up beside the house, wound the reins around the brake, and climbed down from the seat. He released the horses from the wagon stem and led them down to the corral. After removing their harnesses, he rubbed them down, then grabbed a pitchfork and pitched hay into the manger. Karl closed the barn door and walked up a slight knoll where his unpretentious farmhouse sat. He opened the flimsy door and stood on the threshold, his gaze slowly scanning the deplorable room. *Where should I begin? Good Lord, there is a lot to do! There is no true beginning and no quick solution to making this place livable.* Nevertheless, he was home, so he took off his dusty newsboy cap, slapped it on his thigh, and hung it on a peg by the door along with his jacket.

After storing the supplies in the appropriate places, Karl fixed himself a cold supper. Feeling overwhelmed, he decided to postpone the remodel plans for the day. It was getting late and he was suddenly weary. There was something else he needed to do before he slept that night. Karl slid a crudely crafted chair out from the wobbly wood table. He pulled paper and pen from his saddlebag and, sitting at the table, began to write.

> October 10, 1906
> Dearest Leibschen:
> I am sorry I have not written to you before this. Events have been happening so quickly in this new place, I have barely had time to catch my breath. First let me tell you, I think you will like this new land in Wyoming. Lovell is located in a large valley, more than 100 miles across, surrounded by high blue mountains with snow-tipped peaks. The valley does not have many trees, but we can plant trees and crops, and water them from canals. There is a railroad that runs through the valley and it was only completed last year. This is good news because now you and our sons can ride the train to Lovell, instead of traveling by wagon from Montana.
> The people of the town have welcomed me, some not as much as others. I found work on a farm immediately after I arrived. It is in an area called Kane, to the east of Lovell. It is close to large mountains and a river with trees. I helped an old farmer to

bring in his crop and he sold the farm to me at a good price. The house is small with only one room, where I will live for a while. I have plans to improve it before you and our sons make the trip to America.

I bought two black Percheron horses and a sturdy wagon. Now that harvest is over I have inquired for extra work in town over the winter months. While the weather is good, I will stay out here on the farm and make improvements on the house and barn. I plan to dig a new outhouse closer to the house. In the meantime, I will do what I can to make the farm and especially the house better in which to live. I have a few dishes for now; when you and our sons arrive, you will like to choose new dishes and cooking pots.

I do not think it wise for you and our two sons to sail during the stormy winter months. By the month of May, I will have the money necessary to send for your tickets. I count the days; I try not to think of you too often because it makes my heart and body ache with longing. Never forget, you are my life, my day, and my night. Without you I have no purpose. I look at the moon and I see your sweet face.

Ich liebe dich aus herzensgrund,
Your husband, Karl

After finishing his letter, Karl was in a pensive state of incredulity as he sat at the table, looking out the sole window. He sat quietly in the crude wooden chair and watched as the sun slipped down behind the Rocky Mountains to the west, casting its final golden rays across the news papered walls of his unpretentious farmhouse in *Amerika!*

CHAPTER 8

The Winter Alone

★ ★ ★ ★ ★

The next morning Karl awoke to a crispy chill in the fall air. Against his better judgment, he eased out of his warm sleeping bag and stepped onto the frosty dirt floor. "*ACHT*—now I am awake! By gosh, that is the first thing I do today, make a new floor for this shack."

Karl dressed quickly and stoked up the fire in the cook stove. When the surface was hot, he threw a spoon of lard and a few eggs into a cast-iron fry pan along with some dried jerky. As he shoveled down the stir-fried breakfast, Karl thought of the supplies he needed to build a new floor.

After breakfast, he walked down to the barn and fed and watered his horses. He hitched the Percherons to the wagon and headed over to Kane[4] for the supplies he needed. First stop on Karl's list was the hardware/lumber store. He pulled the team to a stop, jumped down, wound the reins around the hitching post, and hurried up the wooden steps of the store. Not breaking stride, he pushed the rough wooden door open.

"Good morning, Bill, here's my list here for lumber, nails, and a few other things I need in order to get my new place in shape before winter blows in and before I can send for my wife. Do you think you can help me out?"

Bill Schneider reached for his glasses and scanned the list. "*Gol dang*, man, this is quite a list. Are you going to do the work all by yourself?"

"*Ja*, Bill, what I don't get finished by November, I will work on it through the winter when I can. I can't afford to hire it done right now. Besides, I need to keep busy—makes the time go by faster."

An hour later, the wagon was full of lumber, nails, tar paper, shingles, and two windows. He had a plan to improve the main features of his new home, first for his comfort, and later for his Katja and their two young sons.

To describe the cabin Homer Runtsch built as rustic was stretching it a bit. Homer had proudly told how he cut and hauled logs from nearby Pryor Mountain all by himself. He never bothered peeling the bark off the logs and the inside was frankly, a mess. Karl figured it would take a little elbow grease to pull off the hanging bark and scrub down the wood. The house was about fourteen-by-sixteen feet. The roof was supported by a large ridgepole with small, rough-cut support poles positioned horizontally, sloping down to the sides and nailed. The log walls were poorly daubed with mud to keep out winter drafts and most insects seeking shelter. Homer had nailed old newsprint and pages from a Sears catalog on the inside walls. He figured its purpose was to insulate and keep out the bugs, but it was filthy and it was coming down.

There was a single doorway with the most pitiful door Karl had ever seen. *There is no way that door could keep out the advancing winter or anything else. Only one window without glass, in the cabin.* Homer had nailed a sheet of canvas across the top of the frame to drop when needed. He used a single kerosene lamp to light the dark interior. Karl decided this was all about to change! Furniture was sparse and limited to the essentials. An ancient iron bedframe, complete with springs and soiled mattress, was pushed against one wall, and the unpainted table with three, unrelated chairs sat in the middle of the room. Karl nicknamed the neglected wood cook stove 'the black beast'; it wasn't the best looking stove but it was the only source of heat.

Interior storage consisted of wooden crates nailed on the wall. Karl didn't mind the packed dirt floor, but he knew in a heartbeat that Katja would not like the floor. Homer had already chopped and stacked the winter's supply of firewood on the south side of the cabin, and Karl was glad for that.

After he unloaded the wagon, he headed for the river to get a couple buckets full of fresh water. He stoked the fire in the stove and sat a large pot of water to boil. While the water was heating, Karl attacked the walls and ripped off the hanging bark, newsprint, and catalog pages. The dirt and dead bugs that had collected behind the newsprint and catalog pages fell in mass to the dirt floor.

When the water came to a boil, Karl added lye soap. With a wire brush, he scrubbed the filthy log walls. As Karl scrubbed the logs, more dead bark and loose chinking crumbled off. He knew he would have to repair the chinking.

The first improvement of the day was to build a sturdy door. Karl tightened up the existing door frame, measured, cut, and nailed new lumber into a primitive, but sturdy, front door. He placed a horizontal crossbar inside that dropped across the door to lock securely. Next, he decided to cut out a second window to the right of the front door. He made an opening the same size as the other window, sixteen by sixteen inches. He had purchased two mullioned (divided) glass windows, which would keep out the Wyoming weather and let in the light.

Ja, my Katja will like these windows; she will probably make some nice curtains for them.

The sun was low in the sky as Karl grabbed a new broom and quickly swept the debris out into the yard. He started a trash heap which he would burn once he was finished reconstructing the house and barn. Karl walked into his cabin, shut the sturdy, new front door and lay down on his bed. An hour later, he woke with a start. Total darkness had descended; at first he didn't know where he was. Finally realization hit him as he rose from his bed and inched his way across the cabin to where he'd remembered the kerosene lamp and matches were stored. After lighting the lamp, he put more wood in the stove and put the cast-iron fry pan on a burner. He cooked up a supper of diced potatoes, onion, dried green peppers, and a couple of eggs stirred in. Unceremoniously, he dumped it on a chipped metal plate he found in the open box cupboard. The stuff on the plate didn't look that good, but it was hot and Karl wolfed it down.

The next day was Sunday and the first thing Karl did was to give thanks to the Lord for keeping him safe and bringing him the good fortune of this farm, his farm. After a cold breakfast, he walked down to the barn to feed and water his horses. He thought about buying a few chickens come spring. First, he needed to build a coop and fence a small yard with chicken wire. He'd heard coyotes howling last night and knowing they were partial to chickens, he vowed not to give them a meal.

When Karl finished with his chores, he started back to the house, wiping his hands clean on the front of his pants as he walked. He moved the rickety furniture, and even the heavy cast-iron cook stove, out into the yard. Karl stacked the lumber for the floor, just outside the door. First, he laid a double layer of tar paper on the dirt floor as a moisture barrier. Next, he spread two wheelbarrow loads of dry river sand over the tar paper to act as a second, absorbing moisture barrier, with another layer of tar paper on top. Next step was to build a wood frame around the perimeter of the room. When this was ready, he began to lay a tight plank floor. As he nailed the wood floor together, he thought of his wife. *Ja, Katja won't have to live with a dirt floor. This is now a good floor that she can scrub to her heart's content.*

By the time Karl moved the furniture and cook stove back inside the cabin, the day was almost over. He did his evening chores and walked slowly back to his house, feeling the long day catching up to him. He walked through his new front door, across the freshly laid, aromatic wood floor and peered out of one of the small glass windows. *Ja*, thought Karl, *I have had a good weekend, I have accomplished much. With winter coming, I don't want any mice or spiders to move in here, too. Maybe a neighbor has extra cats they would give me to keep the mouse population down. Besides, Katja and the boys might like a cat or two.*

As dusk filtered through the remaining yellow-gold leaves of the cottonwood trees, he made himself comfortable on the new front steps of his improved home. He pulled the pipe from his pant's pocket, lit it, and eased himself back against the log wall. Taking a long draw on the pipe, he held the pungent smoke in his lungs for a moment and blew it far out into the cool evening air.

In November as the weather began to take on a definite chill, Karl closed up his house near Kane and moved a few things into Lovell. He made arrangements to board the horses. A neighbor had agreed to tend to the horses in return for the services of Karl's Percheron stud.

His first week in Lovell, Karl walked into the local pool hall after noticing they had a "help needed" sign in the window. He stood at the rustic pine bar and ordered a beer. "I was wondering if I might speak to the owner about the job advertised in the front window."

The bartender looked Karl up and down and replied, "Yor lookin' at him! So your lookin' for a job, are ya? We probably need to talk a bit."

The two men discussed the job and what it paid and came to an agreement. Karl started the job of sweeping up at nights after the patrons staggered out the front door. He rarely shot pool and on occasion, when the opportunity arose, he played cards. He refused to wager his hard-earned money as many of the men did. After cleaning up at night, he was allowed to sleep in the back storeroom on a cot, free of charge.

A couple of weeks after he moved into Lovell, Karl had a day off and, after completing several errands, stopped back at the pool hall for a beer. He was finishing his beer when a woman approached, decked out in a stained, orange satin dress. Karl took one look at her and knew exactly what she was—her breath was ragged and stinking. She reeked of sex and insufficient baths. Her red hair hung around her face in greasy, snarled strands. "Hi ya, darling. Yer lookin' awfully lonely over here, and I can fix that situation real fast!" Her hand slid slowly up his arm.

Karl stood up, leaving payment for the beer on the bar, "No thank you, miss. I am a married man and not interested in the likes of you!"

The hooker got the message loud and clear. With a flip of her filthy hair, she walked away, slowly swinging her hips in an exaggerated sway toward a table full of drinking men.

The only bill Karl had to pay while he was in Lovell was for the board for Sandstone, his bay horse. During the day, he washed dishes in Daisy's Café and usually cleaned up the leftovers as part of his wage. When freight came in on the train, Karl was first to sign up to unload and deliver the merchandise. He sometimes worked as a day laborer at the local brick factory, taking any job that was open. Karl learned many new trades and met a lot of people during the winter of 1907. His straightforward work ethic left a positive impression with most people he met.

One late night in the pool hall, Karl was cleaning up when he noticed several men lingering over by the coal stove, arguing loudly, the result of the amount of whisky they had poured down their throats all night. Suddenly, a wood bar chair went flying across the room, smashing to pieces against the wall, followed by an inebriated chap who staggered to his feet with "blood in his eye." Unfortunately, the first person that came into focus was Karl Kessel.

"What the hell are ya looking at ya dirty, German pig," the drunk bellowed through a whisky-thick tongue.

Karl kept his calm as the man staggered to his feet and lurched menacingly toward him. Keeping on eye on the drunk, Karl continued to swab the wood floor. The drunk seemed further provoked by Karl's disinterest, and made his way across the floor in a zigzag route until they were face to face. Karl did a quick estimate of the situation; he guessed this bloke probably weighed about 250 pounds, but most of it was fat. Slurred, slobbery words sputtered from his foul-smelling mouth as his spit spattered Karl's face.

"Ya know what? I don't like ya and I don't like lookin' at ya German face, and sure as hell don't like breath'n the same air as ya foreign swine. Get the hell back to ya kraut-eatin' kind. Get your ass back on the boat that ya came over on and be leave'n this country to people who belong here," he bellowed through his drunken haze.

As Karl turned to walk away, the drunken slob made a mistake he would deeply regret for several days. Grabbing Karl from behind, the man wrapped his arms around Karl's chest. The drunk's breath was hot and stinking as he began to squeeze Karl's sinewy body with his giant forearms. Karl reacted with fluid fury! In a flash that surprised and dumbfounded the other patrons, as well as the drunk, Karl thrust his right elbow back hard, and straight into the soft belly of the inebriated sot. The fellow gagged, doubled up, and released his prey as Karl spun with the speed of a tornado and drove his left fist with unrestrained fury into the right jaw of the big-mouthed drunk. The man fell back into a table stacked with chairs and Karl continued to go after him. *I'm not done with this rude, arrogant excuse for a man.* Karl might have been mad enough, but he wasn't strong enough to lift the limp body of the man up, so he fell upon him and delivered blow after blow, after blow.

Later, Karl realized he had completely lost his composure, although it was actually something that, subconsciously, he felt compelled to do every time he was subjected to verbal and physical abuse. Karl felt relieved, cleansed from a relentless cancerous anger that had been growing inside of him ever since Arnold was murdered on the streets of Cleveland: *revenge!*

Two of the drunk's companions pulled Karl off the beaten big mouth, who lay motionless on the bar floor in a moaning, crumpled heap. Karl staggered over to the bar and, grabbing a wet bar rag, wiped it over his flushed face. Remorse was immediate and he feared for his job or, even worse, his jobs. He quickly realized he should not have responded as he did, but he had been consumed by instinct that came on him so fast he didn't think. He recognized it as the dark shadowy menace that lived deep inside of him, an evil, automatic tendency for violence that he inherited from his father. *Yes,* Karl thought, *my father taught me well. He taught me to respond violently with hard fists against anything or anyone who would go against me.*

Karl moved toward the four men as they were leaving the pool hall. With fire still flashing from his ice-blue eyes, Karl said, "That should not have happened. He should not have laid hands on me or said those words to me.

We all come from some other place. The only people who were born here are the Native American Indians. This is a free country, open to all who come here to make a new life, like myself. I wish no man harm. BUT, I can, and will, give back as good or bad as I get." Karl locked the door behind the men as they staggered out into the chill of the night.

Two weeks after the late-night pool hall attack, Albert Morgan walked into the pool hall, along with two other men. It was late for a Tuesday night and there were only a few men left playing a hand of poker at one of the front tables. Karl was minding his own business, washing glasses at the end of the bar. "Hey you, behind the bar there!" Morgan called, "I want to have a word with you."

Karl turned and was amazed to see the fellow who had attacked him. He slowly wiped his hands on a towel and stepped from behind the bar. He wasn't sure what was going to happen, but he was ready just the same.

"*Ja*, what is it I can help you with tonight?"

Much to Karl's amazement, the big man extended his hand and said, "I wish to apologize for my actions the other night; I was in my cups and not thinking too good. Obviously, I got what I deserved and would like to forget it and go on. My name is Albert Morgan," and pointing to his two companions, "these are friends of mine, Hector Tennant and Bill Rowe."

Karl walked closer to the man and extended his hand, "Karl Kessel, and I am glad to meet you. I am also most glad we can forget what happened."

The two men shook hands and, turning back to the bar, Karl released an audible sigh of relief as the men walked over to a vacant table for a hand of cards and a few beers.

The persistent Wyoming winds and bitter cold winter months seemed to drag by. Karl tried to keep busy, taking any and all jobs he could find. When there was a break in the weather, he rode out to Kane to check on his place and make a few more improvements. At the end of February, Karl finally received a letter from Katja. He had begun to worry because he had written to her in October, and not heard from her since, even at Christmas.

> February 5, 1907
> My dear Husband,
> Now, it is I who must apologize for not writing sooner to you.
> I hope you had a good Christmas season. Our sons enjoyed their
> Christmas and my parents went to great pains to make sure it was

joyful. They took Jakob and Christian to a concert of Bach the first part of December. The boys loved the music and it made me think of you and the times when we attended concerts together.

I have some wonderful news for you my husband. I did not tell you of this condition earlier because I did not want to give you worry. We have another son! Yes, Karl, I have named him Ralf to honor your friend who gave you the ticket to America. He was born on January 30th early in the morning. He had no trouble coming into this world and his brothers are quite protective of him. I hope that his name is acceptable to you. I think perhaps the last night you were at home you left me with more than your kisses.

Ralf is a good strong boy and always hungry. I hope you will understand why I did not tell you I was with child, before this date. I had no trouble with carrying the baby. My father did not allow me to work in the field during harvest. I have regained my strength now and am feeling well.

I am sure I will be able to travel to America in May. I will use a blanket wrap to secure Ralf to my chest, so I have two hands to hold on to Jakob and Christian. Papa is already making arrangements for our journey. He is becoming more and more upset as the time draws near. I am trying to be cheerful but there are days when I am sad for already missing my family when I come to America. I will be so happy to be with you my husband. Can I be sad and happy at the same time?

Chris and his wife Katharina have a new son named Christian also. Their little daughter Theresia is two years old now and they are a happy family. I am glad my parents have two other grandchildren to love after I take our sons away to America.

Let me know, Karl, when you think I should sail for America. I expect you will send money for the tickets with your next letter. Papa will make all of the arrangements for me so I don't have to worry about anything. He said he would accompany our sons and me to Bremerhaven in Germany as well, to make sure we have no troubles, and for this I am most relieved and grateful.

Ich liebe dich aus herzensgrund,
Your wife, Katja

Karl was stunned as he read the letter from Katja. They had another son—a son named Ralf! Of course, he remembered that last night with his wife, he thought of it so often and the memories physically tormented him. *She did not tell me because she didn't want me to worry?* "*Acht,* that woman!"

He was comforted to know his father-in-law was going to help his wife and sons travel to Bremerhaven, and remain to see them safely aboard the ship. Karl decided to send the money to Christian tomorrow, so he could purchase passage for Katja and his *three* sons to travel to America in late May.

Now, there was a definite time to expect his family, he needed to speed up the numerous improvements he wanted to make at the farm. In the middle of February, Karl gave notice at the pool hall and moved back out to Kane.

When weather permitted, he worked outside, building a small chicken coop and surrounding it with a high, wire-fenced yard. The chickens roamed the yard outside the fence during the day, but had to be locked inside the fence at night.

He planned to build two additional rooms onto the house using adobe bricks. He had heard they made a warm, naturally insulated house. They were a popular building material because they were cheap and easy to attain, compared to cutting and hauling heavy wood logs down from the mountains. Karl fashioned a form to make multiple adobe bricks of mud and straw. He mixed dirt from the clay hills with clean straw and poured the mixture into numerous forms, then left them to dry inside his house until the weather warmed. Every few days he stacked the finished ones against the wall and poured new bricks, until he had a sizeable pile. It took a month, working day and night, to build a two-room adobe addition to the house. Karl and Katja would sleep in one room and his sons would sleep in the bunk beds he built in the other room. While he was at it, he enlarged the kitchen area with a spacious lean-to addition that acted as a parlor. His plans for the farm were slowly coming to fruition. Karl was elated.

In March, Karl sent an order to Billings for additional supplies they would need to set up housekeeping when Katja and his sons arrived. He ordered three more tin tubs for laundry, three feather beds and pillows, two bolts of blue flower cotton fabric for Katja, and a new cradle for Ralf. From the Sears catalog, Karl ordered seeds for the garden along with dozens of potatoes and onion sets. He planned to wait until mid-May to plant the garden or as soon as the frost left the soil and he could get a hoe into the ground.

Karl also had to wait until the frost went out of the ground to dig a root cellar. Around the middle of April, he used a pick ax to cut through the top layer of frost and dug a hole about six-feet deep, and five-by-ten feet in diameter. He nailed together a simple door for the cellar. While he was in the digging mode, he dug a fresh hole for the new outhouse, to the west of the main house and away from the root cellar. Inside the outhouse he built the bench with a large hole for the adults and a smaller, lower hole for his sons.

Before he knew it, it was time to start the spring plowing and preparing his fields for planting. Karl still had a hard time believing these were his fields, his own land. He hitched the Percheron horses to a manure spreader he borrowed from a neighbor. Using his pitchfork, he filled the wooden wagon bed with manure from the corral. It was hard work to lift the damp manure from the corral and throw it up into the manure spreader. Once he had a good load, Karl drove the horses to the field and, sitting on the front of the wagon bed, he pushed the release lever forward. "Haw, boys, HAW!" he yelled at the horses.

Without apparent effort, the huge horses pulled the loaded wagon forward in the field. The rolling action of the wheels turned the revolving iron spikes, throwing the manure backwards over the field. Karl laughed when he looked over his shoulder as the manure flew over ground. "*Ja*, good job boys, good job; keep pulling hard and we will have this shitty job done before noon!" Karl laughed out loud at his attempt at humor.

After all the manure was spread, Karl walked to each end of the field and drove a long stake into the ground. He took a strip of red cloth and tied one to each stake. When he was behind the plow, he kept his eye firmly on the red flag to help him plow a straight line.

Karl purchased his own twelve-inch plow, which one of his horses pulled as he walked behind to guide it. Plowing was not an easy task but Karl made it look easy as he guided the horses while holding the plow at a sharp angle so it cut deep in the soil. He turned over a swath of ten-to-twelve inches in every round. At the end of each row, he moved the flag over about two feet as a guide for the next round. He faithfully sharpened the plow every night so it easily cut through the hard soil the following day. After plowing, he broke up the lumpy soil with a disc, then a harrow, finally leveling it smooth, making it ready to plant.

Karl had almost finished planting the corn that first spring, working near the grove of trees on the lower field. As he drove the team along the edge of the field, a pheasant took to the air in a flurry of wings and frantic squawking. Normally placid, the team of Percherons reared up. As they bolted, Karl flew off the seat of the planter, hitting the freshly planted field with a thud.

"What the hell. Whoa, whoa, there, you damn horses, you are ruining my field!" Karl yelled as he scrambled to his feet and took off chasing after the team. Frightened even more by the planter flying behind them, they headed for the grove of cottonwoods. As they ran through the trees, the planter became stuck, which brought everything to a stop, including the frightened horses. Karl ran up to the team and, breathing hard, grabbed the reins. Angrily, he whipped them both in the head with the leather reins. The mammoth horses reared in fright. Karl had a sudden attitude adjustment as he felt his feet leave the ground and (painfully) return. He decided that perhaps he should take a different approach with the larger horses.

"Okay, okay, boys, you win; but now we go back to the start of the row and finish planting, that is—if you didn't bust up my planter." Karl checked the planter, replenished the lost seed, made an adjustment or two, and led the team back up the field. He finished the final round just before the sun slipped behind the blue range of Rocky Mountains to the west.

Later that week, Karl traveled forty miles south to the county courthouse in Basin to inquire if he could apply to homestead another twenty-five acres of unimproved land that butted up to his farm. Much to his amazement, he had no trouble securing the deed to homestead the land, which he had already decided to plant in alfalfa and corn, after he prepared the virgin soil.

Most of Karl's neighbors also owned only two horses, but frequently needed four to pull the new, larger farming machinery. Karl loaned out his Percherons and in return borrowed their horses when he needed four. It was customary for neighbors to help each other in any way they could. Karl discovered his Percheron stud's "performance" was an excellent form of trade, as his neighbors were eager to build their own Percheron herds. Twice, he agreed to accept a foal as payment, building his own herd. His own herd would increase by four in late June, thanks to the mating of his two Persherons.

As spring approached, Karl built a chicken coop and two lean-to sheds for small animals he planned to buy. He traded for a dozen laying hens and a rooster, two geese and a gander, along with a couple of goats. He secured the fowl inside the wagon and tied the goats to the rear as he traveled back to his house. Later he bought three milk cows from Tom Goodman, whose farm was nestled in the hills to the north of his own place. When Karl finished filling the sheds with animals, he stood and looked at it all with a sense of accomplishment in his heart.

Soon Katja and his sons would arrive. Their passage was supposed to leave Bremerhaven on the tenth of May, arriving in New York on May twenty-fifth. Karl had sent Katja train tickets from New York to Lovell, with as few train changes as possible. He expected his family to arrive around the first part of June. Every day, Karl made another mark on the calendar, crossing off the days and the tasks he needed to accomplish. He worked like a man possessed, making sure the farm and living conditions were as decent as possible.

With the crops and the garden planted, Karl took the afternoon off and went down to the Shoshone River to fish. *Maybe if I am lucky, I'll be frying up a nice catfish for my supper.*

Fishing or taking time off was not something he did often or without a guilty conscience. Frankly, he thought fishing was a waste of time, but today he had a need to sit on the bank and think. Karl found his fishing pole hanging on the barn wall; he dug a handful of earthworms from the soft soil and grabbed his pole. He found a good spot in the shade on a grassy bank, threaded the bait onto the hook, and cast the line in a wide arc out into the middle of the river. Satisfied with his cast, Karl eased himself back onto the riverbank and let his mind drift to images of Katja. *What would she think of Wyoming, Lovell, and their home in Kane?*

Deep in his subconscious, Karl knew Katja would be disappointed in both this barren, inhospitable land and the inadequate house he had tried to make livable. It was not even close to what she was used to. But he also knew she would not let him know if she was disappointed. Karl thought of his three sons, including the baby he had not even seen. "Jakob should be big enough now to have chores and, in a couple of years, help in the field." *Someday, I will have many sons to help with the farm.* German children were expected to work and obey.

Impatient with fishing, Karl picked up his gear and headed back to the house. *What was I thinking, going fishing when there is so much work to do, what is wrong with me to be so lazy?*

CHAPTER 9

Sending For Katja

★ ★ ★ ★ ★

"The Lord will keep you from all harm—he will watch over your life. The Lord will watch over your coming and going both now and forevermore."
~Psalm 121; 7–8

Christian Mehll glanced at the letter from Karl, lying on the table and a shudder of dread rolled down his back. He knew the letter contained money for his daughter's ticket to America. Tormenting thoughts plagued him. *How can I help her do this thing? HOW? I do not want to send her and my grandsons away on that ship because it will be forever. Dear Lord*, he prayed, *Give me the strength to help my daughter and not add to her distress. I know she is torn with leaving her home and I do not wish to make it more difficult for her. My heart is so heavy and it is Karl I blame for this—it is all for his dream, his ambition, that he takes them away from us.*

The night before Katja was to leave, Christian walked down the street to her house. "Katja, are you all packed and ready to go in the morning? I think we should leave as soon after the dawn breaks as we can. We have a long way to travel."

Katja looked up at her father, her deep-brown eyes enormous and moist with trepidation. It troubled him to see her so distraught.

Christian swallowed hard before he continued: "Katja, Katja, tomorrow will come like any other day, but we all know it will not be like any other day. Each of us has many feelings in our hearts; excitement for your new life of opportunity, fear of the unknown, and sorrow for the leaving. Leaving is never easy but we have to embrace the life God gives to us—a wife shall go where her husband goes." Christian turned away in effort to regain his composure, "Our own family, and this German community in Surtschin left Germany many years ago to find a better life. We know what it is like to leave a life and family behind." Christian took his daughter into the shelter of his arms and held her close.

Katja pulled away from her father and turned her small oval face up to him. Tears filled her large ebony eyes and ran unchecked down her face. "Papa, please—I cannot speak of it. I have never been expected to do something so hard. I know Karl is waiting for us and has worked hard to make a home for us in America. He is at last happy, for he has a farm and land of his own. I can't imagine what the days ahead will be like, what my life will be without my family."

Christian laid his large hands on her shoulders. "Katja, you *can* do this thing. I know you are a strong, Christian woman and you love your husband and your sons. It is the life Karl has chosen. Your family tries to understand this. Your sons will have many opportunities to succeed in America. We have raised you to do the right thing as a wife."

He withdrew his hands from his daughter's thin shoulders and reaching down he took her tiny hand in his own. "Katja, you will be happy in America because you and Karl will be building a new life together. You cannot have both lives, Katja; it is your destiny. Pray tonight, my *leibschen*, you know the Lord will give you strength and peace; ask him for this. We may not meet again on this earth, but I know we will meet again in heaven. Now, you need to get your rest my sweet, for tomorrow we have a long journey." Christian drew his weeping, daughter into his arms once again and comforted her as best he could. He gritted his jaw tightly, containing his own emotion.

Predictably, Katja did not sleep well. She tossed and turned with tormented thoughts and visions of leaving. She was at a crossroads in her life; both roads held great sorrow and great expectation. Only the road to her husband held promise of a better future for her and her sons. She knew she had to put them before herself; it was her duty as a wife and mother. She also remembered her wedding vows. Katja pledged to obey and to follow her husbands lead; in spite of everything, she would do what was expected of her.

Finally, Katja rose from her rumpled bed, threw her robe around her shoulders, and quietly padded down the stairs to the kitchen. Perhaps if I read something and drink a cup of chamomile tea, I can stop my mind from tormenting me. Katja put the pot over the lingering coals in the stove to boil the water. As the pot was heating, she stood at the window and looked out. The full moon illuminated the night sky; the gauzy clouds looked so close, so beautiful. She smiled as she gazed out the window, thinking, *The sky looks like cotton batting that Mama and I put in our quilts. But it changes so fast I barely have time to appreciate the wonder of it. It is like our lives—always changing.* The water began to sputter; Katja lifted the pot and poured the seething liquid into a cup and added a tiny bit of chamomile herb.

She took her steeping tea to the kitchen table where her copy of Pastor Bogen's *Handbook for Emigrants* laid. Katja had read and reread the book in order to prepare herself for the long trip across the Atlantic Ocean. She turned again to the advice about children and traveling.

> *Remember, you are in a ship, constantly in motion and therefore you should make your children begin in time, to hang up or carefully place in your berth, whatever they may use as soon as it is done with, and never lay anything down on the deck or you may expect to lose it. Take as little crockery as possible; tin ware is much better. Make one article serve two or three purposes. If you have a small Dutch oven, you will find it of the greatest use when cooking on board the ship. The oven should not be larger than sufficient to cook a slice of bacon, nine inches long. A quart tin pot with a flat side and a hook is the most handy thing you can have to boil a little water in. Your baking pans will serve as dishes. And, all these things in packing will contain some little knickknack or other. For, if you are going far up the country, you will find the expense of luggage a heavy tax on your stock of money, from which you must not draw one single farthing, after you have embarked, without the greatest necessity.*

Katja took a slow sip of the hot tea and felt the warmth slide down her throat, and settle deep inside her tense stomach. Soon, the calming effect of the herb tea soothed her; she began to relax and feel sleepy. Katja carried her empty cup to the washstand, rinsed it and put it back into the cupboard. As she climbed the stairs to her bedroom for the last time, she was ready to sleep.

The next morning the warm spring sunshine promised a pleasant day for traveling. Katja and her three sons hugged and kissed their Oma and other family members as they said goodbye. Not fully understanding the situation, the two older boys were frightened by so many tears and also began to cry. With salty tears running down his rosy cheeks, Jakob pulled at his mother's brown wool skirt, "Mama, Mama, why do you cry. Are you hurt?"

Katja kneeled before her oldest son. Wiping his tears, she cupped his little face in her hands as she said, "*Nein*, Jakob, my love, I am only sad to leave Oma and Opa. But we must be happy, too, because we are going to have a wonderful adventure when we board the big ship to go across the blue ocean waters. Your dear papa is waiting for us in America. Do not worry, *leibschen*; do not worry, now. Come along, it is time."

Jakob looked up with the same ice-blue eyes as his father and said, "Well, Mama, if you are sad to leave, we can write a letter to Papa and tell him to come back so we don't have to leave Oma and Opa." The seven-year-old was sure he had solved the problem.

"*Nein*, Jakob. Papa sent us money to come to him and it is where we will go to live. It will be fine, son. It will be fine. Now, kiss your *grosmuter* goodbye one more time and climb on the wagon with your brother and *grosvater*."

By the time Christian, Katja, and her three sons arrived in Bremerhaven, they were resigned to the task at hand. When she first saw the enormous ship waiting like a bridegroom in the harbor, her body tensed. Soon, she realized she and her children would leave her father on the dock and board that huge ship. Katja watched her father closely; he moved with a heaviness she had not noticed before. It was as though every muscle in his body was tensed for battle. Katja knew he was trying to be strong for them. He struggled to smile and act cheerful.

The dreaded moment came all too soon and Katja found herself standing at the ship's railing, waving goodbye to her father, as he stood alone on the dock. She was glad she couldn't see the inner grief that contorted his face and surrounded him like a shroud.

Christian stood and waved goodbye robotically, until the sturdy tugs released the KronPrinz Wilhelm. Power filled the great steam engines and they came to life, propelling the huge ship out into the open water. Only then did Christian turn his back to the ship to begin his long, solitary journey back to Surtschin. He felt like he was moving in slow motion, as though he was outside his body, watching himself walk toward the wagon. He felt hollow inside; his shoulders slumped and he struggled to move his feet. Life swirled around him like a bad dream. Instinctively, he knew this was what the rest of his life would feel like. It was as though his daughter and grandsons were dead and gone!

On board the ship, Katja was so busy getting Jakob, Christian, and baby Ralf settled in their berth that she didn't have time to think. After the children had fallen asleep, when she sat cross-legged in her berth, she allowed the pent-up emotions to surface. She cried herself to sleep silently that night and the next. Thankfully, the ocean was not as rough through the English Channel as it had been for Karl. She felt a gentle rocking motion that she found soothing, and her sons seemed to enjoy the motion of the sea, too.

Jakob and Christian soon discovered that they preferred to be up on deck in the fresh ocean air. They laughed with wonder as the sharp bow of the ship sliced deep through white-capped waves. Jakob turned to his mother saying, "It's fun, Mama, it's so much fun to see the big waters and I also like to watch the sea birds dive into the ocean. A man told me the birds are fishing! Is that true, Mama, is it?"

Katja smiled, noting the innate curiosity of her oldest son, "*Ja*, Jakob, I believe it is true that they *are* fishing for their supper. Or maybe they are taking a bath, what do you think?"

Jakob laughed at his mother's teasing words, "Maybe they are doing both!"

Katja's two oldest sons knew instinctively they must behave because, without Papa or their grandfather to help care for them, their mother was alone and it was not easy for her. They liked going through the lines for their food as instructed and were careful to mind the ship's rules. Baby Ralf was no trouble as he nursed and slept, then nursed again. Katja was coping, and inwardly proud of her newly discovered ability to care for herself and her three children without help.

When the ship docked at the Rock of Gibraltar, Jakob and Christian begged to go up on deck and watch the hectic activity on shore. Katja agreed, in fact she was curious as well to see the famous "rock" and this foreign country of Spain. The sun shone brightly as the ships crew loaded more passengers and cargo. The atmosphere was chaotic with Spanish-speaking dock workers laughing and yelling orders. Jakob's eyes were wide with wonder; he was delighted with the foreign sounds and feverish activity.

As they stood on deck, a string of men and brown pack mules made their way slowly down a steep hill above the wharf. Each mule carried two barrels of olive oil, one on each side of his back, attached with leather sling straps. Behind the string of mules they spotted five or six wooden carts, each carrying three huge wooden barrels of Spanish red wine. Many passengers were on deck to watch as the ship's crew began to hoist a large steel door on the side of the ship's hull, revealing the area in the ship's belly where the barrels would be stored. Suddenly, a loud *crack* sounded over the frenzied activity. All at once the pitch and intensity of the workers' voices reached a new height and intensity, followed by bloodcurdling screams as men began to run away from the path of a loose cart rolling without restraints, down the hill.

Jakob and his brother gripped the ship's railing, stunned eyes wide with fear and wonder. They looked back at the cart that had been carrying the wine and saw that one of the wooden wheels had broken, spilling heavy wine barrels onto the steep hill. The barrels rolled loose, straight toward the string of mules, picking up speed as they rolled. Missing the mules, the first barrel hit a wood pillion on the dock and burst. Blood-red wine exploded from the broken barrel and covered the dock with a crimson stain. Two other barrels continued rolling in a haphazard route. One crashed over the side of the dock but the other rolled over a stunned Spanish dockworker, crushing him to death.

His mouth open with disbelief and confusion, Jakob turned to Katja, "Mama, what happened? People are running and shouting, the barrel rolled over the man and he is not getting up. Is he hurt? Is he, Mama?"

Katja was horrified by what her small sons had just witnessed, and realized she had to remain calm and unaffected. "*Ja*, Jakob, he is probably hurt, but his friends will take him to the doctor. Let's go down below, now. Ralf needs to take his nap, and a rest might be a good idea for you and Christian, as well." The boys reluctantly obeyed, and followed their mother down the metal staircase into third class.

The next day after sailing out of Gibraltar, the seas began to roll as the wind whipped and howled. The seas were so rough that the evening meal was served on long wooden tables set up below deck. Jakob had gone to eat with friends as Katja wasn't feeling well.

When he returned he told his mother what had happened. "We was eatin' our supper at the long table. They gave us all soup. All the peoples sat there eatin' and all of a sudden the front of the boat went up in the air and went back down. All the soup on that long table was gone. It all fell off onto the floor and onto the peoples. That is why my shirt and pants are wet, Mama. I am sorry, but it was really funny to see how everybody looked!" Katja cleaned him up as best she could and put the boys to bed.

Midway in the crossing, they experienced another day of storm and were instructed to keep portholes latched tight. Jakob was playing tag in the aisles and witnessed the entire thing. "*Ja*, Mama, there is a Slovac woman down the aisle there and she opened the porthole. When the waves got high, the sailor men told her to close it because water was coming in it. As soon as they left, she opened it again and much water came in and about drowned her and all her kids. Those sailors yelled at her, Mama, and they locked that porthole tight so she couldn't get it open. It was funny to see them all wet. Me and Christian laughed and ran away."

The following day dawned bright and clear, the storm had passed and all was calm again. Katja was thankful because she had been afraid of the strength of the storm and how easily it tossed the great ship about. They were three days out from the Rock of Gibraltar when Katja took her sons up on deck to get some air. A group of people were leaning over the side of the ship, pointing and talking with excitement. Katja took her sons to the railing and they were delighted to see huge whales swim close to the ship and spout water. They rolled around on the surface of the ocean as if they were trying to get some sunshine. After a while the sailors made the passengers leave the one side because they were afraid the boat might tip over, or so they said. As soon as the sailors left, the people went right back to watch the whales, so the sailors made them all go below. The next day Katja's sons pestered her until she took them back up on deck and they were pleased to see porpoise leaping through the water. "Mama, look at them, they are playing follow-the-leader. Why are they mostly white and the whales were gray?"

The rest of the journey was uneventful and Katja was grateful for good weather and smooth seas. It was just breaking daylight when the KronPrinz Wilhelm entered the harbor at New York. Katja and her sons were standing on deck with other eager immigrants, each straining for a glimpse of the huge buildings and the Lady in the harbor that Karl had written about. When the passengers saw the Statue of Liberty, many people fell down to their knees weak with emotion; they began to cry and declare, "Ve are free, *Mein Gott*, ve are in a free country at last!"

Jakob asked, "Mama, why are the peoples crying tears down their faces?

Shouldn't they be happy 'cause we will now be free in America?"

Katja put her arm around her oldest son's shoulders and explained, "*Ja*, Jakob, they cry because they are happy and not sad. Sometimes people are filled with so much happiness that only tears come."

Officials herded the people off the ferry boat to wait in long lines in front of the Emigrants Building. The lines entered the building and snaked back and forth until each person stood, ready for their examination. Shots were given when needed and each person was inspected for eye disease.

Jakob was deeply concerned and upset at the fate of people who were rejected. Every time he heard a great lamentation rise from somewhere in the lines, he wrapped his face in his mother's skirts. Both older boys stayed close to Katja, holding tightly to her long skirts. Soon, it was their turn to be inspected by the doctors. They were frightened at first when the doctors began to touch them. When Jakob's turn came to have his eyes examined he wasn't about to cooperate. "NO, NO, MAMA! I don't like the man to hurt my eyes!" Jakob shouted as he took a swing at the white-coated doctor with a botton hook in his hand.

Katja grabbed his arm and spoke sternly: "Jakob, stop this; you must let the doctor look at your eyes or they will send us back on the ship and we won't see Papa! It will be okay, son, I promise. Now, hold still!" Katja sympathized with her son, "I know it doesn't feel good, but you must be brave so your brother Chris won't be afraid."

It was true that none of the children or even the adults especially cared for the eye exam, but they had no choice but to endure it. As Karl had told her, they were given a sustaining snack while they waited in the long lines between the physical and mental examinations. The boys loved the aromatic bananas and cold milk handed out to them by food stewards in the great hall. Neither Katja nor her sons had ever tasted anything like the soft, flavorful fruit.

Jakob turned to his mother and declared, "Mama, I do so like those ba-nan-as. Will they have ba-nan-as in Wyoming?" The little boy laughed. "It's so funny that we must take off the coat first and only eat the inside!"

Even though Katja was an adult female traveling alone, she was allowed to continue on her journey because she had tickets for the train, paid for by her husband who owned property in Wyoming. In order to catch the train west, the Kessel family was taken by ferry across to New York City and the train station. After disembarking from the ferry, Katja was at a loss about which train to board. There were so many trains, going so many places.

Katja's English left a lot to be desired and even Jakob was not a big help in understanding the station signs. Finally, much to their relief they were approached by a kind, smartly dressed man who spoke German. "Excuse me, *Frau*, I can't help but noticed you seem confused. May I help you find the correct train? Let me look at your ticket." It didn't take him a minute and he had them waiting at the right gate for their connection to Wyoming. Much relieved, Katja thanked him for his kindness and they all waved to him as their train pulled out of the station.

The boys thought it was great fun, riding on the black steam train. The clickity-clack of the iron wheels going over the rails was hypnotizing, and the repetitive sound worked its magic in putting all three children to sleep soon after they boarded.

The second day out of New York, they were sitting at a table in the dining car, having just finished their noon meal. The waiter asked Katja if they were ready for dessert. She accepted and the waiter placed three plates of fresh lemon pie on their table. With eyes wide in wonder, Jakob looked at the lemon pie in front of him and bent forward to smell it. The shiny yellow filling wiggled from the motion of the train. The white meringue on the top of the pie looked like snow on the mountains in Yugoslavia. "Can I taste it now, Mama? Can I, please?" Jakob asked impatiently.

Smiling, Katja replied, "Of course, Jakob, taste a little bit first to see how you like it." Jakob's fork slipped down through the lemon pie. He carefully lifted the wiggly confection to his eager little mouth and rolled his tongue around the wondrous tangy lemon flavor. He had never tasted lemon in his life, and he instantly decided this pie was yet another new thing he loved in America.

Later, as Jakob prepared to sleep for the night, he reached up to whisper in his mother's ear. "I think I like this new country, Mama, because it has trains, and bananas, and lemon pie. It is *wunderbar*, Mama, *wunderbar*."

In Chicago, the conductor indicated that all passengers were to get off the train and board a different train going west. Katja felt the acid of fear burn hot in the pit of her stomach, again worried that she wouldn't understand which train and what time it would leave for Montana. *I know my English is not good and, even if it was better, these Americans speak their English so fast I cannot understand, even a little.*

Katja continued to stand where she and her sons got off the train from New York, with her bags and her children at her feet. Her dark eyes darted right and left as she tried to figure out which train was the right train.

A most welcome voice asked, *"Frau, Spreckin sie English?"*

Relief flooding her face, Katja turned to her benefactor, *"Nein,* sir, not good English. I am looking for our train to the west, to Montana, can you help me?"

The station guide motioned for her and the boys to follow him as he carried her bags toward the train to Montana. After Katja and her sons were settled in their berth, and the train was rolling down the tracks, Katja reached up and removed the traditional black scarf from her hair. "I am now in America and, as I noticed in the train stations, the American women do not wear the scarf over their hair." She smiled as she tucked the black wool scarf into her pocket, and felt cool air wash over her neck.

As the train rolled across the farms and the Great Plains of Iowa and on north to the Dakotas, Katja stared out the window, her eyes wide with disbelief. Where are the trees? The land is so barren and ugly, just one brush-covered, rolling hill after another. She felt a building tightness in her chest and a foreboding burn in the pit of her stomach. How could Karl bring me to live in this atrocious country for the rest of my life? Surely, he does not expect me to make my home forever in this ugly, brown, flat land?

Katja's eyes rose upward to the huge puffs of white clouds that dotted the great expanse of blue sky, blue like her Karl's eyes. Everything here seemed so big, like this prairie that just kept coming, mile after mile under the rumbling train. The absence of mountains gave the illusion that the horizon seemed even farther, increasing the size of the land. *Plea-ssse, dear Gott, help me, give me courage and strength to be happy in this new life that you have given to Karl and to me. And please don't let Karl see my disappointment.*

In her heart, she knew she would have to work hard to feel at home in this inhospitable land that was not her beloved loved Surtschin. *Perhaps if I concentrate on the occasional grove of budding cottonwood trees, I will survive.*

She wasn't sure exactly where they were, some place in the Dakotas. The train was just pulling into a small town as Jakob and Christian peered out the grimy window. All at once Jakob let out a whoop, "Maaaaaamaaa, look over there, WHAT is that? Is it a man? He scares me, Mama!"

He and Christian were both in her lap in seconds, holding tightly to her neck. Baby Ralf began to cry because he was at the bottom of the pile. Katja looked up to see about a half-dozen plains Indians with their faces painted and feathers sticking from their hair. They were peering in the windows of the train. They whooped and hollered as they ran from window to window, gleefully scaring the passengers.

"Jakob, Christian, please get back into your seat. You are making Ralf cry. I do believe they are called Indians and they will not hurt you; you are safe here in the train." Katja hoped she was right about being safe on the train. Regardless, she tried to stifle a small smile. For sure, every day held more unexpected experiences, here, in this new country.

As the train rolled on into Montana, Katja looked down at her sleeping children. *What will their lives be like here? As my three sons grow up, will they miss the love and council of their grandparents? Will they be happy and will they have greater opportunity to succeed, as Karl promised?* So many thoughts and fears flooded her mind and heart that it was almost too much to deal with. She was convinced she must have faith and courage to be the kind of wife Karl needed, and to be a good mother to her children. She knew one thing: after her troubles in the train stations, she must work harder to learn English.

It was after two in the morning when the train pulled out of Billings, Montana. Katja tried to close her eyes as the train rumbled south toward the Wyoming border. By early morning, they would be in Lovell. *Will Karl be there to meet us? What will he look like?* It had been a long time since she had seen his face, and a long time since she had felt his strong embrace. Soon she would not have to only dream of her husband, he would be holding her tightly in his arms.

CHAPTER 10

Beginnings, 1907–10

★ ★ ★ ★ ★

"Let there never be an end to your dreams, a road too rough to travel or a sunset that doesn't hold the promise of a new tomorrow. Take hold of that world; explore it, and live it, for you have earned it." ~Mary Jane Cook

Karl paced up and down the wooden walkway in front of the brick train station in Lovell, impatiently waiting for sight of the train from Billings, Montana. His mind was a rotating kaleidoscope of thoughts and doubts. *Will Katja be happy here in Wyoming? Will she like the little house I have worked so hard on to make livable for her and our sons? Did she have a good trip? Had the trip been hard with three small boys?* He couldn't imagine caring for three little ones alone. Would—could they begin again where they had left off with their married life? Or, had they both changed? Would their sons remember him?

He knew the train wasn't due for about another hour; yet he was there, pacing! To pass the time, Karl walked down by the river. The sweet scent of new grass drifted to Karl's nose as he walked across a pasture. At the river's edge, he eased down on a large rock. The river was running high and muddy from the Yellowstone mountains spring snow melt. Karl tipped his head back to look at the sky. High above, a redtail hawk flew effortlessly, playing with the wind currents, keeping an eye out for a possible lunch candidate.

No matter how hard he tried, Karl couldn't sit still for long; he soon rose and headed back to the station. Again he paced, looked at his watch, and paced some more. He was slowly driving himself into a frenzy when suddenly, in the distance, he heard the train whistle. Karl's head lifted quickly as he spotted the black steam train puffing along the track, slowing as it came to the edge of Lovell. His heart pounded in his chest and his breath came in rapid gasps. As the train pulled into the station, Karl moved down the platform, scanning the windows of each passenger car. He froze as his eyes met those of his beloved. *I would know those piercing ebony eyes anywhere. I would know that sweet face and generous smile, it is the same one I see in my dreams every night—mein Katja! She is HERE, Oh, dear Gott, thank you—thank you for bringing my family safely to my side.*

As soon as the train pulled into the Lovell station, Katja had spotted Karl running up and down the station platform, looking at each train window. He was thinner and he looked so anxious. *Oh, mein Gott, my husband, my husband, there he is, waiting for us.* Silently, she offered her own prayer of thanksgiving to God for delivering them safely on their long journey from Surtschin. Her new life was about to begin and she believed she was ready for whatever it held.

Katja smoothed her shiny black hair, pressing stray wisps back into her tight bun. She tidied her clothes and yet again, tucked her sons' shirts into their trousers and adjusted their suspenders. "Hurry now, it is time to get off the train; we are in Lovell and Papa is out there waiting for us. Look there; out the window do you see your papa waving to us?"

Their hands and noses pressed to the window, Jakob and Christian saw Karl. They immediately began to shout, and pound on the glass.

Karl ran to the nearest passenger exit and before he could think twice, Jakob and Christian jumped all over him, laughing and shouting. He hugged and kissed them, held them at arm's length so he could look at them. "I can't believe how big you both are. You must have grown a foot each, in the past year." To himself, he thought, *Ja, they are getting big enough now to help on the farm.*

Karl's eyes devoured the sight of his wife, his Katja. She was right there, standing in front of him, holding Ralf, his newborn son. He reached out for the baby and her, not believing he was actually touching her at last. A few of the locals watched and smiled as the Kessel family rejoiced in their reunion.

After loading their trunks onto the wagon, the family stopped for lunch at Daisy's Café. Karl and Katja were both tingling with restrained emotions and barely touched their lunch. Jakob climbed down from his chair and moved to his father's side, 'Papa, Papa, does this eating place have any lemon pie, do they, huh?'

Katja told her husband about the lemon meringue pie they had on the train. Amused, Karl checked with the cook and reported, "Sorry, my boys, the cook only has apple pie, today. Anyway, it is time we got into the wagon; we have a long way to go to our house. Come along now, my big boys!" He felt blessed to have three sons and a good wife; they would all be of great help in farming the land.

They rumbled eastward out of Lovell toward Kane at the foot of the Big Horn Mountains. On the way, Karl and Katja chatted about the family back in Surtschin, the long journey, and their sons. The two older boys jabbered on about their adventures aboard the ship and the train, until Karl shushed them. A typical German father, he believed children should be seen and not heard; and he was already tiring of their chatter.

All three children eventually fell asleep. Karl's mind was filled with images of Katja, the way she looked when she had first stepped off the train. She had stopped in her tracks and turned 360 degrees. She looked in every direction, her eyes wide in disbelief. Alarm filled her face for a brief moment as she muttered under her breath, *Is this where I am to spend the rest of my life?*

Karl knew the brown, barren landscape was not what she had in mind or had hoped for; it was no comparison to Surtschin. *She is disappointed to think these hills of brown dirt and scrubby-gray brush are now her home. And, she doesn't even know about the ever-present wind.*

Karl reassured her, "Katja, I know this country is not what we are used to, but it is here we have land of our own to farm. Here our sons will have opportunity for success of their own. We don't look back, Katja. The past is done. The future is ours to make of it what we will!"

Karl knew he was talking too fast and loud, but he went on, "We can make the land beautiful by planting trees and some flowers close to our home. Katja, someday I promise to build you a grand house, to be proud of. Please have the patience for me to do this."

Katja turned to Karl and, choosing her words carefully, said, "*Ja*, Karl, this—this land, it is not what I had first imagined. But I had a premonition as I looked out of the train window that this is what it might be like." She noticed Karl's face grow tight and she quickly added, "I will try hard to feel at home in this place; I will work with you to make it better. But I will need time to get used to all of—this."

As her mouth formed the words, her obsidian-colored eyes continued to sweep the landscape in disbelief. In an effort to mask her feelings, Katja snuggled close to Karl, linking her left arm through his as she rested her head on his broad shoulder.

As the massive, snowcapped Big Horn Mountains to the east came closer, Katja noticed more trees and everything looked greener. The trees were not fully leafed out as it was still early spring, but they had promise. Katja vowed silently to discover the beauty in whatever form this land might offer.

"We are getting close to Kane now; we'll be at our house pretty soon. Do you think this looks better out here?" Karl asked.

Katja managed a smile and nodded in agreement.

The black Percherons trotted a little quicker now as they neared the farm, and their hay stalls. Jakob and Christian woke and rubbed sleep from their eyes. They looked around in amazement. "Are we almost there, Papa, huh?"

The boys loved the horses, calling them "giant" horses.

"Papa," Jakob said with glee, "It is more fun to ride in the long wagon pulled by Ebony and Pitch than it was to ride in Grosvater's little pony cart. These giant horses make the ground rumble when they trot, and the wagon goes fast! They are both strong aren't they, Papa? Aren't they?"

"*Ja*, Jakob, they are strong horses and work hard in the fields, pulling the plow, too. Someday, you will be big enough to work with them, would you like to do that, heh?"

Jakob's eyes were large with wonder as he imagined driving the horses in his father's fields. The boys giggled as Ebony lifted his tail and dropped steaming piles of dung on the road.

Christian was the first to comment, "Look, Papa, Ebony is going poop on the road. It is so much bigger than Grossvater's pony!" The boys laughed with glee as Karl smiled.

"*Ja*, Christian, here in America they call those 'road apples.' That is funny, too, isn't it? Ebony's dung is about as big as an apple. Just make sure you boys don't eat any road apples!" The boys laughed into their hands.

Karl drove the team and wagon into the yard of their new home near Kane. When Katja saw the modest log-and-adobe house, disappointment again radiated as her eyes darted to the right and to the left.

Karl couldn't help but notice this and tried to encourage her. "Katja, I know the house is less than what you are used to living in. I know it is not a fine house as your father's, or even the house where we lived in Surtschin.

It is my hope that we will have to live here for only a short time. You must understand this is a beginning for us and we are fortunate to have this opportunity. My success doesn't happen overnight."

Katja could see that Karl had tried to make the farm house livable. His letters had proudly told of all the improvements he had made to the house and farm. At least it was not a dugout house like some she noticed along the road. She did not want to live in a hole in the ground like an animal. She was pleased with the sizeable garden Karl planted, and with the chickens, geese, goats, and cows. Maybe it would not be so bad, once she got used to it. *I can make some cheerful curtains for the four windows and colorful hooked-rag rugs for the floor.*

Jakob and Chris were impressed with the outhouse, and especially the small hole which fit their little behinds.

"Papa, Papa, is this where Chris and I are going to sleep—in here in these beds stacked on each other?"

Karl replied, "*Ja*, Jakob that is where my big boys will sleep. But now it is time to milk the cows while Mama fixes us some supper. Come with me, boys, and I will teach you how to milk the cows, for soon you will be big enough to do this chore by yourself."

Jakob and Chris eagerly ran out of the door after Karl.

After she finished nursing Ralf, Katja laid him in the wooden cradle Karl bought in Billings. She covered the baby with a calico quilt and turned to face what was now her kitchen. In Surtschin, her kitchen had whitewashed walls and blue Delft tiles around the oven. This kitchen consisted of rough log partitions, adobe bricks, and crude storage. She was pleased she and Karl had a bedroom of their own, with the boy's bedroom next to theirs. But there were no doors to shut, only blankets to pull down for privacy. *That might be the first improvement I ask for*, Katja thought to herself.

The stove and a couple of storage crates occupied one corner of the room, with the table and chairs positioned in the middle. The lean-to parlor was to the left and held a couch and two straight-back chairs. Katja stood staring in wonder at the black beast as it "stared" back at her. "Dear Lord," she prayed, "you are going to have to help me make a decent meal in this kitchen. I am going to NEED all of your help and perhaps a few miracles, too!"

After all three sons were tucked in bed that evening, Karl and Katja turned down the kerosene lantern, went into their bedroom, and dropped the curtain. Katja began undressing for bed, taking the pins from her jet-black hair and letting it fall past her soft, white shoulders. The sight was almost more than Karl could bear as he lay in bed watching her—it had been so long, so long. She crawled into the soft featherbed Karl purchased in Billings, and Karl pulled her into his arms.

Afterward, as Karl slept, Katja lay on her back, eyes wide as she listened to the unfamiliar sounds of the night. Through the open bedroom window she could hear the steady chirp of black crickets, the soft hoot of a great horned owl, and the gentle rustle of silky new cottonwood leaves in the night breeze. Trying to convince herself she murmured under her breath, *"This is where I belong; it is where I am, and it is where I will stay beside my husband in this brown, primitive place called Wyoming."* Katja smiled to herself, closed her eyes, and fell into an exhausted sleep.

The next morning after breakfast, Katja walked out to look at the garden Karl had planted for her. In the first of many summers thereafter, she planted large gardens, usually consisting of eighteen rows of potatoes, green beans, cabbage, green peas, sweet corn, tomatoes, turnips, squash, pumpkins, and lettuce. Karl did not allow her the frivolous purchase of flower seeds, but Katja gratefully accepted flower starts and seeds she was given by friendly neighbor women. She became apt at gathering seeds from plants that appealed to her, and she stored them over the winter in the dry root cellar. The deep river sand that Karl had hauled up for the cellar floor was where they would bury root crops like potatoes, carrots, and beets over the winter months, to prolong their freshness.

The first few weeks were hectic for the family as they learned to live together after more than a year apart. Karl was easily irritated by the normal rambunctious activities of the boys and Katja was on edge trying to keep them quiet. She looked forward to her time in the evenings after the children were asleep in their beds. She was determined to make the cabin pretty. In her spare time, she cut the blue cotton fabric Karl had purchased in Billings, and made cheerful kitchen and bedroom curtains.

As Katja sat by lantern light, pushing and pulling the needle through the cotton, she thought to herself, *Ja, I make my curtains like Mama's to remind me of her and also of the home I knew in Surtschin. Someday I would like to have beautiful Austrian lace curtains to hang at my windows, but not in this old house. The delicate lace would look just as well on the horse!* Katja smiled at that mental image of lace on a horse.

One morning after Karl had gone to the fields, Katja washed, starched, and ironed the new curtains, and hung them with pride at the four windows in her little home. *Oh, ja, they are so pretty and even hide some ugliness of this house. I am pleased.*

The family was eating the noon meal at the kitchen table when Karl's blue eyes opened wide. "Katja, what beautiful curtains. Did you make them from the material I ordered? They look good; it helps the room be more comfortable!" She smiled and nodded.

> July 1, 1907
> Dear Papa and Mama,
> Our crossing on the ship was exciting for the boys and they behaved like good children. We had no sickness from the rolling ocean. Ralf slept and ate all the way to America. Jakob and Christian loved the train ride from New York to Wyoming. They especially liked the new fruit they tasted, called bananas, and also to taste fresh lemon pie. We saw many things from the window of the train including some wild Indians, which made the boys at first frightened. They liked much the wild animals called antelope which they saw running beside the train.
> I admit I was disheartened to see the land of western America. It is not nearly as beautiful as our Surtschin. In the eastern part it is quite green with rolling hills and prosperous farms, much as I am used to. But as we traveled farther west, the land became dryer with few trees. In Wyoming, there are large mountains such as we are used to, but the land below is dry and barren. Everywhere I look is brown dirt and short bushes called salt sage and sage brush.
> Karl is pleased with his farm which is near the village called Kane. His farm is good bottomland near the Shoshone River and he is now being successful. We have a yard full of chickens, geese, goats, and two cows. We have a large garden started. The house is poorly and not to my liking but will have to do until we are able to build a better one.
> We have made many friends here, and there are Lutheran people with whom we worship when we can. We must travel forty

miles by wagon to attend church; it is most inconvenient but we try. I miss you all more than I can tell you. Jacob asks often when we are going to see you again. How is it that I explain to my son he may never see you again? This is too hard for me. Please know I love you all and wish you good health. Write to me many letters when you can.

Your loving daughter, Katja

Katja soon learned how to cook efficiently in her primitive kitchen, how to bring in wood and water, how to wash on the scrub board, and how to put a smile on her face so her husband would think she was happy. She taught Jakob and Chris how to gather the eggs, bring in wood, and help in the garden.

Katja treasured the fragrant lilac bushes, white daisies, and yellow bush roses that Mrs. Goodman gave her. She was also thankful for the small apple orchard near the house. When the apples were ready for picking, Katja called, "Jakob and Chris, "*Kommen sie*, sit and wrap each apple in the newspaper and stack them in the boxes. Take them to the root cellar when you are finished and we shall have apples when the snow is on the ground."

Katja made jars of savory applesauce and dried apples from the "wind-fall" apples. The remaining small and wormy apples left on the ground provided tasty treats for the animals, and the boys had great fun throwing rotten apples at each other.

SEPTEMBER 1907

The painted-wagon bus waited at the end of the lane for seven-year-old Jakob to climb aboard for the five-mile ride to the Kane schoolhouse. "Mama, I'm a little scared and a little excited to go to the school. I don't know many other kids. What if they don't like me and make fun of my English?" But that first day after school, Jakob came home, bubbling over with excitement. "Mama, the painted-wagon bus was lots of fun. It is like riding in a little house, except it moves. Did you know that inside the wagon bus there are curtains at the windows and—and a small wood stove to keep us warm when it gets cold."

Jacob loved riding in the wagon bus and he was happy learning in the Kane schoolhouse.

The number of school-age children in the area was growing. Kane needed two log schoolhouses. One was for the grades one through four and the other for grades five through eight. During the cold months, two teachers alternated arriving early in the morning to light the fires in the coal stoves, so the rooms were warm by the time the children arrived. It was difficult keeping the heat even inside the log cabins. Pupils sitting near the stove were always too hot and the ones farther away were too cold. The teachers improvised and asked the students to rotate to another chair about every fifteen minutes, calling it a "pupil rotisserie."

On occasion a prospector or trapper spent the night in the unlocked schoolroom. On those occasions the coal stove was fired up and the room already warm when the teacher arrived in the morning.

Jakob had a hard time in school at first because he spoke only broken English. He was shy with the other children, but made friends quickly in spite of the language barrier. One day in mid-September, he came home from school sporting a sizeable bump on his head. Alarmed, Katja asked, "Jakob, whatever happened to your head? You did not fight in the school did you?"

"*Nein*, Mama," Jakob replied smiling. "Me and Freddy was standing by the coal shed, watching the older boys play a game with a ball and a hard stick, called—a bat. The game is called baseball, I think. One of the big boys was trying to hit the ball and he couldn't hit it good, so he got mad and threw the bat on the roof of the coal shed."

Jakob paused to catch his breath and continued, "And me and Freddy heard someone yell, 'Watch OUT!' Well, Mama, we found out we need to learnt more English because we didn't know what 'watch out' meant, and theys trying to tell us the bat was rolling off the shed roof. It come down and hit me on the head. But I didn't cry, Mama, I didn't."

Katja smiled in spite of herself. *That boy has a way with a story—that he does.* She put her arm around her oldest son's shoulder, "My goodness, Jakob, I am glad you did not get hurt worse. It would be a good thing for your Mama to learnt better English, too. Will you teach me words you learnt in school each day? We can make a game of it—you be *my* teacher!"

A big grin spread across the boy's face, "*Ja, ja,* Mama, I will teach to you my English words from the school. I think we should begin tonight after supper, do you want to do that?"

Mother and son began another bonding experience that night after supper dishes were washed and put away, and the baby was settled in his crib. Katja and Jakob sat at the oilcloth-covered kitchen table. Jakob spread his lessons out on the table and handed his mother a pencil and paper.

"I will make the letter, you watch how I do it and you make it on your paper. The first letter of the English alphabet is called A, then next is B, then C." Jakob carefully and slowly drew the first three letters. "I think also I will write a word that begins with the letter, so you can also learn some words. See, Mama, the word 'ant' begins with the A. 'Bat' begins with the second letter B, and C is the first letter for the word 'cow.' Now, can you think of a word that starts with an A, B, and C?"

Katja put her hand to her forehead in thought, "Uhhh, Annie, and *bun*, uhh, *corn*. Is that good, Jakob? I think your Mama is learning this English good!" They both laughed with delight at their shared progress.

Katja went to bed that night and the next and the next with a big smile on her face and building confidence. "*Ja*, it is good that Jakob teaches me his words and he is getting extra practice on his English at the same time."

She was an apt pupil and practiced her letters and new words every day whenever she had a break in her chores. Jakob enjoyed teaching his mother how to read and write English; he was proud of her and her desire to learn. Jakob was disappointed that his father didn't want to participate in the lessons, but Karl managed to come to the table often enough, supposedly to look at the progression. Jakob didn't realize that his father and his friend Arnold had excelled in their English lessons aboard the ship. Not knowing this, Jakob was amazed at how well his father spoke and read English.

Karl had always been thankful they lived close to the Shoshone River, because it was a convenient water source. The small town of Kane had a cistern for public water storage, but that took precious time away from the fields and work to make a trip into Kane for water. Katja enjoyed teasing Karl about the river, which to her was more like a small stream. "Karl, would you go down to the stream to get more water, please?" She refused to call this unimpressive stream, a river.

In Yugoslavia, the Danube was a river; in Germany the Rhine, the Mosel, and the Elbe were rivers. She could throw a rock across this small river. Regardless, Katja did appreciate having a water source so near to them. She understood water was not something easily found in this country of dirt and wind.

Around the end of September, Katja was working in the garden on a

Saturday morning. She stood up and wiped her hands on her apron as she addressed her oldest son, "Jakob, would you please check for mail when you are in Kane with Papa this afternoon?"

Pleased with the grownup assignment of responsibility, Jakob replied, "Okay, Mama, I will be sure to do that. I can to do that for you!" Flashing his mother a huge grin, he turned and ran out the screen door, letting it slam behind him. He ran as fast as his young legs could carry him, looking over his shoulder as the pebbles and dust flew behind him. He reached the waiting wagon, and climbed up onto the seat beside his father.

"Papa, Mama asked me to go to the post office and check for letters when we are in Kane. I am a big boy now and can do those kinds of errands for Mama." Karl noticed his son's self-satisfied smile.

In Kane, Karl went to the hardware store while Jakob ran over to the post office. He opened the wooden screen door and walked confidently inside. Remembering how his father had addressed the post mistress, Jakob mimicked, "Good day to you, Miz Smith, do you have any mail for the Kessel house?"

Jakob's hand closed tightly over the envelope the post mistress handed to him. "Thank you, Miz Smith, be seeing you," and he was out the door in a flash. He climbed up onto the seat of the wagon and, sitting ramrod straight and proud, said, "Papa, look here, we have a letter from Surtschin!"

Karl took the letters in his hand and looked at the return address. He wasn't excited about letters from Surtschin; they always put Katja in a melancholy mood, which annoyed him.

When the wagon pulled to a stop in the farmyard, Jakob jumped down off the seat with the letter clutched tightly in his little hand. He ran to the house, yelling, "Mama, Mama, you have a letter from Oma and Opa, a letter from Surtschin!"

Katja took the letter but didn't open it at first. She held it to her heart as her throat constricted and her breath came in quick gasps. She took the letter out under the cottonwood tree and sank down on the green field grass. *I am so homesick for Mama and Papa. I miss them all so much, it is hard to bear. Just to hold a piece of paper that they have touched means so much to me.*

Katja's work-worn hands were shaking as she gently tore open the letter. A choked sob escaped her chapped lips as she unfolded the letter written only weeks ago by her mother. She sat for a moment, gazing at her mother's handwriting and savored the warm feeling it invoked deep inside her.

> September 14, 1908
> Our Dear Katja:
> We were so happy to receive a letter from you. We have been saying prayers daily for your safety and for your safe arrival at your new home. We are sorry to hear that Wyoming is not as beautiful as Yugoslavia and Germany. We have heard there are few places on earth as beautiful as our home.
> We miss our grandsons so much. Some day, we would much like to have a photo of them. I am sure they have grown tall and healthy. We are happy with the grandchildren Katharina and Christian have given us. Your father and I are glad to hear that Karl is making a great success of his farming. He should be a happy man with a farm and his wife and children at his side. We wish continued success for you all.
> As we are unsure if you know there is war on the horizon in Germany. There is much unrest and anger not only in Germany, but Austria/Hungary, France, Russia, and many other countries. We fear for a large war in Europe. We have begun to store food and supplies in hidden places to prepare for famine and rationing. Keep safe, pray for strength, and write more letters when you are able.
> Our love, Mama and Papa

When she finished reading the letter, Katja held it to her open lips and breathed in the scent of her mother that lingered on the paper. She was fearful for them and this war talk. Katja knew only too well how easily her people and the surrounding countries went to war; it was almost as if it was the thing that made their blood run through their veins. It seemed war almost a custom.

That fall and all the fall seasons thereafter, the root cellar was filled with more than 250 quarts of canned meats, vegetables, and fruits in preparation for the winter months. When it was canning time, the food had to be picked and canned all in one day and often the wood stove burned far into the hot summer night, processing food in the canning kettles. Katja fermented heads of chopped cabbage in large porcelain crocks. The end result was the favorite

German staple, *sauerkraut*. The crocks were essential when processing pickles and/or pickled meats.

One evening during canning season, the kitchen was suffocating with heat from the stove as it burned steadily all day, covered with dark-blue speckled canning pots. That evening the family sat around the kitchen table trying to eat their supper in the stifling heat from the stove.

"Karl, would it be possible when the field work is finished to build a separate small summer kitchen away from the house like so many peoples have? It is for safety, to not burn the main house down and for comfort from the continuous heat and cooking."

Karl looked up from his meal and nodded his head in agreement. "That is proably a good idea, Katja, I will try to erect some sort of summer kitchen for you during the winter months!"

One of Karl's favorite foods was pickled beef tongue, which Katja made whenever she had the opportunity. She took the tongue, carefully scrubbed it, and slow-boiled it with onion, celery, cloves, cinnamon, garlic, and salt, until it was tender to the fork. In the meantime, she prepared the brine, which consisted of, one cup sugar, one cup vinegar, one tablespoon mustard seed, one tablespoon celery seed, and a stick of cinnamon. She put the boiled tongue in a crock and filled it to the top with brine. After covering the crock, Karl carried it down to the cool darkness of the root cellar where it set and worked for two to four days. When it was ready, Katja removed the cold tongue and sliced it into bite-sized pieces. Any part that wasn't eaten that night was put back into the crock for a special treat on another day. Katja also knew how to pickle animal heart. The whole family enjoyed this delicacy as well. However, her true specialty was sausage making—liverwurst, bratwurst, and bloodwurst.

Katja wrote frequent letters to her parents in Surtschin. Each time she took up her pen, she became melancholy missing the close relationship she had with her mother and sister. Not having her father in her life left an even bigger hole in her heart. She had always felt so loved, protected, and safe in her father's house. Now, her life didn't feel as secure as it had when she was a child; nothing was definite in this new life; it was a day-to-day, week-to-week, hand-to-mouth existence. They had to constantly plan, go without, and scrape their livelihood from the obstinate earth and weather.

FALL 1908

After the harvest, Karl dug a well with the help of his neighbors and erected a windmill to pump the water, and a cistern to store it in. This was a luxury, to have water at a pump in the yard. Now they didn't have to carry water from the river for themselves and the livestock. Jakob and Chris loved to pump the iron handle of the pump; their reward was cold, clear water that gushed from the spout. It was Jacob's chore to carry buckets of water to the house whenever his mother needed it. Karl promised soon he would run a pipe from the well to the kitchen sink, so they would have water in the house and wouldn't have to carry it in.

Jakob liked to sit on the front step in the evening, watching the wind spin the big fan. *At least*, he thought, *there is a good use for all the wild wind that blows. I like to listen to the clickity clack of the blades as they turn in the wind; even at night when I am sleeping. And, I do love to hold my hands under the pump spout and let the clear, icy water wash the dirt of the fields away.*

One evening as they were all sitting at the supper table, Jakob asked to speak. "I saw something really funny today when Ebony and Pitch were playing in the pasture. Ebony kept trying to ride piggyback on Pitch. He was so big that Pitch ran away, but he kept jumping on her back. It was really funny to see, Papa."

Katja flushed and lowered her head in an effort to hide her smile. Karl continued eating as through he hadn't heard what his son said; actually he was trying to think of what to say in response. Karl finally swallowed his food and casually commented, "*Ja*, Jakob, you should not bother the horses while they are playing. After this when you see them play, you go on about your business, do you hear me? All animals like to play sometimes and they don't want us to bother them."

Jakob sat straight in his chair as he defended his actions, "But, Papa, I didn't bother them. I let them play; I was just watching."

Katja welcomed the constant housework, and the farm work she was expected to help with; it helped to keep busy. She soon discovered, because of their isolation, there wasn't often opportunity to purchase things they needed. However, there was the Sears Roebuck catalog. It was advertised as the cheapest supply house and it offered R.F.D., the rural free delivery system.

Ordering was indeed less expensive than a long trip to Billings, but of course it took longer to receive the merchandise. Occasionally Karl allowed Katja to order new clothing for the children and a few things for herself and the house. But she always had to get approval from him first.

Karl chastised, "We must be frugal, Katja; you must make do for a while with what we have. How many shirts do the boys need? How many dresses do you need? You only wear one at a time; do you not?" Still, she enjoyed pouring over the pages of the catalogs, mentally adding things to her wish list, and day-dreaming about things she would like to have someday.

That next summer, Karl took eight-year-old Jakob to the fields and began to teach him how to farm. Early each morning and before dusk in the evenings, Jakob and Chris had chores. They were expected to let the chickens out of their pen and put them back at night. Katja showed the boys how to scare the hens off their nests in order to gather the warm fresh eggs underneath them. She also instructed them how much feed and water should be given to the chickens, geese, and goats each day. Karl and Katja spoke of trading for a pig or two that would eat the garbage and later, when butchered, supply the family with bacon, lard, and the favored pig's knuckles.

Mondays were always wash days. The bigger boys gathered enough wood to build fires for two heavy washtubs. Katja shaved lye soap into one of the huge tubs and separated the dirty clothes into like piles. After the water came to a boil, she added the clothes, one load after another. She allowed the clothes to slow-boil for about a half hour, occasionally stirring them with a wooden paddle. After the washing process, she lifted the clothes out of the boiling tub with a wooden pitchfork and put them into the cool rinse tub. At this stage, Katja bent over the scrub board, working loose any soil that hadn't come off in the boiling tub. The water in the rinse tub was cold to begin with, but became warmer with each hot load of boiled clothes. Katja preferred to have two cold tubs in order to remove all of the soap. The final phase of washing was to lift the clothes from the rinse tub, wring each piece out by hand, and hang it to dry. The backbreaking chore took most of the day.

The entire process of washing clothes was hard enough in the summer months, but in the freezing winter, washing and especially the drying of the clothes was nearly impossible. If the weather was above freezing, Katja carried the heavy baskets of wet clothes out to the clothes line, her wet fingers freezing as she hung the dripping clothes on the wire line. Even though it was so cold, she hung the clothes out overnight, hoping they would dry. The next day Katja took the frozen clothes off the line, handing them to her older sons who delighted in banging them against the wooden fence pole in hopes of knocking off some of the ice. They carried the frozen clothes into the house and stacked them in a far corner like cord wood, waiting for them to thaw and collapse onto the wooden floor, somewhat dryer than they had been a day ago.

If the thermometer dipped below twenty degrees, only a few clothes were washed at one time; they were hung throughout the house and allowed to drip dry onto the wood floors. Katja discovered the additional humidity in the house was a good thing.

During the winter months especially, they only changed clothes once a week. By Friday, the odor of unwashed clothes and bodies was often overwhelming, but they all smelled alike and so nobody seemed to care. On Saturday nights, the family took baths one after the other in the middle of the kitchen in a large tin tub, usually using the same water. Katja bathed first with her youngest child, then Chris and Jakob. Karl was last and Katja always added more hot water before he got in the tub. The water usually wasn't that clean at the end, but it was hot!

Katja had a hard time adjusting to the harsh climate—hot and dry in the summers and bitter cold and dry in winter. Driving snowstorms often left them snowbound for days or weeks. Nothing here was like the home she left in Surtschin. She and her sons had learned quickly about the huge black mosquitoes in summer and the little bugs they didn't see that bit them—the "no-see-ems." She learned from other housewives how to apply a balm of herbs to keep the insects away from her boys' tender skin. Of course, when the insect retardant didn't work, baking soda or even a pack of wet mud stopped the incessant itching.

When needed, they traveled to Lovell for supplies not available in Kane. Jakob and Chris knew if they were good, the store owner might give them a peppermint or licorice candy. On one trip, as Karl was paying for the groceries, he noticed his two oldest sons standing very still and staring at the owner. Mr. Olsen looked down and smiled at the two little boys with the wide expectant expressions. "Well, what can I do for you boys, today?"

Jakob replied without a moment's hesitation, "We've been real good today, sir, and we are ready for our peppermint." Karl was mortified as Mr. Olsen laughed and reached into the jar, handing each boy a peppermint. Jakob grabbed his candy and said, "Thanks, Mr. Olsen, thanks a lot. Be seeing you next time!"

Katja never tired of her view of the majestic grandeur of the Big Horn Mountains. In summer, she loved the feel of a cool breeze as it blew down from the mountains. They seemed to beckon to her, to promise a cool, relaxing day—perhaps a picnic. Unable to resist, one day she approached her husband as he was preparing to go to the fields. "Karl, I have been thinking it would be wonderful to take the family on a wagon ride up on the mountain some day soon. We might even take a nice picnic and make a day of it. What do you think of this idea?"

Karl looked at his wife in disbelief. His reply was short and abrupt, "Katja, do you think I should stop my work and ride off to picnic in the mountains? Who is going to do my work? The sight of them will have to satisfy you for now. I have two fields to irrigate and beets to thin. There is certainly no time for foolishness like a wagon ride and a picnic!"

Katja was taken aback by Karl's abrupt and brash attitude. She had only asked for a needed break in their daily drudgery and routine. It would have been good for all of them to take time off the never-ending work. For months now, she had been haunted by the growing notion that Karl had changed. He used to be pleased to take her to the woods for a hike or a picnic—he used to like to have fun once in a while. Now, Karl didn't have time for a picnic, a box supper, or a community dance in Kane—even a neighborly visit. To him there was nothing but work and more work. She was beginning to see another side of her husband, and it was disturbing.

CHAPTER 11

Building a Life In America, 1911—14

★ ★ ★ ★ ★

One Sunday after harvest season, Katja noticed two wagons rolling up the dusty lane toward the house. She smoothed her black hair and wiped her hands on her apron as she quickly straightened the small house for company. Tom Goelbe and his wife Emma, along with the Schneider family, climbed down from their wagons with smiling faces and arms filled with baked and canned goods.

Karl had been working out in the barn and, when the two wagons rolled into his farmyard, he put down what he was doing and walked up to the house. He was more than a little irritated by the uninvited interruption of his work, but he managed to put a smile on his sweating face as he twisted the corner of his mustache. The neighboring families had brought a picnic with them, hoping for a communal Sunday visit under the cottonwoods. Jakob and Chris ran from the house and immediately the yard was filled laughter and squealing children playing tag.

Karl put on his "company" face and helped the men move the kitchen table out in the yard, in the shade of the old cottonwood tree. They found various stumps and a few chairs to sit on. The three women hurried into the kitchen to finish preparing the baskets of food they had brought to the Kessels. When the food was ready, they all said grace and sat together as they enjoyed their picnic meal under the blue summer sky and cool shade of the spreading cottonwood tree. It was good to spend time with their neighbors and Katja was grateful for the female company.

All too soon it was time for the visitors to begin their journey back to their homes. Katja stood in the doorway, watching wistfully as the neighbors rode back up the lane. *What a lovely afternoon this was, a chance to sit and visit, to be happy and relaxed. I'm grateful to them for bringing a little joy into our world, but I fear they are leaving and taking that joy with them.* Katja shivered with that thought and at the coldness that seemed to seep into the cabin as Karl stomped back toward the house.

As soon as the visiting neighbors and their wagons rolled up the lane out of earshot, Karl shouted, "That is enough, everybody get back to work! Now we have to work twice as hard because we wasted half the day sitting under the trees. Jakob and Chris, clean up this yard, now. Katja, you have chickens and geese to tend to!"

Katja went about her chores, thinking of how relaxed and happy she had been with the unexpected visit from their neighbors. Karl had spoiled their afternoon of joy with his domineering tirade; if felt like a bucket of cold water had been thrown on their joy. A foreboding chill ran down Katja's back as she thought of how her husband continued to change before her eyes. All he seemed to think of was the land, work, and money except when they were in bed. Of course, their tender moments together didn't last long anymore, either. Once he was satisfied with her, he rolled over and promptly fell asleep. This was not the way she had thought their life would be and she shuddered with disappointment. She had never felt so alone.

In January 1911, a daughter, Louise, was born to Karl and Katja. She was a beautiful, healthy baby, and again blonde and blue-eyed like her father. Remembering the relationship she had enjoyed with her own mother, Katja was pleased that at last she had a daughter.

When they weren't busy in their fields and when weather permitted, Karl and Katja joined their Lutheran neighbors in making the thirty-mile trip across sagebrush-covered hills and gullies to the white clapboard Zion Lutheran Church in Germania. They usually spent the night, returning to Kane as soon as the sun rose over the Big Horn Mountains the next morning.

Germania was a German Lutheran community settled by Missouri Synod Lutherans from Seward, Nebraska, around 1898—six years before Karl and family arrived in Lovell. In the spring of 1911, when Pastor Germeroth traveled across the sage-peppered hills to Kane/Lovell to conduct Lutheran services in the schoolhouse, the Kessels asked him to baptize their infant daughter.

As time past, Karl required Jakob to do more chores than other farmers expected from their young sons. This situation did not go unnoticed by Katja. Jakob was only ten years old when Karl first showed him how to harness up the massive Percheron horses. The boy was so small that he had to stand on the corral fence to throw the harnesses over the horses' heads. Soon Jakob was sent out into the fields and required to drive the massive draft horses while they pulled harrows and wagons. It was a good thing they were so obedient and docile, otherwise the small boy could not have handled them.

Katja saw how often Karl raised his voice and belittled his sons. She tried to speak to Karl about this, but he would not listen to her. "Katja, you do not tell me how to be the father. Do your job as the mother and care for the children, the house, the chores, and when I need you in the field. I know how to farm my land and you do not stick your nose into what I do. I will hear not more on this!"

This was just one more situation where Karl pushed her away and humiliated her. In Karl's world, Katja had defined purposes. She most certainly was not a partner in this marriage as she had considered. Of course she accepted the husband as the head of the household. But when they courted and were first married, it had been so different.

Frequently, when Katja was expected to help in the fields, she had no alternative but to take her baby out with her. She would fashion a gauze tent over the cradle/box, and leave the baby and toddler, Ralf, at the end of the row as she worked the crops. She often left Chris to watch the younger ones while Jakob helped her work. Katja checked on them each time she came to the end of the row to make sure they were safe. She worried for her children as she worked, and often put their safe-being into the hands of her Lord. She did what she had to do in the best way she knew. Karl was not concerned about the babies because that was "woman's work." The only thing he was concerned about was when Katja should help with the field work. He was pleased with how hard she worked, but he never bothered to compliment her. He rarely noticed how difficult field work was for Katja, nor that she did what he asked without complaining.

SPRING 1911

Early one morning, Katja led her children to the north field of young sugar beet plants; Karl was planting corn in the field next to them. As she was used to doing, Katja left her sleeping baby nestled in a wooden orange box at the end of the row with Ralf and Chris in charge. Thinning beets was backbreaking work—Katja was bent over with a short-handled hoe, chopping out a section of beet shoots every twelve inches. Jakob crawled behind, thinning the clump of remaining beets to one plant. They worked steadily for several hours.

By mid-morning they were startled to hear screams and yelling at the end of the row. Baby Louise joined in the vocals with her frightened wailing. Jakob jumped to his feet and saw dirt clods flying through the air and exploding in clouds of dust as they hit an intended target. Chris' and Ralf's faces were covered with angry tears as muddy streams of snot ran from their noses, and yet they continued to throw the clods of dirt at each other. Without being told, Jakob dropped his hoe and began to run to the end of the field toward his brothers and baby sister.

As Katja jerked to a standing position, twisted her body, and started for the end of the row, she took only three steps before the breathtaking pain ripped through her belly. She froze, doubled over, and dropped to hands and knees as she cried out, "Ahhhh, *mein Gott, ahhhh, nein*." Beads of perspiration appeared on her forehead. She began to crawl, trying in vain to get away from the pain and reach her screaming children.

As he was running, Jakob turned and saw his mother down on all fours and the look in her eyes shot fear through his gut. For an instant he didn't know whether to hurry back to her or keep running to the dirt clod war at the end of the row.

She saw Jakob hesitate and look back at her, "*Nein*, Jakob, go and see what is the matter with your brothers—go, hurry, son. I will be okay, I just hurt my foot!" She struggled to crawl in spite of the pain ripping through her belly like a thousand knives. That was when she felt familiar, sticky warmth running down between her legs. Katja turned her head and saw a trail of blood seeping into the dirt. She stopped crawling and lifted her head, trying to see if her oldest son had reached the young warriors. Whatever it was, he seemed to have gotten them calmed down and now was running back up the row toward her as she doubled up on her side.

"Jakob, *nein*, stop and go find your father, quickly, son, run! I need your papa!"

The boy didn't know what was wrong, but he didn't stop to ask questions, especially when he saw the dark bloody dirt. He ran and ran until he got to the field where his father was working.

Karl had reached the end of the row with the team of field horses pulling the planter. As he turned the team to head back up the next row, he noticed something moving on the other end of the field—he squinted trying to see what it was. *It is Jakob, running, running fast, and he is yelling something. What, what has happened? Something is wrong.* Instinctively, Karl pushed the brake forward, wrapping the reins around the lever, and jumped from the planter. He began to run up the row toward his son.

"Papa, Papa—come quick, something has happened to Mama and she can't get up. She is crying and crying and, and there is blood on the dirt, I think. Hurry, Papa, this way." Jakob had turned before Karl could respond and was running back toward his mother.

Jakob reached his mother seconds before Karl did. He took one look at her curled up in a ball between the rows of beet saplings; beads of sweat and tears dotted her face. He was about to speak when he saw more red stains on her clothes and he knew for certain it was blood. Out of breath from running, and frightened beyond words, Jakob bent over as the contents of his belly spilled to the ground. Karl rushed past his oldest son to where his wife lay in the field.

"*Gute Gott* in heaven, Katja, what has happened to you? How did you get hurt to make so much blood?" As Karl bent down to his prostrate wife, the answer exploded in his mind. She was having a miscarriage and was losing his child, right here in this field of brown dirt and beet saplings.

Karl yelled to his oldest son, "Jakob, get up now, go and get the baby and your brothers, take them to the house." He bent to pick up his wife. Karl wasn't a big man, but he was strong and he was scared. He scooped her up in his arms and trudged through the beet field to the end of the row, and carried her up the short rise to the house. He could feel the sticky blood as it seeped through her skirt onto his work clothes.

As Karl neared the kitchen door, he called to his son, "Jakob, hurry now and saddle the bay—ride to Kane to fetch the midwife, Grandma Bittner. Hurry, son, hurry now. Your mother is in much troubles."

The lad did not hesitate as he ran out the door toward the barn. He was mounted and galloping up the lane in the blink of an eye, hell bent for Kane.

About an hour later, Jakob and Grandma Bittner rode into the yard at a full gallop, reining in their horses and skidding to a stop in front of the small house. Jakob grabbed the reins as Grandma Bittner got off her horse and made a beeline for the house. Realizing the house was probably not the place for the children, Jakob gathered his brothers and baby sister, took them outside to play, and waited under the shade of the cottonwood trees.

After several hours Grandma Bittner came out of the house carrying a basket. She walked slowly to where the Kessel children sat under the tree. She sat the lunch basket down and plopped down on the grass gathering her skirts around her ample bottom. Scooping up the wailing baby onto her lap, she reassured the children as she handed out lunch. "Your mama is going to be fine. She will have to stay in bed for a few days to get her strength back. You must be good children and not make her upset, do you understand me?"

Not wanting to miss out on any love and affection, Ralf crawled up onto her lap as well. She wrapped her strong arms around both children as she continued, "I will stay here with you until your mama is able to take care of you. It is getting near to supper time, what can I cook up for your hungry little tummies?"

Jakob stood, eyes wide with fear, looking at the midwife as she spoke to them. "Grandma Bittner, can I go in and see my mama? I will be really quiet and I won't stay long. I just want to give her a kiss."

Grandma Bittner nodded her head with approval. Jakob crept silently to the kitchen door and peered in. Not seeing anyone, he tiptoed to his parents' bedroom door, pushed it open and slowly walked across the floor. Katja lay in her bed with covers pulled up to her chin. Her black hair lay in soft waves across her thin shoulders. Jakob thought, *Mama looks like an angel, a white-faced angel!*

He stood by the bed for a few minutes, and when Katja didn't open her eyes, Jakob bent over and gently kissed her on the forehead with his soft lips. The laudanum Grandma Bittner gave Katja had taken full effect and she did not know her son stood by her bed. When his mother didn't respond, Jakob turned and walked reluctantly out of the room.

His father was sitting at the kitchen table with his head in his hands. Jakob walking quietly across the floor, "Papa, Papa," he touched his hand gently to his father's shoulder, "Papa, is Mama okay? Is she going to die?" He was sure that his father had been crying and that frightened him even more. He had never seen his father cry.

Karl raised his head, his eyes were red and bloodshot and his cheeks were wet, "*Nein*, son, she will be okay. She needs to rest now for she is fragile. Your mother has lost another baby and needs to rest in bed for a week; soon she will be well and strong again. You must be brave and help care for your brothers and sister. Grandma Bittner will stay here to cook; she will take care of the house and your mother until she is ready to leave her bed."

Karl almost never exhibited tenderness to his children, but he had been badly frightened that day. He reached out, putting his hand on Jakob's shoulder. "Thank you, Jakob, for being such a good son this day. You did a fine job getting help for your mama."

Grandma Bittner stayed with the Kessel family for a week, taking care of the children, washing their clothes, cooking their meals, and caring for Katja until her strength returned. One evening after the children were tucked into their beds, the midwife approached Karl. "Mr. Kessel, I must tell you that Katja does not respond as quickly as she should. She had not regained her strength from the last baby and hard work in the fields was too much for her. She has lost much blood with this miscarriage. You would be wise to hire someone to help you with the field work until she is completely recovered. I think you do not want to yet lose your wife, too; is that right?"

Karl didn't like any woman telling him what to do; however, in this case he accepted the direction of the intimidating midwife. He knew Grandma Bittner was wise and competent in what she did, and that her words rang with truth. Reluctantly, Karl accepted what she recommended. "Grandma Bittner," Karl humbly addressed her: "I am so appreciating of what you have done for my wife and our family in taking care of us while she heals. Here, I want you to have this twenty-dollar gold piece in payment for your work. And, thank you, thank you!"

The Christmas season was usually a time of happiness for the Kessel family, although happiness was temporary at best. Karl usually rode to the base of the Big Horn Mountains, cut an evergreen tree, and dragged it into their home several days before Christmas. The pungent aroma of the fresh evergreen branches enhanced the fragrance of cinnamon and molasses as Katja baked her German Christmas cookies and holiday strudel.

Gifts for the children were most often things Karl and Katja made. When there was money to spare, Karl bought simple gifts in Lovell or allowed Katja to order gifts from the catalogs, but only one gift per child. The children enjoyed making decorated chains of colored paper, and stringing juniper berries and popcorn. They decorated the tree with their chains adding a few carefully placed pieces of store-bought tinsel. Katja had a special punched-tin star that she had packed in the traveling truck when they left Surtschin. Every year, she made a great ceremony of placing it at the top of their tree. When they could, they attended Lutheran church services; but, more often than not, they conducted their own family service with prayer and song.

When Christmas Eve came, they took out the unique German-made copper candle holders Katja parents sent to them as a gift from Yugoslavia. The candle holders consisted of a small round holder, which held the candle, while a clothespin-like pincher was attached to the branch of the tree. After they attached the candle holders to the far end of a sturdy branch, they put white spiral beeswax candles in them. The candles were not lit until Christmas Eve and only for an hour or so. The tree was never left unattended as they all knew how fast a tree could burn.

The family gathered around the tree, breathing in the fragrant pine scent as they absorbed the visual wonder of candles burning brightly. Joyfully, their voices filled the little house with favorite Christmas songs like "Silent Night" and "Oh, Christmas Tree" or "Oh Tannembaum." On Christmas Day, the Kessel family enjoyed a slow-roasted goose, accompanied with garden vegetables from the root cellar. It wouldn't have been Christmas without their beloved *sauerkraut* sprinkled with brown sugar. For months they looked forward to boiled chicken feet, which they peeled and ate, taking care to suck the tender meat from each toe.

That next February, 1912, Katja gave birth to another son. This child was not blond and blue-eyed, but had dark hair and eyes like his mother. Katja was happy for this, a child who looked like her. They named their new son, Johann, but changed it to the American version, John. As the child grew he acquired the nickname of Johnny.

That August, about a month after Jakob turned twelve, he got up the courage to ask a favor of his father: "Papa, if I finish my work early, may I ride my pony up the river a ways to fish?"

Jakob knew his father didn't especially like the idea of him spending part of the day fishing, but Karl reluctantly agreed. Jakob hurried through his morning chores, saddled his pony Freckles and, grabbing his fishing pole, headed upriver with his dog Gabby close at his heels. Jakob still had memories of fishing with his grandfather Christian back in Surtschin. His grandfather had taught him that fish like to spend their afternoons in quiet, shaded pools, and this was exactly what Jakob was looking for as he walked along the grassy river bank.

He knew there wasn't much to fish for in the muddy Shoshone River, but he enjoyed it anyway. Jakob rode his horse about a mile up river until he found a good spot. Jumping off Freckles, Jakob threw the reins loosely around a low branch, untied his fishing pole from the saddle, and put a couple of squirming worms on the hook. He walked a short way back to where he had noticed a deep, shady pool. He whipped the pole back and the line sailed forward in a wide arc. Not happy with where the sinker landed, he tried again. Jakob liked the sound of the weighted line as it whistled through the midmorning air and settled in the middle of the targeted pool. He tried the pool for around ten minutes without luck and decided to head back up the river, close to where he had tied his horse. He crawled out onto a rock and threw the line out into another promising spot. Suddenly the line went taut; Jakob pulled and reeled, pulled and reeled the line until he landed the wriggling catfish. He caught another catfish in the next ten minutes and, with a smile, tied them onto the saddle. *Mama will like these fine catfish; maybe she will cook them for my supper.*

As Jakob headed back to the river, he spotted Gabby digging frantically at a large hole in the river bank. He went over to investigate just about the time an angry skunk decided to protect his hole. Instinctively, the skunk sprayed them both with his defensive scent. The smell was so bad that Jakob could hardly breathe—he wasn't aware that his dog was whining and throwing up. Jakob started to cry as he staggered toward the river, trying to wipe away the tenacious stink from his body. After splashing in a shallow part of the river to no avail, he lifted his head and, through his watering eyes, noticed movement on the bank. He rubbed his eyes with his fists and as they cleared he saw a shabby, bearded man standing next to a cottonwood, watching him. "Having a bit o'trouble are ya, lad? Smells to me like you got the worse end of an ole skunk; that ya did! Do ya liv around these parts?" He started making his way down the bank toward the reeking boy. Gabby stood close to Jakob as a low growl rumbled deep in his throat.

Jakob tried to talk, but ended up being sick right there in front of the old man. He tried to apologize but started crying with embarrassment and frustration.

The old man said, "Well, don't think you are goin' home in this shape, so looks like we'd better be building a sage tent for ya lad, to get rid of that thar stink. Tis the only thing that will cut the skunk spray; bring your dog long— he smells as bad as you do! Come on now, follow me up the hill to ma shack, and I will be a fix'n you up."

He started off up the hill and Jakob stumbled after him, still crying and puking as he went. They walked about half a mile to a sandstone bluff above the river. The back half of his hut was carved into the bluff while the front was made of logs and hidden by thick brush and junipers. If he didn't know it was there, Jakob would never have seen it, and that was the way the old hermit wanted it.

When Jakob finally got a good look at the old man who said he wanted to help him, it scared the dickens out of him. He had a nasty red scar across the right cheek that was obviously responsible for the missing part of his left ear. His eye was about a half-inch lower on his face than it had been before somebody's Bowie knife ripped across his face, years ago in Georgia. His hair was matted and filthy and he carried the biggest ole gun Jakob had ever seen. A shudder ran through Jakob as he realized this old man must be the "crazy" Jebediah Jordan, who he had heard people talking about. Folks said that when Old Man Jordan came back from the Civil War, he built a secluded hut and kept to himself, but nobody knew exactly where it was. He was strange and made it clear he didn't want any human contact.

The boy thought to himself, *I sure hope he doesn't plan on having me for dinner; course, I smell so bad that maybe he won't want to eat me yet. He might wait till I get to smelling better!* Jakob said a little prayer to the Lord, asking him to fill the old man's belly with something other than him.

Jakob watched the old hermit tear sagebrush out of the ground and pile it around a tent-like structure that he had built with cedar poles. With a chuckle, he lit it on fire. Now, Jakob was quite sure he was going to be roasted for dinner. He started to stand up to make his getaway, when the old man grabbed him by the belt, lifted him off the ground, and pulled him back. "Take them thar clothes off; just leave them thar drawers on. Give 'em to me now boy so I can get that stink off 'em!"

Okay, my clothes are off and I'm thinking I am ready for the pot. Jakob was scared to the bone now as more tears welled up in his blue eyes. The sage fire flared up, then seemed to settle down, producing thick smoke which boiled and rolled into the sky.

The old man put Jakob's clothes on the ground in the middle of the sage tent as he said, "Hey thar, lad, get yourself ovar here and sit ya rear end on that thar short stump in front of that thar sage smoke."

The lad did what he was told; the hairy old man didn't have to say it twice. Jakob could hardly breathe, the smoke was so thick, but he figured he better stay put on that stump. After the intense smoke died down and only ashes were left, the old man told Jakob to rub the warm sage ash onto his skin. The smell was strong, but not as bad as the skunk smell, so Jakob did as he was told. Frankly, he was still afraid something really bad was going to happen, especially if he didn't do what the old man told him to do. After he rubbed himself all over with the warm ash, Jakob began to feel better; he couldn't smell that relentless skunk odor anymore and relief flooded over his face and his stomach settled.

By now it was getting dark and Jakob wasn't sure how to get home. He knew his father would be angry with him and he would probably get the belt again. The old man finally spoke, "Well, laddie, looks like the day is done. Tis too dark to be trapsin' down that thar path now; s'pose ya might as well spend the night har and in the mornin' I will help ya find your way home. What is your name anyhows? Ya got folks round har I 'spect."

Jakob's faith in his rescuer had improved and he managed to speak up. "Sir, my name is Jakob Kessel. Karl Kessel is my pa and we live on a farm to the south of the butte. My dad will be mighty worried if I don't come home tonight, especially since my horse Freckles ran off home when the skunk sprayed."

Jebediah Jordan smiled in spite of himself as he replied, "Well Ja-kob, I can't help if yor pa is worried, we can't be takin' a chance on that thar dark trail. I ain't got no lantern to light tha way, and thar is no moon either. So, here is a straw mat for ya to sleep on, in the mornin' we can be a-gettin ya on home. Don't s'pose ya are hungry are ya? Got a bit of roastin' ears here and I was cookin' a rabbit on the spit when I heard ya hollaring dawn by that river. Go ahead now, fill ya belly and get sum sleep."

The boy was scared, but hunger won out as he filled his plate and his belly. He slept fitfully that night, filled with worry about what his papa and mama were thinking.

Karl had been working out in the field that afternoon. He had been on his way to the house for supper around dusk when he saw Jakob's pony trotting down the road without the boy on his back. He hurried up to the horse, grabbed the reins, and pulled him to a halt. There was no sign of Jakob, but Karl was quick to smell skunk odor. He spotted two catfish tied to the saddle—but what had happened to the boy? Where *was* Jakob and that blasted dog? He took the horse to the barn, removed the saddle and put the pony in the corral.

When he got to the house, he told Katja what happened. Of course she was upset, frantic was more like it. Karl assured her that Jakob was a smart lad and if he wasn't home by morning, he would go out looking for him. "There's nothing we can do tonight; its pitch black out there with no moon and all."

"Karl, what is wrong with you? Jakob is just a boy, out there alone in the dark night. Something has happened to him. He is a good boy and he would come home if he could. What if he lays hurt on the ground all night? We need to search for him now and not wait until morning! We could take a kerosene lantern to light the way. Do something, Karl, do something!"

But again, she realized that it didn't matter what she thought. More than once during the night, Katja slid out of her warm bed and quietly walked in bare feet to look out the window. She moved from window to window, straining to see something in the moonless night. "Oh, dear God, please, please keep my son safe. Watch over him if he lies injured on the cold ground. Bring him home safe to me; please hear my prayer." Katja murmured this prayer again and again.

Karl slept soundly that night, but as soon as the sun edged up over the Big Horn Mountains he was out of the house and on the back of his horse. He rode out at a gallop, down toward the river in the direction Jakob had gone the day before. He had gone about a mile and half when the smell of a skunk led him to the place where Jakob and Gabby had been sprayed. Karl noticed the disturbed hole in the bank and saw a trail leading up the hill. He took his horse by the reins and followed the path on foot.

As soon as morning light began to creep through the leaves of the trees surrounding the hidden hut, Jakob was awake. He smelled the salt pork frying and coffee boiling on the fire. With his back to the boy, Jebediah was bent over the fire pit, cooking breakfast. "Okay, boy, get yar butt outa that bed and grab yar plate if'n ya want any of this har grub," he growled.

The boy had taken the first bite of food when his father burst through the brush, his face was flushed with anger and worry. When he saw Jakob sitting on a stump beside the cook fire, calmly eating breakfast, Karl didn't know whether to whelp him there or hug him. He grabbed Jakob by the arm as the breakfast fell to the ground. "What in the hell is going on here, you just decide to spend the night up here and make your mother sick with worry?" Karl tossed Jakob to the side and went after the grubby old man standing in the doorway of the hut.

Knowing trouble when he saw it and not wanting any part of it, Jebediah pulled a menacing knife from his belt in one fluid motion. "Jus' hold it right thar, friend, ya ain't gonna lay a hand on me as long as I'm upright. That thar boy got hisself in a passel of trouble yesterday, and I come ta help him out with the skunk stink and all. He couldn't even hardly breathe, so I built a sage tent and we smoked the stink off'n him. It were a black night and we couldn't make it down the path in the dark; now, could we? So he spent the night here'n my protection and I even fed tha lit'l squirt. I knows what peeple around har says of me and they have a right ta theys opinion, but I didn't hurt the boy, I only helpt him. Just you ask him, now."

Karl had stopped in his tracks, first persuaded by the threat of the huge knife and then the old man's words. The boy spoke up before his father had a chance to open his mouth. "Pa, it is true what Mister Jebediah says, he saved me, Pa; he truly did. Gabby was going after the skunk in his hole and that ole skunk came out and sprayed us both real bad, as he was gettin' away. It was so awful Pa that I puked and could hardly see. Mister Jebediah found us and smoked me and Gabby in the sage smoke to get rid of the skunk stink. It was like he said—about coming home in the dark, and we didn't have a light to see the trail, but I wanta go home now, Pa."

Jakob turned to Jebediah and said, "Thank you, sir, for saving me and smoking me in the sage smoke. I am sure glad you found Gabby and me. And, and—it was nice to meet you Mr. Jebediah, thanks!" Jakob climbed on the back of his father's horse as Karl mumbled some sort of appreciation directed at Jordan. They headed back down the bluff toward home. Karl didn't utter a word to his son on the long ride home. He was still furious and determined to teach the boy a lesson for not coming home last night—a lesson he would not forget.

His father's mood was something Jakob knew well; he had experienced it before and he never doubted he would suffer another beating when they got home. *It is so unfair,* Jakob thought, *I did my best to get home, but all along I knew that any excuse would not be good enough for Papa.*

When they arrived at their farm, Karl told Jakob to take the saddle and reins off the horse and wait in the barn. Katja ran into the yard when they rode up. Karl got off the horse and thrust his forearm across her chest, stopping her before she could see to her son. "Katja, your son is fine; I'll tell you later what happened. You have chores to do and I need to deal with the boy!"

Katja tried to object as Karl shouted at her. "Katja, you are becoming like the Americans with their softness toward their children. You know my rules. I'll be damned if my children fail to learn that I am the head of this house and they will do as I say! I AM the boss, the authority, not them or you! Do not argue with me, Katja; remember I am over you as well!" He ripped his belt out of his pants as he strode toward the barn.

Jakob waited against the far end of the shadowy barn. Tears already rolled down his young face in anticipation of the beating he was going to get. He heard his father stomp across the yard and saw his silhouette momentarily in the door as he stood, belt in hand, eyes adjusting to the dim light. Karl wasted no time in administering what he called discipline. The first blow came as Jakob turned and tried to get away, knocking him forward onto the barn floor. The big leather belt came down twice more before Jakob cried out, "Dad, no more, DAD!"

The belt froze in mid-air as memories surfaced of the beatings he had endured as a child, from his own father's rage. The blood drained from his contorted face and his eyes narrowed as guilt crawled up his spine. "Next time you do something like that I'll give you a real threshing! When you stop your crying, wash your face, and get your chores done before you come to the house." With that Karl turned and strode out of the barn door, threading his belt back through his pant loops as he walked.

The boy lay motionless on the straw-covered floor of the barn, while pain throbbed and chewed in his back and buttocks. *I do not think Papa loves me anymore and, and I am quite sure I don't love him, either. How could he beat me so, if he loved me? Why couldn't he understand I wasn't able to come home last night? Mama does not beat me like that. She might give me a slap on the head or a light kick in the pants, but she never uses a belt on me like he does*. Jakob decided there and, when he was old enough, he would leave the farm and his father's injustice—and that day couldn't come too soon for him.

His mother waited and watched out the window for her husband to leave the barn. After he saddled the bay horse and rode out of the lane, Katja grabbed her basket of salves and herbs as she hurried to the barn. Slowly, she opened the west-facing barn door and peered into the filtered light. Tears welled up in Katja's dark eyes as she knelt beside the curled and crumpled form of her oldest son. Her hands reached behind his head and slipped down to the nape of his neck, as she began to lift him. "Jakob, oh, my son, my son," she sobbed. "I am so sorry I cannot protect you. I do not know how to stop your papa or to make him understand that this much beating is wrong. I promise; I will find a way. Can you sit up, son? I have brought salve to put on your wounds."

When Jakob tried to sit up on his own, his face grimaced in pain. Finally he managed to move to a sitting position where his mother could apply the herbal salves to his broken skin. She felt his pain as her hands gently smoothed the salve over his open and bruised flesh. Tears of anger and her own guilt rolled down her face, tears her son could not see. When she finished, she asked, "Do you want me to help you up to the house?"

He looked up at his mother, "Did he leave? I don't want you to get in trouble for helping me, Mama."

"*Ja*, Jakob, he rode out a few minutes ago; I don't know where he went and I don't care! We don't worry about your papa now. I will help you; you are my son. Come now, take a deep breath and push yourself up on the hay bale."

It took mother and son about ten minutes to walk the short route from the barn back to the house. Katja helped Jakob into the bedroom where he lay on his bed without taking his clothes off. "Lay on your side, son, so the herbs have a chance to work into your wounds. I will apply more before Papa comes back."

Chris, Ralf, and Johnny peeked into the bedroom, concerned with what had happened to their older brother. Chris asked, "Mama, should we go out and do Jakob's chores for him?"

Katja turned her head to look at her sons standing in the kitchen, "*Ja*, that would be good of you; be sure to gather all of the eggs, don't forget any of the nests or the skunks will get them and your papa will be more angry!"

Later that night after she put the other children to bed, she applied more salve to Jakob's back before giving him some supper and tea laced with laudanum. When Karl finally returned to the house, Katja was waiting for him as she sat at the kitchen table with a hot cup of tea in front of her, and a thousand thoughts going through her head. He threw open the door and stomped into the kitchen. "Where is that boy, did he do his chores?"

Katja stood so quickly her chair fell back onto the floor. She replied with an icy tone, "Chris and Ralf attended to Jakob's chores; he is in his bed." Katja sneered, "You must be so proud Karl, to beat your son like that. I may have to call the doctor; you hit him so hard!"

Karl's eyes widened at the word doctor and he quickly tried to defend his actions. "Well, I had to teach him to obey. I am his father!"

Those words were all Katja needed. She moved, blocking Karl's path, her ebony eyes flashing with anger. "Karl, what kind of father are you? What kind of man are you to beat a child, our child, like you do? It was not his fault what happened, it was an accident and a kind man cared for him when he was in trouble. And for this you beat him? I don't know who you are anymore, Karl. You are not the kind, sensible, loving man I married and who lived with me in Surtschin, the man who worked in the fields beside my father. You have become something I know nothing of. You have become as brutal to your sons as your father was to you!" Her burning eyes did not leave her husband's flushed face as she accused him of things he already knew, but had tried to ignore.

Shoving her roughly out of his way, he strode into their bedroom and began undressing for bed. Katja was not through with him, she followed him, continuing to question his ruthless brutality against their oldest son until Karl whirled and slapped her hard across the face. "You will not speak to me like this, woman; you will respect me because I am the head of this house. There is one way to do things in this house, MY WAY!"

Katja was stunned, Karl had never hit her, or even acted like he might. Besides, she was pregnant again; her fifth child was due in a few months. She held one hand to her stinging face, while the other moved instinctively down in protection to rest on her bulging belly. Tears of frustration and shame rolled down her face.

Karl glanced momentarily in her direction without concern. "Don't start with the tears to think you will soften my heart; it will not work. Now shut up, Katja, and get in the bed. I have much work to do tomorrow."

That night, after Karl was asleep, Katja left their bed and walked quietly to the next bedroom where her son lay in his bed. She gently ran her hand over his forehead. "Jakob," she whispered, "Jakob, my son, are you all right? Are you able to sleep? Do you need more salve?"

A hushed voice, edged with pain, whispered back in the darkness, "*Ja*, Mama, I am sleeping a little. I think the salve and the sleeping herb is helping me. Don't worry, Mama, I will be all right; you go to bed. Mama, I knew he would beat me today; he never understands. I don't know how much longer I can stay here, how many more beatings I can take. Someday, I will leave his house, but never you, Mama, never you."

Katja put both hands around his young face and leaned to kiss her oldest son, her first born. "Thank you for the fine catfish, Jakob; I saved them to cook tomorrow for your supper. I love you, my sweet son!"

Leaving him, she crept back to her bed to lie beside the man she no longer cared to call "husband." Yet another part of Katja's heart grew cold against this man who had fathered her children. She laid next to him that night, in his bed, and thought of what he had become. A shiver shot threw her as she saw the years ahead and wondered how she and her children would survive. She also knew that things would never be the same between her and her husband.

CHAPTER 12

The Middle Years, 1915–18

★ ★ ★ ★ ★

In 1915, the Kessels had a second daughter, Dorothy. She was a pretty baby girl with brown eyes, light-brown hair, and a fiery temper like her father. A month after Dottie was born Karl made a trip into Lovell for supplies. When the wagon rolled back into the yard at the end of the day, they all went out to meet him, each hoping for some special treat. Karl was in great spirits as he climbed down from the wagon, handing peppermint sticks to each child. He climbed into the back of the wagon where a canvas tarp covered something large. His eyes lit up as he announced, "This is for you, Katja." With a sudden jerk, he threw the tarp off, exposing a new black coal-burning cook stove.

Katja's hand flew to her face in amazement. "Oh, Karl, oh *mein Gott*, look at that beautiful stove. Thank you—thank you so much."

Karl and the older boys disconnected the old black beast and replaced it with the shiny new cook stove. Katja was thrilled to cook their supper on her new stove.

Although Katja had given birth to six children in fifteen years of marriage, Karl still expected his wife to help out in the fields whenever he needed an extra hand, even after what Grandma Bittner had told him. The hard work kept the extra pounds off, but Katja noticed that with each birth, her body was beginning to thicken and sag. She also noticed she became tired easily from tasks that never bothered her before. The backbreaking field and housework, along with numerous pregnancies and miscarriages, were taking both a physical and mental toll on Katja.

Trying her best to cope with her situation in life, she searched for ways to keep from being pregnant. Like many women of her time, Katja heard of a special herbal tea that would bring on bleeding and possibly abort an unwanted pregnancy. But she felt in her heart that doing so would be a sin and something she could never do. She realized she had only one alternative, to nurse her children for two or more years. Katja didn't understand why this seemed to work as a type of birth control but it helped to keep the number of her pregnancies down.

> June 18, 1915
> Our Dear Katja,
> We hope and pray that this letter finds you safe and well. We are so happy with the good news of the birth of your sixth child, Dorothy, in April. We hope that you are feeling your strength back and the baby is doing well. The Lord is good and has blessed you and Karl with six children, we are so thankful.
> Your father and I are grateful you and Karl are not living in this country anymore. So many have died, including several of your cousins. Your cousin Heinrich and Wilhelm were both killed on the western front. Your brother is safe and is coming home to help with the farm. He was also fighting with the army but the government has decided to send him home now so he can work the land to raise more food for the armies. His wife Katharina and their children are restless until they see his face.
> There is much talk among the village for moving back to Germany after the war is over. There are many farms now for sale because so many men were killed in the terrible war. It will be good to go back to Germany, but sad to leave the many friends that we have made here in Yugoslavia and who wish to stay. We are not sure if we will leave now, perhaps we will wait for a while. Give all of our grandchildren our love and thank you for sending the picture of you, Karl, and the children.
> Our love always, Mama

That evening as the family sat around the supper table, Karl noticed Katja was unusually quiet and withdrawn. "So Katja," Karl began, hoping to break the ice, "what was in the letter from your mother?" Katja's eyes lifted from her plate, but she didn't look at her husband, instead she gazed out the window to the distant Big Horn Mountains.

Annoyed at her obvious dismissal Karl said, "Katja, did you hear me?"

"Yes, Karl, I heard you but I don't think you want to hear me." She turned and faced him. "I am saddened and fearful of how hard it is for my parents and their life in Yugoslavia and it promises to become worse." Katja hesitated, choosing her words carefully as she continued, "I wish, Karl, with all of my heart I could see my family, and especially Papa, just one more time. I need to do this before it is too late; I feel it in my heart."

Katja was quick to recognize the answer she would get by the look on Karl's face and, before he could reply, she pushed back from the table and hurried out the front screen door. Katja twisted her hands up in her cotton apron as her face turned side to side in frustration. To her horror, she felt a wave of hot tears erupt from her brown eyes and course down her cheeks.

Karl watched her leave the table and, shaking his head in disbelief, he also pushed back his chair and followed her out into the front yard. He caught up with her as she stood under the cottonwood trees, facing the mountains. "Katja, have you lost your common sense? There is no way you can make such a journey. First, we cannot afford it; there is no money for such an expense. Second, you have just birthed a child; and third, there is war everywhere over there. So, NO, Katja, you cannot go to Surtschin for a visit and frankly I am surprised you would even think of anything so unrealistic, so foolish." Karl turned his back on her and walked toward the house but stopped and turned back before sternly adding, "AND, we will not speak of this again!"

She had expected as much from him, but was still disheartened by Karl's response. For days, she went through the motions of caring for her family, her heart and mind not involved in her physical activities. In the evening she sat still in her rocking chair, listening to the small Victrola, and the records of classical music. Katja was normally comforted by listening to the music, but now it made her even more upset and homesick.

After more than a week, Katja resigned herself to her plight and willed herself out of the depths of nagging depression. She had received absolutely no comfort or sympathy from her husband, only impatience and indifference. Something deep inside Katja began to change, she felt more alone than ever. She was convinced her future would hold no more than it did at that moment. Katja lost hope—in her marriage, in her future, and finally, in her husband.

October 1, 1915

Dear Mama and Papa:

I am sad to hear of how you suffer from the war. It never seems to change or get better with war after war, somewhere in Europe. The United States is feeling the effects as well, but not on our soil as it is on yours. I am thankful that none of our sons are old enough for the government to tell them to go to war.

Karl is always busy with working on the farm and also the sugar factory. He has three sons to help him in the fields, but always he has to tell them what he wants them to do, so he is pleased. Karl is hard with Jakob, always expecting so much. I fear he is turning into his own father. He is not so strict with the other sons, only Jakob. There is no time to be spent on fun as there is always more work, more money, and still no fine house. I should be thankful we live in this country and have a good farm and much opportunity. It is the same for everybody; life is not easy.

I miss going to the concert, I miss hearing the music in person. I have not heard of such music concerts in this country. I do not think people here know of the beauty of music, only perhaps in the large cities like New York. For me, this is sad.

We now have electricity on the farm and it makes my work much easier. Karl bought a Victrola and records to listen to the music. Many of our friends do not appreciate listening to the records. It leaves me sad for their ignorance of this wonderful thing.

I would like to travel back to see you all again, but Karl tells me that it is not possible with the war. This makes me upset and sad for many days now. Please stay safe and give my love to all the family.

My love to all, Katja

The day-to-day disillusionment and reality Katja experienced was silently degenerative. She still lived in what she considered a hovel, while Karl ignored her wants and needs, only buying more land and machines with the money that came from his crops and the animals. In the early years, Karl had been a considerate and loving man, especially when her father had been watching, but now he was demanding and cold. The only joy in her life was supplied by her children, and occasionally those rare evenings when there was time to listen to the wonderful music on the Victrola, after her work was done. Frequently, she sat alone working on her needlework, mending, or rocking a restless or ill child on her lap.

More often than not, Katja felt as though she was just going through the motions of living. *This was not the life I dreamed of nor is it the life I thought Karl promised. When we were first married, I was filled with such innocent love and consuming desire for my husband. I have been loyal and done my duty to him and my marriage, and that is what brought me to this godforsaken land. Now, all I feel is the emphatic duty and drudgery of the marriage which is only countered with the joy of caring for my children and my flowers.*

The winter was a hard one with constant, howling winds driving blizzard after blizzard from the north. The temperature stayed below zero for weeks on end. The roads were constantly drifted shut with incessant snow and wind, trapping rural families within the confining walls of their homes with what food they had stored for the winter. Katja prayed there would be no severe illness in house, because it was almost impossible to ride for the doctor.

Every morning, Karl and the boys had to chop through the ice in the animal's water troughs. Washing clothes was near to impossible and so they wore the same clothes for weeks on end, only changing their long underwear once a week, on Saturdays. Their lips cracked and bled, and their skin was so dry and itchy that Katja was forced to concoct a relieving salve from lard and herbs. When Karl came in from feeding the animals, his mustache was frozen to his lips and the little hairs in his nose hung stiff with thin icicles.

When the weather finally broke, Katja encouraged the children to play outdoors, building snow forts and snowmen, and throwing snowballs. The six children didn't like to be cooped up in the small house, even though Katja tried to keep them busy with school lessons, whittling or carving wood, cooking, cleaning. She even taught them to knit—anything to keep their little minds and fingers busy with productive things.

One day in late March, Karl had been able to get through the road to drive into Kane for supplies. He returned that afternoon with only a few things because deliveries to Kane were few and far between as well. He did bring treats for the children. He also had news. "Katja, I will wait until the children are asleep to tell you of some terrible news I heard in Kane today."

The rest of the day, Katja went through all sorts of scenarios in her head of what the "terrible news" might be. After she put the children to bed that night, Karl and Katja sat at the kitchen table with steaming cups of tea.

"Remember when we met Astor and Martha Rudolph and their five children last summer? Something terrible has happened to them all. Bill Schneider at the grocery told me Astor had been in, buying shells for his gun and told him he was going out on his horse to hunt for food. They think he and his horse must have fallen through the ice on the river, because they found the spot where he had probably gone through. His horse was found dead further down on the bank, with no signs of Astor. They think he was swept under the ice, drowned, and pulled down stream with the current!"

"Oh, *mein Gott!*" Katja's eyes were wide with concern and horror. "What about Martha and the children?"

Karl took a sip of the hot brew. "It gets worse, Katja. Bill and Jim Stott rode out to tell her about what they found. They said she just stood and stared out the window, no screaming or crying, nothing. They had to get back to town and so they left. Two days later they went back out to take her some groceries. Bill said they knocked and knocked, but nobody came to the door. It was unlocked, so they went in." Karl paused again to compose himself. "Katja, Bill said the children were all in their beds, dead! Martha had stabbed each one with a butcher knife as they slept. After writing a note, she cut her own wrists and bled to death!"

Katja sat, stunned and motionless with the horror of the news, as her hand rose to cover her open mouth.

"The men in Kane have to wait a month before they can dig the graves in the cemetery. Astor's body was found twenty miles down stream two days ago."

Later that spring when the children were able to go back to school, they came home with a note from the teacher.

TO THE PARENTS

Unfortunately, because of the cold weather and insufficient or improper hygiene, we have had an outbreak of head lice at the Kane School. School will be suspended for another two weeks. It is our hope that while the children are home, the prescribed treatment will be followed to rid them of the pest. Children will only be readmitted to school after a thorough examination.

Shave the child's head and apply a warm diluted mixture of tar to the head. Leave on for about an hour and remove with kerosene. Please apply this treatment every five days. Thank you for your cooperation in this matter. School will restart on April 14th.

Sincerely, Mrs. Ruth Waters and Miss. Audrey Meyers

Katja hated the regiment prescribed to rid her children of head lice. She knew when it was time to initiate the "cure," there wouldn't be any volunteers. At the end of the two-week treatment, the lice and their nits were decimated and the children were thankful to be back in school—bald, but lice free.

Jakob's relationship with his father had not improved over the years. He steered clear of him as often as he could and tried his best to do the work expected of him. All of the children had been taken out of school when they completed the sixth grade. Karl made the excuse that it was more important they should work full-time on the farm, rather then spend time learning useless nonsense in school.

Every once in a while Jakob risked asking for an afternoon off, to go fishing or to ride horses up into the foothills of the Big Horns with his friends. He was almost sixteen and doing a man's share of the work on the farm, without pay. It seemed to Jakob that no matter how much he did, it was never enough nor was it done as his father wanted it done. Leaving the farm was becoming a daily thought as he tried in vain to please his father.

Two weeks before Jakob's sixteenth birthday, their relationship faced an inevitable and ugly confrontation. Earlier in the month Jakob had decided to shorten the German pronunciation of his name to the American version, Jake. This did not please his father and the displeasure had festered for weeks, Karl refused to call his oldest son, Jake. "I will call you by the Christian name your mother and I gave you at birth, Jakob!"

Jake had worked hard all week driving the team of draft horses as they pulled the plow through the fields. When that task was finished, he followed up with the disc and later the harrow, all implements meant to break the soil into fine particles in which to plant the seeds as his father taught him. One day after he had finished harrowing the upper field, he was hitching the Percherons to the planter, preparing to put the corn seed into the prepared ground. Karl came around the corner of the barn and saw what Jake was doing. His lips pinched tight and his eyes blazed as he approached his oldest son. "What the hell do you think you are doing there?"

Jake turned around in shock and, defending his work, replied, "I am getting ready to take the team out into the north field to plant corn. I finished harrowing that upper field and you said you wanted the corn planted there."

Karl's fury was as red and hot as his face. "What makes you think you say when it is time to plant the corn? You don't even have the sense to prepare the ground right. I have looked at the field—is that what you call *prepared* for planting? What about leveling after you harrow? Did you forget about that? I want that ground leveled before planting. It's not ready!"

"Dad, I have been working hard all week on the field and, yes, I thought the soil was worked fine enough to plant the corn without leveling. You have told me you wanted me to start taking more responsibility and that is what I thought I was doing."

Karl threw down his shovel and shouted at his son, "You do not have the sense of a sheep, you know nothing, and you will never know nothing! You are an absolutely worthless and lazy BOY!"

That was the final straw for the young, strapping Jake Kessel. Every defensive emotion and every rebellious thought that had come into his head during the last eight years roared back in his mind and out of his mouth, "What's the use in trying to please you? I have never, and I will never, do anything, *anything*, that pleases or is good enough for you, Dad. I have tried so hard to farm like you want me to farm, to be who and what you want me to be. I wanted to work with you and to someday inherit this farm and make you proud of me, your oldest son."

Karl began to laugh mockingly, "You actually think I would give you my farm, this farm, that I have worked so hard for? Never, nev-er, do you hear me? Never, will you inherit this farm. I am not giving this farm to any of my sons. That might be how it is done in the old country, but this is America, and, if you want this farm, you will have to buy it from me! But I know you will never have enough money to your name to buy this farm, because you are too bullheaded to learn how to do things the right way, like I do them."

As his father's words registered, anger flared and spilled as Jake spit his words, "You stand there and tell me, as your oldest son, I will never inherit this farm, but I can buy it from you? You can say this after what you went though with your own father and how his treatment affected your whole life? You are doing worse to me—you won't give the farm to me your oldest son, but you will sell it to me? This is what you are all about, isn't it, Dad? The work, the money, the control, and the power. You have no heart anymore, Dad; you are consumed with what you want and what you can get out of the land, my mother, and your sons. We are no more to you than slaves!"

Karl took a step closer to his firstborn son, raising his fist to strike him but, before he could bring it down, he felt a steel grip around his wrist. Jake stood cold, blue eye to cold, blue eye with his father, as he held tight to his father's wrist. Through clenched teeth he warned, "Never again, Dad, will you hit or beat me. Never, do you hear me?"

Karl's eyes widened in disbelief; this was the first time Jake had ever even tried to defend himself against his words or fists. Karl jerked his arm away from Jake's grip, his ice-blue eyes glaring cold and his nostrils flaring wide. "You dare to touch me? That is the final straw, get off my farm, NOW!"

Jake's face was glowing with anger, the ice-blue eyes he inherited from his father were flashing with explosive emotion and his hands shook with indignant rage. "Now, I will tell you something. Just as you left your father's house, I am leaving your house because I want to leave, not because you tell me to leave! I want no more of your judgement, no more of your control, no more of not being good enough for you, no more of your beatings, and hearing you belittle my brothers, of being cruel and dictatorial to my mother. No more of you! I am packing my clothes and I am leaving today, now! I will show you how lazy and stupid I am and I will show you what a mistake you make this day!"

In mid-stride, he turned facing his father again, "But, of course you have never made a mistake; have you, Dad? Or at least one you would admit to? Someday you will see that you made a mistake this day, a bad mistake."

With nothing left to say, his heart pounding and his breath coming is ragged gasps, Jake turned and strode to the house. He didn't need to explain things to his mother because she had heard the bitter argument coming from the yard. She knew this moment would happen sooner or later, and now it had come. Jake slammed the screen door as he crossed the kitchen and went directly to the small bedroom he shared with his three brothers. He packed his few clothes into a canvas bag, and only minutes later, carrying the bag, he re-entered the kitchen where Katja stood in her faded work dress and apron, her hands twisting with anguish.

Jake looked at her. Somehow, she seemed smaller than he remembered; her eyes were moist with tears. Katja held out her arms to her firstborn. He walked quickly to her and folded her aging body in his work-hardened arms. Only then did he allow the tears of frustration and hurt to spill from his eyes; Jake struggled to speak in spite of the rock-sized lump in his throat. "Ma, it has happened. I can't work with him anymore. There is no pleasing him and I don't want to even to try. I have had a gut-full of him! He is such a hardheaded man; he knows only work and money and what he wants. I have no choice but to leave; I have to get away from him. I love you, Ma; and I promise to stay in touch and let you know where I am. Thank you for loving me and for all you do for me; I won't forget it." He pulled himself out of his mother's consoling embrace and walked quickly out the door.

He trotted down to the barn, hesitated as he looked around for his father. Satisfied that he wasn't in the barn, Jake saddled his roan horse. *He'll probably be mad that I took my horse and saddle, but it is mine. I just don't give a damn anymore how he feels or what he thinks.*

Karl had returned to the field to level and plant the corn his way. He did not care or give another thought to the harmful and cruel words he and his oldest son had exchanged or what he would now do. *What does it matter anyway if he really leaves? I still have Chris, Ralf, and young Johnny to help with the work. With Jake gone Katja will just have to do more work in my fields. Good riddance*, he thought as he shoved the lever on the planter forward, and slapped the reins onto the backs of the Percheron team.

By the time he rounded the end of the first row, Karl's conscience had surfaced and he was forced to come to terms with what he had done. Was history repeating itself? Wasn't this the same thing that happened between his father and himself years earlier? He still felt the sting of betrayal and humiliation he had felt that day; today he let the same thing happen between himself and his firstborn son. It was something he had vowed never to let happen and now it had. Karl still tried to justify everything that had happened; he couldn't, or wouldn't accept that he was wrong. His last words with his own father came roaring back into his mind. "If God ever gifts me with sons, I will never treat them as you have treated me!"

What have I just done? I have treated my oldest son like my father treated me, and maybe even worse! Karl shuddered as he realized his entire life consisted of an exterior appearance and an interior agenda. *Well, it is done, and there is no turning back or making amends. I will not grovel or apologize, ever! I am the father and my word is law.* Karl clenched his jaw and vowed to himself: *So, let it be as it is!*

Back at the barn, Jake tossed his meager bag of clothes over the back of the saddle and tied it in place as Chris and Ralf walked into the dimly lit barn. "Suppose you heard, I have to get out of here; I have to get away from him. You know I do. Take care, you two, and stay out of his reach. Watch out for each other and take care of Ma, please! I will let you know when I find a job and get settled."

Jake put his foot up into the stirrup, swung his right leg up and over the saddle, took the reins into his hands, and gave the horse a gentle kick in the ribs. He trotted the roan toward the lane and in a cloud of dust, he was gone. As he galloped toward Lovell, he admitted to himself, *I'm scared, I'm real scared to be doing what I'm doing. It was the only thing left for me to do; he pushed me to the edge time after time!*

Katja stood in the doorway for a long time after her firstborn son galloped up the road toward Lovell. She had tried to prepare herself for this day, but there was no preparation for watching a child leave like this. Jake took a little piece of her heart with him. She felt it in her chest, just as her father had felt it when she left Surtschin. She wondered, *At what point, will there be no more heart from which to lose these little pieces? How long will it be and how many more heartaches will I have to endure, before I have no more heart for this living, this life with Karl in America?*

She didn't wait for her husband to come in from the fields that day to eat his supper and sleep in his bed. No, today she wouldn't wait on him; today she would go to him, in the field where he worked, because there was something she would say to him, something he needed to hear from her, in private.

Katja talked out loud to herself as she stomped down the dusty field road, verbally rehearsing what she was feeling, what she would say when she was face to face with Karl.

This is America; I have a right to speak what there is to say, what I am feeling, what I am thinking? I already know Karl probably will not listen to what I say, because it doesn't matter to him. I don't matter. He has made that point clear, more than once. I am going to say it anyway, he must hear from me—that he does have to deal with me. I am the mother of his children and his wife of too long. He is going to realize that I will matter and his children will matter.

Karl was surprised to see his wife standing at the end of the row with the late afternoon sun behind her, illuminating a halo around her small frame. He didn't know why she was there waiting for him, but he did know it was something she had never done before. His guilty conscience told him it was probably not good for him that she waited so patiently, so calmly, at the end of the row.

He pulled the horses to a stop, wrapped the reins around the planter lever as he remained sitting on the seat. "What is wrong that you come into the field at this time of the day; don't you have the evening meal to prepare?" Karl asked as stayed where he was, safe on the seat.

Katja locked eyes with him. "Come down from the planter, Karl, come down and stand before me. We are going to talk."

Slowly, Karl climbed down and walked toward her. Katja didn't wait for him; she moved deliberately across the field, until she was three feet from his face. Karl felt a twinge of fear when he saw her eyes, black orbs of fierce blame piercing into him.

"Karl, I have come into the field to speak to you, without our children to hear." She took a moment to choose her words carefully as she lifted her face in confidence, not losing eye contact with her husband. Karl felt himself step back as her eyes narrowed and her mouth twisted with the accusing words, "What you have done to our firstborn son, Jakob, will never be forgotten. You are a cruel and unforgiving man, Karl; and I think you have been this kind of man for a long time. This is what America did to you. This is the kind of man you have become since you become owner of your own farm, and *more* land, and *more* cattle, and *more* money. All from this land, land you call yours alone! I tried not to see it, but I do see it and I see you, now! I see it all, and I wish to God I didn't."

He turned his back on her and walked around to the other side of the planter, but Katja did not intend to let him turn from her again. She was not through with him; he was not going to get off the hook, not yet. "You have no heart for your own children. You have regarded our oldest son in a worse way than your father did with you. You have become a vengeful, willful bully. Jake has only wanted to please you, always, always to please his father and make you proud. And how do you return his love and respect? You have beaten him, talked cruelly to him, and made him feel as though he is worth nothing. So now, Karl, he has left his home and I do not know if I will ever see him again. You, Karl, YOU have made this day happen. You have done this thing to the son whom I bore for you in my pain and innocent love!"

Karl started to open his mouth to speak, but Katja held up her hand. "*Nein*, Karl, do not spill out your empty words to me. I do not believe any worthless words you say. But, I tell you this—as of this day, you will not beat my other sons as you have beaten Jake; you will not speak to them bad. You will not take your belt off and lay it across the backs of any more of my sons. You will be fair to them, and kind. IF you do not do this thing that I say, Karl, I will take my children and we will leave you, alone on this land of yours. I did not suffer in the birth of these six children for you to beat them and to treat them in the ways you have. It is right for a parent to teach the child and to be strict, but it is not right to purposely cause them harm. What do you think our Lord Jesus would say to you this day, Karl Kessel? HUH? What would you say to explain to him how you treat his gifts of children? You beat them like animals!"

Once more Karl opened his mouth to respond, but his guilt and common sense stuck him dumb. His face was flushed and his fists were clenched as tight as his jaw, but yet he did not speak. Katja turned and started to walk back to the house and hesitated. She turned her head toward her mute husband standing where she had left him, "And Karl, do not speak to me of this, there is no way that I will change on this because I am right, and I will have it no more! It is all the blame of you, Karl, all of it! If you push me, if you want to know how serious I am, keep being as foolish and stubborn as you have been, and you will know. I only hope you believe what you hear today and that you do not have to learn the hard way from me."

As she marched up the path toward the house, Katja found herself shaking and weak from the anger she had expressed toward her husband. She knew one thing, however; she felt cleansed, she felt empowered, and she felt a guilty weight lift from her heart. As the mother of her children she had done something to protect them as she should, and it felt right!

As the weeks passed, Katja kept thoughts of her oldest son to herself and in her prayers. She found solace and time to think when she tended the growing plants in her garden. This entire situation with Karl and Jake brought the hurt of leaving her family in Surtschin back to the forefront of her mind. She thought of her father so often lately, images here and there for no reason. Her heart had never healed from the circumstances of leaving him. On the day she sailed with her small sons to the west on the KronPrinz Wilhelm, a black emptiness filled a corner of her heart and remained.

As the weeks turned into months, Katja addressed her chores like a robot—scrubbing clothes, cooking meals, cleaning house. At harvest time she had additional chores, canning and putting away food for the winter. Karl hired a man to help with the harvest this year, which meant one less thing for Katja to do.

One balmy fall day as she digging potatoes in her garden, Katja felt a sudden and certain chill. Initially she thought it was the cold easterly wind that often blew down from the slopes of the Big Horn Mountains, but this breeze wrapped frosty fingers around her. A deep shiver ran through her body, a foreboding chill she didn't understand. Katja lifted her face to the darkening sky and was forewarned of a late fall storm that was building steadily to the east. As the wind blew colder, she gathered the bags of potatoes and dragged them to the root cellar.

"Ralf, Louise, get the kids together and hurry to the house, there is a bad storm coming." They ran through swirling dust and ice-cold drops of rain toward the house. The dark clouds seemed to come in out of nowhere as the icy rain turned to marble-sized, pounding hail. Safely inside the house, Katja went to the window and watched as small balls of ice fell and bounced in the yard, pounding her garden and the fields that lay beyond the fence. She was glad most of the garden had been harvested. She felt another severe shiver ran from the back of her neck, down to her tailbone. She wondered to herself, "*Was ist das?* Am I getting sick?"

Later that October day, as the family sat at the supper table, Katja felt a sense of gloom that did not leave her. Her dreams that night were dark and strange, with intermittent images of her father. Even the next morning she felt disoriented and concerned, for what, she did not know. She remembered these emotions and premonitions weeks later when she received a letter from her family in Yugoslavia.

October 29, 1916

My Dear Katja:

It is with a heavy heart, daughter, I must tell you of a sad thing. Your papa has met with a bad accident in the fields this past week. The horses have dragged him and he now lies in his bed. The doctors say he will live, but he may never be the same health. If he walks again, he will do so with a cane. It does not help him in his mind, that he never recovered from your leaving your home here, for to live in America. From that day he has been different. He has been sad and thinking of you and his grandchildren. He loves you and his grandchildren much. We pray he has the will to go on with his life.

Your brother and sister and their families are working hard to help your papa and they send their love to you and your family. I know this news will be not good for you, daughter, as you too love your papa. Trust in the Lord and take to him your prayers to restore Papa's health. Stay strong as we must also.

My love, Mama

The letter slipped from her hands and fell to the floor. Katja's face was tight and her jaw was clenched as she slowly walked out of the screen door. She walked as though in a dream. *I knew, I knew even before the letter came that something was wrong.* She thought of the shivers she felt that day of the storm; her heart had known of her father's accident. She stumbled and almost fell as she made her way to the grove of cottonwood trees near the river. She found a secluded spot and sunk to the soft cool ground. As soon as her skin felt the coolness of the grass, the tears came in huge, choking waves. Sobs wracked her body as she thought of the last time she embraced her father. *That day when I left him and sailed on the KronPrinz Wilhelm to America, was the last time I felt his arms around me. Now, he lies in his bed, his body broken. Of course I already know Karl will not allow me to travel to visit Papa. Now he has a broken body to match his broken heart. It is my fault, my fault, I am so sorry, Papa, so sorry. If I had it to do over again, I would not go to America. I would not go!*

Katja dried her tears on her apron and walked back up the bank of the river, back to her utilitarian life. She stopped at the pump and cranked until a cold gush of water sprang from the spout. She cupped the icy water in her hand and washed it over her tear-stained face and the back of her neck. Lifting her apron, she wiped her face and hands dry before she walked into the kitchen and began peeling potatoes for supper. As Katja stood at the sink, she thought about how empty she felt; she was just going through the motions of living. She really didn't want to be here, in this country, in this life.

Katja had realized late that summer that, once again, she was with child. *Dear God, when is this childbearing time going to end? I am now forty years old and going to have a seventh child.* Even though she and Karl didn't make love as often as when they were young, she was still fertile.

MARCH 1918

Katja gave birth to her fifth son, Edward or, as everybody called him, Eddie. Again, the boy was blond and blue-eyed, but his long body promised he would be taller than his brothers and his father. Katja smiled; perhaps he will be tall and thin like my papa.

Karl saw this fifth son as yet another helper in his fields and was happy. To his way of thinking, fathering children, especially sons, was a necessity in order that he might have the manpower to run a large farm. He gave himself all the credit for his children, especially his five sons.

Katja did not recover from this birth as quickly as she had from the others. She knew part of it was her growing despondency and her concern about her father's health, and missing Jake. Her marriage and life with Karl was difficult and a daily, bitter disappointment. She felt all he wanted from her was her back to work, and her body to satisfy his carnal needs. He was spending many hours, and sometimes several days in Lovell where he performed managerial tasks for the sugar factory. She did not mind his absence, especially since it meant she would benefit from a good night's sleep, without his demands on her body. Her life consisted of caring for her children, her garden, and her home, which was another point of constant dissatisfaction to her. It was difficult to care for a house like the one she was forced to live in. Keeping it clean and neat was almost impossible, and it frustrated her daily.

The Kessels still lived on the farm in Kane, and Karl only occasionally remembered his elusive promise to Katja about building her a grand house someday. He decided she would just have to make do with this house until he had all of the land, cattle, and machinery he needed and wanted. *At least this house is a roof over our heads and she should be thankful for that.*

Whenever she asked for something extra or special, his answer was always the same. Every time he threw spiteful rejection at her, she felt as though her husband slapped her face, again and again! She felt the flush of embarrassment and humiliation wash over her cheeks, as disappointment and anger filled her soul. Then came the night when Katja turned away from her husband when he reached for her in their bed. Karl grumbled, but wisely decided not to force himself on his wife; besides, he was tired!

Karl owned more than 180 acres along the Shoshone River. He still had three sons old enough to help him farm the land, and he worked them hard. Even though he did not beat them as he had beaten Jakob, he still expected perfection and complete obedience to his authoritarian instruction. They all knew they were expected to obey all his commands and never question his judgment; they also learned how to avoid his temper, most of the time.

Karl began to scout available farms for sale that were closer to Lovell. Plans to build the sugar processing factory in the town were progressing and this was yet another reason he wanted to live closer to the town. He was still obliged to help the owners in Cleveland and area farmers to participate in the construction of the factory in Lovell.

Karl Kessel had built a fine reputation for himself in the Lovell/Kane area. He was a strong, knowledgeable leader; he paid his debts on time and expected those who owed him money to repay their debt in like manner. Even though he was known for his strong work ethic and initiative, he rarely worked on Sunday, no matter what the situation or conditions.

Karl Kessel felt the same as most farmers; they did not relish the effort it took to grow sugar beets, but the payoff was good. Growing sugar beets was a grueling business. The grower's tasks required skill and experience to operate machinery to plow, plant, cultivate, or harvest. Many farmers hired beet labors, usually migrant families or Volga Germans who were needed only for the dirty and backbreaking hand labor. That fall when it came time to harvest the sugar beets, Karl or his hired man loosened the ground with a lifter machine. Migrant laborers followed the machine, pulled the beets by hand, topped them with a knife, and threw them on a waiting wagon. The beets were hauled to a local beet dump, weighed, and put in railroad cars for the trip to the Billings processing factory.

Karl had spent several days in the Lovell that week, attending to sugar factory duties and looking at yet another farm he heard was for sale. When he rode back to the farm in Kane that day, the first thing he did was hand Katja another letter from Yugoslavia.

In her usual manner, Katja first held the letter to her heart and slowly opened the wax-sealed envelope. So much had happened in the world and Katja had been worried about her family because, as they had predicted, war had come to Yugoslavia and Hungary/Austria. German emigrants who had accepted free land in Hungary, Romania, and Yugoslavia were caught in the middle. Part of their original agreement with Austria/Hungary stated they did not have to serve in war, but Katja's mother reported that many were kidnapped and forced into service anyway. After the passenger ship Lusitania was sunk, Italy declared war on Austria/Hungary and, just a year ago, the United States declared war on Germany. The entire world was fighting and this terrible time was known as the The Great War.

Katja went down to sit in her favorite spot by the river and thought about her mother's letter. If she and Karl had stayed in Surtschin, their own sons may have been some of those kidnapped to fight and die for another country. Katja put her face into her hands and asked herself, *Are any of us safe? Is there any place where we would not feel subject to the government?*

Jake was working on the Martin farm, training and caring for the prize stable of Percherons. He lived in the loft of the barn, enjoying his freedom and his life. He missed his mother and his brothers and little sisters, but he didn't miss the black cloud of tension between him and his father. He realized deep in his heart that he still loved his father; he would always love him. He admired his father and all he had sacrificed, coming to this country alone and working so hard to buy land, farming it as a free man.

All I ever wanted from Dad was his respect and, yes, to be loved and needed. I know German fathers have a reputation for beating their children, especially their sons. It's their way. Their code teaches that children should be obedient, and that it is not honorable to spoil children, that only weak Americans "spare the rod and spoil the child."

CHAPTER 13

Making Their Way, 1918–28

"Always bear in mind that your own resolution to succeed is more important than any other one thing. I do the best I know how, the best I can; and I mean to keep on doing so until the end." ~Abraham Lincoln

Their cherished subscription to German publications came every month. Karl and Katja read the news religiously in order to stay abreast of what was happening in the old country. Native language publications were established in part to aid the immigrant population in the process of their assimilation to the American culture. But when war was declared against Germany in 1917, many things changed for German immigrants and their newly acquired way of life in America, including cancellation of the German newspapers.

General hysteria, mostly directed at German Americans during the war in Europe, was inevitable. Karl was both afraid and angry when he heard of the new attitude toward Americans of German heritage. "Katja, we are denied the right to speak German in public or private, even on the telephone. German publications are also denied, this means we won't be able to read any papers from the old country. Even German teachers are being investigated, pastors are forbidden to preach in German, and there will be no German taught as a second language in the schools. I have read that musicians are refusing to play any music composed by German composers. *Gott in Himmel!"*

Karl threw his wool cap onto the floor as he continued, "Many peoples who have German names are changing them to make them more American. What really upsets me is that our German foods are banished and not served in restaurants. I even heard that some German man in Lovell was forced to kneel on the main street and kiss the American flag. What is going to happen next? Beatings, whippings, and jail, too? The final straw is our favorite food, sauerkraut—it has a new name, 'liberty cabbage'—liberty cabbage! Have you ever heard of anything so crazy?"

Everyday in the newspapers, they read of further disturbing actions taken against German Americans. President Woodrow Wilson encouraged every community to establish a "home guard" which was supposed to root out and expose all unpatriotic Germans.

"Katja, have you heard of this? Remember Pastor Germeroth at Zion Lutheran Church in Germania? While he was away in Worland tending to the Lutherans there, some patriotic men raised the Stars and Stripes above the German Lutheran church. Pastor Germeroth's two teenage sons didn't like that and so they tore the flag down and nailed it to the church's outhouse. Before they knew what happened, the home guard in Greybull demanded that Pastor Germeroth be lynched and he wasn't even there when it happened!"

Karl and Katja found out later in the day that before a mob materialized, other more rational members of the home guard made a trip out to Germania. They stopped at the first farm on the east end and talked to John Davis who headed up the Germania Bench home guard. Since this involved a Lutheran pastor from the west end of Germania, Davis directed the group to the home of John Wamhoff, a respected elder and member of the church and the community. After meeting with Mr. Wamhoff, the home guard concluded that the pastor's sons had shown great disrespect and poor judgment by nailing the national flag to the church outhouse. Even though the Germeroth family has purchased Liberty Bonds and declared their patriotism, and they were still the targets for a lynching. In order to avoid a visit from a drunken lynch mob from Greybull, the pastor and family were asked to leave Germania before the sun set. In a matter of hours, the Germeroths hastily packed their Model T and drove off in a cloud of dust. They were gone, just liked that.

"Now, the home guard and certain U.S. government officials have strongly suggested that residents of Germania change the name of the settlement to something more patriotic. Just yesterday, the residents unanimously voted to change the name to Emblem. Many people wanted the name of Liberty Bench, but the U. S. Post Office wouldn't accept that name because too many towns and communities were already named Liberty, something or another. What next is going to happen? I hope nobody bothers us about being German—we are American!"

The Kessel family tried to maintain a low profile, leaving no doubt in the minds of their community that they were loyal Americans. Karl and Katja decided this was a good time to travel to Basin, the county seat, and apply for citizenship. It was something they had discussed at length and both had wanted to do since they arrived in the United States more than ten years before.

When the Kessels arrived at the court house in the county seat of Basin, they presented the appropriate papers to the clerk. She inspected their papers and made a shocking statement, Katharina Kessel would indeed be a candidate for citizenship to the United States of America; however, Karl Kessel was not a candidate because he had entered this country illegally under another man's name, the name of Ralf Nimitz. Karl was bitterly disappointed and somewhat indignant. Becoming an American citizen was something he and his friend Arnold had talked about—it was important to him, and now he was denied—because of *the ticket*.

Katja Kessel proceeded with the process and eventually became a citizen of the United States of America; her husband did not. He was legally, a man without a country. The Kessels rode back to Kane that day in silence. Karl was crushed and humiliated. AFTER all the years of living in this country, working hard to be a good citizen, now, a woman behind a desk could crush his dream—like that! The situation would haunt him until the day he died. But he vowed he would not stop being an American in his heart. He WAS an American in every way, except on paper.

In the spring of 1918, another letter came from Surtschin. Katja's hand trembled as she opened the letter, remembering the news that the last letter had brought. Since receiving the last letter from her mother, there hadn't been a day that Katja didn't think of her injured father and offer a prayer for his recovery. What kind of news would this letter bring, good or bad?

June 12, 1918

Dear Katja and Karl;

As the entire world is suffering with this terrible Spanish flu and many are dying, so it is here in Yugoslavia and Germany. We have received word from your parent's home in Pancevo dear

Karl, your mother and your father have both been taken by the flu. They were buried together in the cemetery of the Lutheran church in the village. Your brother now lives in their house with his wife and six children. I know you have had little or no word with them for many years, but it is right you should know they no longer live. We are sorry to tell you of this news, Karl.

We have further bad news, here in our own family. Your brother, Christian's son, Jakob, who was only eight years old, has died. He was never a strong boy and the doctors said they think it was his small heart, which stopped beating with the flu. Katharina has been in her bed for over a week with her grief. It is the same as when they lost their Ludwig right after he was born in 1909. At least with Jacob they had some years to love and care for him. They have Theresia who is now thirteen, Christian who is eleven, Katharina who is six, and baby Adam. I do not know how hard it is to lose a child and I thank God I never have known this. It is a test of faith, as I know, to lose a grandchild and I say many prayers for Christian and Katharina. I am sending to you a picture we had made before Jakob passed on. It is of Katharina holding baby Adam. Next to her is our brave angel Jacob. Also in the picture are daughters Theraisa and Katharina, Christian is sitting beside me. We are in our mourning dressing because of Jacob, and for Karl's parents.

Now the summer months are upon us, the flu has almost stopped and we hope that it does not come back. Many of the village people and also soldiers have died as well from this terrible flu. It will take a long time and much work to regain our village and our way of living. Much has been lost from the war and now from this terrible sickness. We want you to know too, that your papa is much better now and is recovering more than the doctors thought he would.

We also hope and pray that you and your family are safe and well.

With our love, Mama and Papa

After washing and drying the dishes from the noon meal, Katja wiped her hands on her apron and went out to sit on the front porch. She eased down onto the first step and reached into her pocket to pull out the letter from Surtschin. Katja held the letter from her mother in her chapped hands, and slowly unfolded it again. She smoothed the letter out on her lap, gazing at the picture of her mother, sister-in-law, her nieces and nephews, most of whom she had never seen. Katja read the letter again, trying to digest what the words said. She sat for a long time on the front step. Salty tears rolled down her face and fell on her cotton-print apron. She cried for her brother and sister-in-law and the loss of yet another of their sons. She and Karl had not lost a grown child, but she had suffered several miscarriages over the years. Karl had, by choice, driven Jake away from their home and it felt to her like the same sort of loss. Lately, she had begun to notice little signs Karl's conscience might be bothering him. He made small, casual inquiries of Jake, asking if she had heard from him. But Katja did not share any of the things she knew about their son—she decided Karl did not deserve to know.

Though the family continued to live on the farm near Kane, Karl was becoming even more eager to find land closer to Lovell. He had a buyer for the farm in Kane, but would not seal the deal until he found another farm to move to.

In 1919, after nine difficult months of pregnancy, a weakened Katja gave birth to her last child, another son they named Henry, or Hank. He was strong and healthy, but the birth almost took her life. It was the longest labor she had ever experienced and she lost a lot of blood. At her age, it was normal for a woman to take longer to regain her strength after giving birth. Katja allowed the baby to sleep in her bed, something she had never done before. She discovered it was easier to nurse him during the night while staying in her bed. She needed to conserve her strength and this arrangement worked well for her.

One night when the baby was about a month old, Katja finished with the three a.m. feeding and laid her son across her shoulder to encourage him to burp. After a healthy belch, he didn't want to go back to sleep and was fussing so, in the dim light of the bedroom, Katja held him in her arms, singing and lulling him back into slumber. Her own head nodded with sleep as she eased her sleeping son down into the bend of her arm. She buried her nose in the fuzzy hair on his little head, breathing in the pure scent of him. In the darkness of the house, she lay back, listening to the steady rhythm of his breathing and savoring this tender moment alone—with her last baby.

After the birth of his sixth son, Karl had again resented the fact that he was forced to hire a woman from town to come in and care for the other children, to cook and help with the housework. He did not understand why Katja did not get her strength back and why her mood was not as he thought it should be. He was certainly happy with a sixth son, because again it eventually meant more help for him.

Late in the night, about three months after Katja gave birth, she finished nursing Hank and laid him back in his cradle. Exhausted, she made her way through the dark bedroom to her own bed and quietly climbed in, trying not to disturb her sleeping husband. But, Karl was not sleeping and, when he reached for her, Katja was startled and impulsively pushed him back, hard. "*Nein*, Karl, NO MORE, no more will I do this thing because there will be no more children. I have done my duty with giving you six sons and two daughters; there will be no more children. Do you understand my words?"

Karl was stunned and vehemently responded to her rejection, "Katja, it is a woman's duty to love her husband, and I want you to do your duty, now."

The blood drained from Katja's face and her ebony eyes froze in a stare as she replied, "Do you not understand what I say to you? I will not have another child; I do not care about what you think is *my duty*. How many children do I have to give to you, Karl? How many will be enough for you? As far as I am concerned, I have done my duty to you, so stay away from me. Do not take lightly what I am saying, Karl. I mean every word; no more! Is it dead that you want me? That is what will happen if I am to bear one more of your children!"

She pulled the covers up tight around her neck and turned her back on her husband, as she had seldom done in their married life. Karl lay stunned and rejected, staring at the ceiling in the dark. He was shocked by her attitude, but he didn't put much stock in what she said, he figured she would forget and return to what he considered was her duty as a wife.

Meanwhile, the Kessels' oldest son, Jake, was courting a lovely Volga-German girl, Raisa Schutz, the daughter of David and Sofie. She was a fine young woman with the most beautiful head of wavy auburn hair Katja had ever seen. She was tall and graceful, with soft blue eyes set deep in a sweet oval face of creamy skin. Raisa came from a fine Lutheran family who farmed to the south of Lovell. Jake had been working on David Schutz's farm from time to time and that is how he met Mr. Schutz's attractive daughter.

Jake was making a fine reputation for himself as a hard worker, willing to take any job he was offered. Unlike his father, he was good humored and thoroughly enjoyed his free time with his friends. They called themselves "The Gang," and spent weekends going on picnics, driving around in a Model T, riding horseback, and making camping trips to the Big Horns. They had fun together, just being young. Frequently, Jake invited his younger brother Chris to go along with the young bunch. All of this warmed Katja's heart; she was happy for her son and delighted that he was enjoying his life.

In January of 1920, Jake rode his horse out to Kane, to his father's farm. His brothers and sisters saw him coming and ran up the road to meet up him. Jake slowed his roan horse to a walk as his siblings ran alongside, laughing and chatting like a bunch of magpies! Jake took quick notice of his mother as she walked out of the little house with her new son Hank straddling her left hip. Jake was shocked at her appearance. Her normally well-restrained hair had come loose from her bun and lay in strings onto her collar. Katja had dark circles underneath her ebony eyes and she looked exhausted.

"Jake, how good it is to see you. Hurry and come into the house before you catch your death. Your papa is out in the barn tending to the animals." Once inside the toasty house, Katja pulled out a chair from the kitchen table. "Here, sit and tell me of your news. How have you been doing?"

"I wanted to see this new brother of mine before he goes to school! And, yes, Mama, I do have wonderful news to tell you. Raisa has agreed to be my wife; we are to be married next month at the Lutheran church in Lovell. I am so happy, Mama; she is a good woman." Jake was obviously excited about his future. "Can you come to the wedding and bring my brothers and sisters with you? I don't know if Dad will want to come, but for sure, I want you to be there."

A luminous smile crossed Katja's tired, weathered face and her eyes lit up with the news, "Oh, *ja*, Jake, we will be there and I do think your papa will want to come as well. We are happy for you, son; this is wonderful news."

The front door opened and Karl walked in on the joyous exchange that was taking place in the warmth of the small kitchen.

Katja turned as her husband came in the door, "Karl, Karl—Jake has the wonderful news—he and Raisa Schutz will be married next month and he wants for all of us to attend!"

Unexpectedly, Karl extended his hand to his oldest son, saying, "That is good news, Jakob; it is good you will take a wife. She will settle you down and make a *man* of you."

Jake smiled in spite of the implication of his father's comment. "I am glad you all will come to the wedding. We plan to have a wedding dance in the Schutz barn after the ceremony. Mr. Schutz has hired a good German polka band and we will have tables of food and good beer for all to celebrate *Hey Ho Hockzeit*. I will see you, but now I better ride back into town. Raisa and I have a lot to do to prepare for our big day." He turned to embrace his mother, "And Ma, try to get more rest; you look awfully tired. Make those kids do more of the work. Love you, Ma, see you later." With that, Jake strode out the front door, leaped onto the back of his horse and galloped back down the road toward Lovell.

Jake and Raisa were married the first week of February. Both families and their many friends were there to help them celebrate their marriage. When Karl had reached out to shake his son's hand a month before, the ice in their relationship began to melt. Karl approved of Jake's new wife and wished them both well. All of the wedding guests had a good old-fashioned celebration at the *Hockzeit* polka dance after the wedding.

Katja and Karl danced the polka until they collapsed onto the bench to drink a glass of cold German beer. "*Ja*, Karl, it is times like this that I feel like a girl again." She laughed gaily and Karl noticed the happy smile on her face and wished he could see that more often.

In early summer it was apparent Raisa was expecting. Karl commented to Katja in the privacy of their bedroom one night, "*Ja*, I see that Raisa is going to have a baby. Jake is a good planter of the Kessel seed!"

In November 1920, Karl and Katja became grandparents for the first time. Their new granddaughter was christened Elizabeth, but everyone called her Beth. She was a healthy baby with those sky-blue Kessel eyes, a tiny cherubic face framed with thick, straw-colored hair. Jake and Raisa were living close to the Schutz farm, so Raisa had lots of help with her new baby.

She was the first grandchild for both sets of grandparents and all of her aunts and uncles couldn't help but spoil her.

When their new grandchild was around, Katja saw a different side of Karl, a gentler side that she had not seen with his own children. This attention had not been given to his own children, and especially to his new son, Henry, who was less than a year older than their granddaughter. It was almost as if he had taken the children she had borne him, for granted. With the passage of time, Katja softened her attitude toward "her duty" in the marriage bed; but, she limited sex to those few days during her month in which she knew she could not conceive. Karl was not completely happy with this new arrangement, but it eased the strain in their relationship and they had fewer arguments. During this time, Katja noticed that her body was changing, punctuated by persistent and irritating night sweats and more headaches.

One spring day while watching her granddaughter and son play in the yard, it suddenly occurred to Katja that this unconditional love she felt for her granddaughter was what her father must have felt for his grandsons, before she took them from him. Because of that, they had grown up without the kind of love and support given to children by their grandparents. Had her parents loved her sons as much as she loved Beth? Katja recalled how her father played with and doted on her sons. Of course he loved and cherished them; he showed that in everything he did—even traveling far to make sure they were safely on the ship to America. Katja vowed to love this child as her parents had loved their grandsons.

That April, before the farmers could get into their thawing fields, Karl saddled his buckskin horse and headed into Lovell. He had heard that Ned Turner was talking about putting his farm up for sale. Karl knew that it was a good farm about five miles out of Lovell. He turned the horse off the main road and down the lane into Ned Turner's farm. Karl spotted Ned down by the corrals pitching hay to his cattle. He reined in his horse, climbed down from the saddle, tying the reins to a corral post. "Ned Turner?"

The man turned and answered, "You bet, that's me, and what be your name?"

Karl put on his best smile as he extended his hand. "I'm Karl Kessel from Kane, and I thought I'd stop by today to see if the rumor I heard, about you selling out, was true."

Ned Turner stuck the pitchfork into a pile of hay and jumped the corral fence. "Oh sure, I have met you before I think, a couple years back. *Ja,* Karl, it's true, the wife and I want to move up to Montana where her people are from. This here is a darn good farm; do you have time to take a look at it?"

The two men walked to a nearby field where Karl bent down and scooped up a handful of soil. He rolled it around in his hand for a bit, and squeezed some between his fingers. To Ned Turner's surprise, Karl lifted the dirt to his nose and smelled it. "Some say this is river bottom ground. It might have been river ground a long time ago, but all the farming has taken the sediment's nutrients out."

Ned Turner was quick to defend his farm. "I'm sure at one time it was riverbed ground; the river runs a mile to the north now. But looking at those bluffs, this whole valley was once a river bed. It's still darn good ground, Karl. I have about eighty irrigated acres here and am thinking of asking around $75 an acre. If that sounds like something you'd like to talk about, we can go in and sit at the table, have a cup of coffee, and talk business?"

The two men walked back to the adobe and log farmhouse. Karl made a mental note that Katja would not like this house any more than she liked the one they lived in now, but he couldn't worry about that now. The two men sat at the kitchen table with their cups of hot coffee. Karl spoke first. "Frankly Ned, I was looking for a place I could buy for around $60 an acre. I'm interested in your farm, if you could come down a little on the price, that is."

Ned Turner took a sip of coffee and scribbled some figures on a pad of paper on the table. He looked up and smiled as he said, "I've heard that you're a frugal and shrewd businessman, and you drive a hard bargain. The best I can do is around $65 an acre; will that work for you? The price includes the house and all the outbuildings as well. I don't think you are going to find a better deal anywhere!"

A bright smile spread over Karl's face and crinkled his sky-blue eyes as he slapped the table, "DONE!"

Later on, the two men rode into town to arrange a follow-up loan to the $3,000 Karl gave Turner as a down payment. He didn't have any trouble securing the rest of the loan plus interest for the next four years. He agreed to repay the bank after the fall harvest for the next four years. Turner told Karl that he wouldn't be ready to move until later in the fall after the harvest was in and they could get packed up. Karl agreed that would work well for him, too.

On the ride back out to Kane that day, Karl thought about telling Katja. *I already know what that is going to be like. She never understands that I have to get to a certain point with the land and money before I'm able to build her the house she wants. Well, I will just keep it to myself for a while, waiting for a good time to tell her.*

By harvest time in the fall of 1922, Karl still had not told his wife about the new farm. He knew he was putting off the inevitable and would have to tell her soon—a deed he didn't relish.

Karl had decided not to buy one of the new open-geared gas tractors to pull the wheat threshing machine. He thought they were experimental and was satisfied to work with his Percherons, and with what he knew. However, his knew his friend in Emblem, John Wamhoff, had purchased a massive, iron Minneapolis Moline tractor in 1918, and he claimed the tractor did the work of four horses! In fact, John often rented out the great iron beast to his neighbors. The enormous tractor made the ground shake and rumble when it was fired up. That was not something Karl was ready for; he wasn't one to take chances or experiment. But John was; he had purchased one of the first automobiles in Germania in 1914, the same year his youngest son, Arnold, was born.

Katja did not look forward to harvesting the wheat. It was a hot, dusty job and she and the neighbor women were expected to serve up gigantic amounts of food to the *Meitheal,* or workers, who went from farm to farm to help with the threshing. Neighbor helped neighbor during harvest, which made the difficult work go easier and much faster. The threshing machines were powered with steam tractosr with a large belt running between it and the threshing machine; the machines did a good job of separating the wheat from the straw. The wheat or grain flowed out of the long tin chutes at the rear of the mill where four or five men would be ready with grain bags. The grain was carried to a waiting wagon and taken to the farmer's granary or a nearby town to sell.

As if there weren't enough minuses about the job itself, threshing grain was also an itchy job. Little grain barbs twisted and turned, burrowing deep in the sweaty skin of the workers necks and backs, usually where it was difficult to scratch. Threshing wasn't all work, however; and in the evenings, or especially on the night the threshing was completed, the farmers and their womenfolk held a dance. There was always someone who played the fiddle or accordion. When the joyful music began everyone grabbed a partner to dance a jig or the polka. Of course, the beer flowed down parched throats and managed to ease and fuel tired muscles. During harvest, beer was often served at the noon and supper meal—most Germans were proud to call it German water.

Celebrating the end of threshing was the one rare occasion when Karl Kessel and his wife came together to dance the polka. Katja looked forward to the harvest dance all year. It was the one night that she felt young and gay again, like in the old days when she and her husband had fun together.

Katja had taken their new baby with them and nestled him down in a stack of discarded coats which lay on the wood benches. He was a good baby; all he needed was a full tummy. The noise from the music and people having fun did not wake him; he was used to a lot of noise from his brothers and sisters. He slept for several hours in his nest of coats while his parents danced the polka. On the way home that night, Katja found herself in an unusual giddy mood as she commented to Karl, "Wasn't that great fun tonight, to see all of our friends, to celebrate the harvest and dance the polka? And the children had much fun, too, with dancing the polka and playing games outside!"

Karl responded gruffly, "*Ja*, Katja, it was fun and a good way to end the season, but now it is over. We have yet to harvest the corn. One night of fun will have to satisfy you for the rest of the year."

Katja looked to the side of the road as Karl spoke. She did not want him to see the effect his coarse words had on her. *Why does he always seem to have a word or a black mood ready to squash my rare joy? It was almost as if he can't stand to see me happy. He has to be in control of me, even my every emotion.* A familiar cold shiver slipped down Katja's back as they continued down the moonlit road toward their home. As they rode, Katja thought of her parent's relationship, of their happy marriage. She had never noticed anything other than complete devotion to each other, so unlike her marriage. Katja felt that she and Karl were always at odds, that they rarely agreed in any of the decisions. He made all the important decisions, rarely confiding in her or asking her opinion. That lack of communication made her feel as if she was nothing more than his servant—certainly not his cherished wife or confident.

Karl's mind was on the weather and the coming corn harvest, an entirely different procedure from that of wheat. Early the next morning, Karl hitched the team to the mowing machines and drove them into the cornfield.

Addressing his sons and a new hired man, he said, "*Ja*, I will cut the corn about six inches above the ground level and you boys walk behind and collect the stalks into bundles or sheaves. The younger boys and the girls will tie about six to eight sheaves together and leaned them against each other to form the tent-shaped stook."

In a few days, the older boys and the hired man went back to the field and selected about thirty sheaves and put them into stacks like round huts. Karl rode his horse into the field after the men had been at work for three hours. "I marked three stacks that you will have to rebuild to allow the corn to dry; they are not arranged as I like. Remember also, to build them so they will not let in any rain."

Karl and some of his neighbors had jointly invested in a "threshing set" that consisted of a steam engine, a threshing mill, and an elevator for lifting the corn onto the rack. When the corn was ready to be threshed, Karl sent word the next evening to Henry Goetz, his neighbor. Henry brought the equipment to Karl's farm so it would be ready to go in the morning. The next day Henry and his son arrived before breakfast and, after filling the tank with water, they lit a fire in the engine. When the fire boiled the water, it produced steam and the power to run the engine. The farmers were just finishing up with the huge breakfast Katja prepared, when the steam whistle on the engine blew. It was *TIME* to thresh!

Two or three men on the mill opened the stacked corn sheaves and threw them into the hopper. Karl volunteered, "I will work on the mill with Christian and Henry, because I want no accidents to happen on my farm." Two weeks earlier, at another farm, an accident had occurred during threshing. One of the men on the mill wasn't paying attention and was caught by a moving arm and severely injured. Accidents were not rare when working around the crude machinery, especially when men were tired from the grueling physical work and long hours.

Always during threshing, Katja's job was to provide meals for the harvesting crew when they were on their farm. After the noon meal, she looked at the stack of dishes in her kitchen sink. *Mein Gott, when is this endless hard work going to get slow or become easier? I do not have the energy as I once did. It is good that I have my daughters to help in the kitchen, but I am still getting tired of it all, year after year.*

After the harvest was in and the work had slowed to a crawl, Karl was in an unusual jovial mood. He walked into the kitchen on Friday evening after chores and announced that the next morning the Kessel family would pack a lunch and drive their wagon to the Big Horns for a picnic. "*Ja*, tomorrow will be an Indian summer day and we should take advantage of the good weather; winter weather will blow in before we know it."

Katja thought she must be dreaming. She turned her weary face to her husband in disbelief and asked, "What—what did you just say? Are you making joke with me, Karl?"

With his blue eyes twinkling and a rare smile softening his face, Karl turned to her and the rest of his family as he repeated his offer to take them on a picnic to the mountains. Katja was elated. At last a relaxing day and a trip to the mountains, the mountains she only had time to only look at, month after month, year after year. Now, with the news of a picnic she suddenly didn't feel quite so tired. With a luminous smile on her face, Katja cheerfully instructed Ralf, Johnny, and Eddie to go to the chicken house and kill three of the young fryers. The boys didn't have to be asked twice as this was one of their favorite tasks.

The two older boys opened the gate to the chicken coop and selected three fat, young chickens. They each grabbed a chicken by the feet and with a rapid twist, broke the neck, and released the chickens to do their wild death dance. Karl had shown them how to gut the chickens and with a swift slice of the knife, Ralf and Johnny opened the bellies of their respective fowls. This was not one of Ralf's favorite chores so he let his younger brother Eddie gut his chicken.

Katja had a sizable pot of water boiling when the boys brought the gutted chickens to the kitchen. She plunged them into the pot to loosen their feathers, and took them back into the yard to pluck the feathers off. They made sure to put the feathers into a special bag that Katja would use later, adding to the goose feathers for their beds, comforters, and pillows.

Katja sent Louise and Dottie to the garden to bring in cucumbers, tomatoes, and potatoes, so she could prepare the rest of the picnic. The entire household had difficulty getting to sleep that night in anticipation of the frivolity of the next day. However, Katja did not drift off to sleep as quickly as the rest of the family, she thought of how Jake would have loved to go to the mountains with his family when he was a boy. Although she knew he now enjoyed going with his own wife and young friends as often as they could.

The next morning the Kessel household arose early and, after a hearty breakfast, loaded the aromatic picnic lunch and some old blankets into the wagon bed. Karl sent Johnny and Ralf down to the barn to hook the black Percheron team up to the wagon. When the horses were ready, the family climbed into the large, iron-wheeled wagon. Katja put on her sun bonnet and sat beside Karl on the front seat while the children found a seat in the wagon bed among the picnic paraphernalia. With a flip of the reins, Karl drove his prize team of horses down the lane and turned east toward the Big Horns.

Katja had to pinch her arm to realize this was not a dream, but a trip she had dreamed of for years. The sun was bright and fell warm on her face as she looked out over the fence to the stubble of the wheat field they had recently harvested. The cluster of cottonwood trees, which bordered the field, stood in sharp contrast between the golden wheat stubble and the destination of the day, the cool slate blue of the Big Horn Mountains. On the lengthy, bumpy trip to the mountain, the nearness and heady aroma of the fried chicken and potato salad eventually proved to be too much for the children, who were sequestered in the rear of the wagon bed. First one, then another child slid under the cover of the blanket with a juicy piece of fried chicken clutched in their greasy fingers. Their parents were busy talking and enjoying the beautiful day, oblivious to what was happening to their picnic lunch in the rear of the wagon.

When they arrived at a shady grove of aspens, Karl pulled the team to a stop, jumped down, and tied them to a tree. "Okay, let's get out of this wagon and have us a picnic!" Karl reached up to take Katja's hand and helped her down from the wagon; he dropped the tailgate so the children could climb out. They each carried a cloth-wrapped dish of food to the large blanket which Katja spread on the grass. She uncovered the bowls of food, then stopped and began to laugh, "I think somebody was hungry and could not wait to arrive for our mountain picnic!"

Six little guilty faces were suddenly serious and fearful as their mother discovered what they had done. Katja smiled and gathered them in her arms, "Don't worry, there is still plenty for our picnic and I am glad that you liked my cooking so much!" With their appetites suddenly renewed, they all plopped down on the blanket to have their long-awaited picnic in the mountains.

Later that day, after the family had consumed the wonderful picnic lunch, the children were amusing themselves, exploring the rocks and woods, Karl and Katja relaxed on the blanket under the grove of ponderosa pine trees. Karl reached for his clay pipe, lit it, and took a long drag of the smoke. Katja looked up at her husband and began to reminisce. "Karl, this day reminds me of the old times back in Surtschin, when we went on secluded picnics in the great oak woods above Papa's farm. Do you remember those days, huh, Karl?" In that particular moment she felt happy, and for a time almost forgot her many disappointments and the never-ending caustic brutality of farm life in Wyoming.

Karl propped himself up on his elbow and, smiling at his wife, said, "For sure, I do remember those sweet days." He took a deep breath, "Katja, I have been saving some good news to tell you. It is about our future."

Katja looked at Karl, her eyes wide, she thought, *Oh, dear Lord, he is going to tell me of more land or another piece of machinery that he needs. When is he going to have enough machines, enough land, enough cows? I've had enough of this all!*

Karl reached over and took her hand in a rare display of tenderness, and continued, "Katja, I have bought a wonderful farm only five miles east of Lovell. I received a good bargain on the land. It has a barn, granary, chicken coops, and a small house. Before you see the house Katja, I must tell you, it is not much. It is an adobe house, large, but old." He quickly added, "I know, I know, you are not fond of the adobe, but it will have to do for a year or two. I am thinking we can move to this new farm after the holiday season. I have a buyer for my farm in Kane and he is willing to wait for it until we move to the new place."

Karl's inner alarm rose as he glanced at Katja's ashen face and her clenched jaw—*this is not going well.*

Karl rose to his feet and paced back and forth as he continued. "We can live in the house that is there on the new farm until I am able to begin to build the house I have so long promised to you. I hope you will be happy with this move, I know we have lived in Kane for many years and have many memories on this farm. But Katja, I believe this move will be a good one for us, in every way."

Katja was stunned. She couldn't move. Thoughts on top of thoughts raced through her mind, especially of the adobe house. *At least it isn't a dugout, perhaps I wait until I see it.*

In her mind she went over and over the news Karl had cleverly introduced during their picnic. *Of course he would do something like take me on a picnic, to catch me unguarded, to drop the news of another farm on me. Such a foolish man to think he could soften me up. Time will tell if this is a good thing; time is running out for him to build me this good house he promises for twenty years.*

The family agreed that the day on the mountain had been wonderful, a rare treat. But Karl pouted most of the way home that day because he had anticipated a more exuberant response to his exciting news. *Acht, that woman, what does it take to make her happy? I do not think I know anymore!*

FEBRUARY 1923

Karl and Katja packed up their children and everything they owned and moved to the new farm near Lovell. Katja did not adjust easily to the adobe house. She hated the constant, fine dust that sifted through the thatched ceiling onto her furniture and floors; it was near to impossible to keep things clean. Of course she had known what to expect because half of their house in Kane had been constructed with the mud bricks.

Karl was more than pleased with the new farm and the harvest yield that next fall, the return was more than he had hoped for and he had no trouble making the first payment to the bank. He had six huge Percherons in his stable and he needed all of them to farm with. Karl made the decision to buy more cattle; feeding cattle was a smart way to make more money on the farm. He had around twenty head of Herford cattle and when the price of cattle dropped from $75 to $25 per head, Karl decided it was time to *buy more!*

That spring, Karl traveled to the stockyard auction in Billings and bought twenty head of yearlings to fattened up and sell. He settled on another thirty head of Herford heifers and one prize bull. He bought when the price was low and would feed them sell when it went up, making a fine profit. He planned to graze the cattle in the Big Horns in the summer months, bringing them down in the winter and feeding them hay, sugar beet and corn silage. This was a good moneymaker, but he knew he had to be smart and not over-extend himself. Every year his herd doubled in numbers. His success was intoxicating and Karl loved it.

Karl and Katja farmed the new location for several years. Katja tried to keep her discontent to herself, but disappointment and frustration rolled, festered, and seethed deep inside her. She was determined to be patient and wait until her husband was ready to build the house he had promised. As before, years went by and Karl always had one reason or another why he couldn't build the promised house.

In 1926, Jake and Raisa moved to Michigan in search of their fortune. They had two children, Beth and a son Arnold who was named after Karl's lost friend. Jake wanted to try working at something other than farming. Raisa had an uncle in Port Huron, Michigan, who promised there was work for Jake. When their son and his family moved away, Karl and Katja learned for themselves what it was like when their grandchildren were taken from them. Now it was their turn to feel the effects of this void in their lives, even though the move was good for young Kessel family. Their letters were full of their success and happiness.

By summer of 1926, Katja realized she was at the end of her patience and listening to Karl's infinite excuses. Karl never once considered he had used up excuses and time for not building the promised house; his day of reckoning was drawing nigh.

On an especially hot and sultry August day Karl walked into the cool, dim light of the kitchen in their adobe house, expecting his midday meal to be sitting on the table, waiting for him as usual. However, he found Katja sitting ramrod straight in a wooden kitchen chair, staring out the window with no expression on her face.

If Karl had looked into her smoldering ebony eyes, the fear of God would have struck him, but he didn't. He simply reacted as he always did—his fiery temper flared because he was tired, hot, and hungry. "What the hell are you doing woman? Where is my food? I am coming in to eat my noon meal and you are just sitting, looking out the window."

Karl was beside himself, but he soon learned that the anger he felt did not compare with the encompassing rage which was about to explode from his wife, like red-hot lava from a volcano. With one look at his wife's face as their eyes met, Karl knew he was in for BIG trouble—for what, he had no clue.

Katja rose from the chair, never taking her dark eyes from her husband's face. She walked slowly and purposely toward him, stopping inches from his face. "Karl, I am done with living in this hovel! You would keep me living in this dirt hole on top of the ground forever. Always one excuse after the other. I know now that the farm is paid for—it is PAID FOR! How do I know this? The banker congratulated me last week when I was shopping in town."

Karl felt his knees grow weak, and his bowels threatened to let loose.

Katja continued, "I know this grand house you promise is nothing more than a hollow promise, which you have used to keep me away from your other plans for more than twenty years. TWENTY years, Karl! Soon I will be dead, and *still* there will be no house. All these years, asking for a decent house in which to live, asking for anything extra I wanted or needed, always you with an excuse why not! For many years I believed someday you would build me this house you promised." Katja took a deep breath as her eyes glowed black with her rage, "But no, Karl, everything is for you, it has always been for *you*, Karl, what Karl wants, when Karl wants, where Karl wants! You always say to me, 'Oh, Katja, wait until I buy more cattle, more machinery, more land—I will build you a fine house.' I no longer believe anything you say to me, Karl, NO MORE!"

Karl almost made a feeble effort to respond, but Katja's small fist struck his shoulder, pushing him backward. "I left my parents and family in Surtschin. I left the music, a good house, and fine garden to follow you. You, my husband—I followed to this godforsaken land. I have tried so hard to be a good wife and helpmate to you, and what do I get? First one dirt house to live in, now another! I have worked myself to the bone, I have given you eight children and none of it is enough that I should have a decent house to live in? If you are going to build me this house, you had better do it NOW, because I will not live in this hovel one day more, I WILL NOT! I will go to the hotel in Lovell to live, and I go now!"

Katja moved around her husband, walked to the front door where she picked up her suitcase. She shoved the old door open and walked out. She was a sight to behold—a tiny, middle-aged woman, dressed in a fresh blue-print house dress, her salt-and-pepper hair pulled back in a tight bun, clutching a small suitcase securely in her hand as she marched toward the road, putting one little black shoe in front of the other.

Karl could not believe his ears or his eyes. *Who is this woman? This raging female could not be my wife, my Katja—what has happened to her, is she crazy?*

He didn't know that the female change of life had given fuel to Katja's innermost anxieties. Raging hormones gave her courage, stubbed out her patience, and created a formidable force, which was not going to dissolve with another promise.

Karl was absolutely stunned when his wife walked out the front door of their adobe house. Panic punched him in the gut. He ran after her and yelled, "Katja, Katja! Okay, let us speak of this thing and make the plans now for the house. I have been thinking it is time to do this thing. Put the suitcase down now and stay here so we can make the plans, today—now!"

Katja turned around to face her husband, "I told you, Karl, I don't believe your words. You say you have plans for this house? Okay, what plans do you have? Let me see them."

Karl hastily explained that he would go now, into Lovell, and talk to a man about building a brick house for them. He knew brick would not cost too much because the brick factory was right there, in Lovell.

Not about to let Karl off the hook that easily, Katja turned to walk toward their car and said, "Good, I will go with you. If there are no plans, you can drop me off at the hotel!"

In the spring of 1927, Karl presented Katja with a 2,500 square foot, red-brick house. He sold forty head of cattle so he could pay cash for it. The house was beautiful, with a wide, north-facing front screened porch where they could sit on warm evenings. There was electricity in their new house and Katja enjoyed her large, modern kitchen, especially the white refrigerator. Next to the kitchen was a formal dining room, bright and cheerful with light from four east-facing windows. The spacious parlor was between the dining room and the front porch. One of the greatest luxuries was the indoor plumbing. The indoor bathroom contained a sink, stool, and large, sinfully deep bathtub. When Katja saw the bathtub, her face lit up with excitement. "Oh, Karl, I can hardly wait to take a hot bath. I have waited so long for this house and I am pleased."

Karl brought new furniture from a store in Billings—a formal dining set, maple with walnut insets, including a hutch for the new dishes. He bought a sofa and two chairs, tables, and lamps for the living room. They slept in a new store-bought walnut bed and everything matched. Katja had fine furniture on which to put her crocheted doilies. They looked beautiful against the dark wood of the table, and on the arms and backs of the soft chairs and sofa in the parlor.

Hanging at the windows in the parlor and dining room were exquisite Austrian lace curtains, a gift from her family in Yugoslavia. She loved the way the sunlight filtered through the intricate pattern of the ivory lace—it was all so beautiful! She smiled to herself as she thought, *Now my dreams of a better life, an easier life have come true. I am living in the new house Karl promised since the day I stepped off the train.*

The house had three bedrooms upstairs and a full basement where the boys slept. There was a special cool room for the canned goods in the basement. One evening as they were sitting in their new parlor, Karl handed Katja the Sears Roebuck catalog. "Katja, I think you should choose new dishes, cooking pans, and linens for the beds. You decide what you want and I will order them for you. Would this please you?"

Katja was stunned, "*Ja*, Karl," she stammered, "I will be happy to look through the catalog and actually be able to order some of the things I look at." Katja spent the rest of the evening sitting in her easy chair and pouring over the pages of the catalog, happily making her decisions.

Karl realized Katja had been right to insist on the hew house. It had been time and even he was enjoying the comfort and prestige it brought him. Deep inside, he realized how hard she worked during their life together. He would never realize how hard it had been for her to leave her family behind, because he had no problem leaving his own family behind. Karl came to America with an agenda for success and THAT had always been at the head of his list, everything else was secondary. He had hoped his wife would understand this, but now realized he had asked too much of her and he feared for their marriage. Karl blamed himself as he took a long and hard look at how he had handled everything and prayed it wasn't too late for them.

After they moved into their new house in 1927, Katja was busy as usual with house and garden. No longer did she have to go into the fields. Chris had married and moved to Nebraska with his wife Martha, and Ralf was engaged. Katja was more content than she had ever been since coming to Wyoming. Her happiness was evident and she frequently told Karl how pleased she was with her new home. Karl was relieved the house issue could be put from his mind and now felt at liberty to devote all his effort to farming.

It had been months since they had settled into their new home. Karl had expected, even hoped some of Katja's new-found happiness would carry over into their bedroom. Persistently, he continued to try and have a greater degree of physical intimacy with his wife, but her unrelenting rejection became the basis of intensified disagreements between them.

Karl did not understand why she acted like she did, especially now that she had her house. She was his wife and she should do what a good wife does: submit to her husband. However, Katja was most definitely *not* of the same mind, and she dug in her heels when it came to the frequent intimacy her husband desired. She recognized the symptoms of "the change." More often than not, she woke in the night, drenched in her own sweat. She suffered from sudden migraines, mood swings, and her time of the month was erratic and heavy. Karl simply was not tuned into his wife's problems and didn't

understand how this, or any bodily change, could affect her duty to him.

Jake and Raisa returned from Michigan with the children in 1928. Times were getting hard in the east and there was no work. Jake told his family about endless lines of desperate men hoping to get work, any work; but there was none to be had. There were food/soup lines everywhere, for people who were out of work and hungry. They made the trip back from Michigan in a used, black Ford car, pulling a trailer filled with their household goods. Jake told his father about the hordes of people on the roads and in roadside camps. Everywhere, people were out of work, out of luck, and out of food, with no viable options. Jake had hoped to find work on a farm around Lovell, since the Depression wasn't as severe in Wyoming yet, especially in the rural regions.

The children, Beth and Arnold, had grown so much. Beth was eight and Arnold was five. Karl and Katja were so happy to see them and invited the little family to move into their new brick house until they found a house and work in the area. Jake was reluctant at first, but finally agreed this would be the best thing for now. He would work with his father on his farm, but only until he could find other work.

Late the first night, as he and Raisa and the children were settling into their rooms in the basement of his parent's home, Jake told Raisa, "I want to keep working here on the farm with Dad; maybe we can forget the bad feelings we have had. Besides, we need the work and the money. I promise it won't be for long. I know you want and need a place of your own—so do I."

Raisa knew that Jake still had deep-seated memories of the way his father treated him growing up. Yet he desperately wanted a relationship with his father, whom he secretly admired. She agreed that Jake's decision made sense. The couple lived with Karl and Katja for the next six months until Jake found another farm to work.

That year Karl and Katja had been married thirty years and their wedding day in Surtschin had been on her mind for days. One evening as they were sitting in their parlor, listening to Mozart on Victrola, Katja spoke. "Karl, I have been thinking it would be nice to have a party here at our house to celebrate our thirtieth anniversary. Maybe the children could help bring in the food, and—we could have the Lovell Bakery to bake a big cake. What do you think of this idea?"

Karl didn't respond immediately and Katja took this as a negative response. "Karl, would you stop please stop reading and listen for once to what I am saying to you?"

Karl peered over his wire-rimmed glasses, slightly irritated. "*Ja*, Katja, I heard what you said and was only taking time to think about it. A party you say, I don't think people would come to celebrate an anniversary; those things are usually a private, family thing."

"*Nein*, Karl, we have many friends who have had such parties and we could also have a polka band in the barn. It would be much fun I am thinking."

Karl's blue eyes twinkled as he nodded his balding head, "Okay, Katja, you go ahead and invite our friends and our children. We will have this party you would like. I have to see if I can also buy some kegs of good German beer, which we will probably have to keep hidden in the barn because of the prohibition laws."

They invited their children and many friends from the church and community. People carried in food and they danced well into the night, fueled by the German beer that Karl had smuggled into the back horse stall of the barn. Several reported that Karl and Katja probably had the best time of all as he whirled her round and round in time to the music. Katja's face had a perpetual smile the entire evening and Karl's blue eyes twinkled as they celebrated their marriage.

They went into Lovell later in the week and had a photograph made. It was the first picture they had taken with just the two of them since their marriage in Surtschin. Katja sent a copy of the picture to her parents and family in Yugoslavia, so they could see how the years had treated them.

CHAPTER 14

The Great Depression, 1929

"There will never be a road so rough that it will defeat you or a dream so far away that it will escape you. When things seem to be getting difficult, pull forth your belief and confidence in yourself." ~Mary Jane Cook

TUESDAY, OCTOBER 29, 1929

Karl and Katja were listening to the large walnut radio which occupied a position of importance on the carpeted floor in their parlor. They couldn't believe their ears—the announcer was calling this day, Black Tuesday.

Later that afternoon, Karl returned from a trip into Lovell where he bought the local newspaper. He hurried into the kitchen and not seeing his wife, called out. "Katja, Katja, where are you?"

Katja ran up the basement stairs, practically out of breath, she managed to answer, "Here Karl, I was down the basement putting away my grape preserves. Whew—let me catch my breath. What is the matter that you call for me so loudly? Are you sick?"

Karl's eyes were wide with alarm. "*Nein,* Katja, but I have just read here in the *Lovell Chronicle* that the stock market in New York City has crashed. Katja, men are jumping from skyscrapers to escape the fact their fortunes are lost. Also many banks made poor investments with savings of their clients— their money is all gone and peoples at the door want their money!"

Karl sat down in a chair beside the kitchen table. Katja moved into the kitchen, wiping her hands on her apron, "How is that possible, Karl? How can they use other people's moneys and lose them. Do they not remember where they put them? I don't understand how moneys are lost?"

Karl pulled out a chair and spread the newspaper on the table and began to read. "It says here that blame for the disaster is directed at over-production in both industry and agriculture. We have too much grain and automobiles and the like—along with high war debts, high tariffs, taxes, and unequal distribution of wealth in the nation." Karl paused to explain. "Unequal distribution of wealth means that there are only a few who are rich, some who do okay, like us, and many who are poor. Financial panic and collapse have rampaged throughout the United States and other places, too."

Several weeks after Black Tuesday, Karl and Katja sat at their kitchen table, eating an early breakfast. Katja pushed her plate back. She didn't seem to have an appetite; something was bothering her. She wrapped her hands around her coffee cup as she sipped the hot brew. She hesitated for a thought-filled moment and said, "Karl, excuse me, please, would you? Do you have time to explain to me what this word 'depression' means? I don't understand why there are no jobs and people are hungry. What is happening?"

Karl looked up from his bowl of hot oatmeal and laid his spoon on the oilcloth-covered table. "*Ja*, Katja. The government calls these troubles 'depression' because our whole money system is sick; it is broken and going down like a big hole in the road, like a depression or big down hill in the road. Or, when peoples are down in the dumps and they don't want to do anything. It's a bad, bad thing, it is!

Karl ran his palm back over his forehead. "The American banks use customers' money for investments and the operations of big companies— but they weren't as smart as they thought they were. Our country is in big trouble. I heard in town the other day that big companies and factories back east had to lay off workers because they have no business. Those workers had no work, no paycheck to pay their bills or buy goods. Many of those men couldn't pay their bank loans and lost their businesses, houses, cars and the like. It is like when you stack cards on end, one leaning against the other. When the first card goes down, it knocks down the one in front of it. Pretty soon they are all lying down."

Karl was indignant as he explained further, "*Ja*, that is what happens when you borrow too much money, borrow here, borrow there, and pretty soon it all comes down on top of you. I don't have a good education, but I know *better* than to do this."

Karl lifted his cup to his lips and took a drink of coffee and continued.

"They are saying that this problem is spreading to Europe, too. Has your mother mentioned anything that they know of this Depression?"

Katja's face wore a grim expression as she replied, "*Ja*, Karl, in the last letter I received from Mama, she said Papa told her they needed to be careful with their money, also bad times were coming to Yugoslavia."

Daily, Karl and Katja read in the newspapers that over twenty-five percent of Americans, who worked for wages, were unemployed. If people still had jobs, they had to work twice as hard for half the wages—employers had to cut back, reduce wages, or simply close the doors. The Kessels were relieved they had paid cash for their new house, and their farm was paid off.

One day about two months after Black Tuesday, Karl walked into the kitchen and sat heavily at the kitchen table. Katja looked up from her work at the sink. "Karl, what is the matter? You do not have a good look on your face."

Karl put his head down and shook it. "*Ja*, Katja, we now have two farms, because the fellow who bought our farm in Kane could not make the payments to the bank and so it is again ours. I will have to pay taxes on all this land, too. I hope it will not be a problem to us!"

The drastic drop in agricultural prices hit Wyoming farmers and ranchers later than the rest of the country, but it hit hard just the same. Bumper wheat crops from 1924–28, caused a glut in the market that caused prices to drop dramatically. Many farmers, who had purchased land and machinery on credit, were in trouble. Thousands of farmers refused to harvest their crops because of the low prices—it simply didn't pay to spend more money on something that was almost worthless. It made no sense to unemployed people suffering from hunger in the cities, why farmers refused to harvest their crops—people were hungry! Where were they supposed to get food if the farmers wouldn't plant any?

For years, Karl's friend John Wamhoff, from Emblem, hauled dozens of eggs from his large flock of chickens, into Greybull every week to sell. He usually sold several dozen eggs to local grocers, restaurants, and regular consumers; but now, few could pay for the eggs. Not wanting the eggs to go to waste, Karl heard that John had put the boxes of eggs on the street with a "FREE" sign propped up beside them. At first people were hesitant to take the eggs without paying, but finally with John's urging they helped themselves to the food. There was food, but nobody had money to buy it. Eventually the farmers stopped planting.

The Kessel family realized they were in a good place, living on a farm when the economy was depressed. They were used to living in a frugal manner; now they just pulled their belts a little tighter. They put cardboard in their shoes, and cut down old clothes for their kids, but they were able to grow their own food unlike those folks who lived in the cities.

Kids and even some adults went barefoot in the summer months, saving their precious shoes for cold weather—if they still fit. There were clothing co-ops where people traded outgrown clothing for larger or smaller sizes. People became better friends and neighbors, helping each other and using their ingenuity and wits to survive. As Karl mentioned to Katja one winter's night, "*Ja*, these bad times brings out the good in most people."

During the 1920s and well into the 1930s, society was ablaze with jazz music and the limits of Prohibition. People were eager to find something, anything, to take their minds off their troubles. One evening as Karl and Katja sat in their parlor, Katja was in a talkative mood. Karl listened and nodded occasionally as she chatted.

"Karl, have you seen the new clothes that Ralf and Johnny are wearing these days? The pants, they are so baggy with cuffs and creases down the legs, and they hold up their pants with belts instead of suspenders."

Katja was amazed as she looked through the Sears and Montgomery Ward catalogs. She couldn't envision herself wearing the clothes they showed. When Jake and Raisa returned from Michigan, Raisa was sporting a fashionable short, sassy hairstyle and a comfortable tube-style dress that stopped just below the knees. She was proud to say that she had made the dress herself from a Butterick dress pattern. She also had a new *cloche* hat which looked like a bucket and was pulled down to her eyebrows.

Katja mused, "I don't know if I like this new modern look of the clothes—this 'flapper' style."

Before Christmas 1929, another letter came from Surtschin, a letter written by Katja's father. When Katja saw the letter had been penned by her father, her breath caught in her chest. Her hands shook as she opened the letter. *Something serious has happened.*

Karl was feeding cattle in the barn when he heard Katja scream. He dropped the pitchfork and ran to the house. He found her down on her knees on the kitchen floor, a letter clutched in her hand. She was screaming and pounding the floor with her fists and her face was contorted as tears rained from her eyes.

"Katja, *mein Gott*, what has happened? Is that a letter that you have in your hand? Who is it from? Tell me, woman; what is it?"

Katja looked at her husband and in a grief-stricken daze, put the letter in his outreached hand. Karl took the letter and smoothing it out, began to read Christian Mehll's words.

> December 15, 1929
> Dear Daughter Katja:
> I am filled with sorrow that I must tell you of the saddest of news. Your mother's heart stopped to beat. When I came in from the field, I found her lying on the kitchen floor and she was gone. We have laid her to rest in the church cemetery in Surtschin.
>
> We know that this will be of great shock and sadness to you, dear daughter. But you must live your life and care for your family. Christian and Katharina, as well as Elizabetha and Helmut, are taking watch of me. I will be fine as time goes along, but right now it is hard not to miss your dear mother. She was a fine woman and wife to me, and mother to our three children. I am blessed that she was a part of my life.
>
> I am sending you a picture we had taken at the funeral. This is so you can see your brother Christian, his wife Katharina, their seven children, and young Christian's new wife, Sophia. As you will see, my hair is now white as the snow that lies in the fields. We are all well and trying to get on with our lives without your mother. We hope you and your family are the same.
> Your loving Papa

Karl bent over and slipped his hands under Katja's armpits, gently pulling her to her feet. He wrapped his arms around her small quivering body. "Katja, oh, Katja, I am so sorry, this is terrible news from your papa. Here, here, come into the living room, sit here in the soft chair."

Karl didn't really know what to do for Katja, but he knew this was the worst possible news from Surtschin—something she had always dreaded hearing. He knew how much Katja loved her mother and how close they had been.

"Oh, Karl," Katja sobbed into her hands, "I knew this would happen someday, but now it comes, and I am not ready for it. I feel so—so, empty and sad and I cannot be there with my family to grieve as I should. It just doesn't seem right. I am certain my papa needs me now to help comfort him."

Karl took Katja's trembling, work worn hands into his own and held them firmly. "I am here with you, my Katja; I will help you to get through this sad news. Your papa has Christian and Elizabetha to watch over him. I also loved your mama—she was a good woman, always kind to me. Do you remember when she made me the good suit of clothes to wear to the concert before we were married? We will pray together and ask our Lord to bring us peace."

Karl quickly added, "You realize, of course, that it is not possible for you to go to Surtschin in this Depression. So, you must be strong now; this is the way of life and we must accept it." Karl bent to kiss his wife's damp cheek. "Would you like for me to go to the kitchen and make some tea to help you feel better? I think it would be good; just stay in the chair and rest."

Karl was uncomfortable when Katja was not herself. He knew what a strong woman she was and yet, when something happened to crack her strong demeanor, it shook him to the core. Karl left the parlor and walked quickly to the kitchen. He wasn't good in the kitchen, but he did know how to make tea. Soon it was ready and he carried two steaming cups of the hot brew into the parlor, carefully handing one of them to his wife.

"Okay, now we will drink our tea and perhaps feel better. We will have to tell our family of this news when they come in from the fields for supper, this evening. Would you like for me to call Mrs. Cooper to come and prepare the evening meal, so you do not have to think about it?" Karl asked.

Shaking her head, Katja responded, "*Nein*, Karl, I want to make the supper myself. It will help me to not to think about the letter; we will tell the children about their grandmother later."

That afternoon as Katja busied herself in her kitchen, she thought of how kind and loving Karl had been to her. *This* was the Karl she had married, the Karl she fell in love with. That man had seemed to disappear from her life until this moment, this day. She hoped and prayed he would stay or at least reappear often, but she knew it probably would not happen.

When Ralf, Johnny, and Eddie came in from the fields, and the three youngest children arrived home from school, they walked into a different house than the one they had left earlier that morning. Katja was in the kitchen preparing every sort of favorite dish she could think of. She was almost frantic in her preparations, trying desperately to blot out the fact that her mother was dead. Her children stood watching as she literally flew around the kitchen. She was not even aware they were observing her. Finally, Johnny spoke up. "Ma, Ma, what are you doing? Why are you cooking so much food? Are we having company to supper?"

Katja whirled around, startled by their intrusion into her private world of grief. "What? What are you doing just standing there? All of you go now into the parlor where your father sits waiting for you."

One by one they filed into the parlor. Their eyes were wide with bewilderment as they questioned why their parents were acting so strange. Karl was sitting in one of the soft chairs and Katja went to stand near him. Karl waited until everyone was seated and he spoke. "We have received bad news from Surtschin. *Grosvater* Christian Mehll has written that your *Grosmuter* Theraisa has died of a tired heart. They have buried her in the church cemetery in Surtschin. This news has been hard for your mother."

One by one the children went to their mother, kissing her cheeks and embracing her in their arms. They did not feel the gravity of this news because they had never known their grandparents, and had only seen pictures and heard stories of them and their home in Surtschin, Yugoslavia. They were, however, concerned for their mother and how she was taking the news. This coming Christmas celebration might not be like the other ones they had known. It would be hard for their mama to celebrate the holiday season and be joyous with her family.

When Jake heard the news of his grandmother's death he hurried to his parent's home. On the way he thought about his Oma, he only had misty memories of her. He remembered her kitchen had smelled like dough and chicken soup and that she had loved classical music. But he had only been six years old when they left Surtschin and his brother Chris had been four.

Jake pulled up to the farmhouse and walked into his mother's kitchen, where she stood at the sink. He gently folded her in his arms and whispered in her fragrant black hair, "I'm so sorry, Ma, I know you want to be over there with your family. You will see her again; you know that and you've got to hang onto that thought."

As it turned out, Katja poured herself into holiday preparations, hanging homemade and store-bought decorations throughout the house. She urged

Karl to go to the mountains early to cut their tree so she could decorate it with electric lights and glass ornaments. She was obsessed with making this Christmas special for her family. The harder she worked, the more she hoped for a distraction from her loss, and thoughts of the Christmas seasons she knew as a child in Surtschin.

The kitchen was steamy and fragrant with baking Christmas strudels, molasses and sugar cookies, and the pungent dried fruitcakes. Katja plunged her hands into the bread dough; she pounded, kneaded, and rolled it with fury, in an attempt to release her incessant grief. She was grateful she had her memories and held tight to them, reliving them in her mind again and again.

Katja had saved all her mother's letters and stored them in the bottom drawer of the dresser. One afternoon, she pulled out the drawer of the walnut dresser. She drew out the string-tied packet of letters from her mother and added the final letter from her father and the picture he sent.

Her mother's death haunted her like a bad dream. Katja realized the death had consumed another portion of her heart. She knew the day would come when her father's death would take even more of her heart. *How much heart do I have left to keep on living?*

After Christmas, Katja had more time on her hands and she acknowledged her grief in her own private way. She didn't want her children to worry and fuss over her. *It is better this way. Let them think I am coping well, let them get on with their lives and not worry over me.*

But, frequently, she returned to the privacy of her bedroom and the dresser where she kept her mother's letters. Bending over, she removed the photo her father had sent of himself, her brother Christian, his wife Katharina, and their children.

Her finger reached out to trace the form of her father's aging face. She sat and stared at the photo, saying to herself, *Oh, Papa, look at your hair, it is like a cloud on your dear head, so white. I can still see the papa I remember inside that aging face and under the white hair. Please Papa, stay well, I can't lose you, too, not for a long time.* Katja shook her head in disbelief. *I was so worried you would be the first to go to your reward, especially after you were injured and in your bed for so long. Now I sit here, looking at the picture of my family and it is my mother who is missing. You sit alone without her at your side, oh, Papa, Papa!* Katja allowed bitter tears to fall from her eyes and the sadness to seep from her heart.

Later in the month, Karl and Katja invited Jake and Raisa and their family to Sunday dinner. They arrived early so Raisa could help her mother-in-law in the kitchen. The children went out to the barn to see the huge Percheron horses. Karl said, "Jakob, come, come out to the front porch and let's have

a smoke before the dinner is ready. There is something I want to talk to you about."

Jake followed his father out onto the front porch; they each took a seat in a green, wooden chair. As they lit their pipes, Karl asked, "*Ja,* Jakob, so how is that farm doing out by Cowley? Did you have a good crop?"

Jakob, sensing that something was up, spoke slowly and deliberately, "*Ja,* Dad, we had a pretty good harvest, but we did not get good prices for the wheat and all. We are struggling and I am not sure what we are going to do. I think we will be looking for another farm or another job since Mr. Riddell wants us off the place by spring."

Karl took a deep pull from his pipe and said, "Well, I think I might have a solution to your problem, if it is one you want to consider. You know I have the old home place back, since Mel Rogers couldn't make the payments. He tore down the old house and put up a pretty good wooden house. You and Raisa could move out there and you could farm that place. I wouldn't take a percentage of your crop, either. Talk it over with Raisa and let me know."

Jake didn't know what to think at first. Here was his father making an offer to him about farming some of his land. Jake wasn't sure how everything would work out, but he realized this farm was far enough away so his father wouldn't be looking over his shoulder all the time, not to the extent he once did. That night after Raisa put the two children to bed, she walked into their small front room. Jake was standing, looking out the window.

"Jake, what are you looking at? Is there somebody out there?"

Jake turned and held out his arms to her. Raisa moved quickly across the small space and embraced her husband. "Jake, what is it? Is something bothering you? Tell me."

Jake gently pushed her at arm's length. "Let's go out on the front step. There is something I have to tell you."

They settled down on the worn wooden front step and Jake lit up his pipe. "Raisa, today, Dad made me an offer, to farm the old place in Kane. I know it's a ways out there, but we would be farming for ourselves and I don't think we have any better options or opportunities, especially in these bad times. Dad said he didn't expect us to sharecrop the farm, and that's good. But—it's just that Kane is so far from Lovell, and the children would have to go to a small school out there."

Raisa reached down and picked up her husband's labor-hardened hand and buried it in her own. "Jake, we need to have someplace to earn a living. You know I hate farming, but I don't think we have much of a choice now, do we? At least we would have the opportunity to make some money and have a roof over our heads, which is more than a lot of folks have."

In January 1932, after the first of the year, Jake and Raisa moved out to the old family farm. They were happy to have a place of their own, even if it meant living way out in Kane. The new house was not large, but it was fresh and clean, and seemed to be waiting for the little family. As time grew near for twelve-year-old Beth to receive her Lutheran confirmation instruction, Jake and Raisa decided to let their daughter live near Lovell with her grandparents. She could attend school and confirmation classes in Lovell with her Uncle Hank, who was a year older than she. Karl and Katja were delighted to have their granddaughter living with them. There were certain adjustments but things were working out fine, until around the first of November.

Beth came running into the kitchen where her grandmother was busy canning. The girl's eyes were red from crying, her face tense with alarm as her hands pressed against her tummy. Alarmed, Katja asked, "Landsakes, Beth, what in the world is the matter with you? Are you sick?"

Beth looked up at her grandmother and sobbed, "My stomach hurts and when I went to the bathroom, there was blood. I don't remember hurting myself down there. Oh, Oma, I think I am dying!" Beth wept convulsively.

Katja put her arm around her granddaughter and without a lot of pomp and circumstance, said, "Oh my, you aren't going to die, you have just gotten your first 'time of the month.' It is not anything to cry over, it will happen to you for a few days every month. It happens to all women—it is your body getting ready for you to have babies someday. Stop crying now, and help me tie some rags around you to soak up the blood."

Katja took her granddaughter into the bedroom and opened a drawer full of old rags. She pulled one out and tied it diaper-style around her granddaughter. "Now, when that is soiled, take it off and put it in the soaking bucket out on the back porch, and put on a fresh one. Be sure to wash yourself every morning and night."

Katja's sister-in-law Katharina now wrote the family letters, telling of the news from Surtschin and the family there. She didn't write often, perhaps only once or twice a year, usually when she sent Christmas greetings. Katharina reported that Katja's father was doing well, but he was lonesome. As a remedy, she and her husband Christian had insisted that *Grosvater* move in with them and their children. He was no trouble at all and his grandchildren loved having him there.

In 1930, Karl and Katja's daughter Louise and their son Ralf both married people from the Lovell area. Katja and Karl were pleased with their new son-in-law and daughter-in-law. Left at home were: Johnny, eighteen; Dottie, sixteen; Eddie, fourteen; and Henry, who was twelve but looked sixteen. Johnny helped his father in the fields on a regular basis and of course, Eddie and Henry were expected to work as much as they could. Their father finally saw the light and agreed they should finish grade school and even go on to high school. He now realized that an education was important because he had seen what the lack of education had done to his older sons and their opportunities for work. Eddie was proving to be a born farmer. He couldn't get enough of the farm and was an apt pupil, following Karl's every word of advice.

Beth noticed a lot of things around her grandparents' house, and one of them was how her Uncle Johnny never seemed to do his share of the work. He stayed out late at night, often not arriving home until the sun was coming up. One day, as Beth was cleaning up in the kitchen, her uncle sat at the table, getting a head start on his Saturday night activities. Curiosity got the best of the young girl as she inquired, "Uncle Johnny, why do you stay out all night? Mama says you go dancing and drinking beer till the sun comes up—with girls."

Johnny sat down his glass of beer, glared at his niece, and snapped, "Why don't you go study your confirmation lesson and keep your snotty nose out of my business? You are getting a bit too big for your britches!" With that, he slapped Beth across the face. Her hand flew to her reddening cheek; tears rose in her blue eyes and threatened to roll down her freckled face as she turned and fled to her bedroom.

Katja had just walked into the room and witnessed everything. She flew at Johnny like a hen off the nest, grabbing him by the collar and slapping his back. "What do you think you are doing, slapping a little girl like that? Get out of my kitchen and go do something worthwhile for a change. But before you go, you listen to me: don't *ever* slap Beth again, do you hear me? If you do, you will feel my hand as well and it will have a board in it. Now, OUT! OUT!"

Karl heard about what his son had done and shook his head in disgust. He was disturbed by many things this son had done lately, and he was irritated by Johnny's arrogant, devil-may-care attitude. Karl had also noticed his middle son had a reputation around Lovell and spent his nights drinking and chasing women. But he had more important things to concern himself with; as long as the Johnny showed up to do his share of the work in the fields, Karl couldn't be bothered.

One spring morning, Karl had gone to the fields to instruct Eddie and Hank with their tasks for the day. He knew he could count on them; they were always where they were supposed to be and both worked hard. They were good sons. Johnny was also supposed to be in the fields at sunup, but once again he was absent. After Karl and his two younger sons had been working in the fields about an hour, Karl noticed Johnny lurching across the rough-plowed ground.

As Johnny came closer, Karl didn't waste words. He was angry and had enough of this kind of behavior. "Where in the hell have you been? You were supposed to be out here in this field when the sun came up, like the rest of us!"

Johnny lifted his head and looked at his father through bloodshot, squinted eyes and snarled, "Oh hell, Dad, I just woke up. I'm here now, so don't get all worked up."

His indifferent attitude and shoddy appearance was all Karl needed to throw him into a fit of rage. Carrying his shovel, Karl quickly closed the space between them. Johnny had turned his back and started toward the tractor when Karl bellowed, "You irresponsible, ungrateful sloth, there is no way that someone like you came from my loins!" With that Karl wielded the long-handled shovel and landed a hard blow right between his son's shoulder blades, knocking him face first into the damp soil. "You are a disgrace and an embarrassment to this family. Look at you, unshaven, your hair still speaks of the pillow, and you reek of bad booze and cheap women."

Johnny staggered to his feet, reeling and coughing. He was no innocent when it came to fighting and he whirled toward his father, "Why the hell did you hit me with that shovel? You crazy old man! I'm not going to take another minute or another day of your abuse. You drive away all of your sons, don't you?" Johnny drew in a deep breath and thought, *why quit now? Let him have it all.*" You have always treated all your sons like your workhorses—oh hell, you actually treat your horses better. At least you care about your horses!" Johnny bent to pick up his hat and took a step closer to his father.

Karl took the opportunity to raise the shovel once more to what he considered "intolerable disrespect." He shouted, "I will not stand for this kind of talk from a son of mine. It's time I taught you a lesson you won't forget!" In mid-swing, before he could land his second punishing blow, Johnny closed the space between them in a flash. He grabbed the shovel, savagely wrenched it from his father's grip and threw it to the ground. "That was the last time you'll strike me, old man! That's the last time you order me to do your work. You know what I think? You should never have been given sons!"

As he strode from his father's field, Johnny turned and shouted back, "Kiss my ass, old man! I am out of here. And, if I were a betting man, I would put money down on the fact that the day will come soon, when you will stand alone in your fields, with all of your things—and all of your money. You will be alone someday, old man! Remember my words. ALONE!"

Karl screamed his response after his retreating son, "That is enough! Now get the hell off my farm and don't come back, not ever! We don't need the likes of you. You are an embarrassment to your family—especially to your mother and me!"

Throughout the entire ugly scene, Hank and Eddie stood and watched, dumbfounded. There were times they were ashamed of their brother, Johnny, ashamed when he acted like he did, especially when he spoke hateful and disrespectful words to their father. Yet they had to admit they had had good times, too. But a lot of what their brother had said was true. However, they had a different relationship with their father than Jake had, because Karl had mellowed toward his sons as he grew older, all except for Johnny who never backed down from a fight, because he was Karl Kessel's son in every way!

Eddie said under his breath, "I would never have the guts to talk to Dad like that. I don't know how Johnny thinks he can get away with all his runnin' around. He's getting a real bad reputation around Lovell."

Hank took his hat off, rubbing the sweat from his forehead. "I know what you mean; he's always drunk or in the process of getting that way. Maybe it's good he's leaving; it'll be easier on the folks this way. I don't think he will ever bend to Dad's will; he's too much like Dad, isn't he?"

Eddie and Hank agreed that their father had a mean streak and was known to be ambitious and hard. They both remembered times when their own efforts hadn't met with their father's standards. However, they were proud he was well-respected in the community and the church. Karl had done amazing things, coming to this country with so little and now they could look at the farm and the riches he built. They feared and yet admired, hated and yet loved their father. But, he was their father, and they knew they were expected to honor him.

Karl Kessel never paid much attention to his daughters. Females were too complex and weepy for him. He didn't understand them and wasn't about to take the time to do so. He never cared much about anything they did, only concerning himself with whether or not their actions brought honor and respect to the Kessel name. He never expected them to do the things he expected of his sons. Louise was safely married, and that left Dottie at home (who was sixteen, "going on twenty.") She had a temper to match her father's and was not afraid to go nose to nose with him, which vexed yet, in a strange way, pleased Karl. He liked a person with some vim and vinegar in their blood, not a milk toast.

Since moving closer to Lovell, Karl was more active in their church. He became an elder and a respected leader in the church council. He also kept busy with the Great Western Sugar Company, although his duties were now limited. The land for the factory had been purchased, the factory had been built, the workers hired, and it had been in full swing just in time for the Depression. In spite of the hard times, it provided many jobs for desperate people, and put money in the pockets of Lovell's breadwinners, keeping a lot of households afloat.

Karl and Katja enjoyed being grandparents and, by the mid-1930s, they were blessed with eight grandchildren. They all lived in the Lovell area except for Chris and Martha who were farming in northern Colorado around Greeley.

By 1933, Franklin Roosevelt was president of the United States and the banking system, as it was previously known, ceased to exist. Business people could not get credit to buy inventory and checks were virtually as worthless as the banks that issued them. President Roosevelt was called the "Moses" of the Depression, gradually instilling confidence in the nation and the world, pulling the people out of the depths of the economic black hole with his New Deal.

As if things were not bad enough during the Depression, Mother Nature also had a few tricks up her sleeve. It was almost as though she was getting even with the farmers of Southern Colorado, Oklahoma, and Kansas, for plowing up the prairie grasslands. The blowing "dust bowl" filtered into homes and buried the hopes of farmers trying desperately to hold on to their homes and farms. No moisture came from the skys. Barren, over-plowed and unplanted fields released the dry topsoil into the atmosphere, where ceaseless wind carried to wherever it happened to land when the wind finally stopped blowing. Tenant farmers, sharecroppers, Mexican and African American workers were the first to be excluded from farms struggling in an effort to make ends meet. Those who could find work often supported their families on as little as $1.75 a week. Still, they were thankful for even low-paid work.

Although the Kessel family was better off than most, Karl spent endless hours and weeks planning new ways to survive. Katja canned large amounts of vegetables from her enlarged gardens, and when there were no crops to attend to, Karl helped her. Lately Katja had more than the usual amount of time to think about her family and their individual problems. She had always been secretly proud of her middle son's devilish good looks. Johnny was their only child to inherit her dark hair and deep-brown eyes, and he had a reputation for using them to his advantage. Katja smiled to herself as she remembered all the times he used his charm on her to get his way with something.

Karl and Katja heard frequent rumors of their son's reputation around Lovell—a lusty reputation with the ladies. In May of 1935, two months after he turned twenty-two, he arrived unannounced at the house one evening as Karl and Katja were eating their supper at the kitchen table. Johnny had a stunning, raven-haired young girl on his arm. With pride, he announced, "Ma and Dad, this is Edie, my new wife. We were married today by the justice of the peace."

Karl and Katja were stupefied; Edie couldn't have been more than sixteen but she had the curvacious body of a twenty-year-old. Karl said nothing to either of the young married people, nor did he meet their eyes. With a stony expression he pushed back his chair from the table and left the room. Katja tried in vain to smooth over her husband's departure. Johnny and his bride did not stay long after that, saying they had a party to attend.

Karl and Katja later discovered that their new daughter-in-law came from a Frannie family and she was not only young, but pregnant! In early January 1936, their granddaughter Emma Jo Kessel was born. The baby was not well from the day she was born and, early in 1937, they buried her in the small Kessel Cemetery, south of the farm.

Several years earlier, Karl had designated a particular portion of his land under a grove of cottonwood trees as a Lutheran cemetery. The Mormons had their own cemetery and local Lutherans also wanted a designated burial area for their dead. Karl didn't attend the burial services but later, after everybody left, he went to the cottonwood grove cemetery and stood at the fresh grave of his infant granddaughter. He had not even had the privilege of holding her in his arms. Tears of sorrow and shame clouded his sky-blue eyes. *She is the first of our family to die and be buried in American soil!*

Johnny and Edie had another daughter, Mollie Jo, born later that same year. However, their marriage was not on stable ground and it ended shortly after the baby's birth. Johnny discovered he wasn't ready to settle down with one woman or be a father. Karl and Katja heard that their son had left for Texas, where he later filed for divorce. His parents were not happy with the actions of their son. But, as Karl put it, "What else can we expect from him? He's not learned responsibility; he made his bed and he should lay in it!"

But Johnny wasn't fazed by what his parents wanted or expected him to do; he never had been. He didn't write often, and when he did it was addressed to his mother. His parents didn't know what he was doing in Texas, or even if he was actually still there.

In April 1936, Karl walked into the kitchen one evening with the day's mail in his hand, and asked Katja to come into the parlor and sit down. She was mystified and somewhat alarmed by his request, but did as he bid. Slowly, he pulled a white envelope from the stack of mail and handed it to her. "There is a letter from Surtschin. It is from your brother."

Katja froze. She did not move; she did not reach for the letter. She could barely breathe. Karl thrust the letter closer to her, and still she did not take it. Karl finally spoke in a soft, calm voice. "Katja, it is addressed to you. Do you want to open it or do you want me to do it for you?"

She slowly lifted her ebony eyes to look on her husband's face. "Karl, I do not know what the letter will say; I only know my brother has never written a letter to me and there is only one reason he would write the letter! I fear the worst. I do not know if I *can* open the letter, I do not know if I *want* to open the letter. It is always bad, Karl, ALWAYS!"

Karl also felt alarm in his belly and his mind was racing, trying to figure out a way to ease what he also expected to be bad news. "*Leibschen*, I am filled with dread as well, but if you want me to, I will read this letter to you. Is this what you want?"

Katja sat in the chair, holding her shaking hands together tightly in her lap, "*Ja*, Karl, go ahead—read the letter, please." Sitting in her soft parlor chair, her tiny hands folded in her lap and her dark eyes wide with fear and anticipation, Katja waited in dread for what was coming. Her breath came from her chest in short, quick gasps as Karl slowly tore open the envelope. Katja watched his every movement—as though he was moving in slow motion. Karl pulled the letter out, unfolded it and, taking a deep breath, began to read the words Katja's brother, Christian Mehll, had written on the white vellum paper.

> February 15, 1936
>
> Dearest Katja and Karl,
>
> It is with deep sadness I must tell you of the news that I know will be hard for you to bear. Our papa, Christian Mehll, has gone to his final resting place, where our mother has already gone before him. He died in his sleep on the 9th of February. We were all shocked and saddened by his death. But you must know he had been in good health, not with pain or distress in the days before he died. He went peacefully and did not suffer. We have had the funeral and laid him to rest beside our mother in the church cemetery. There were many, many people at the funeral too many

to each have a seat. He was loved by many peoples.

Katja, I know that always you and Papa were close. When you sent the pictures, he sat for hours and looked at them. He carried them to the village to show his friends of his grandchildren in America.

The Depression has hit us hard. Now, we find ourselves on our own; we no longer have the support of the Austrian government. We are trying to make the best of a difficult situation. We are also alarmed with increased pressures and political manipulation from Germany, namely Adolf Hitler. We believe that it is not a good thing and war clouds loom again as we have so often witnessed here in Yugoslavia.

We all pray for your peace, my sister. Our papa was in our lives for many years. He enjoyed a long and blessed life and we must rejoice in his final reward.

Your loving brother, Christian

Karl looked up from the letter, fearing how Katja was taking this news. She sat like a stone in her soft English chair for several minutes as her mind struggled to digest the words. Suddenly, without any warning, her face contorted and a most horrible wailing scream came from deep inside her body, as she pitched forward onto the floor, falling on her hands and knees. Her body arched and tensed with each continuous scream reaching such levels that Karl was near panic himself. Never had he heard or witnessed anything like this; it made the hair on the back of his neck stand up. Karl did not know what to do; he was afraid she might actually go out of her mind, have a heart attack, or perhaps even a stroke. He ran from the room and telephoned Dr. Craft to come quick to the farm. Karl hurried back into the room where Katja was prone on the floor, now curled into a fetal position—still screaming and sobbing uncontrollably. He went to her side, gently touching her and smoothing her hair, speaking softly, "Katja, *mein* Katja, please try to control yourself. I am afraid for your health. I have called Dr. Craft to come to the house to attend to you and give you help."

Katja's eyes were wild and unseeing and her breath was coming in uneven gasps. Unexpectedly, she reached up and slapped Karl—she beat his chest with her fists and kicked him with her little black shoes. Finally, he simply backed away, getting out of her reach. He let her be, hoping that the doctor would hurry.

Katja continued to writhe on the floor, not hearing anything Karl said to her. Wild thoughts raced through her mind—tormenting thoughts. He was her husband, the one who had forbid her to travel to Surtschin to see her father when he had needed her and now he was dead. She would never see her father's face, or feel his embrace, never for sure, on this earth—and it was all Karl's fault!

Katja was completely consumed with grief; there was nothing else in her mind but the knowledge that first her mother and now her father were no longer on this earth. She had completely lost control and she did not care; she felt completely alone. She was not aware when Dr. Craft and Karl lifted her from the floor and carried her to their bed, or of Dr. Craft giving her an injection. She quieted shortly and slept. Karl called the children and told them of their grandfather's death and of their mother's condition. Jake and Ralf came immediately to the house to be with their father. Their wives, Raisa and Lottie, arrived to take care of the household work and feed those who still lived at home.

That evening, the Kessel house was steeped in mourning. The electric lamps were low; the Austrian lace curtains were drawn; a black shroud hung on the front door. Katja remained sedated in bed for several days. Karl was worried about her; she was not a weak woman. If anything she was the strongest woman he knew.

As she had aged, Katja had always tried to keep her feelings subdued and was usually successful, except when it came to the family she left in Surtschin. This was why Karl was now so terribly worried. "I am afraid she might give up all together and will not want to be in this world without her parents."

It was true that Katja had grieved long for her mother, but this situation was different. She was completely devastated, consumed with grief over her father's death—this death was different and it frightened Karl. That night Karl prayed for his wife as he had never prayed before. He called their pastor to come to the house and pray over Katja. Karl did everything he could think of doing to try and ease his wife's grief.

It was a week to the day that Karl and Katja received the news from Surtschin that Katja rose from her bed, washed herself, and dressed. She was in the kitchen, preparing breakfast when Karl came in from milking the cows. Karl found his wife standing at the stove and exclaimed, "Katja, I am surprised to see you up. Are you sure you are feeling strong enough?"

Katja turned slowly to face him, and Karl noticed that she spoke without facial expression and her eyes were dull. "*Ja*, Karl, it is time for me to get out of the bed and get on with my duties." That was all she said to him as she continued to cook breakfast. The days that followed were much the same. She did what she had to do, and nothing more. She did not speak unless spoken to; she did not smile, she did not laugh. Katja merely existed. It was as though she was there in the flesh, but was not there—not in her mind.

Her father's absence from the earth was all that occupied Katja's thoughts. The news of his death had sucked the breath from her bosom. She could never have imagined how his loss would affect her. Without her father, she seemed to lose her will to exist. She ate little and lost weight at an alarming rate. She did not sleep well. Her dreams were agonizing, and she woke often, so haunted that further sleep would not be hers for the rest of the night. Katja felt it, knew it—her father had taken another part of her heart with him to his grave.

One night after such a dream, Katja rose quietly from the bed she shared with her husband, slipped on her worn navy chenille robe. In bare feet, she padded silently across the glossy hardwood floor in the darkness. She walked to the large windows that faced east, where the moon sat high in the night sky. The mere sight of the moon sparked more agonizing thoughts in her fragile mind. She stood in front of the window for a long time, gazing at the moon and thinking of her father. *Oh Papa, before you left me, I was okay as long as I knew we both looked at the same moon, the same stars. I could go on when I knew we both breathed the cool night air, and felt the warmth of the same sun. As long as I knew you lived and breathed, I had the courage to live as well. It was what inspired me to bear it all and be the daughter you expected me to be. Now, nothing matters to me, nothing.*

Katja reached for the Austrian lace curtains hanging in the window, curtains her parents sent as a gift to her and Karl. She bunched the lace into a ball and buried her face in it. After a few minutes, she pulled back and wound a length of the lace curtain around and around her body, wrapping herself into a cocoon of lace, feeling safe and secure. After a time, she unwrapped herself and smoothed her precious curtains as they fell back to the floor. Tears rolled down her weathered cheeks and onto her blue chenille robe. *Papa, oh Papa, you were the whisper in the wind that caressed my face as your hand once did. You were the beat in my heart, the smile on my face, the laughter in my voice. You were the reason I got up every morning; I lived to please you. Now, you are no more and I feel like you have taken my breath with you.*

Katja was never sure whether she actually heard the voice or had just dreamed it, but it seemed real just the same. Hearing his voice in the night was the catalyst that enabled her to go on with her life:

> *"Katja, daughter, listen to me now, as I speak to you. I am still the whisper in the wind that caresses your face and your beautiful raven hair. I am the memory in your beating heart and the smile on your sweet face, the laughter in your voice. I am the sun that shines and warms your skin. I am beside you, a part of you, as I always have been. But now I am your guardian angel and I will never leave you. You must be brave as you always have. Take heart and live the rest of your life as you should. Your husband and your family still need you; you are not finished. Do not grieve, daughter; I am at peace with your mother."*

Katja stood at the window for a long time. When she turned, her face was relaxed and glowing, and her heart was more content than it had been for a long time. She returned to the bedroom she shared with her husband; removed her robe, and quietly slipped between the sheets. Katja turned onto her side, moving close to Karl; she laid her arm across his sleeping body and closed her eyes in sleep.

The next morning, Karl noticed something different about his wife. She seemed lighter in her mood, not as distant as she had been. Karl bravely gave her cheek a quick kiss after eating his breakfast and hurried out the back screen door to his waiting fields. As the next weeks and months went by, Katja appeared to be feeling better. Karl was relieved, and once again his work and other duties received his full attention.

Life was still hard and the country remained in the grips of the Great Depression. Occasionally there was news of a bank reopening and crop prices were gradually creeping upwards. But nothing came quickly or easily. Jake and Raisa had left the farm in Kane and were struggling, moving from one farm to the next, trying to scratch a living from the reluctant soil. Everybody was in debt to the grocery store, the doctor, each other, and the government.

Finally, in 1938, Katja received a letter from her son Johnny, it was from Texas. "I'm working in construction and am making a lot of dough," he said. "Well, Ma, that's about it—oh, I got married, she's a real swell gal; her name is Maribelle. Hope you can meet her someday." Love you, Ma. Johnny. Well, at least they heard from him, he was alive and married again.

One day Katja was at her sink, preparing vegetables for the evening supper when she saw a shiny car drive into their yard. It rolled to a stop and she couldn't believe her eyes when she saw her husband open the door and climb out. She rushed to the back door and out onto the porch. "Karl, Karl what are you doing with that car? And, when did you learn to drive?"

Karl walked toward the house beaming, "*Ja, das is gute, huh, Frau Kessel?*" He laughed his familiar chuckle, and a merry twinkle radiated from his ice-blue eyes. "Katja, oh, Katja, you will not believe my good luck. I was in town to see my banker and when we finished with the business he asked me if I would be interested in this car here. It is a 1935 Plymouth and in good condition. The previous owner could not make his payments and it is over half paid for. The bank had taken it back and was now looking to find someone who could make the monthly payments. I think it is time we got a decent car to drive. So, what do you think? Do you want to get in a take a little drive with me?"

Katja just stood there for a moment. "Why, Karl, would you buy a car during this depression? You know money is scarce and many people are having a hard time of it. What will they think of us when we show up in a new car?"

Karl smiled back at her, "We are not many peoples; we are doing okay and this was a good deal. I could not pass it up. So, what do you say, *mein leibschen*? Come on and get in and let's try it out."

Katja went around to the passenger side, wiping her hands on her apron as she walked; she opened the door and climbed in. She rubbed her hands over the leather seat, "It *is* a nice car and I think it would be good to go to church in the comfort of this car, also to drive over to Emblem once in a while."

They drove up and down the country roads for over an hour, enjoying their new possession. Katja enjoyed seeing her husband when he was happy, when he was proud. "It reminds me of the old days in Surtschin when we were so carefree and so happy. Oh my, that was so long ago, so many things have happened in our lives. At times it almost seems that we are living some other people's life."

After their ride, they drove into their farmyard and Karl said, with a twinkle in his blue eyes, "You know, wife, now I will have to build a garage to put this good car in, I cannot leave it out in the bad weathers!"

He let her out at the back door and drove on through the farm yard toward the barn where he got out, opened the barn doors, and drove his new treasure inside, where it would be out of the weather until he could build that garage.

CHAPTER 15
A Time of War, a Time of Peace

"For everything there is a season, a time for every purpose under heaven; :
A time to kill, and a time to heal; A time to love, and a time to hate; a time
of war, and a time of peace." ~ Ecclesiastes 3:1,3, and 8

SEPTEMBER 1939

Karl and Katja were stunned along with the rest of the world, when their morning news was interrupted by a "flash" announcement. The radio announcer said, "Germany has invaded Poland. At 4:45 a.m. on September 1st, more than 1,250,000 German troops, including nine armored divisions, smashed through the Polish border. Using an entirely new concept of warfare called *Blitzkrieg*, the German military seemed invincible. Having no other choice, England and France have immediately declared war on Germany." At that moment, the United States began a discreet and badly needed buildup of their armed forces, which had dwindled to almost nothing during the Great Depression.

In May 1940, the world was again stunned and outraged when Hitler attacked to the west. Karl and Katja had been eating breakfast at their kitchen table when the news came over the radio. "I can't take anymore of this craziness; is that Hitler insane? What in the hell is he thinking? That he is going to rule the world and kill any who oppose him? It's like the end of existence Katja, I tell you, the end of days!"

German forces breeched the Netherlands' new defensive lines and were heading toward Rotterdam, Antwerp, and Paris. After holding out for only twenty-seven days, France could see the writing on the wall and asked for armistice terms. After hearing the latest news, Karl commented. "It is like a line of standing dominos. One push and they all fall—boom, boom, boom!"

Katja was alarmed. "When and where is this going to end, Karl? I am so afraid that the United States is going to get in this war in Europe. Do you think they will tell our sons to go to the war, too?"

On a beautiful fall day in early September, Karl and Katja were sitting at their kitchen table, eating a light supper when Katja approached her husband. "Karl, our oldest granddaughter is to be married the end of this month and I was thinking I would like to have a new dress to wear to the wedding."

Karl looked up from his supper plate. "*Ja*, Katja that is a good idea. I think I can afford to buy the grandmother of the bride a nice new dress. Would you like me to drive you to Billings on Friday to shop?"

Katja almost fainted with shock. Karl had actually agreed to buy her something she had asked for, but really didn't need. She smiled to herself. *Miracles do happen; yes, they do.*

After the wedding on September 28, everything went back to the original routine. The leaves were beginning to fall from the trees as Katja walked out to the mailbox by the highway. She pulled the tied bunch of letters from the box, tucked it under her arm, and walked up the gravel lane back toward the house. It was a cold fall day and the wind had a hint of winter as it blew in from the north. Katja sniffed the air and thought to herself, *It smells like snow already. I think I will start a pot of chicken soup for supper. It'll taste good with some fresh-baked wheat bread.*

She reached the back porch and stomped the dust off her shoes before she entered the kitchen. Laying the mail on the kitchen table, she took off her worn brown sweater and removed the printed silk scarf from her head. She poured herself a cup of coffee as she turned and sat down at the kitchen table to look through the mail. There, right on top, was a letter from their son Johnny, a letter from Texas. Katja picked it up with shaking hands she quickly opened it.

> Dear Mother and Dad,
>
> I am writing to tell you that on the thirteenth of August, I enlisted in the United States army in Sacramento, California. We had only a month in basic training, to get us all ready to ship out. By the time you get this letter, we will be on our way to the

Philippines.

I know that you may be upset by my decision, but I believe it is my duty to serve my country. I wasn't doing much anyway, and so decided that this would be a great adventure! The scuttlebutt is that things are brewing in the Pacific and, if so, I want to be one of those Americans who kicks Japan's butt all over those islands. I sure as hell am not going to miss this battle. It looks as though the Americans will be fighting in Europe before long, as well. If I get sent over there, I might be fighting some of my cousins. Want me to say "Hello" for you? Ha!

As far as I know right now, I will be stationed in the Philippines. I will try to write you more when I get there. My wife is going back to live with her parents in Houston. Say some prayers for me, Ma, and know that I am going to give it my all. You taught us how to be tough and how to get in there and fight for what we think is right, and never give up. That is exactly what I am going to do. Say a prayer for your "black sheep"! Ha! Had my picture taken and wanted you to have a copy.

Don't worry—I'll love you forever,
Johnny

Katja's head bowed to her chest as she clenched the letter to her bosom. Her worst fear, that the war would somehow touch their family, had just become real. Her chest felt tight with foreboding and her heart beat faster, as she thought, *It now begins, with this letter, it all begins.*

Katja turned as Karl came in from the barn. He stopped on the back porch to take off his boots and work jacket. Katja walked slowly toward him with the letter in her hand. Karl looked up and was startled by the expression on his wife's face. "What is it, woman? Why do you look like that?" Karl spotted the letter in Katja's hand. "It is another letter? I hope to God nothing more has happened to your family in Surtschin!"

Katja handed the letter to him as she said, "It is from Johnny, and he has joined up to fight in the war. He said he thought they were going to the Philippine Islands!" Her face was tight and strained with concern as she said, "Is this why we came to this country, Karl, for our sons to go to war and die like they did in the old country? NO, it is not; and now our son is fighting in the war, and who knows what happens?"

Turning to face his wife, Karl said, "Katja, *nein*, of course not, you know better to say that. But it doesn't matter where people live; the ugly clutches of war can always reach. There is no place on this earth that is free from war, and there never will be. Johnny is doing what he believes is right. We must be thankful he is the only one of our sons who is going. We have five other sons who are safe and we must be thankful for that, Katja."

She shook her head, "*Nein, Karl*, I cannot be happy, even if only one of my six sons is going to war. To me, that is one too many. *Ja, ja*, I do understand we all must help; we must all do our duty to our country. It is too hard. It makes me too worried and to have a rock in my stomach; it all makes me tired." She put her head down and went into their bedroom to lie down on the bed. Katja did not sleep well that night, or the next, or the next. Her dreams were filled with visions and memories of her son, the only son who looked like her, with his flashing dark eyes, straight nose, and slick black hair.

On a Sunday morning in December 1941, Karl and Katja were dressing for church services in Lovell when they heard more unbelievable news flash from their radio. The Japanese had bombed Pearl Harbor in Hawaii. The announcer reported it was feared that thousands of American servicemen and women had perished in the surprise attack.

"Katja, we must hurry to church and pray for our country. This is a terrible thing that has happened and I fear greatly for what may come," Karl said. They drove into Lovell where they joined the stunned congregation, as Pastor Siebert led a special prayer service. Many were crying as they bowed their heads and prayed for their country.

After services, Karl was standing with the other men and heard them talking. "It doesn't look good, does it? Looks to me like the United States will now be pulled into another war. The situation in Europe isn't getting any better and, with this vicious attack in Hawaii, America's got no choice but to go to war with Japan."

Karl heard someone else say with savage bitterness. "Our boy's lives will be avenged; we'll show those Japs what a beehive they just opened up, we sure as hell will!"

On their way home from church, Karl reminisced, "Katja, this feels so much like what we left in the old country, wars looming from all directions. I am thinking in our life, we can never really get away from the wars, because it is a human situation of greed and revenge. There are always those who want what someone else has, and are willing to take it by force. There always has been, and always will be, evil in our world. I pray, oh, I do pray for our country and all those who suffer from this war. I have a bad feeling we will have a second great war!"

Katja nodded her head in silence. What more was there to say? This war and threat of war was dark, cold, and constant. Katja shivered as unnerving thoughts passed through her, but she did not share them with her husband. Perhaps if she didn't acknowledge these black thoughts, they would cease to exist.

The following day, the president of the United States, Franklin D. Roosevelt, gave an unforgettable message to the outraged people of the United States. He began, "Yesterday, December 7, 1941—a date which will live in infamy—the United States was suddenly and deliberately attacked by naval and air forces of the Empire of Japan."

Not long after this, the United States responded to Germany's declaration of war. America not only declared war on Japan, but now would also go to war with Germany, Italy, Romania, Bulgaria, and Hungary! The people of the United States rallied behind their president and Congress. "We will show them what Americans are made of and they all better know they are in for one hell of a fight!"

Fueled by the fear that Japan might attack the West Coast of the United States, and also the fear of sabotage from within our country by people of Japanese origins, the government voted to round up Japanese-American citizens and send them to internment camps. One of these camps, the Heart Mountain Relocation Center was to be built in Wyoming, between the small towns of Cody and Powell in the Big Horn Basin. At one point, 10,000 Japanese-Americans, mostly from California were uprooted and sent to this remote Wyoming camp. The harsh climate of northwestern Wyoming was difficult at best for people who were used to the temperate climate of California.

There were a handful of men around the area who would have nothing to do with building the relocation center, claiming it was wrong to imprison people because of their cultural heritage. Karl and Katja recalled the harsh prejudice they experienced during the last war even though they were citizens of the United States.

Jake and his teenage son, Arnold jumped at the opportunity to help build the Japanese relocation center at Heart Mountain. Jake told Raisa, "Right or wrong, we are doing what we have to do, and that's that. It pays real good and God knows we need the money!" Work of any kind was difficult to come by and this was the perfect opportunity for them and for others to get out of hovering Depression debt.

Jake and Raisa's children both worked at any jobs they could find and gave their paychecks to their parents to help pay the family debts, as was true in most households still reeling in unpaid bills. Raisa was happy, living in town with oiled streets and no fields to work in. She took any work she could find—a house cleaner, a laundress, and a checker at the grocery store while Beth worked at the local Rexall drug store. The Kessels were determined to get out of debt and repay those who had generously allowed them credit during the hard years.

With Jake and Arnold's substantial paychecks from the internment camps, Jake and Raisa were able to stucco their tar-papered house in Lovell. The day they paid off their last debt, Jake drove to Billings and bought his wife a stylish fur coat. Later that year, he accepted a full-time job in the oil fields. Major new oil discoveries had been made in the Bighorn Basin, especially around Byron. Jake went to work for and would stay with the company until he retired. He found his niche where he could hold his head high and be proud of the man he was—he was a success.

Ranchers in Wyoming were encouraged by the increased demand for beef and farm products. Karl Kessel was quick to pick up on the need for cattle and began at once to increase his herd of Herford cattle. He bought various breeds of range cattle from farmers, ranchers whoever had cattle for sale. He corralled the cattle, fattened them up, and sold them to the government at a good profit.

Men who were farmers were exempt from military service because the government needed farmers to grow food for the war effort, to feed the troops and the country. Karl and Katja assumed that none of their sons would be asked to serve because they were all farmers, all that is, except Johnny. He was not a farmer and he was going to fight. When asked about his son, Karl commented, "That Johnny, he always liked a good fight; I remember this!"

Jake and Raisa's only son, Arnold, was to graduate from high school the end of May. Lovell was crawling with recruiters who were talking hard and fast to any eligible young men. Raisa was beside herself with the thought that her eighteen-year-old son might be shipped away to fight in a war.

Karl and Katja read the newspapers and listened to their radio every day, hoping for some news of the war in the Pacific and also in Europe. The war was not going well in the Philippines, where their son Johnny had thought he was going. They hadn't heard from their son since he left so they listened to their radio and the war news at every opportunity. The Philippine Islands had been lost to the Japanese after three solid months of battle. General MacArthur was being pulled out, leaving General Wainwright in command of thousands of American troops. Karl and Katja were concerned. *What about the men left behind on those islands? Where is our son Johnny?*

On April 9, 1942, Karl and Katja were busy planting the spring crops in the fields and the garden and taking a break, when there was time, to enjoy their grandchildren. They were happy with the news that they were about to be great-grandparents. They had no way of knowing of the unthinkable ordeal their son Johnny was facing that day in the Pacific.

On April ninth, Private Johnny Kessel was one of almost 12,000 American prisoners of war being ordered to begin marching in what was later known as the Bataan Death March. Their chance of surviving what they were about to experience was one in three. After the fall of the Philippines, the Japanese had thousands of prisoners, no place to put them, and no supplies to feed them; the group of prisoners consisted of about 60,000 Filipinos and Allied forces. The Japanese forced them to march long and hard in the extreme humidity and heat of the island, exhibiting no empathy, mercy, or humanity for their prisoners. In fact they hoped many would die, relieving them of the responsibility of feeding and guarding them.

In the morning Johnny and the other prisoners struggled to stand up from wherever they happened to fall the night before. Their captors beat and bayoneted those who rose too slowly from the road. As he was being marched along the road, Johnny thought, *I guess there's no point in asking for a hot cup of coffee, we'll be lucky to get water.* Prodded by bayonets, they began another day of forced marching in the unbelievable heat and water deprivation. Guards took great pleasure inflicting pain, humiliation, hardship, and death, berating 'the dogs, the enemies of Imperial Japan.' Surrender for a Japanese soldier was the ultimate humiliation and cowardice deed; better to die than surrender.

Johnny wasn't surprised by the extreme cruelty they were suffering at the hands of the Japanese; their reputation for brutality was well known, but just how far and to what extent they would go—he could not have imagined.

Thousands of prisoners sat beside the main road, slowly dying in the sweltering tropic sun; they were, experiencing the infamous Japanese torture, "sun treatment." Many prisoners were wounded and twice as many were sick from malaria due to the heavy infestation of island mosquitoes.

Late on the second day, the prisoners saw dust boil up from troop trucks approaching in the distance. *Will we finally get to ride to wherever it was we are going?* The troop trucks rolled to a stop near the irregular line of prisoners; the back flaps opened, as more guards joined the ranks.

The Japanese guards pushed and prodded their prisoners into groups of one hundred, in columns of four abreast. Guards on both sides of the columns continually jabbed the prisoners with their bayonets and screamed "Speedo, speedo!" If anyone fell or complained, they were beaten, shot, or bayoneted at the discretion of the nearest guard.

Johnny was horrified to see guards behead prisoners with their heavy swords. *That goon just chopped off some guy's head like my dad topped a sugar beet—no emotion, no difference!* The heads and bodies were kicked to the side of the road or left where they fell.

When the columns stopped, nobody was allowed to sit except when the guard was changed. Prisoners could not lie down, ask (or beg) for food, water, or mercy, without fear of being beaten, beheaded, or shot. American and English officers implored the guards to have mercy on the wounded and sick, but the guards' only reply was some version of: "You are not worthy of food, water, or medicine; those are saved for our brave soldiers. You are dogs; you are enemies and you will die while we watch. And if you don't die, we will help you die. Every prisoner who dies saves us a bullet."

Like his fellow prisoners, Johnny Kessel couldn't believe this was happening; it was surreal. Basic army training sure as hell hadn't prepared them for this. But Johnny was determined to do what he had to do to survive. He noticed what irritated the guards and he learned to avoid their eyes and weapons. At night he lay awake, dissecting lessons from that day and he began to make a plan.

The following morning, April 10, 1942, Karl and Katja sat down to a hearty farm breakfast of ham, eggs, and hot steaming coffee. They listened to the radio for news as they ate, but the war news they received was censored and usually days old; still it was new to them.

Halfway around the world, night was falling and their son was being forced to march along some darkened road on the island of Bataan. He had been one of the lucky ones to fill his canteen with a little bug-filled, murky roadside water before the march resumed.

"Speedo! Speedo!" the guards screamed and jabbed the closest bodies with their bayonets. Johnny's body flexed every time a shot rang out, as blood and life spilled from hundreds of bodies that fell every day and were left along the roadway. Johnny thought to himself, *Are they ever going to stop screaming that—speedo-speedo shit?*

But they didn't stop; the shrill shouts of "Speedo, speedo!" continued to pierce the humid air. Just before midnight, the order to halt punctured the senses of the zombie-like prisoners. When the guards motioned for them to lie down on the road, they dropped like flies, desperate for sleep.

The next morning and the morning after that, Johnny thought about his parents as he put one foot in front of the other. *They are probably asleep and safe in the comfort and warmth of their goose-down bed. I need to think about something other than what is happening!*

Midmorning each day, the march was halted and prisoners were handed a golf-ball sized, fly-covered rice ball. Almost immediately, they were forced back into columns and driven back out onto the road. One morning, Johnny was able to partially fill his canteen with ditch water. *It'll probably make me sick but at this point I'll take the chance—got to have water.*

After four excruciating days of marching, death, and horror, the prisoners came to a railroad station, where they were stuffed into rail cars. The men were jammed so tightly against each other that they couldn't move—they could only stand in one spot. Even when they couldn't stand any more, even when they died, they remained, entombed in that place! Johnny couldn't move; he couldn't raise his arms, or even squat to defecate or urinate. He heard someone wail in humiliation, "Oh my God, I'm sorry I gotta take a dump; I can't help it. Oh, dear God, I'm sorry."

They all stood, sealed in place, as vomit, diarrhea, and urine ran down their bodies and the bodies of those around them, ending in repugnant puddles. The heat of the brutal tropic sun against the metal boxcars was relentless; the prisoners felt like they were being cooked alive. Someone whispered through swollen lips, "I'm so dehydrated I can't even sweat. Someone else added, "This damn heat is cracking my lips and my tongue is startin' to swell. I need water; please, for God's sake, just give us some water."

Johnny concentrated on taking short breaths but it was difficult. Each man experienced the same suffocation, the intense heat, nauseating smells. Some fainted and some died. The living, the dead, and the dying remained upright, packed in the boxcar, mile after excruciating mile. Only when the train stopped and the doors of the boxcars were unlocked and opened, did the exhausted, sick, and the dead spill out onto the ground. Guards stood on the perimeters and took pot shots at random prisoners; they used their bayonets on those too weak to stand or move out. They kicked and shoved bodies into a huge pile and a guard threw kerosene over it as another torched it.

Johnny turned to steal a look and instantly turned back. *Shit, I hope they were all dead before they lit that thing.* But he knew they weren't.

The Bataan Death March covered ninety-one miles in just over four days. Sixty-three miles of the march were on foot, which turned out to be the easy part compared to the twenty-eight miles they rode, crammed tightly together in the boxcars.

Johnny was paralyzed with outrage. *Never in my life have I seen things like this or would have believed any man could be this cruel to another. If I'm going to survive this nightmare and whatever else is ahead, I've got to use my wits and German tenacity.* He knew he had to be smart and harden himself to the horrors going on around him. *I can't afford to lose it, and sure as hell ain't gonna give those bastards the satisfaction!* He went to sleep at night thinking about his German heritage and the country he was born in. *I will show them—I WILL beat them at their own game! I am Karl Kessel's son and I have been taught how to survive brutality!*

On the evening of April 12, 1942, Karl and Katja were glued to the radio, listening to the latest reports on the war in the Pacific: "The peninsula of Bataan, namely the allies' stronghold of Marivales in the Philippine Islands, has fallen to the Japanese. We have reports that around 12,000 American soldiers became prisoners of the Japanese, along with 60,000 Filipino troops." The report provided no details about what the prisoners faced; because no details were known.

Karl and Katja Kessel had not officially learned of their son's capture until the first notice came, months after the battle, listing him as "missing in action." Nobody, even the military was aware of what the men on Bataan were going through and they wouldn't for months, even years. By the end of June, the Kessels received official word that "Corporal Johnny Kessel is officially listed as a prisoner of war, on Bataan." By this time, the world had some reports of the Bataan Death March and the cruelty of the Japanese. Everybody knew the war news was censored, so only selected horrors were revealed to the public.

The more Karl and his family read and heard of the horrors, from sketchy news reports, the more they were convinced Johnny might not be among the living. However, Karl was not persuaded. "*Nein, nein*—he is MY son and he is a fighter. I KNOW my son and he will not give up. He is smart and strong and he will find a way!"

Katja merely sat and stared at her husband with her sad, fear-filled eyes. She spent much of her time alone, in her garden, on solitary walks out to the cottonwood grove and the small Lutheran cemetery where Johnny's first daughter was buried. She felt better when she was alone. She didn't have to be cheerful, or hopeful, or make small talk. She preferred to be alone with her thoughts, remembering conversations with her son. Katja didn't believe he was dead because she could feel him breathe, she could feel her son's torment and fear.

The end of May their grandson Arnold Kessel graduated from high school. Many of the young graduates immediately went down to the recruiting office in Lovell and joined up. When most of the boys from his graduating class decided to sign up, Arnold was with them and they all "did the deed" together. He chose the Army and was sent to basic training in early July. When it was time to say goodbye, Karl merely slapped him on the back and instructed him to "Give 'em hell!" In the darkness of night, he prayed his son, and now his grandson, would come back safe.

CAMP O'DONNELL, PHILIPPINES

When Johnny and the other prisoners heard they were going to a camp, they had great hopes that things were going to level out. So far, Corporal Johnny Kessel was surviving the odds, surviving the daily awlfulness of their lives. Food, water, medicine (such as quinine for malaria), and decent treatment were rare; but could sometimes be bought if a particular guard wanted what was for sale or trade. American officers were singled out by Japanese privates who took delight in humiliating and punishing them. If an American officer did not bow and salute them; there was no end to their cruelty. Lt. General Homma, commander of the camp, made his hatred of Americans in particular, quite clear.

Johnny noted that when the prisoners were in large groups, the men on the fringes seemed to be easy targets for the guards' incessant punches, jabs, and slaps. Seeing this, he made a point of moving to the interior of a group, attracting as little attention to himself as possible. He stopped exercising because it made him perspire more and increased his thirst, and he knew he needed to retain as much moisture as possible. During the first forty-five days at Camp O'Donnell, more than 1,500 Americans died; by July, 25,000 Filipino prisoners met the same fate.

One afternoon, as they were rounded up for some sort of inspection, Johnny noticed a Japanese guard who bent over to help a prisoner who had fallen to the ground. Without hesitation, the guard was shot and bayoneted on the spot. Johnny looked at the ground thinking, *That act of charity, that moment of sympathy, cost that poor bastard his life. These Japs don't even have empathy for their own.*

When several thousand prisoners were rounded up and forced into yet another lengthy march, many were hesitant and fearful to leave the camp. Only weeks before, guards loaded up a group of ill prisoners, took them to the edge of the jungle, and machine-gunned them. Johnny didn't know how many more had died that month but it was a couple of thousand anyway. The Japanese plan was working; the infidel prisoners were dropping like flies. Infected wounds, malaria, and the lack of adequate food and water rapidly aided the death plan.

During the second march, prisoners from Camp O'Donnell were joined by prisoners taken from the recently fallen island of Corregidor. To this point, the prisoners from Corregidor had been more fortunate in avoiding the atrocities and starvation in particular and they were shocked by the physical condition of the survivors of Bataan. The newcomers were in much better shape to withstand the abuse; however, it didn't take long before they all shared the horrors of Camp Cabanatuan.

For the prisoners from O'Donnell, things seemed better, now they had all the water they needed. But there was still no medicine, and the meager portions of food were still crawling with vermin. Malaria was relentless, followed by beriberi, scurvy, pellagra, and dysentery. The prisoners knew they needed more protein, so they caught dogs, rats, lizards, snakes, anything that moved, and they ate it, usually without cooking. Johnny had always been lean, but he dropped another twenty pounds and his ribs were starting to show. By the fall months, the rate of prisoner deaths had fallen to around twenty-five a day.

Johnny tried to steel his mind against the daily horrors. Everywhere was the odor of human waste and of the smell of death. The prisoners who lost their minds and stared off into space, totally unresponsive or uncaring, were the men who troubled him the most. Dreams of revenge filled Johnny's mind. *Someday, someday—these Japs will pay for what they are doing.*

Johnny didn't have a deep religious faith to fall back on. *I never really bought into that stuff when I was growing up. My folks insisted I go to church, even got confirmed, but all that religion never got a grip on me, no siree—not old Johnny.* Instead he was fueled by his innate charm with the ladies and steely defiance to anything that rubbed him the wrong way.

In November, Johnny was among several hundred men loaded into a truck and taken to a farm labor camp. He was chosen because he told the guards he had experience working in the fields. As Johnny surveyed the fields, he hoped he'd be able to steal a radish or carrot when the guards weren't looking—and he did.

That October, Arnold Kessel came back to Lovell to visit his family before he left for Europe. He told them, "I'm excited about the training I've had to operate a Sherman tank. You can't believe what it's like, to ride inside one of these babies and fire those big guns, wow!"

Arnold had been assigned to General Patton's Third Army, Armored Division. He was in high spirits and his parents tried to savor every moment they had with him. He had a sweetheart, too, a pretty Lovell girl, Noreen.

The troop train pulled into Lovell in mid-October. The entire town turned out to send their sons, husbands, brothers, and lovers off to war. The high school band played loudly as American flags flew from each storefront and from the hands of small children and old men. Thirty young soldiers, looking smart in their new uniforms marched down Main Street to the railroad station. Occasionally a young girl darted out and laid a sweet kiss on the cheek or lips of a departing soldier.

After the parade, the officer in charge dismissed the soldiers; they broke ranks and rushed to waiting families. Departing hugs and kisses were given to mothers, wives, and sweethearts. Many couldn't contain their fear and grief. Unchecked tears ran down many cheeks as their loved ones boarded the train. Fueled by adrenaline-pumped dispositions, excitement, fear, and the uniform, soldiers leaned out the windows of the troop train and waved—it was going to be a long goodbye.

The train whistle blew as steam poured from the bowels of the black iron horse, the wheels slowly began to grind and turn as the train headed east out of Lovell. Those left standing on the platform waved and waved until they couldn't see the train any longer. Jake and Raisa watched in numb disbelief as their only son was taken away from them, to Europe and war.

Jake had a flashback: *I arrived on a train with my mother and brothers— in this depot. I was six years old. Now, my only son is leaving on a train out of the same depot, to go back across the Atlantic to fight the people I called my own. Perhaps he will even fight against a cousin he never met. This is all craziness, madness.*

Jake and Raisa received a letter from Arnold every week or two. Raisa and his sister Beth wrote to Arnold each week. They sent boxes of baked goods and other hard-to-get items. Three of his buddies from basic training were assigned to his unit. Things were a little easier for all of them to have familiar faces around.

Early in 1944, Arnold landed in England where he received a promotion to corporal. Soon, he became commander of his Sherman tank. He wrote: "I've seen General Patton, commander of the Third Army, and his ugly white dog. We've heard scuttlebutt that we might be gearing up for a big battle, but nobody knows for sure, where or when. Don't worry. I'm in a tank and a damn good one at that; it's not called a Sherman for no reason!"

The Kessels saw some images of the war when they went to the movies. The war reports were all too real and terrifying, especially to those with loved ones serving in the Pacific *and* in Europe. In most American homes, it was an evening ritual to sit around the Philco radio and listen to the world news, disturbing as it was. All they could do was pray.

One day as Katja was working in her Victory Garden, Karl arrived back from a trip into Lovell to have the car fixed. He climbed out of the car and headed for the garden where Katja had a basket of tomatoes for him to carry to the house. "I'll be a son of a gun, you'll never guess who worked on my car at the garage today—a woman! Never thought I'd see that but I guess woman are filling in for the men who are gone to war. Just isn't normal though."

One night in the Philippines, Johnny woke up on a sweat-drenched sleeping mat. He knew, oh, he knew only too well what the symptoms were for malaria, and he had them all. Fear rose in this throat along with sour bile. Weak with fever, he crawled out of the huddled mass of sleeping prisoners and staggered to the camp hospital. They called it a hospital, but they had no medicine or drugs to help the sick. But there was the black market even in this godforsaken hole, and Johnny had watched as men hocked their jewelry, anything the Japs hadn't already taken. Some even gave the ragged shirt off their backs in trade for medicine or food. Johnny looked down at the watch he had hidden from the guards; he hoped he'd be able to trade it for quinine for his malaria.

The medicine helped Johnny make it though the bout of malaria. Lying in bed, recuperating, he worried, *Am pretty sure this damn disease will come back; it usually does. I'll have to hock my wedding ring next. I doubt the little woman is still wearing hers. I'll do what the hell I have to; anything, for a chance to survive this shithole.*

As each day passed, Johnny and his fellow prisoners experienced escalating physical torments as the result of nutritional deficiencies. The ravages of beriberi caused men to wake in the night, screaming with the pain. Johnny spent many a night massaging a buddy's legs and arms hoping it would give him temporary relief from the stinging agony of the disease.

As months dragged on, the hospital ward filled with beriberi patients, taking valuable manpower out of the fields. Surprisingly, the camp furnished a concerned Japanese doctor who tried to administer to the needs of the prisoners, to no avail. In desperation, he went to the camp commander and suggested they give the prisoners more protein or they would lose their needed workforce. The guards finally issued small portions of protein, mostly beans, to the prisoners. Soon most were back in the fields.

If the coast was clear when Johnny worked in the fields, he pulled up a vegetable, any vegetable, and gobbled it down, leaves and stems included. He didn't care if it was covered with dirt. If there was a worm in it, he was glad for the extra protein. However, it was never enough; nothing seemed to help as he grew weaker, as the pounds dropped from his already starving body, exposing more ribs and bones. It was the same with all the prisoners—they were slowly dying from overwork and starvation. They didn't need mirrors to know how bad off they were; they just looked at the guy next to them.

In mid-March 1943, the prisoners received their first ration boxes packed with food from the Red Cross, it was like Christmas. To this point, none of the men had even received letters from home. They had hope but no proof that anybody knew they were there, which had been particularly demoralizing. The extra food helped build, or at least sustain, their bodies. Still, 10 to 30 more men died every day. Some escaped into the jungles, but many more were shot trying. Johnny never knew if those who made it past the guards actually survived the jungle itself.

Prisoners were constantly being moved from one camp to another, in an attempt to demoralize them. They began to hear rumors that the Americans were making strides in brutal battles to take back the Pacific islands. The Japanese guards denied this, declaring that *they* were winning, and the men would be prisoners and slaves to the Imperial Japanese—*forever!*

In February, Jake and Raisa were notified that Arnold had been slightly wounded. His tank suffered an indirect hit in the battle at Bastogne and he was blown out of the tank. But Arnold healed quickly and was soon back in command of his tank, as Patton's army continued north to the Ardennes Forest and another fierce battle.

Around that same time Johnny stood in a group of prisoners, waiting as Red Cross workers called out names at mail call. "Johnny Kessel," the voice called out. Johnny's heart began to beat so hard his ears rang as he made his way to the front and claimed his letter. He eased back through the pitiful group of men and crept into a secluded corner by himself. He felt pangs of guilt that he had received a letter from home while so many of his buddies hadn't. He couldn't get their faces out of his mind, faces filled with dejection, faces with need, without hope.

Johnny and the rest of the guys took this as another sign that the Americans were making progress in the war and opening the mail lanes. They all knew most of the mail and boxes from home didn't reach them—that the guards opened the boxes and ate the food themselves. Johnny saw the stack of mail that wasn't claimed and hoped the Red Cross would get the message back to their people that these guys were gone.

Recognizing his mother's handwriting, he was immediately flooded with images of her, how she smelled, her soft embrace, her striking ebony eyes, her generous smile. Slowly; Johnny opened the letter from home, the letter from his mother.

October 3, 1944

Dear Son Johnny,

We want you to know that everybody in your family is praying for you to survive being a prisoner and to come back home to us. We do not know exactly where you are. We were told you are being held by the Japanese somewhere in the Philippines. I hope that they are treating you well and you are not sick with the malaria sickness we have heard so much about. We have read much in the newspapers, heard the war news and reports over the radio, and also at the moving picture show, they always show scenes of battles. Oh, Johnny, how I wish you had not signed up and gone away to this war. What is done is done, and now all of us have to get through it, whatever way we can.

Today is your birthday and I am thinking of you and when you were born and how you were such an eager little boy. I know you had a hard time growing up, but you did it as you wanted, not as your Papa wanted. I wish you a happy birthday! Do you remember the dirt clod fight you and Ralf got into out in the field that time?

The biggest news from home is that your brother Eddie has married a good girl, Marguerite Wilson. They are living here at the farm and Eddie is farming with your papa. Papa has increased the size of his herd of Herford cattle. He has done well selling the beef to the government. We are still on war rations, which is sometimes hard, but we know it is what we have to do to help our troops in Europe and where you are. I have decided not to plant such a big garden next year. Working in the garden and all the canning is getting hard for me.

We are visited by your daughter often and we are all happy when this happens. Also, she is not so little anymore. She is now twelve and is a pretty girl. I do not know if you know or not, but she is small with dark hair, like me. She is not big like her mother. Well, I think this is all the news I have in this letter. I pray you are safe and well, son; we wait and hope for the day you come home again.

With our prayers and love, Mother and Dad

For a long time, Johnny just sat and stared at the letter from his mother. He allowed the memories to come forth out of the depths of his mind. Most were comforting memories and they were all he had for now. He tried to remember the smell of his mother's clean black hair, how she washed it in rain water and rinsed it with vinegar to make it shine. He tried to remember the soft scent of her favorite soap and powder. He thought about the wonderful meals she so effortlessly prepared for her large family, for days, weeks, months, and years. His favorite had always been the pungent German sausage, with fluffy mashed potatoes, savory sauerkraut, and the hearty beer his dad brewed in the cellar of the barn. Oh, what he wouldn't give to be home and to experience these little things. He knew he would never again take them for granted, and after this experience would appreciate them even more.

Johnny didn't think much about his wife, he was sure she had divorced him and moved on—*I never figgered her to be one to wait around for me or any man. It doesn't bother me a bit, she isn't worth thinking about. I do wonder what my little girl is like, sure hate it that she is growing up without me. Ma said she looks like her—like me? How big is she? Would she even know me and does she miss me? Will I ever put my arms around her again?*

Soon after receiving this letter from his mother, Johnny Kessel heard news in the camp located in Manila that there would be yet another selection of prisoners. The healthiest men would be loaded onto a waiting, rusty Japanese freighter anchored at the dock. Everyone knew why these boats were named death or hell ships. By October 1944, recognizing the aggressive advancement of the allied armies and the possible loss of the war, the Japanese decided to speed up the exportation of the healthiest prisoners to Japan, to work as slave labor in their mines.

On the 24th October 1944, Johnny Kessel was one of the 1,775 prisoners selected to board the next ship out. They were encouraged with bayonets to board and were packed into the lower cargo holds of the floating junk/barnyards. During the day the men literally boiled in the heat and humidity. At night they shivered with relentless chills in the depths of the death ship. On average, twenty men or more died per day. Their corpses were quickly stripped of any good clothing. Dead bodies were stacked like cordwood in the middle of the dank cargo hold. The decomposing bodies were hauled on deck in a net once every four days and thrown overboard, lunch for the sharks.

A chaplain or one of the other prisoners said prayers for the dead. Johnny uttered his own kind of prayer in the privacy of his mind. He still wasn't sure whether there was a God but, just in case, he prayed. His mind was filled with doubt, and he felt abandoned, forgotten.

The Japanese guards seemed to take great pleasure in announcing, "There will be no food today. American submarines sink Japanese supply ship, and so you must suffer more, compliments of your aw-mee."

An American officer called up to the guards standing at the open hole, "We need water and food; we are starving and dying down here!"

The guard answered, "That is good! We want you to die. American planes sink our ships, so you die, too. We want you to die!" They could hear the guard laughing as he walked away.

Most prisoners didn't smell any better than the animal feces they bedded down in. All they knew was—that it was softer and warmer than the cold, bare iron floor of the ship. More space became available as more prisoners died.

Word was—they were heading for Japan. Death ships stayed close, skirting island vegetation during daylight hours, venturing out into open seas during the night. All lights were extinguished so allied planes wouldn't spot them. Day in and day out, the confined men heard the drone of low-flying airplanes on missions to bomb Japanese-occupied islands of the Pacific. The Japanese crew disguised their ship as a neutral freighter, in order to slip under the eyes of the allied forces, but the prisoners knew this tactic did not always work. American planes dropped bombs on anything that looked Japanese, especially one of these rogue ships.

Johnny had survived, or simply existed, on numerous death ships for what seemed like weeks. Prisoners were put on one ship, taken off, and transferred to another. None of the ships were fit for human transport and the guards couldn't have cared less. The endless days of hiding along the beaches of the jungle-filled islands were followed by long nights running the darkened waters, always inching their way toward Japan.

Johnny wasn't quite sure of the exact date anymore, but thought it was probably mid-summer. He had been on the same ship about fourteen days in the storm-swollen South China Sea, when they were roused by the intense drone of airplanes—many airplanes—and they were flying low! They could hear the ship's crew scrambling as orders were shouted, and covers were ripped off hidden machine guns in a frantic attempt to defend themselves.

The half-naked, emaciated prisoners heard the rattle of anti-aircraft guns, of men on deck being hit, the screams and shouts that settled down into the cargo hold. Deep inside the belly of the ship, the prisoners' eyes were wide with terror as they crouched with arms shielding their heads. Nobody spoke, many held their breath until someone yelled, "Give 'em hell, boys; give 'em hell." Cheers went up and reverberated through the cavernous belly of the floating prison, as the high-pitched whistle of falling bombs came closer. Johnny thought, *There must be a hundred planes up there and it's obvious they've spotted this tub of bolts; they just don't know WE are in the bottom of it.* He was scared and he knew he wasn't the only one. Johnny had an ominous feeling in the pit of his belly that this was it!

Johnny couldn't wrap his mind around the fact that God, if there really was one, cared a damn about their terrible suffering. *If He does exist, IF He really cares, where the hell has He been? Doesn't He hear our screams, our suffering, and our dying? Why does He let this shit happen to all these good men?* It just didn't make sense, nothing made sense anymore.

But on this day, the moment came when it was all he had left, when reality, bravery, resistance, defiance, and even survival ceased to matter. His involuntary memories, and the faith he hadn't recognized, took over and he began to recite the Lord's Prayer, *"Our Father who art in heaven."* The planes and bombs sounded like they were right on top of them. *"Hallowed be thy name, Thy kingdom come, thy will be done on earth as it is in heaven. Give us this day our daily bread."*

The prisoners heard and felt ear-shattering explosion after explosion as they vibrated through the thin metal of the rusty old ship. Relentlessly, exploding bombs and rough seas rocked the ship in succession. Johnny prayed faster and louder now, *"and forgive us our trespasses, as we forgive those who trespass against us."* He was screaming now, *"and lead us not into temptation."* The entire side of the ship opened up with a deafening white-hot explosion. *"Deliver us from EVIL, for thine is the kingdom and the power and the glory forever. Dear Jesus –help me, help us—please."*

The metal sheathing of the ship peeled apart like an orange skin, as an intense blue-red flash ripped through the aft part of the ship, directly above and then down into the cargo hold.

Johnny heard the terror-filled shouts of his buddies, "My legs, where are my legs?" "Make 'em stop, dear God; make 'em stop!"

Hatch covers, machinery, fire, and large red-hot pieces of iron flew through the air, bouncing off rusty interior walls of the ship like ping-pong balls, tearing into flesh and bone of the trapped prisoners. "Oh, dear God, it hurrrrts, it hurts—help us, someone please help us!"

Johnny tried to see something, anything, through the choking black smoke and fierce flames. The gruesome sight came in flashes of light from more bombs and more fire. The pieces of bodies, arms, legs, heads, and limbless torsos were scattered and floating over the cargo hold of the ship. The sea water that rushed into the hold was blue and when it went back into the South China Sea, it was red, red with the life blood and bodies of dying men. Johnny was moving forward, holding men's heads above the water, trying to help in any way he could. These were his buddies, with their bodies blown apart and ripped open as they screamed in agony, until blessed death came to call, that's when he let them go.

Death and horror covered the floor of the cargo hold as well as on the upper decks. Johnny finally acknowledged a searing pain in his left thigh, as the salt from the sea water washed over his flesh. From the dim light that came through the holes in the ship, he saw the jagged piece of metal wedged deep in his thigh. He reached for it and barely touched it as the pain tore through his leg, shooting down like white-hot lightening to his foot. He heard his own voice scream, "Oh, damn it, I can't get it out, I can't get the sons-a-bitching thing out!"

On the upper decks, the barbaric and arrogant Japanese guards lay wounded and dying, sharing the same fate as their prisoners, down in the stinking cargo hold. The only difference was the Japanese could *see* the American planes; they could *see* hundreds of the enemy planes and the falling bombs, so many bombs. In the South China Sea, a few on board saw the telltale white path of unstoppable torpedoes, as they fished through the warm blue waters toward their waiting targets. Now, these Japanese soldiers, these guards were experiencing the same terror, agonizing pain, and death that they had so eagerly inflicted on their American prisoners.

Screams of agony and terror from the once-brutal guards filled the upper decks. Their captives down in the darkened hold below heard the screams, and were glad. The men still alive down in the depths of the ship didn't see the next wave of American planes. However, they did hear the unmistakable whistle of more bombs as they fell through the sky, and through the ship. Johnny heard someone scream, "They are killing us, our own planes are killing us, but at least the Japs didn't get us, did they, huh?"

They were nearly insane with mounting fear, pure terror, and the white hot, atrocious pain. Yet, through their hysteria and death throes, they were elated that finally, finally the Americans had come, reinforcements were here and they were giving 'em hell! The water of the South China Sea was spilling in faster now, finding new holes in the ruptured sides of the rusty old freighter as it began to sink. It came in rapidly and went out slowly, lifting up the weak and limp bodies of the dead and the near-dead, carrying them out through the large jagged metal holes.

Through his own haze of pain, Johnny heard more than one maimed and dying man scream, "Mo-ther, oh, Mama!" He thought of his own mother and how he wished he was safe inside her embrace, as he was as a child. He could see her face, the black hair, always swept back into a tight bun, and those piercing ebony eyes. Suddenly he felt her touch and opened his eyes wide, actually thinking she was there with him. But, it was only the body of a buddy who had brushed past, as the water tried to pull him out. Johnny reached out his arm to grab his friend, but the pain in his thigh stopped him. In mid-reach, a torpedo stopped everything. An incinerating blast filled the entire ship—exploding, ripping, tearing, dissolving with the screams and endless flashes of all-encompassing light, first red light, then blue. Everything was spinning downward, so fast, so hot. Suddenly there was another light, cool and comforting; Johnny saw the hand of his Lord Jesus and he reached out and took it. Then—a deafening silence and encompassing cocoon of white as the cool blue water of the South China Sea took their bodies to her depths.

Sleep, my sons, your duty done,
for Freedom's light has come;
sleep in the silent depths of the sea,
or in your bed of hallowed sod,
until you hear at dawn,
the low clear reveille of God.

~ inscribed on The Pacific War Memorial,
Corregidor Island, Philippines

CHAPTER 16

Freedom's Debt

★ ★ ★ ★ ★

WYOMING, 1945

It was a particularly balmy, spring day that makes people want to be outdoors in the sunshine; the kind of day which gave farmers early access to their thawing fields. The shiny, lime-green cottonwood leaves were slowly opening as their fuzzy seedpods sent the discarded shells spiraling down to the warming earth. Tender spears of new grass pushed up through last winter's mat of dead, butter-colored grass. The air was pungent with the unforgettable odor that only comes from damp soil and matted leaves. The earth was waking as were its people, reviving after the horror and losses from a terrible war, which had consumed Europe. The war was not yet over in the Pacific, but hopes were high that soon those boys would be coming home, too.

When Arnold Kessel came home from Germany, his grandfather Karl noticed the taut, haunted look in his grandson's eyes and face. He had been a boy, an easygoing, fun-loving kid, when he had left for the war. But a man returned—a tense man with a hard set to his jaw and wary eyes, always searching for the danger. He had witnessed terrible things. He just wanted to forget what he saw and did; he wanted to start living the rest of his life.

Jake and Raisa threw a family party for Arnold so his relatives could see him and welcome him home. All the aunts, uncles, and cousins carried in traditional German dishes for the meal, and of course there was plenty of cold beer. Arnold put on a cheerful, devil-may-care appearance for the family.

"Hey, buddy, tell us about killing those *krauts*. How many notches do you have on your belt?"

"How many Panzer tanks did your Sherman blow to smithereens? Bet you saw some real grizzly stuff, huh?"

Question after question, they all wanted to know about the war, how many Germans he had killed, all the details. But that wasn't something Arnold needed or even wanted to talk about, and his family soon got the message. Late in the afternoon, he pushed open the screen door and walked out into the backyard. He needed to be alone.

Karl Kessel had observed how his grandson reacted to his family's questions and comments about the war. One minute on top of the world, cutting up, and then in a flash, Arnold's inherited blue eyes had grown dark with memories. Karl followed him outside. He wanted to speak to his grandson in private.

Karl attempted to put his arm around the shoulders of his tall grandson, but settled for his waist. "Let's walk out this way, away from the peoples. I have been thinking there is something I want to say to you." Karl took a deep pull on his pipe before continuing, "Arnold, I saw much war in the old country, and also the men who returned. They had the same look on their face as you have this day. I do not know what you saw in the battles; I have never been in a war, but I do know you will never forget it. Arnold, you must learn how to put it away from your life, to be happy with your wife and son. We both know it will not be easy, and there will be bad days. But, it is the only way you will have a normal life again. I just wanted you to know, I understand. I have seen the fearsome results of war, in the old country. I know our weapons are even more terrible today, but I also know war, battles, and the dying never changes—it is always bad. Just between you and me, I want to tell you that I am proud of you for doing your duty for your country. And, I love you, my Arnold. I am thankful you are home, safe and whole."

Karl reached up and briefly embraced his grandson. He turned abruptly and walked swiftly back to the house and the celebration, as emotion began filling his chest, his throat, and his own ice-blue eyes.

Arnold stood, rooted to the spot, watching his grandfather walk back into the house. His grandfather had just told him he loved him, and he understood. Arnold had always heard the stories about the old man's fiery temper and of his stern, stoic concepts regarding his life and family. Karl Kessel had never shown a lot of affection to him in the past, much less told him he loved him. Arnold's own emotions sprang to the surface and his own blue eyes filled with tears. Even though his grandfather was out of earshot, Arnold declared, "It feels damn good—DAMN good, that somebody understands what my days and nights are filled with, and somebody cares enough to speak the words. I'll try hard not to let you down, *Grosvater*. I'll give it a hell of a try." Nobody told him it would be easy to put what he had seen and done behind him; he knew it was now a part of who he was. The startling sounds of shells exploding, the faces that were contorted with terror, pain, and death; the smells—*oh good Lord, how will I ever forget the smells*.

By the end of May, Karl and Katja still had no word about their fourth son, Johnny. The war in the Pacific was not over but when it was, they understood that the process of releasing prisoners of war was a particularly slow one. They had to be patient, but the waiting was agonizing. As days passed without any word, their worry and unrest began to elevate and made them edgy. The nagging concern would not leave their conscious thoughts or their dreams, but neither Karl nor Katja addressed this worry to the other. Privately, they held onto the hope that one day their handsome, charming Johnny would swagger through the kitchen door.

Early morning, October 7, 1945, Katja carried a heavy wicker basket of wet clothes down the wooden steps to the backyard clothesline. This was one chore she enjoyed, hanging up the clean clothes she had just washed in her prized, wringer washing machine. As she pinched each piece with two wooden clothes pins, her thoughts went to the coming winter and what it would bring.

Karl had been working in the corral for nearly an hour, pitching hay to the cattle. Neither noticed the black sedan with government license plates, slowing as it approached the driveway of their farm. The driver signaled as he made the right-hand turn off the highway into the lane of the Kessel farm. The black car decelerated and rolled across the gravel, finally coming to a stop in the yard.

Hearing the crunch of tires on the gravel, Katja instinctively turned toward the sound, and froze with recognition. "Oh, *mein Gott*," the words rose from her throat in a choked sob, "*Mein Gott, NEIN—NEIN*, the *black* car."

Everybody knew who was in the black car—the government, military men, officials who brought news. And, it was never good news. They carried the official documents that announced the death of a son, a husband, a father. Katja's knees began to shake and buckle as she reached for the clothesline pole to steady herself. A pair of Karl's work pants hung by one clothes pin, dripping onto the grass, as Katja forgot about what she had been doing. She heard Karl running from the barn and, in a moment, he was by her side, his chest heaved as he tried to catch his breath. They stood still together by the clothesline, rooted to the ground. The black car's gears shifted to neutral; all was quiet as the motor died, and the Kessels' perpetual hope turned to alarming despair.

Two uniformed men stepped from the car. The men were uncomfortably aware of the elderly couple who stood together, holding hands in front of the wet clothes. They did not relish their orders; the two men had often discussed the unspeakable difficulty of their military assignments.

Karl left Katja's side and walked toward the two men, extending his hand. "Karl Kessel, but I think you already know my name."

"Yes, Mr. Kessel, Mrs. Kessel, we know your names. I am Staff Sergeant Melvin Cooper and this is Lieutenant John Urmhoff."

After more hand shaking, Karl said, "Please, please come into our house."

He turned and motioned for Katja to come with him. She hesitated, but walked the few steps toward her husband. Her legs and feet felt like they had lead weights in them; she could hardly put one foot in front of another. Karl reached for her hand and they climbed the wooden steps to the back porch together.

Karl pulled out a couple of wood chairs from the scrubbed kitchen table, for the two men, as Katja offered them coffee and apple strudel. The government men graciously declined and slowly opened their briefcases. The tall one adjusted his glasses and began, "On behalf of the government of the United States of America, we regret to inform you that your son, Corporal Johnny Kessel, has died in the service of his country and was buried at sea, shortly before the end of the war."

Katja's face and body froze and her ebony eyes stared unblinking. She appeared as though she did not comprehend what the man had declared. Slowly, her work-worn hand rose from her lap to cover her quivering mouth, in an attempt to stifle a gasp or sob. It was true—her worst fears had come true. Her Johnny was dead. The son who looked like her would not be coming home, not ever; he was *dead!*

Hot, salty tears filled her eyes and rolled uncontrolled down her weathered cheeks, past her quivering chin and onto the bodice of her green, cotton-print dress. Katja struggled to suppress her emotions and retain her dignity. Her head and shoulders shook as she tried in vain to contain her grief. Karl reached over, a grim, stunned expression on his face as he put one arm around his wife's shoulders, gently patting her upper arm. His other hand was clenched into a tight fist as he also struggled to control his shock and the rising bile in his throat. The harsh reality of the government man's words hung in the air.

Katja's mind frantically searched for some logical explanation for what she was hearing. *This has to be a dream; it has to be a dream*. Had she thought of this possibility so often that now she was dreaming it? Silently, she pleaded with her maker, *Pleeease, let this be a dream, dear God, please!*

Karl's mind was racing, searching, as he questioned the two men, "What happened to our son? Do you know how he died and when?"

The government men looked at each other before one of them spoke. "We are sorry we do not have detailed information. We only know that Johnny Kessel and approximately 1,774 other prisoners of war were forced to board Japanese ships. Their destination most likely was the mines in Japan, to work as forced labor. The unmarked ship was assumed by American fighter pilots to be a Japanese warship. Many of these ships were torpedoed as enemy vessels and, according to our reports, most on board perished. There were a handful of survivors from the ship your son was on and that is how we obtained our information."

Katja's buried her face in her tiny hands. She felt light-headed and afraid she might faint.

"Within the past month, the Japanese government supplied our war department with lists of prisoner-of-war survivors, as well as the names of those prisoners who died during the war. As near as our government officials can determine, Corporal Johnny Kessel died sometime near the end of October 1944, aboard a ship headed for Japan. We have also received verification of this information from five American prisoners who survived the sinking of the ship." Lt. Urmhoff didn't volunteer that the information was also verified by the American pilots who bombed the Japanese ship.

As sweat began to bead on his forehead, Staff Sgt. Cooper paused to collect himself and continued, "Corporal Kessel survived the Bataan Death March after being captured. He was imprisoned by the Japanese for over two years. Thousands of prisoners died, but your son survived the POW camps. The terrible and unfortunate circumstances of his death are indeed regrettable. Corporal Kessel was a hero and his country is eternally grateful for his ultimate sacrifice."

The facts exploded in Karl's mind—his son had survived the infamous Bataan Death March and the brutality of the Japanese prisoner of war camps. He had almost made it, *he had almost made it. He had survived everything, until our planes bombed the Jap ship where he was being held prisoner!* He had not survived American bombs, and he wasn't coming back home to them. Karl Kessel sat there at his kitchen table with thoughts of his son racing through his mind; *I am proud of him and the man he showed himself to be when things got bad.*

One of the government men said, "If the family prefers, we will arrange a special ceremony of respect and honor for your son. At this ceremony we will present the Medal of Honor and the memorial flag of the United States of America to Corporal Kessel's family."

It was agreed the men would return in a week for a memorial ceremony on the front lawn of Kessel home, weather permitting. Dazed, Karl walked the two men to their car, thanked them for coming, and graciously bid them goodbye.

Watching the car turn left and disappear down the highway, Karl walked back to his house, into his kitchen to speak quietly to his wife. "Katja, I know this is not what we had hoped and prayed for, but the government has now made it official. Our Johnny has died in the war; now we know what has happened. If you want me to, I will call our family to tell them of the news. I will also ask them if they will like to come to the memorial service next week. Do you want me to do this?"

Slowly, Katja lifted her head and her words came with difficulty, "*Ja,* Karl, I knew when I saw the black car; I knew it was the government men who came with the terrible news, news we hoped we would never have to hear." Katja's numb response was monotone, "But now, we must do what is proper for our son, and honor his memory. If you want to call our sons and daughters, you should be the one to do that. Also, please call Johnny's daughter and her mother and ask for them to come to the ceremony, too."

"I cannot prepare supper for you, Karl. If you want something to eat, you will have to fix it for yourself." Katja's face sagged with grief as she waved off any further conversation. She turned and slowly walked out of the kitchen and into the solace of her bedroom. She put her hand around the white porcelain door knob and pushed the door shut, inspired by some internal effort to shut out the unspeakable horror of the death of her child.

Katja sat down on the edge of the bed and bent over to remove her black shoes. She put her face into her hands and wrenching sobs came from deep within her body. She stood and removed her dress and slip, letting them lay where they had fallen. Katja was usually fastidious, but she just didn't care anymore. She gave no further thought to the half-full wicker basket of wet clothes she left beside the clothesline. They didn't matter; nothing mattered. She opened the drawer next to the bed and took out a small white pill from the bottle that Dr. Craft had given her to take for hypertension. She laid it on her tongue and swallowed it with a sip of water. She laid back onto the bed and hoped for blessed oblivion to cover her mind.

Karl sat for a long time at the kitchen table that evening with a lukewarm cup of coffee, trying to digest the information the government men had brought into his house. After awhile, he rose and quietly opened the door to the bedroom and found Katja on the bed. He reached for the chenille blanket and gently covered her.

Back in the kitchen, Karl's eyes went to the black phone that sat on the cabinet. It almost seemed to mock him, "*Pick me up. I am here waiting for you—use me to call your family, to tell them of the bad news. Come on; pick me up!*"

Karl didn't wait long, *better to get it over with*, he thought. He reached for the receiver, lifting it off the hook, and dialed the first number. He spent over an hour calling his children, telling them the terrible news, "Johnny will not be coming home. There will be a service, a ceremony on Friday of the next week. Your mother and I would like to have the whole family there.

Karl left the brick house as the sun was setting and walked out to the barn where he had privacy. There in the shadows of his barn, and only there, he allowed his heartbreak and grief to leave his heart. Karl Kessel had not cried often in his lifetime, but this was different. He had lost a son whom he had loved. Memories flooded his mind, memories of the kind of father he had been to his dead son, to all of his sons. *I know I was particularly hard on Johnny because he was too much like me with his bad temper and defiance. We had so many bitter words and disagreements.*

He remembered that morning in the field when Johnny showed up late, still drunk and smelling of women. Karl remembered how he had chastised his son and, when he attempted to smash the shovel against his back a second time, Johnny had grabbed it and tore the shovel from his father's hands, throwing it to the ground.

Karl recalled his son's words: "THAT was the last time you will strike me, old man! THAT was the last time you order me to do your work. You know what I think? You should have never been given sons, because you've done nothing but abuse us! Someday, you will be alone old man. Remember my words, ALONE!"

Johnny had always been defiant, not a follower. He was his own man with his own ideas of how things should be done. He had always lived for the day, not living his life with goals and dreams—only the moment. Karl shook his head, trying to rid his mind of tormenting thoughts. *I must be strong for the rest of my family because I am the head of this house, of this house which had now lost a son.* He folded his leathered hands and prayed God would give him strength to do what he had to do, and to forgive him for his sins. He slumped to his knees and, falling forward, wept bitter tears.

The next morning Katja made a feeble attempt to get up, dress, and make breakfast for her husband. Everything she did seemed to be in slow motion; nothing seemed real. Each leg felt like it weighed a hundred pounds. Her heart literally hurt. *All I want is to rest, to sleep, and try to forget the news the government men brought to our door and our lives yesterday.*

Later in the week, Karl became more concerned about how Katja was taking the news of the death of her son. When she had lost her parents, she had taken it badly and had shown immediate, strong visible emotion and grief. But this time was different. She sat; she did not speak, scream, or cry. She just sat with a stony, numb expression on her aged face. This worried Karl and he did not know what to do for her when she held all her sorrow inside, but he knew this was not a good thing.

The day for the memorial came, and their children, grandchildren, Johnny's daughter, and her mother all came to the Kessel brick farmhouse for the ceremony. Pastor Siebert spoke reassuring words to the family and asked God's blessing and forgiveness for their dead son, Johnny, and for comfort to his family in their grief.

Staff Sgt. Morrow and Lieutenant Urmhoff presented the emotionally numb parents with the war medal and placed the folded American flag into

Katja's arms. Reporters and photographers were present from the *Lovell Daily Chronicle* to take pictures for the paper. The Lovell Florist shop sent a wreath, which was placed around Johnny's picture. After a simple lunch, everybody left the ceremony at the farm for their respective homes. It was over. Their waiting and wondering about the fate of their son and brother—was over.

Jake and Raisa stayed for a few moments after the ceremony. "Are you two going to be okay? Do you want to come into Lovell and stay at our house tonight?"

"*Nein,* Jakob; we will be fine. However, it might take some time to get used to the idea. Your brother Johnny is not coming home. But that is the way it is and we have to accept it." Karl's jaw remained clenched tight against the inner turmoil that ate at him daily. Katja's gaze was blank.

Jake and Raisa kissed each of them goodbye and drove back to Lovell. As he turned onto the highway, Jake glanced in his rearview mirror at his parent's fine brick farmhouse, and thought to himself, *They are alone now, in that big house with only their memories of Johnny. How are they going to cope with this kind of grief? What is this going to do to them?* A shudder ran down his spine.

Karl and Katja walked up the steps into their brick house. The ceremony had been nice, the government officials were nice; their sons and daughters had been nice, and the weather had been nice. Everything was as it should be, except for the fact they would never see their son again. Knowing he had endured terrible torture and endless suffering in his last months, made it even more terrible. They had read newspaper articles of unbelievable atrocities done to the prisoners of war. They were haunted by mental images of Johnny's suffering, horrible images that filled their minds again and again.

After a light supper Karl and Katja retreated to their dimly lit parlor, not sharing their thoughts or emotions. They sat in silence, both struggling with their personal version of grieving and the horror of their son's suffering.

Karl rose from his easy chair and walked over to the Victrola and pulled a recording of classical music from its protective sleeve. He put the black disc on the turntable and placed the sharp needle on the disc. Beautiful, soothing music drifted through the house as they sat in their easy chairs with white crocheted doilies protecting the arms and backs. *There are many other peoples who have lost someone; we have to learn to live with it, but it feels so heavy in my heart. Perhaps if we just sit quietly and get through today, tomorrow, and the next day—this pain will be less each day and it will be better again.*

Karl looked up to see more tears falling down Katja's cheeks. "Katja, what is it? Does the music make you more sad? I will turn it off you want me to."

Katja looked up at her husband, "Karl, do you wonder what we were doing WHEN our American planes bombed the ship Johnny was on? Do you think about such things? I do. I think about it all the day and night, too. Was I cooking supper? Was I hanging clothes out to dry? Was I working peacefully in my garden? What was I doing when the life went from our son's body?"

Shaken, Karl responded, "*Nein*, Katja, I try hard not to dwell on what has been; it does no good. It is over, it is done and there is nothing we can do to bring him back. He almost made it through all of the bad things, he just ran out of time!"

During the days that followed, Karl seemed to manage grief better than his wife. He kept busy in his fields and caring for his cattle and working the earth was his savior, for a while at least.

On Thursday afternoon, two weeks after the memorial ceremony for their son Johnny, Katja sat motionless and quiet on her chair in the living room. Her head was tipped back against the crocheted doilies that were pinned to the back of the chair. Her ebony eyes were closed, seemingly in rest. Her breath came softly and gently, moving her chest up and down. The telephone rang, and rang again before Katja responded to it. Startled, she rose from the chair and ran across the hardwood floor to reach the phone on the dining hutch.

"Hello, hello," she said breathlessly.

"Am I speaking to the Kessel house? Is this Mrs. Kessel?" The voice on the other end of the line was young, and male.

"*Ja*, this is Mrs. Kessel, who is this?"

"Mrs. Kessel, my name is Lt. Stewart Morrow. I am now living in Powell." The voice on the phone paused, as the man took a deep breath.

"Mrs. Kessel, I would like to come to your home and speak with you and Mr. Kessel. I was on Bataan, in the Philippines and in the Death March. I was in the prisoner of war camps with your son, Johnny. I knew your son. He was my friend; he was my good friend."

Katja froze at the words that came from the telephone; they entered her ear, and struggled to find their way into her mind. "Mrs. Kessel, are you there? Mrs. Kessel…?"

Katja shook her head as if to clear it and responded to the voice on the other end of the phone line. "*Ja, ja*, I am here. This is such a surprise that I cannot find the words. You knew my son, and you were his friend in the war, *ja*?"

"Yes, Mrs. Kessel, that is true and I would very much like to come to your home. I have some things to tell you about your son that may give you comfort. May I come for a short visit tomorrow, say around two o'clock?"

"*Ja, ja*, Lt. Morrow, that would be fine, I will tell my husband and we will be expecting you. Do you know how to get to our farm?" Katja hands were shaking as she struggled to gain control of her emotions.

"Yes, Mrs. Kessel, I do know where you live and I will see you tomorrow at two o'clock. And, Mrs. Kessel, thank you for seeing me, it really means a lot to me, goodbye."

The line clicked dead and Katja replaced the phone in its cradle. She stood, rooted to the spot, trying to digest the words she heard. *The soldier knew Johnny and had been his friend!*

When Karl came in from the fields and barn that evening, Katja met him with the news. At first, Karl didn't understand what she was saying and thought perhaps she had another dream about Johnny. He heard the part about this young man coming to speak with them tomorrow, to tell them about their son.

Neither Karl nor Katja slept well that night, they were both anxious about the visit that was to take place the next day. *What would he say about Johnny? Would it be things that would make us feel happy or make us sad? Why, oh why did this soldier make it back to his family and our son is dead, dead at the hands of his own countrymen?*

The next morning, Karl left the house early to attend to his chores in the barn and Katja tried to keep busy with her housework and laundry, but found herself looking at the clock every few minutes. Around noon, the back door swung open and Karl walked into the kitchen, ready for his noon meal. He washed up and sat in his chair at the wooden kitchen table. Katja brought two steaming bowls of chicken soup and freshly baked wheat bread to the table. They sat and ate in silence. After the noon meal, Karl went into the bedroom to change out of his soiled work clothes. Katja washed the dishes, tidied her hair, and smoothed her dress. She took off her apron and hung it on a hook behind the kitchen door.

The Kessels went into the living room and sat in their respective chairs. Karl turned the walnut radio on, spinning the dial, and tried to find a particular station. Finally, he was rewarded with the classical station he was searching for. Waves of soothing music from Bach rippled through the room, comforting their nerves. After a while they heard Lt. Stewart Morrow's car pull into the gravel driveway and roll to a stop.

Karl and Katja hurried to the back door as the uniformed young man walked up the sidewalk.

Karl spoke first, "Lt. Morrow? Please, please come into our house. We are so happy that you called and have come to speak to us."

Stewart Morrow extended his hand to the small, elderly man who stood framed by the doorway. Stewart thought to himself, *Mr. Kessel has the same slight build as Johnny, but Johnny had his mother's black hair, and yeah, he sure did have her dark eyes, but they twinkled just like his dad's.*

"Mr. and Mrs. Kessel, it is so good to meet you, I appreciate the opportunity to come and talk with you about your son."

Karl and Katja ushered Lt. Morrow into the dining room and motioned for him to take a chair. Katja spoke first, "Lt. Morrow, can I get for you a cup of coffee or something to drink?"

"Please call me Stewart and, yes, I would appreciate a cup of hot coffee; black is fine."

Karl and Stewart made small talk until Katja returned with coffee for the three of them, accompanied with her famous strudel. Stewart waited until they were all settled and he began. "Johnny and I met during basic training in Sacramento, California." A wide grin spread across Stewart's face as he recalled his friend. "Yeah, he was a good-looking son of a gun and tough as nails. Whenever we were lucky enough to get some time off and get off that base, the dames were all over your son. Not sure what his secret was, but he *was* popular with the ladies!"

A knowing look passed between Karl and Katja. Sure, they knew of their son's reputation. He knew how to use his dark good looks and smooth way with words to get whatever he wanted.

Stewart Morrow took a sip of the hot coffee and continued, "Johnny and I were lucky enough to be assigned to the same regiment when we were sent to the Philippine Islands in March 1941. I suppose you read all about it in the rags, about the battles and stuff. We fought like hell on those cursed Philippine islands." Lt. Morrow paused as he turned to Katja, "Sorry about the bad language, Mrs. Kessel, but guess I just got used to talkin' like that in the war!"

The black memory crossed Morrow's face as it all came flooding back; the horror they faced almost daily still haunted him. Both Karl and Katja noticed the difference in the young man's face as he clenched his jaw and continued, "Johnny and I were stationed on a small island called Corregidor it was at the entrance to Manila Bay. The island was said to be shaped like a tadpole, it was about four miles long and about a mile-and-a-half wide at its widest point. The entire island was a fortress and many of its facilities were underground in a huge concrete tunnel. It was pretty interesting how that place was set up."

Lieutenant Morrow went on to tell how in late fall of 1941, their unit had been moved from Corregidor to Clark Field, an Army airbase located inland, on the main island of Luzon. "Johnny and I were at Clark Field on December 8th; it was a Monday I think. The big brass had summoned all of us officers to the headquarters building early that morning and told us the Japs had bombed Pearl Harbor, but they didn't know many details about the attack. They said we'd all better get our men ready for action, and they told us to go back to our units and await further orders. I kept my men busy all morning moving ammunition and guns to where we thought it should be if something came up. We could see all the bomber and fighter planes taking off, but other than that things didn't seem much different than usual on the base."

Morrow continued, "Finally, it was around eleven o'clock when the bomber and fighter plans returned from their scouting mission and began to land at the base. In the meantime, I got orders to send my men to lunch. When we was marching over to the mess hall, I happened to notice all the airplanes were parked together in straight lines near the fuel tanks. While the fuel crews got busy refueling the planes, the rest of us got in line for chow. The first twenty men had just sat down when the Jap fighters flew in out of nowhere. The sirens began to scream and we all ran outside to have a look."

"They were already over the airfield by the time we got outside. That was a hell of a bad feeling, to look up and see the sky filled with those fighters with that red sun on their tail! They caught us with our pants down, pure and simple, just like Pearl Harbor. They took out fifty percent of our planes in that first attack. You just can't imagine how those crazy bast...sorry, Mrs. Kessel."

Lieutenant Morrow lifted the cup of coffee to his lips and took a long slow sip of the hot brew. "Bombs were falling everywhere, one hit right in the middle of the platoon that was stationed next to ours. We could hear screams from guys that were wounded, and I, I don't mean to make you sick, but we could see pieces of our guys scattered around everywhere!"

"About ten of us ran like hell across the base to where our unit had placed a couple of machine guns; big ones, fifty-caliber. At that point it looked like all we had left were about six P-40s, our best fighters. They were just getting them warmed up when a whole of a bunch of them Jap Zeros, fighter planes, came in low with their guns blazing. Johnny was the only one ready for 'em, and he was firing his machine gun like a madman every time they made a strafing run over us. He put holes in a lot of those damn Zeros, and a couple of them started smokin' like hell and went down in a fiery spin after he hit 'em. I'm pretty sure some of those Japs never made it back to where they came from."

Morrow wiped the perspiration from his forehead with his handkerchief, shook his head as if to shake the memories from his mind. "That awful day spilled over into that night. Death and the smell of it was everywhere, and believe me, Mr. And Mrs. Kessel, when I tell you there was no sleeping around Clark Field that night. Once we got hold of our guns, we didn't make it easy for them. But, at the end of the day, they got us pretty good!"

Katja and Karl sat rooted to their kitchen chairs as the young lieutenant told them how hard Johnny and the rest of the men had fought that day at Clark Field. "After it was over, we just sat around, pretty much stunned. We snapped back to life as the screams of the wounded, sirens, and general commotion pierced the otherwise eerie silence of death and destruction. The next few days are just a blur 'cause we were so busy trying to help the wounded and bury our dead. Then, on December 22, we got word that over 40,000 Jap troops under General Homma had landed on beaches about a hundred miles to the north of Clark Field. The platoons began to prep to face the enemy, and we were just starting to get dug in when we got orders to get the hell out of there, away from Manila. None of us knew what was going on, 'cause we hadn't seen any Jap troops yet. But pretty soon we would see plenty of them bastards."

Lt. Morrow paused as he turned to Katja. "Sorry about the bad language again, Mrs. Kessel, guess I need to learn to talk around women again!"

Morrow went on to tell the old couple about how it had been when their unit had been sent to the Bataan peninsula, a hot muggy place that was mostly jungle, and one of the most heavily mosquito-infested areas in the entire world. He told them how their ragtag army held out against the Japanese for almost four months. At first, according to the lieutenant, things weren't too bad, even though food seemed to get pretty short at times; but, as the hunger increased and food rations were decreased, morale began to decline. "Morale got even worse when the men began to hear stories that McArthur, our commanding general, was eating well and living 'high on the hog' in his fancy headquarters in the tunnels on Corregidor. We called him Dugout Doug—among other things," Morrow told the Kessels with a slight smile. "Before long, the guys at the front began running out of quinine, the only remedy we had for malaria. Soon hundreds of our guys were sick with those chills and the fever, and under heavy attacks by the Japs, the troops had to withdraw to new positions further down the peninsula."

He went on, "The Japs knew the pickins was good and we couldn't defend. For the next few weeks, they pounded the living hell out of the airbases and the Cavite Naval Yard, and took out even more of our fighters. For three weeks without ammo or fresh water, we hung on through all that. We hung on only because of our pure ornery! But you know, by Go--, we hurt those damn Japs, and we hurt 'em bad. We smashed their Fourth Division, the same Jap troops ole Homma planned to use against us in New Guinea and the Solomons. We intercepted their intelligence 'bout where they were plannin' on goin' in the Pacific and that hurt 'em, too. We protected Australia, by damn, the Japs never got to the shores of Australia, for sure!"

Karl and Katja sat like statues in their chairs, barely drinking any of the coffee, barely breathing as they listened to what their son had experienced in the Philippines. Lt. Morrow raised both hands to his face, rubbed his eyes, and raised them higher, running them through his hair. "Whew, just talkin' about it all, is bothering me a bit, just brings it back, you know!"

"We didn't—we simply couldn't hold those Japs off much longer," Morrow said. "They had more bullets, more men, more water, more medicine, and more food. In March, McArthur got his orders to get the hell out of there—like the brass could see the writing on the wall and they wanted their best boy in a safe place. He just went off and left the rest of us there. All the time we were waitin' for that convoy, with fresh troops, replacements whatever they could send us. But nothing, nobody came, except more Japs."

Morrow stood up and walked to the dining room window, and turned as he continued, "We knew; we all knew at that moment we would all probably die or become prisoners. It was one of those no-win situations, you know? We hung on doing all we could do. Then, on April 3, 1942, the Japanese got their reinforcements and we didn't get ours. They launched a new offensive. We had nothing with which to fight back, and they quickly overran positions still held by our outgunned and hungry American and Filipino soldiers. By nightfall the roads going south toward Marivales were clogged with soldiers pulling back from the frontlines. Many had been injured, while others were sick and weak from malaria and could barely walk. Zeros swept in unmolested and strafed the slow-moving columns. A few American units remained cohesive enough to stay behind the refugees and provide supporting fire to slow up the Japanese infantry, who were in hot pursuit and gaining fast on the fleeing soldiers and civilians."

Lieutenant Morrow told the startled couple, "Your son was one of the soldiers providing covering fire for his comrades. That's when Johnny was wounded."

With those words, Katja's emotions got the best of her, and she tearfully cried out, "Oh, my God, I did not know that he was wounded! Was it bad, Lt. Morrow?"

"No, Mrs. Kessel, it wasn't really bad. It was more or less a flesh wound in the soft under part of his left, upper arm. He could still fire a rifle with his right arm and he did, by damn, he was a sight. In fact, he was still a good marksman using only one arm."

Both Lt. Morrow and Karl Kessel smiled at this thought, as Karl reported, "*Ja*, I taught him to shoot the rifle when he was ten. He was always good with the gun and he sure liked to shoot."

Morrow slapped his leg and let out a subdued chuckle. "Just before dark that night Johnny picked off a monkey that was way up in a tree quite a ways from our position. We hadn't had anything to eat all day and probably the thought of eating boiled monkey doesn't sound all that appetizing to you; but, let me tell you, that monkey tasted pretty damn good to us!"

Karl and Katja just looked at each other without commenting on their soldier's dinner menu. Morrow continued, "A little while later, we saw Johnny looking up at another tree, and suddenly he fired off another round and something big fell out of that tree. I thought, *Oh crap, I don't really need another monkey, right now.* BUT, what fell out of that tree was a Jap sniper! Ole Johnny could really shoot."

Morrow went on to tell the parents of his buddy that on the 8th of April, he and Johnny were among some of the last American troops to reach the Marivales area. Up ahead they could hear explosion after explosion, which they found out later were not caused from Japanese shelling, but instead were American demolition teams blowing up the remaining ammunition and fuel supplies. Some two thousand persons managed to get aboard barges and small boats and escape to Corregidor, but that left around twelve thousand American troops and almost sixty thousand poorly trained Filipino troops trapped at the southern tip of Bataan. "Our ammunition had almost been used up and we had orders to blow up what was left. Our food supply, if you can call it that, was about exhausted as well. Continuous bombardment and artillery barrages by the Japanese went unanswered. To prevent a total slaughter of our troops, our battlefield commander, General King, opted to surrender."

"Well, finally on the 9th of April we surrendered," Stewart Morrow told the

Kessels. "We were out of everything and there was no other choice. I think some of the guys purposely got themselves killed because they didn't want to become a prisoner of the Japs. We had all heard of their cruelty and weren't looking forward to it. But, little did we know it would go beyond what we Americans call cruel! When those Jap troops learned we'd surrendered they started running toward us. It was the creepiest thing I ever saw—thousands of them gooks running and screaming with rifles raised. It just made the hair stand up on the back of your neck!"

Katja noticed that Morrow's coffee cup was nearly empty, and interrupted his story to ask if he wanted a refill. While she took his cup back to the kitchen to refill it, the lieutenant leaned in closer to Karl and said, "I found out after I got home that the war correspondents had begun calling us the Battling Bastards of Bataan."

Karl grinned and said, "*Ja,* I think that was a good name for you guys, and I know Johnny would have had a good laugh over that one!"

Katja sat the fresh cup of coffee on the table in front of the lieutenant and he took another sip. "I am not telling you these things to upset you, Mr. and Mrs. Kessel. You indicated you wanted to know of your son's last days and months in the war. I will stop at anytime you want; just say the word."

Katja looked across the kitchen table at her husband as he lifted his head, "*Nein,* Lieutenant, we want to know what it was like for our son. It is not easy to hear, but it will put our minds to rest, I think. The *not* knowing is the worst. Please continue, go on; go on."

Morrow's head went down as he began, "Well, I guess you have heard the rest of the story. When we surrendered and they rounded us up and put us in a barbed-wire fenced yard with guards posted all around. They got their kicks out of jabbing us with their bayonets, spitting on us, hell, hurting us any way that they could. We stayed penned up like that for about five days until they figured out what to do with us. Frankly, I don't think they knew what to do with so many prisoners."

"In a day or two, they rounded us up again and forced us out of the yard. They yelled and screamed at us that we had to march to another camp," he imitated them, "You run fast, or you die!"

He went on, "The Bataan Death March had begun. I had been wounded in that final battle, too, and was not in good shape. If it wasn't for your son, I would not have lived through that march. What can I say? It was bad and the Jap guards were purely vicious." Morrow paused, trying to regain his composure, and took another sip of coffee and a bite of the strudel.

"When they started marching us, Johnny put his arm around me, let me lean on him. I got so weak in that damn heat; I had a hard time walking. If he had not done that, if I had fallen—I would have been bayoneted or shot on the spot. We saw it time after time; those guards were determined NOT to pick anybody up who couldn't walk! In fact they got all excited and smiled when they had an opportunity to shoot or bayonet one of us who had hit the road. They especially liked shooting us Americans!"

Stewart paused and lifted the cup to his lips, "Sure is good coffee and apple strudel, Mrs. Kessel, thanks!" He took a deep breath and continued, "After we got to the first camp, my wounds healed slowly in all that humidity. Johnny was always right there giving me part of his rations and doing anything he could for me. I told him not to give me part of his food, because he needed the nourishment to do the work the guards were forcing on him and the others. But Johnny would not hear of it; he insisted I take part of his food if you can call that slop food. He insisted on trying to help me get well, and I did get better, but slowly. One day the guards came after me for not being able to work; it wasn't clear if they were going to beat me or shoot me. So Johnny jumped in front and took a swing at a guard, and of course they forgot about me and went after him. They beat him up pretty bad, but nothing that didn't heal."

"Johnny and I shared many days and nights talking about home, about our families, about the freedom we were fighting for. Your son loved you so much. He admitted he had not been the best son, and felt guilty for causing you so much grief when he was grown up and livin' at home."

Stewart folded his hands together as his head bowed. Finally, he raised his head and, looking directly at the Kessels, said. "Your son was a good man; he was the best friend a man could have, and I miss him—I will miss that man until the day I die! I will always be grateful to Johnny Kessel for saving my life. The last time I saw him was when they were loading the prisoners onto one of those stinking boats, one of the hell ships. The guards always chose the heartiest prisoners to ship off to Japan as slave labor."

"Before he left, Johnny made an effort to find me in the camp and shake my hand—hell, he hugged me and I hugged him. He was like a brother to me. I cried when that ship pulled out of the harbor, 'cause I had a real bad feeling. We all knew some of those ships were being bombed and torpedoed by our planes, and that is what happened to the ship Johnny was on. It was a terrible, terrible thing." Morrow paused.

"He almost made it, Mr. and Mrs. Kessel, he almost came home with me, and I wish to God he had." The tears were coming now, and Morrow didn't even try to stop them. "Johnny deserved to come home, especially for everything he did for me and other prisoners who were in trouble. I just wanted you to know that your son was a hero. He did his best to help his fellow Americans, and in particular helping me to survive. Without Johnny, I wouldn't be sitting here, telling you about what happened over there."

Stewart Morrow wiped his large sinewy hand across his brow, "There is one more thing I have to tell you—something Johnny told me early on in our ordeal. He said, 'Stu, we all know we are living though a Jap hell here, right? There might be times we want to just give up and die. If and when that time comes, remember this—tragedy can bend or break you—YOU decide which it will be!' I will remember those words the rest of my life."

He added, "Lots of those prisoners only cared about themselves; hell, I don't blame 'em. Those were tough times and we were each just trying to survive!"

Throughout the entire visit, Karl and Katja sat like stones in their respective chairs and listened as Stewart Morrow told them about their dead son. Obviously shaken with emotion, as he finished his story, Stewart stood and walked over to shake Karl's hand. "Thank you for seeing me today, Mr. Kessel, and Mrs. Kessel. I am forever in your son's debt and if there is anything I can ever do for you and your family, please call me. I certainly hope I have given you some comfort in hearing about Johnny and his life in the Philippines. I know few letters and information got through, and I just felt you deserved to know what a fine soldier and damn fine man he was. He told me once that you had a parting of the ways before he left home and he felt bad about it all. He changed. I never knew a better, more honorable man."

After Stewart Morrow drove off in his car, Karl went out to the barn to be by himself, while Katja went to her bed. She sat on the edge of the bed and then swung her feet onto the bed and laid back. She stared at the ceiling, thinking of the things Johnny's friend had told them. It was good to hear their son had done his best, that he was honored and appreciated by those he helped. But it didn't change the fact he wouldn't be coming home. His body was at the bottom of the China Sea, but now—she was sure his spirit was in heaven with the Lord. Katja had her memories—they were all she had now, memories of her dark-haired son.

Out in the barn, Karl thought especially about the final thing Morrow had said to them—something Johnny had told him. "Tragedy can bend or break you." It was something he had told each of his sons, a lesson for their lives; his Johnny had remembered it and it had helped when he needed it.

The Kessels grieved for their dead son, but they grieved separately as they lived their lives. Perhaps a tragedy in itself, they didn't turn to each other for comfort; they turned away. Karl dealt with the loss of his son by working longer hours in his fields and caring for his stock. Katja secluded herself in her house, not leaving to see or talk to others, even her family. At night she escaped reality by retreating to her bed and the gift of mind-erasing sleep the little bottle of sedatives gave her.

CHAPTER 17

When Love Dies

★ ★ ★ ★ ★

"Sometimes a thing can hurt too much for the heart and soul to bear, and deep inside something breaks, falls apart, dies, and there isn't any feeling left at all. Just cold, empty cold, like ice, or vacant space, or the darkest depths of the ocean floor. Sometimes the pain can be so large as to overwhelm even the ability to cry. Silence, taking advantage and exploiting the opportunity, surges into the newly created void, drowning, suffocating the last small vestiges of self until all that remains are bittersweet memories of the past." ~Author unknown

Following the memorial service for their soldier son, and the visit from his friend Stewart Morrow, Katja moved through her days like a zombie. It was just the two of them in the brick house now and she performed her chores robotically—cooked their meals and cleaned the house, all without emotion. She continued to feel like there was a cold stone inside her chest. She couldn't pass the photo of her son Johnny without stopping to stare at it. She didn't realize how often her index finger rose to trace the shape of his handsome face, as though she might actually feel him live. She had a difficult time wrapping her mind around the fact that her Johnny was dead. Katja had never experienced this kind of grief or pain; she knew it was eating her alive but she didn't care; she gave in to it and let it have its way. She simply stopped caring.

In Surtschin, when she was young, she had lived with zest and eagerly embraced her life. Now, she sat in solitude on the front porch and thought, *It's a burden lifted to admit I am ready for it all to be over. Sometimes I see myself like sand in a bottle; I am all run out, there is no more.*

The same questions rose to the surface of her mind again and again. *What is there to live for? What purpose do I have in this world? My other children are grown and living their own lives. My marriage—it hasn't been the same for Karl and me for a long time; I no longer have feelings of love left for my husband.*

She recognized with numb acceptance that Karl was submerged in his own world of farming and success, while she surrendered completely to grief and hopelessness. He seemed to be a constant source of irritation to her, especially when he acted young and virile. *He is old and dried up, just like me*, Katja thought. She shuffled into the living room and eased her body down into the familiar comfort of her easy chair as her eyes fell to the crocheted doilies she had pinned to the arms. *They don't even matter anymore; I take no pleasure or pride in any of it.*

After a few minutes, Katja went over to the dining room window. She gently pulled back the intricate Austrian lace curtains and peered out. Her eyes fell on the dried, empty stems sticking up in what had been her glorious, summer flower garden. Memories filled her mind. The once beautiful, fragrant flowers had been resplendent in their brief life. They brought so much pleasure to our eyes and their gift of fragrance especially in the warmth of a summer evening was gratifying. When their time was over, one by one they began to fade and wilt; the petals and leaves first shriveled and covered with brown spots as they released their attachment to the stem and fell to the ground. The gift of life was no more; it existed only in the memories of those who had witnessed the beauty and the glory.

Katja thought to herself, *My life feels like those flowers. There is no more life in them, no beauty, no purpose or reason to exist. Soon the snows and winds of winter will cover them as they lay down to sleep.*

Katja returned to her chair and laid back her head. *I find no reason for being, no reason to breathe, no reason to live in this house, or to exist on this earth. I'm an old woman, without purpose in this life. Oh, how I remember the days when I had reason to live, when I believed my whole life lay ahead–a wonderful life with Karl. When I arrived in America, I faced the life I was given and its harsh demands, even though it wasn't the life I dreamed of. I embraced the opportunities and blessings it had to offer as I was filled with thanksgiving. What has happened to me? Why do I no longer have the desire to go on living my life with Karl in this beautiful brick house? Now at this time in our lives, we should be reaping the harvest of everything we worked for. This house was my dream. Karl realized his dreams. We had success in America; we realized the American Dream. The responsibility of raising our family is over and now we are supposed to take the time to enjoy these years, to smell the roses, they say. But I have no joy left. I have no zest for life, no anticipation for tomorrow.*

Katja sat in her chair with her eyes closed and her hands folded in her lap, reviewing their life. She went over and over it all again in her mind, trying to make sense of this black weight.

Katja's gaze fell to her aging and gnarled hands. *These hands have worked so hard and done so much. They have caressed in tenderness, in the heat of love; they have scrubbed clothes in hot tubs of water until they were raw, worked in the fields until they dried and bled, prepared a million meals, and wiped the tears from my babies' faces. So often they were raised in anger and, at night, folded in prayer. Now, I sit here, looking at them and all I see are two hands, shriveled and gnarled with arthritis. I can't believe these are my hands, covered with wrinkles and brown spots; so ugly but with so many accomplishments and memories.*

All she wanted to do was to lie on her bed and close her eyes; she was so tired of—of living.

Katja knew in her heart that for years she subconsciously blamed Karl for ignoring her dreams. *It has always been about his dreams, what he wanted, when he wanted. I was expected to be at his beck and call, to be a good wife, to bear and care for his children, help with the brutal work in the fields, expected to give up everything I dreamed of—all for Karl! I did everything expected of me and more—and for what?*

Katja made her way down the front steps of her brick house as the sun sat low in the western sky. She walked slowly out into the north-facing yard. She paused near her cherished purple lilac bush, remembering how beautiful and fragrant it had been during the past spring. Katja walked a little further and turned her head to the right, to where the fields lay brown and bare. The crops had been harvested; the fields lay in well-earned rest until the spring sun warmed the soil and new life would begin again.

She gazed up at the elegant shapes of the cottonwood and elm trees that grew so tall in her yard, their graceful limbs now bare of golden leaves that had fallen to the ground in the last few weeks. The leaves had fulfilled their purpose and, when their time came, had released their hold and drifted slowly in anticipated death, to the waiting ground where they shriveled and died. It was the way things were; it was the circle of life.

Katja held these thoughts in her mind for a long time. I am like the leaves that fell from these trees. *My purpose is over; I don't need or want to keep on with this living, I want to drift slowly to the ground like the leaves. I want to see Mama and Papa, and now my son Johnny, too. I am so tired, so tired. Life is not easier, it is harder and I do not have the strength or the will for it.*

During the weeks and months following the ceremony for their son, Karl was aware of how his wife went about her household duties without showing emotion of any kind. It worried him, but he didn't know what to do except leave her alone. Eventually, one day, feeling he had endured enough of what he considered her moping, he approached her. "Katja, enough with this *way* you are. How long are you going to grieve for our lost son? What is wrong with you, do you want another son? Let's go into the bedroom and I will put the seed of another son into your belly." Frustrated and angry, he grabbed her by the arm and shuffled her across the kitchen toward their bedroom.

Katja's eyes opened wide with shock and revulsion; she resisted and pulled back. Karl hung on and in the process tore her dress off one shoulder. Backing away, Katja began to scream at him. "Leave me alone, you crazy old man! I do not want your touch; I do not want even to see your face anymore. You cannot put your seed into me; you cannot even perform the act. Are you crazy? We are both old. I have experienced my body torn apart, giving you eight children, Karl, EIGHT, and you think I want more? You make me sick with your dirty mind!"

Katja was losing control; she knew it and she didn't care. Adrenaline pumped through her aging body as she whirled to face her husband. "Karl— you want to know what is wrong with me? You really want to know? Now you listen—you listen for once in your life to what my words are! What IS wrong with me is that my life is over—O-V-E-R! The life *I wanted*, had *hope*d for, had *dreamed* of, it never happened. What I got in return is the life you wanted—this all is now no good; it is done."

Karl stared at her as she continued to yell at him, "If only I had realized at the time, but when I boarded the ship to come to America; I was leaving my good life, my happy life in Surtschin. I left it all to come to live with you in a godforsaken land, in a dirt house where I was nothing more than your slave and brood-sow, all so YOU could have your dream, *your* success!"

Katja walked away from her husband to stare out the window. Her disappointment and betrayal fueled her rage. "Remember when we became engaged? You said that I would never be sorry to become your wife. Well, Karl," she said as she turned to face him, "you were wrong—I am sorry, and I have been sorry for a long time!"

Karl's weathered cheeks were ashen with raw shock. "Katja, how can you say these things, after what our life together has produced? Eight children, a beautiful brick house that I promised to you, fine furniture, our own land, and a proud reputation! Is this not enough for you? What more is it you want from me?"

Katja again turned away from her husband, bowing her head as she spoke, "*Nein,* Karl, it is not about whether it all was enough for me. It is because I had to give too much of myself for you, for your dream!"

Katja's face was pallid and her breath came in great heaves as tears of resentment and disappointment rolled over her soft cheeks, "You don't understand this, Karl, because it is easier for you to deny it, not admit it. It was ALL for you; it was all—YOUR dream. When I learned of my parent's deaths, parts of me died, my dream of seeing them again was shattered. Johnny was taken from me. I can NOT bear this life with you any longer; it is filled with too many disappointments!"

Katja began to move toward her husband, her eyes wild, perspiration on her forehead, and her hair had come loose from the bun and hung in disarray. Her jaws were clenched tight, and her tiny hands balled into firm fists as she screamed, "Get out of this house and get away from me! You have brought nothing but unhappiness and drudgery to MY life! You used me, Karl, and now I am all used up!"

Stunned and not knowing what to say or do, Karl ran from the brick house. He hurried to the garage and got into his car and headed out of the lane, onto the highway. Sweat beaded up on Karl's forehead as he drove toward Lovell. "What in God's name have I done to my wife? I have never heard Katja talk like this in all my life. Have I really caused her to want to stop living?"

Questions raged through Karl's mind as he drove to Jake's house in Lovell. He didn't know what else to do, where else to go; maybe Jake and

Raisa would know what to do. All Karl knew was that he was at his wit's end with his wife. It was almost a year since the ceremony for Johnny. So much had happened. Nothing was good anymore and he simply could not understand why.

Pulling to a stop in front of his son's house, Karl got out of his car and walked quickly up the front walk. It was late, so he knocked softly on the front door. After a few moments, Jake opened the door, surprised to see his father standing there. "Why, Dad, what brings you over here this time of night? Do you know it's after ten?"

Forgetting at first why he was at his son's front door, Karl suddenly remembered and panicked. He grabbed Jake's pajama top and began to pull him out of the door, "Hurry, hurry, your mother has gone mad, and she won't stop screaming. She doesn't want to live. She doesn't want me anymore in her life!" A frantic sob burst out of Karl's quivering lips as he put his head into his hands.

"Dad, Dad, calm down and start at the beginning. What is wrong with Mama?"

Karl went over it all, leaving out the part about him trying to force Katja into the bedroom to make another son. "Get Raisa and come to the farm with me. Maybe you should call Louise and Bill to come, too."

Jake had a nagging suspicion he wasn't getting the whole story. He had never seen his father in this condition; he was usually so controlled and in command of every situation. Jake knew something was really wrong so he called his sister Louise and her husband Bill, asking them to meet him at the farm right away. Jake and Raisa threw on some clothes. "Come on, Raisa, you drive our car and I'll go with Dad in his car."

"Dad, I'm going to drive; you're in no condition to get back behind the wheel. Go on and get in the passenger's side."

A short time later, the five of them pulled into the Kessel yard and hurried into the house. They could not believe their eyes. Katja sat in the dark, in the middle of the hardwood floor of their dining room. Her dark eyes were red and swollen from crying; saliva drooled from the corner of her mouth. Her graying ebony hair had pulled loose from the tight, perfect bun and hung down around her contorted face. The top of her dress had been torn and hung from her shoulder, her apron was askew and one of her shoes was missing. The four of them stood frozen to the spot for a moment, shock paralyzing them.

Karl started to move toward his wife, but she began shrieking, "Get away; get away you crazy, dirty old man!"

Horrified, Jake asked, "What in the hell has happened, Dad? Why is she like this?"

Karl's eyes opened wide, and he responded, "How am I supposed to know why she is like this? She has gone crazy, telling me she doesn't want to see me anymore and she doesn't care about living. All this is because of Johnny dying. She just can't forget about it!"

Louise and Raisa gently touched Katja's shoulders; lifting her up, they led her to the bedroom. Louise got the sedatives out of the bathroom medicine closet and gave her mother one. Raisa dampened a washcloth and gently wiped Katja's flushed face.

For a moment Katja seemed to regain her rationale, but her eyes opened wide as she implored her daughter and daughter-in-law, "Please, take me home with you. I have to get away from that crazy man. I don't know who that man is, but he is crazy, *I know!* He wants to touch me; he wants to have another son to replace my Johnny. He can't even perform the act anymore and yet he thinks we can have another son. I don't understand him. I don't know him. I am old and used up, yet that man will not let me be. He is pawing at me day and night. I have not told anyone of this shameful thing; I cannot live another minute under the same roof with him." She began to weep softly into her bed sheet. "Pleeeeeease, take me to your house, Louise, so that I may have some peace. Please."

Louise and Raisa were alarmed by her vehement words and accusations, the pallor of her face, and the wildness in her dark eyes. Louise reached down and felt her mother's pulse; it was rapid and that was not good. Dr. Hartman had cautioned them about her stressed heart and she should not become overly agitated. They looked at each other and without words they knew they must do what she requested. They had to separate Karl and Katja.

Louise went to her mother's closet while Raisa got the suitcases. They packed Katja's clothes as she lay on her bed and drifted off in a light sleep as the sedative took effect.

Louise and Raisa went back out to the kitchen where their husbands were tending to Karl. Louise spoke first, "Jake, Raisa and I think Bill and I should take Mama back to our house to stay with us, for now anyway. She is unhappy here with Dad and says they cannot get along; he won't let her be. He is acting strange and Mama can't defend herself. Raisa and I think it is best to split them up or they might end up killing each other. We all know what the doctors have said about her heart."

Jake's eyes opened wide. "I don't understand. What is going on? What did she say to you to make you talk this way?"

Raisa spoke up quickly, "Jake, your mother does not want to live under the same roof with your dad. She says that he is at her day and night to make another son to replace Johnny. She needs some peace and quiet; she can't take much more."

Jake's eyes opened wide in disbelief. He wasn't the only one who was shocked at the circumstances and events of the night.

Jake addressed his father. "Dad, is this true, what Louise has said about you not leaving Mama alone, wanting to make another son? That is shameful, Dad! What in the hell is in your head that you are acting like this? You know she has a bad heart and yet you are pestering her to go into the bed with you? That is NOT right, Dad, not right; we are going to have to do something about it."

Karl did not react as he usually would have to a rebuke from his oldest son. He bowed his head in shame and replied, "I, I guess she should go to stay at Louise's house for now, until she gets better. I only wanted to help her and I thought she might want to have another son. You don't know what it has been like around here. She won't talk to me. She has no joy; she doesn't smile. I don't know what to do with that woman; she is making me crazy, too! So take her, take her to your house, Louise; maybe it will help her to think better!"

Jake looked at his sister and her husband. "We all know they haven't been getting along for a long time now. These arguments obviously have gotten worse since Johnny's death. We've all witnessed their loud fights or heard their angry voices through closed doors. Now it has come to this. We have to make a decision here, today. Louise and Bill, you go ahead and take Mama to stay with you. We can't leave Dad here in this house alone; he is not capable of taking care of himself, so Raisa and I will take Dad. I'll ask Eddie to look after the animals."

Raisa sat, unmoving, stunned; she looked at her husband, thinking this was all moving too fast. She realized what he proposed was probably the only solution to this difficult situation. But, to have her father-in-law live under her roof for the next few weeks or even months; she didn't know how it was all going to work out, but she had a pretty good idea. *I am going to be taking care of Karl while Jake goes off to work every day. Dear Lord, how am I going to do that?* Raisa could not imagine everything she was going to have to do. She would have preferred to take Katja and let Louise have her father. But Jake had spoken and it was decided the best thing for now was to split them up in the manner he suggested. Both Karl and Katja were too distressed to really understand what was being said and how it was going to change their future.

Bill picked up his mother-in-law's suitcases and carried them to the car while the women dressed Katja and walked her down the steps and out to the car. Karl just sat at the kitchen table with his hands in his lap; his sky-blue eyes were gray as they stared in disbelief at the oil-cloth covered table.

The decision the four of them made that day was supposed to be for "just a while." As it turned out, it was much longer. Jake and Louise soon discovered it simply was not possible to allow Karl and Katja to be in the same room. Karl would not leave his wife alone; it was just as she had described to them. He kept asking her, "Why don't you want to live with me? Why don't you want to kiss me? Why don't you want to sleep with me?"

Katja reacted to his awkward questions and demands with hysterical, wild-eyed emotion, which alarmed their grown children.

After a thorough medical examination, Dr. Hartman warned them again. "Katja's heart is not good and she should not be placed in situations that are stressful for her. I think it would be wise not to continue to limit their communication."

Eddie and his wife Mary moved into the brick farmhouse Karl had built for Katja and took over operation of the farm. Later, after it was certain that Karl would not be able to return to his farm, Eddie made arrangements to buy the farm from his father.

Katja settled into her new life with ease; she slept well at night and her appetite began improving little by little. She was relaxed and at peace, she seemed to enjoy her solitude and the time she devoted to her needlework.

Winter came into Lovell, wearing a heavy white coat that made it difficult for Louise to take her mother outdoors for a walk. Katja moved slower and became winded with little physical activity but she enjoyed the spacious safety of the front porch. In cooler weather Louise wrapped her with blankets and Katja nestled down into the rocking chair. She was content to sit quietly with her hands in her lap, looking at the cars as they drove up and down the street. She had no idea Karl lived right across the street or that he spent hours watching the house, waiting for her to come out.

At Jake and Raisa's house, Karl had taken the front spare bedroom to the right, off the living room. Soon after he moved in, Karl realized the living conditions were crowded and needed to be improved. "Jakob, I have been thinking maybe I could give you and Raisa some money to fix this house up better. I don't like it that I have to go outside to do my business in an outhouse."

Jake smiled and nodded his head in agreement. "Dad, it's almost like you read our minds. Raisa and I were talking about that the other night. We could put a nice bathroom between the bedrooms; some larger windows in the living room and dining room; we would also like to enlarge the kitchen so we can eat in there and Raisa would appreciate having a laundry porch as well."

Karl nodded his head and smiled. "*Ja*, Jakob, why don't you call somebody to come give us a price and we can get busy while the summer is here. I am also thinking I want you to get my good bedroom furniture at my farm and bring it here to my new bedroom."

Jake called a handyman the next day and by the end of August, they were able to enjoy their improved house. Karl was pleased with the remodel and how comfortable it made them all feel. "Raisa, I am thinking you need a nice dining room set in the new dining room so we can have the big family dinners there. Would you like to have the dining room set I bought for Katja after we moved into our new brick house? It is mine and I can do with it what I want. I would like to give it to you, for taking care of me. Would you like that?"

Raisa was hesitant at first; but, when Karl insisted, she accepted his offer with pleasure. "I'll take good care of it in case some day you may want it back."

Karl nodded his head and a smile lit up his blue eyes. "*Ja*, that is good; you are a good daughter-in-law to take such care of me, Raisa. *Ja*, you are the good girl you are!" Karl was adamant he and his wife, wherever she was, didn't need the furniture anymore. "After all," he declared, "I bought that furniture for Katja and for our brick house. Now, she has left the house and does not want to see me, so I will give away her furniture. No ME, no furniture!"

As the months past, it was just as Raisa had feared: much of Karl's care was left to her; because Jake was on shift work, his schedule was chaotic at best. When Karl became anxious, Raisa helped him out to the car and drove him around Lovell, even out to Kane where he liked to see the old homestead. Of course the drive included a stop at his farm outside of Lovell. He liked to make sure Eddie was doing a good job farming the place. As the weeks turned into months, Raisa was first to notice when Karl seemed easily confused, not always able to digest all that was happening in his life.

Raisa tried to explain to Jake what having his father in the house entailed. "Jake, it is like having a small child around again. I have to constantly keep track of him and what he is doing and where he is. He is so sneaky, always waiting until he thinks I'm not looking to do something he knows he isn't supposed to. Have you noticed the disgusting mess he makes every time he goes into our bathroom, which I have to clean up?"

Jake soon experienced the discomfort of sitting on a wet toilet seat in the middle of the night. "Damn it to hell—who pissed all over this toilet seat?" he shouted, fussed, and fumed as he wiped the dampness from his butt.

Raisa lay in their bed, listening to Jake's swearing as he cleaned the toilet seat. She pulled the white bedsheet over her head as she developed a bad case of the giggles. *Now, he knows firsthand, what I have told him for the last several months. We have a problem with his father, and that it is getting worse.*

Karl knew Katja was living right across the street and he asked almost daily to be allowed to visit; several times he attempted to cross the street by himself to see her. Fortunately he was usually spotted and convinced it was not a good idea to visit because Katja was ill and Dr. Hartman said she needed rest. Karl was frustrated. "How long is that woman going to need more rest?"

They were all thankful that Karl had a hard time keeping track of time and reality. For him, one day was beginning to slip into another. The family managed to keep Karl and Katja apart for months, but when Christmas time rolled around, Karl again asked to see his wife. Jake tried to redirect his father's thoughts. "Dad, Ma is still too ill to see you, but how would you like to send her some flowers for Christmas?"

"*Ja, ja*—I guess it would be a nice thing to do; do you think she would like to get flowers from me?" Jake ordered the flowers for his father and had them delivered across the street.

The night of December 28, Katja went to bed early. It was snowing lightly outside as she lay in her bed and looked at the beautiful flowers that Karl sent to her. She thought, *He probably is trying to get me to come back to him, to get me back into his bed. But I will not do that, ever again I do not want him to even touch me.*

Growing sleepy, she turned out the lamp on her nightstand and settled underneath the goose down quilt. She slept peacefully until near morning when she began to have terrible nightmares. She tossed and turned as Karl chased her, pawing at her, tearing her nightgown and pulling at her hair until it fell from its tight black bun. She hit him and slapped his face, but he only laughed and laughed. With his ice-blue eyes twinkling in merriment, he just kept coming after her. She kicked his knee but he would not stop. She tried to hide from him behind the drapery, but he found her and continued to chase her. She could not run and her feet felt like lead weights; it was becoming hard to breathe, she felt like someone was sitting on her chest—and he was gaining on her again. "Help me, help me," she screamed weakly, "Make him leave me alone, make him go away from me, *nein*, Karl, *nein*, go away from me now!"

Katja thought Karl had grabbed her by the shoulders and was shaking her; she was trembling with fear. All at once, Katja's ebony eyes flew open and she saw the face of her daughter Louise in the dim morning light. "Mother, Mother, wake up, you are having a bad dream! It's only a dream, please take a deep breath and try to rest. Bill is calling the doctor. Your pulse is high."

Bill hurried to the phone in the kitchen, as Louise remained by her mother's side. "Doc, this is Bill Franks; can you come by the house? Katja just had a disturbing nightmare and her pulse is extremely rapid. She doesn't look good doc; she doesn't look good at all."

A few moments later, Doctor Hartman pulled up in front of the Franks' house. He opened the door of his black Ford sedan, grabbed his medical bag, and rushed up the sidewalk to the front door. Dr. Hartman's immediate evaluation of Katja Kessel was that her situation was not good. She was pale and her pulse was indeed rapid, too rapid. He put his stethoscope to her chest and listened to her heart. Slowly, he removed the stethoscope, put it back into his black bag, and looked up at Louise and Bill, who were standing close to the bed. "Your mother has had another setback, Louise; I think it wise to put her into the hospital for a couple of days to keep an eye on her.

Doctor Hartman called an ambulance to take Katja to the hospital. It ran without the siren, but Jake saw it stop across the street when he opened his front door to get the morning milk. Not wanting to alert his father, he went back into his house where his wife was still sleeping. "Raisa, Raisa, shhh. I don't want to wake Dad, but something is going on across the street. I'm gonna run over and see why the ambulance is there."

Jake trotted across the street as the attendants were rolling the gurney to the waiting ambulance. "Louise, Bill, what happened?" Jake stopped dead in his tracks as he saw the pallor of his mother's face. Her ebony eyes were closed as a result of the injection the doctor had given her.

Doctor Hartman addressed Katja's son, "Jake, your mother had a bad fright from a nightmare and as we all know her heart is weak. I think a few days in the hospital will do her a lot of good. Give her a day or two to settle down and you can come to see her, but do NOT bring Karl; she gets too upset when she sees him."

Jake returned home and told Raisa what had happened to his mother. They said nothing to Karl because they knew he would fuss and argue to go to the hospital. As far as he knew, his wife was still across the street at Louise and Bill's house.

After a few days, Katja recovered enough to be released from the hospital and was allowed to return to her daughter's home. She had her good and bad days for several months. Katja was well aware she was weak; she knew she was not well and it was often hard for her to breathe.

As the days grew warmer near the end of May, Karl liked to sit on Jake and Raisa's front porch facing Louise and Bill's house across the street. He told Jake he wanted to sit out there because he liked the morning sun and he liked to watch the different cars go by on the busy street. He had a secret agenda—he sat out there hoping to catch a glimpse of Katja. Day after day he sat quietly on the porch, watching the cars drive by but also watching the house across the street.

The first week in June as Karl was sitting out on the front porch he noticed movement from around the corner of Louise's house across the street. Karl sat stone-still in the green metal spring porch chair. He smelled the sweet aroma of Jake's rose garden, drifting across the yard in the early summer heat. Karl narrowed his failing eyes to see who was moving around in Louise's front yard. He squinted harder as a slow, smile crinkled the loose skin around his ice-blue eyes—it was Katja, his Katja. She was walking slowly and carefully, looking at the pretty flowers in Louise's front garden.

Karl became excited sitting there, watching as his wife enjoyed the garden. He scooted his bottom to the front of the metal porch chair, almost tipping it over. He gripped the arms of the porch chair and edged forward a little further, trying to get a closer look. She still looked good; her dark hair was streaked with gray and pulled back, tight into the perfect bun she always wore at the back of her neck. She had on a pretty, dark-blue dress with a white collar, one he did not remember seeing before.

Katja was oblivious to the fact her husband was ogling her from across the street. She often forgot he lived over there at Jake and Raisa's house. In fact, she was happiest when she forgot about Karl Kessel altogether.

He worked himself into such a state that he was determined to smell the fragrance of her neck. Karl had it all figured out in his mind how they would go into the house and make love right over there, across the street! What Karl didn't know was his son Jake was around the side of his house, pruning the young roses.

Jake had also noticed his mother across the street, carefully walking in the yard, looking at the flowers. He knew his father was sitting on their front porch, in the metal spring chair. He also figured that his father had probably spotted her. Jake waited, bent over, pruned another rose bush, and another. He started to tend to another bush when he caught a slight motion out of the corner of his eye. His father was shuffling down the sidewalk. Karl had already gotten to the edge of the street before Jake reacted. He threw down the pruning tool and pursued a course straight toward his self-propelled father who, at this point, was halfway across the street.

A blue Ford sedan was coming fast down the street and almost hit the old man. The driver slammed on his brakes as he honked his horn and yelled out the window, but the old man seemed not to hear or to care. Karl only turned his head and looked back over his shoulder. He saw Jake running across the lawn after him and shifted into high gear, nobody was going to stop him from seeing his wife. Luckily, no more cars were coming down the busy street at that particular moment, because Karl Kessel was on a mission and was not paying any attention to traffic. He was *determined* to see his Katja, and he was going to embrace his wife and smell her sweet neck, and everything would be good again!

Karl made it to the sidewalk leading up to Louise's white-frame house before Katja looked up and saw him. She opened her eyes wide with recognition and the slight smile that had been on her mouth disappeared as she stopped what she was doing. "I know who that old man is. That man with the brown hat on his head and the icy-blue eyes—it's my husband. Go away, go away," she cried as she swatted the air. Katja turned and tried to get to the front step leading to Louise's house, all the time waving her hands, screaming for him to get away.

Louise heard the commotion and was out the front screen door just as Jake crossed the street. She hurried to her mother's side as her father shuffled almost nimbly up the sidewalk. "Dad, stop right there, can't you see that Mother does not want to see you? She just is not ready yet, Dad, you frighten her. Please stop and go back to Jake and Raisa's house."

Karl stopped and looked in astonishment at his daughter. "Who are you to tell me I can or can't talk to or even give a hug to my own wife? You are my daughter and you will not tell your papa what he can or can't do; now, get out of my way!" With that he continued making his way toward Louise and toward his wife.

Fortunately, at that moment Jake reached the threesome. He reached out and gently took hold of his father's arm. "Dad, Dad, stops this, listen to me for a minute."

Feeling someone grab his arm, Karl whirled and threw a pretty good punch for an old man. But, Jake was younger and quicker; besides, he was used to evading his father's punches. "Dad, for God's sake stop, get a hold of yourself. Can't you see you are scaring Ma?"

Karl paused, first he looked at Jake and then at Louise; finally he turned to Katja. Her head was buried on Louise's shoulder, sobbing softly as her little hands frantically clutched at her daughter's dress. Jake motioned for Louise to take their mother back into her house. Louise guided Katja by the arm as she led her slowly up the steps into the safety of her house.

Karl was completely bewildered. "Jakob, why can't I see my own wife? Why is she afraid of me? Why does she scream and tell me to go away? I am her husband and it is her duty to see me, to hug and kiss me. We, we love each other; we have been married a long time. What in the hell is wrong with that woman, huh? You tell me, what in the hell is wrong with her?"

Jake put his arm around his father's shoulders, turned him around, and slowly began to lead him back across the street to his house. As they walked, Jake explained, "Dad, I know it is hard for you to understand, but Dr. Hartman has told us she has a bad heart. She is just not herself and she needs rest. She becomes upset when she sees you because something has happened to her mind as well. You just have to be patient; try and understand she is not well. We will pray, Dad, pray that she gets better soon and, when she is well, you can see her."

Karl accepted his son's explanation and reluctantly walked back across the street, back to the house he now called home. Jake slapped his father affectionately on the back, "Hey, Dad, I have the day off tomorrow, how would you like to go fishing? We can get up early and drive up to the North Fork. The guys at work said the fishin' is pretty good up there. Would you like to do that, Dad, huh?"

Karl nodded his head in the affirmative as the two men reached the screen door and walked into the house. Karl had forgotten all about Katja—tomorrow, he was going fishing with his son!

Karl simply did not understand why NOW she was rejecting him—what did he do to deserve this treatment? In order to evade owning any part of the reason, Karl's mind began to wrap around itself, shutting out the world, its judgment and humiliation. The only way he could go on breathing without his Katja was to create another world in his mind where they would always be together.

Two weeks later, around two o'clock in the morning, the silence of the slumbering house was shattered by a loud crash that came from the front bedroom. Bill was out of bed before Louise, racing through the dark house to the front bedroom. He threw open the door to Katja's bedroom and saw the little pink porcelain lamp that had been on her nightstand, lying on the floor broken in pieces. Bill threw on the overhead light and to his horror, saw his mother-in-law in obvious peril. He yelled to his wife, "Louise, get to the phone and call for the ambulance, I think your mother has had a heart attack; tell them to hurry!"

Jake and Raisa both woke as they heard the scream of the ambulance's siren as it raced down the street and screech to a stop at his sister's house. Jake ran to the front window and saw the ambulance sitting outside the house across the street, "MA!" He hurried into their bedroom and pulled on his pants, grabbed a plaid shirt, his jacket, socks and shoes. "Raisa, please stay here with Dad in case he wakes up. It's Ma, they are taking her to the hospital again; I have to go with them, Raisa."

Raisa was wide awake now and standing in her pink chenille robe. "Of course, Jake, you go with Louise and Bill. Do you want me to call your brothers?"

Jake replied, "Thanks, honey, not yet, first let me find out how bad it is. I will call you and let you know if you can do anything else."

Jake ran out the back door, hopped into his new Mercury, and had it backing down the driveway before the screen door slammed shut. Raisa watched him go and bowed her head. *Dear Lord Jesus, please, if it is your will, keep Jake's mother safe, heal her heart, and give her the will to live. This I ask through Jesus sake. Thy will be done, oh Lord. Amen.*

Jake got to the hospital and met Louise and Bill in the waiting room. "Mom—how is she? Is she going to be okay?"

Bill put his arm around his brother-in-law's shoulder. "Jake, the doctors are working on her. Doc Hartman said he thinks she had a massive heart attack. They are going to try and do all they can. We just have to pray.

"I am going to call the rest of the family right now; they will want to be here," Jake said as he rose and headed for the pay phone. He also remembered he had promised to call his wife. Together, Katja's family sat in the waiting room, until the sun was slowly rising over the Big Horn Mountains in the east.

After a long, tense night, Doctors Hartman and Kraft came into the waiting room to address the Kessel family. "We have done all we can for your mother. Frankly speaking, we don't have much hope she will survive this heart attack. There is a lot of damage and she is not a young woman. She doesn't have the will to live; she is tired and obviously giving up."

Jake rubbed his face with both hands, trying to clear the cobwebs, "How long do you think she has, Doc? Is she awake?"

Dr. Kraft looked at the concerned people sitting there waiting for some positive word that their mother would live. "Your mother is in a coma and, frankly, we do not think she will come out of it."

Ralf looked at the rest of his family and said, "I think we should bring Dad over here to say goodbye to Mother. He would want to do that; she won't even know he is there. Do you think it would be okay, Doc, to bring our father over to the hospital to see his wife for the last time?"

The doctor nodded.

Jake went home, told Raisa what had happened, and she in turn helped him get his father out of bed, dressed, and in the car. As they were driving to the hospital, Jake told his father, "Dad, we are taking you to the Lovell hospital because Ma is there. She had a bad heart attack and she is in a coma. Dad, do you know what a coma is?"

Karl didn't respond for a moment as he concentrated on the words, "*Ja*, I know it means my Katja is deep asleep and she is sick; is that right?"

Jake cast his blue eyes to the side of the road briefly, as he drove down the town's main street toward the hospital. "*Ja*, Dad, that is what it means. She is sleeping deeply and she will not know we are there. You don't have to be afraid to wake her; she won't wake up."

When they arrived at the hospital, Jake and Ralf each took an arm of their aging father and guided him to the sterile room where their mother lay. When Karl recognized Katja in the hospital bed with the railings up on the sides, he shook loose of his sons and rushed to her.

Karl's ice-blue eyes opened wide in terror. "Oh, Katja, Katja, *mein leibschen*, Katja, please wake up. I am here now; I will take care of you." His hand rose to her face and with his index finger, traced over her eyes and slowly down her cheeks. Karl spoke softly and tenderly to his wife, "I want you to be awake, so I can look into your beautiful yes once again. I have always loved your eyes; they are dark like the night; so deep, so beautiful. It has been a long time that I told you this."

The adult Kessel children were engrossed in their own conversation about the condition of their mother and what the days ahead might hold. Karl ignored them as he continued to speak gently to his comatose wife. "I will be so happy when you are awake; you can give me a nice smile with your sweet mouth. Oh, my Katja, it is good that you are having a rest. Get better and tomorrow I will come back to see you." Karl reached again to stroke her face. "Your skin is so cold, Katja, so cold. Here, let me pull this blanket up to cover you and get you warm!"

Karl pulled the extra hospital blanket up and tucked it gently under her chin. Then, to his children's amazement, Karl nimbly hoisted himself up onto the hospital bed and curled up next to Katja, cradling her tenderly in his arms. He moved so his face was nestled in the soft folds of her sweet neck. He stroked her face and spoke softly, "There, my Katja, now we will get you warmed up—there, my girl!"

Louise took a protective step toward her mother, sputtering, "We can't, we can't allow this—Jake, do something, what if...?"

Jake looked at his younger sister with a smile, "For Pete's sake, Louise, it's all right, she won't wake up, she's in a coma. Dad has the right to comfort her and to say goodbye in his own way. Just leave him be for now; he needs to do this."

Karl lay next to his beloved wife, his faced buried in the fragrance of her neck—something he had long dreamed of doing. He laid next to her, undisturbed, for what seemed to his children like a long time. Finally, Jake walked over to the hospital bed and gently laid his hand on his father's shoulder. "Dad, I hate to bother you, but we need to let Ma get her rest. You can come back tomorrow. Come on now, here take my hand and let me help you down off that bed."

As Karl Kessel and his oldest son left the hospital room, the rest of his children could hear him say, "I have been wanting to do that for a long time, to smell the sweetness of your mother's neck, but she would not let me, until now." A contented and satisfied smile spread across Karl's face as he shuffled down the hospital hall and out to Jake's waiting car. Chris had offered to spend the day at the hospital and Ralf would take the night shift. They agreed that one of them would be at their mother's side until the end.

That evening as Jake was helping his father prepare for bed, he noticed Karl was especially agitated. With his bedclothes and bathrobe on, Karl paced the floor, often going out onto the porch and looking across the street at Louise's house then he moved to the bay window to look across the street. Finally Jake said, "Dad, remember that Ma isn't over at Louise's house now. She is in the hospital. We went to see her today—do you remember that, Dad?"

A blank look initially appeared on Karl's face until his son's words registered! "Oh, *Ja, ja*—I remember that. I need to go see her again—come on, Jake, you drive me."

He hurried back into his bedroom and came out with his hat on his head. "Okay, I am ready for you to take me to see *mein* Katja!" Karl was pushing the front screen door open before Jake reached him.

Jake put his arm around his father's thin shoulders to detain him. "Dad, look outside. It's dark and a bad storm is coming from the east. I will take you in the morning—first thing, I promise."

Father and son stood for a moment, looking out the door as the sky darkened and a cold wind tossed the weeping branches of the willow tree. A bolt of lighting crashed across the sky and thunder rattled the windows as Jake closed the front door against the storm. Another bolt of lightning shot to the earth, from the fast-moving, ominous storm clouds as the electric lights flickered. Jake turned to Raisa. "She's not going quietly!"

Inside the coma, Katja was at peace, she was floating, just floating away. She saw her papa at the foot of her bed. There was an aura surrounding his body. Katja had forgotten he was so tall; he looked young and handsome. Christian Mehll smiled at his firstborn daughter and his hand reached out for her. She heard his voice, "Katja, my daughter, I have come to take you home to be with Mama, your son Johnny, and me. We have been waiting for you my *leibschen*. Katja reached out to take her papa's hand; it was warm. Together, they walked toward the intense tunnel of light. Katharina Mehll Kessel knew no more of this earth, of its disappointments, of its joy, or its sorrow. She died on June 15 at the Lovell Hospital, without ever regaining consciousness.

The funeral for Katja was held on the 19th of June. She was seventy-one years old and had been married to Karl for fifty years. Pastor Siebert performed a beautiful funeral service. The church was filled with her favorite flowers and the members of her family, including her husband Karl and seven of her eight children. They gathered to celebrate her remarkable life.

She was buried in a cemetery near Lovell in a plot she and Karl had chosen, where they would lay next to each other for eternity. Her course on this earth was run; she had lived her life with love and the best intentions. Toward the end, she was not sure of many things, but she was sure of where she was going when she closed her eyes for the last time.

CHAPTER 18

In The End

★ ★ ★ ★ ★

"I have fought the good fight. I have finished the race. I have kept the faith." ~II Timothy 4:7

Karl sat in the passenger seat of Jake's Mercury as they drove to the cemetery for Katja's burial services; immediate family and friends gathered near the open grave. Jake went around to the right side of the car and opened the door, but Karl refused to get out. There were too many cars and too many people at the cemetery; Karl didn't like to be around crowds anymore, but he didn't know why.

As Karl sat in Jake's fancy car, he entertained himself by looking around the groomed lawns of the cemetery. The trees were fully leafed out now and the fragrant lilac bushes were rich in bloom. Lilacs reminded him of his wife. Katja had always loved lilacs.

Impatiently, Karl turned his body to the left, looking out the side window of the car, then back to the right across the driver's side. Finally, he turned around and inspected the backseat of the Mercury; to his surprise, nobody was there. Outside the car he could see a crowd of people standing together; some looked like they were crying. Karl didn't know most of the people and he couldn't remember why Jake brought him here.

Karl thought to himself, *I wonder where Katja is today; she should be here in Jake's car with me. Maybe she is still at Louise's house.* Karl rubbed his forehead as a different scenario slipped into his turbulent mind. *I think my Katja is in the hospital, I think I remember her in the hospital bed. Ja, I do! I will have to go see her tomorrow. Maybe I should take lilacs to her.*

Karl ran his hand over the dashboard of Jake's car. *This is a pretty nice car,* he thought, *maybe I will go to town tomorrow and buy one for myself. I can drive by and take Katja for a ride in my new car. She would like a fine car like this.* Karl glanced down at his suit. *I don't remember buying this suit.* He ran his hand over the rich tweed. *Maybe I will just keep this suit, it fits me pretty good.*

Karl's mind continued to ramble: *Where is everybody? I am ready to go home! I am going to have to fix up that old house before Katja will want to come and live there with me. I know she won't like the old adobe and log house. Those purple flowers are so pretty and there are so many. Maybe I will dig a well, so she will have running water. I think she will like that idea. Ja, that is what I will do for my sweet wife!*

Karl reached up to swat a fly buzzing on the front window of the Mercury. Panic began to take over as he reached for the handle of the door. He pulled it back, nothing. He pushed it forward; still the door would not open. In his frustration, Karl pulled the handle toward him and the door swung open, releasing him. With some effort, Karl lifted his right leg and, with the help of his hand, he pushed his sleepy leg the rest of the way out the car door. He pulled his left leg out so both feet were resting on the grass beside the road. He thought to himself, *I will go over to those people and tell them I am tired of being here and want to go home.*

Karl grabbed onto the car door with his left hand attempted to push his body up and off the seat of the car. He fell forward onto the grass, coming to rest on his hands and knees. Stunned, Karl remained on his knees for a moment, trying to figure out what had happened. Karl turned his head from side to side, angrily looking in vain for the person who might have knocked him down.

Out of the corner of his eye, Jake had been keeping watch on his father as he sat in the car. Jake closed his eyes for the pastor's final prayer. After AMEN, he opened his eyes and again, glanced at his car and couldn't see his father. Jake moved quietly but quickly toward the car, not wishing to disturb his family. He went around to the passenger side of the Mercury and stopped in his tracks, seeing the open door. He moved around the open door and stopped dead in his tracks, not believing what he saw.

"Dad, Dad! What happened? What in the hell do you think you are doing?

Here, let me help you get up; grab onto my arm, Dad. Come on now, Dad, help me here. Stand up."

With Jake tugging on his arm, Karl struggled to stand but his legs were still shaky from sitting in the car. "*Ja*, Jakob, I think I must be sick; I am weak in the legs here. Help me sit back in this nice car. You get in and drive me home, now. What are all of those people doing over there? Come now, Jakob, get in the car and drive me home. I want to take a little nap. *Ja*, that is what I want to do."

Jake started to walk back to the family who was gathered around his mother's grave. Karl didn't like that one bit. "I told Jakob I want to go home. Now where is that boy going?" Karl started to yell and hit his hand on the dashboard of the car. "Ja-KOB, come back here; I said I want to go home, NOW! *Kommen sie hier*," he demanded. "Come here Ja-KOB, Ja-KOB!"

Quickly, Jake ran back to his car. "Dad, please, will you relax? Stop yelling and hitting the dash; give me just a minute to tell the others that I have to take you home. Now hold on, I will be right back. Here, let's get your legs back inside the car and let me close the door. I will be just a minute, Dad, I promise."

Jake hurried back to where the family members were still gathered around the open grave site. He glanced at his mother's bronze coffin, as it rested on supports above the waiting hole. A shudder ran through him as he digested the entire scene. It was so hard to think of his mother down there, in that hole in the ground. Emotion welled up in his throat, constricting the muscles yet again. *Damn, my throat hurts from trying to keep these feelings contained. I thought I was through with the sadness and grief, but obviously I'm not.*

He quickly wiped the tears that clouded his blue eyes. Jake moved close to Raisa and whispered in her ear. "I think we better get Dad home; he's really disoriented and talking crazy."

Jake and Raisa said their goodbyes and walked quickly toward the car. Raisa sat the backseat, while Jake got in behind the wheel.

Not remembering anything that had happened five minutes ago, Karl was furious now. He turned to his son and demanded, "Jakob, where in the hell have you been? I have been waiting here for half the day. Now turn this car around and take me home, I want to go to my nice brick house!"

Jake turned to look at Raisa in the backseat, with a "see what I mean?" look on his face. When they pulled in the driveway beside Jake and Raisa's house, Karl looked at the stucco house, he turned to the house next door and back at his son. Now, agitated even more, he began to shout, "Ja-kob, damn it to hell, I want to go home. I don't know whose house this is, but it isn't mine!"

Jake said, "Raisa, you go ahead into the house, I want to talk to Dad for a minute." Jake turned to his father, who was still sitting on the passenger side. "Dad, listen to me. This is *my* house; you are staying here with Raisa and me for a while, until you feel better. You have not felt good lately and we are trying to help you. Do you remember that, Dad? When you are better I will take you to your house, okay? Now let's get out and go in, so you can take a long nap in the nice bedroom Raisa fixed up for you. You have your bedroom set here, which we brought from the farm. Do you remember that?"

Jake went around to the right side of the car and, opening the door, offered his father his arm. Together they walked to the back steps and into Jake's house.

This day was only the tip of the iceberg in the demise of Karl Kessel. There were many mornings when Karl woke and laid in his bed, looking around the room where he slept, not knowing where he was. Finally, partial realization dawned as he recognized the bedroom set he had bought many years ago in Billings. He remembered the glossy walnut wood of the bed, the dresser, and the bureau. It was his furniture, but why was it in this room? Whose house was this? Mornings seemed to be the worst, until Raisa got him to eat some breakfast. He always insisted on the same thing: two eggs fried and turned sunny-side up; two pieces of wheat toast with currant jelly; and a cup of black coffee. After eating breakfast, Karl liked to go out into the yard or just sit on the front porch, looking at the cars on the street and the people as they strolled up and down the sidewalk. Occasionally he looked across the street to see if he could spot Katja in the yard. But he didn't look for her as often anymore.

Jake and Raisa noticed many things about Karl as the months went by, things that were not normal. At the top of the list was his attitude about his wife's death. Karl had not grieved at the hospital, the funeral home, the church, or the cemetery where he had refused to stand with the rest of the family at her grave. He had taken her death in stride, or so it seemed. He didn't cry; he didn't seem to be upset.

Late one afternoon, Raisa was in the kitchen fixing dinner while Jake and his father were out on the porch having a smoke. "Dad, do you realize what has happened to Ma and where she is?"

Karl took a pull on his pipe and, without emotion and without looking at his son, he replied, "*Ja*, I know she is gone. She went and left me here all alone and I don't like it!" Karl had never been a matter-of-fact man, so this reaction of his was not what Jake had expected.

One day, after a particularly difficult morning with her father-in-law, Raisa called the doctor to discuss his emotional condition. "My father-in-law doesn't seem to have a grip with reality, Doctor. He walks around as though he is in a fog. He responds most of the time when we speak to him but, other than that, he just sits and stares into space. His gait is also different. He used to take quick purposeful steps, but now he only shuffles, not lifting his feet at all, and frequently he stumbles and falls."

Later that day, after Karl went to bed, Jake and Raisa were sitting out on their front porch in the green, metal spring chairs, enjoying the peace and cool of the summer evening.

Raisa said, "Jake, I called Dr. Hartman, today, to talk to him about the changes in your dad. He thinks we should bring him in for a complete checkup as soon as we can."

Jake took a long draw on his pipe and exhaled the fragrant smoke into the evening air. He looked across the street at his sister's house, where his mother had lived her last years. "*Ja*, Raisa, I know Dad has changed; I just don't like to think about it. I think what upsets me the most is the way he is dealing with Ma's death."

Raisa breathed in the familiar scent of her husband's pipe. She preferred the aromatic pipe to his Camel cigarettes. Jake knew he wasn't supposed to smoke and had tried to quit several times, but when he had to have a smoke, he elected to pick up his pipe. He kept a tin of Sen-Sen breath fresheners in his pocket, to munch after smoking.

"Jake, there are more situations, things I haven't mentioned before, that have happened around here when you are at work. Your dad is getting worse, Jake. I don't think I can take care of him much longer; I can't stand it! Every time he goes into the bathroom, I have to go in after him and clean the entire toilet with disinfectant cleanser. He can't seem to wipe without getting it all over the toilet seat and lid. What's worse, he is getting it on himself and his clothes, too. In fact, today, he came out of the bathroom with his pants down around his knees. Jake, I just can't do this much longer." Tears of anger and frustration welled up in Raisa's eyes as she continued, "And I am the one to clean up the shit. It's not fair, Jake, not one bit fair!"

Jake scuffed his feet on the painted wood floor of the porch. "Oh, Raisa, I know he's getting bad, but you are right; I don't have to take the brunt of his care. It is up to you and you are not even blood kin."

Raisa took a sip of her ice tea. "Jake, this morning your dad was sitting out here on the porch like he always does. I was busy cleaning the bathroom after his bath, and making the beds. I glanced out on the porch and he wasn't there. I dropped the dusting cloth and hurried out the front door, onto the porch and down the steps. I ran around the side of the house into the backyard, thinking perhaps he wandered back to sit under the willow trees. But he wasn't there. I called and called for him, there was no answer. I hurried back around to the front and looked up and down the street. I saw him shuffling down the sidewalk toward the church."

Raisa continued, "I ran after him, down the sidewalk, calling and calling for him to stop. He turned around once and looked at me, but kept going. When I finally caught up to him, I tried to take him by the arm. He threw my hand off his arm and yelled at me. 'Who are you? Get your hands off me, get away from me!'—Jake, the look in his eyes was frightening. He really didn't know who I was!"

Jake had stopped smoking and was listening intently to his wife. "What did you do?"

"Well, I calmly told him I was his daughter-in-law, Jake's wife, Raisa. He tipped his head to the side and looked at me with those ice-blue eyes. He said, 'Well, Raisa, you have on a pretty dress today, what are you doing out here in the street by yourself?' Then he took my hand, turned around and allowed me to take him home. I never found out where he was going; he probably didn't know himself!"

"I guess I hoped things would work themselves out and he would snap out of it, but it's pretty obvious he isn't getting better; in fact it sounds like he's worse. I'll make an appointment with the doctor and let's hope he can figure out what is going on with Dad."

Two weeks later, Jake was sitting in his chair in the living room, reading the evening paper when Karl shuffled into the room. He took one look at Jake sitting in the chair, and shouted, "Who the hell are you? Why are you sitting in my chair? Who are you? Who are you? Get out of my house!"

Jake was absolutely stunned. He was rooted to the spot, unbelieving as he stared at this man, his father, who apparently didn't recognize his own son. Raisa heard the commotion from the kitchen where she had been preparing supper. She hurried to the living room to see Karl tugging on Jake's shirt, trying to pull him out of the chair. "Who are you? Where am I? Whose house is this?"

Despite more frequent episodes like this one, Jake had still not scheduled a doctor's appointment for Karl, fearing what the doctor might say.

Raisa struggled on. She was adamant about cleaning the bathroom right after Karl used it. Her daughter, Beth, could see that taking care of her grandfather was wearing her mother out. It was making her a nervous wreck. Beth cornered Raisa in the kitchen while they were making Sunday supper. "Mom, you can't continue taking care of Grandpa like this; you are going to make yourself sick. Doesn't Dad see what is happening, and how hard you have to work to take care of his father? It's shocking to me, to see how he has deteriorated since the last time we were here. Have you taken him to the doctor for his yearly checkup?"

Raisa didn't say anything for a minute as tears welled up in her soft blue-gray eyes. She busied herself preparing the meal and replied, "Your dad does see the things that happen, and I have told him I don't think I can care for his father any longer. But we don't know what else we can do. It is expected we take care of our parents, as they once cared for us."

Beth was furious, "Then let Grandpa's children come and at least take turns caring for him. They are using you, Mom, and they need to experience just how hard it is getting to be. You aren't a nurse and that's what he needs. Grandpa isn't even your parent, yet they expect you to take care of him, to do things they don't want to do themselves. I am going to say something to Dad. I just can't stand by and watch you do this anymore, Mom. You are going to get sick; I can see it!"

At that moment, Jake walked into the kitchen for another cup of coffee. He smiled affectionately at his wife and daughter as he joked, "So what is all this quiet talking in here, aren't you women making my supper?"

"Dad, we were talking about Grandpa and the care he needs. Mom will keep trying to do it all until you tell her she doesn't have to take care of him or she ends up in the hospital. Why can't your brothers and sisters help with his care? Why does Mom have to do it all? She isn't even his daughter!"

Jake's face flushed red as he turned to face his daughter. "Beth, who do you think you are? This is none of your business. Your mother agreed to take care of my dad. Look at all the nice furniture he gave her, and the money he gives us each month to take care of him. What do you think we should do, just put him in one of those terrible homes for old people, to rot?"

Beth knew her father's quick temper affected her like this; she burst into tears. "No Dad, no, I am just so worried about Mom. She isn't as young and strong as she once was, either, and I don't want anything bad to happen to her. Why can't you see this?"

Jake turned and angrily left the kitchen, forgetting his cup of coffee. His daughter's words had hit a sore spot, even if he didn't want to admit it. He knew the day was coming when he and his family would have to make a decision about their father.

The rest of the evening went by without further upset. When the time came, Jake walked his daughter and her family to the door, as Raisa got Karl ready for bed. Beth took her father by the arm. "Dad, please try and work something out with Grandpa, or you will have to put Mom in the hospital. She is just about to collapse. I am really worried about her, Dad."

Jake nodded his head in agreement but didn't reply. Frankly, he knew what to do, he just had a hard time admitting it, and acting on it.

The next day was Jake's day off, so he made an appointment for his dad with Dr. Hartman. The doctor had an opening at three o'clock that afternoon. Jake loaded his father in the Mercury and drove him over to the doctor's office. After an extensive examination the doctor told Jake (out of his father's earshot) that his dad's heart was strong, but there was obvious evidence of serious mental deterioration, regression, and confusion. The doctor confirmed that Karl no longer had the ability to completely control his bladder or bowels. Jake had confided to the doctor that this particular problem was becoming almost impossible for Raisa to deal with, and he was beginning to worry for her health as well.

Doctor Hartman suggested that Jake and his family consider putting their father into the hospital for a few days for further tests. Jake didn't need to confer with his family. He made the decision to go ahead as the doctor suggested; they had to find out what was going on with him. "That's fine, Doc, let me take my dad back home first. Raisa can get a few of his things together and I will have him back here in the morning."

The doctor cocked his head to the side and looked at Jake over his wire-rimmed glasses. "Jake, we are equipped to take your father now, right now. All he is going to need is a hospital gown, and we have plenty of those. You can go back home and put together a few of the toiletries he might need. Other than that, we've got it covered. I don't see any sense in asking Raisa to do anything more at this stage."

Jake said, "Sure, Doc, that's fine with me if you think you and your nurses can handle him. How long do you think he will need to be in here?"

The doctor replied, "I don't know for sure, Jake, we just have to see what the tests show us. So, take him right down that hall and tell the nurse to admit him, and you can tell him goodbye."

Jake paused, "Well, Doc, I have a slight problem. You see, I promised Dad a drive in the car when I was bringing him over here. Do you think I could take him out for just an hour and bring him right back?"

Doc Hartman looked at him over his glasses and said, "Yes, of course."

So Jake and his father left the doctor's office in the Lovell Hospital and walked out to his Mercury coupe, parked at the curb. Karl perked up when he saw the shiny car. "Jakob, look at that fancy car. I wonder who owns this fine piece of machinery."

Jake looked at his father with emphatic sadness as he replied, "Dad, this is *my* car. Would you like to get in and we can take a spin around Lovell before we come back here?" His father didn't catch the "come back here" part, which was probably for the best.

"*Ja*, Jakob, I would like to take a ride in this nice automobile."

So, Jake drove his father around Lovell, out to the Great Western sugar beet factory, which Karl actually remembered building many years ago. "I like all the roses they have planted around the factory; they are pretty and they smell so good. Can you stop, Jakob, and let me pick one so I can smell it?"

Jake pulled the car to a stop and went around to the other side to open the passenger door for his father. Karl climbed out and Jake walked with him as he chose a red rose that he liked. "Here, Dad, let me cut it with my pocket knife; we don't want you getting a thorn in your finger."

Karl put the velvety red rose to his nose and inhaled deeply. "*Ja*, Jakob, it smells good." Karl had a happy smile on his face.

His wife was in the kitchen in her apron getting supper ready when Jake walked in the back door, alone. "Hi Raisa, well, Doc Hartman said he wanted to keep Dad in the hospital for about five days for observation and tests. I hated to leave him there. I expect he will give the nurses a bunch of trouble." He took his hat off and hung it on a hook in the laundry room.

"Do you think you could put a few of his things together in a small suitcase, when you have a few minutes? I can run it over to him tomorrow. Probably best to leave him be for tonight—we don't need to confuse him anymore than necessary."

This was all music to Raisa's ears—*five days without Karl underfoot!* In the morning, she handed the packed bag to her husband and set off by herself for a leisurely walk. That afternoon, she went to the beauty shop and had her hair washed and styled, something she had not had time to do for herself in the last several months.

Jake arrived at the hospital the next morning and the nurse directed him to his father's room. Jake didn't know what to expect from his father. In fact, they never knew for sure where Karl's mind was from one minute to the next. Jake opened the door to his father's room and found Karl sitting up in bed, eating breakfast. Jake approached his father, "Well, good morning, Dad, and how are you today?"

Karl just nodded and continued to eat.

"Dad, the doctors want to keep you here a few days to do some tests. The more you cooperate with them the sooner you can come home, do you understand?"

Karl took another bite of scrambled eggs and spoke with a mouth full of food, "I don't like how it smells in this place. My Katja's house doesn't smell like this place, and I don't like it."

Jake was amused, and he replied, "Dad, it is just some new cleaning stuff they use here. You don't like dirty houses, do you? I know you like to be in a clean house and besides, you won't be here that long so don't worry about it. I am sure after a while you won't even notice the smell. Hey, I see they have some pretty nurses here, too, which I think you probably like, *ja*, am I right?"

Almost as if on cue, a portly, older nurse opened the door to the hospital room and proceeded to check Karl's blood pressure. Karl looked at Jake; he looked at the nurse and back at his son. "Jakob, you said they had pretty nurses here; this one doesn't look so pretty—*nein!*"

Jake blushed with embarrassment. The nurse obviously didn't hear or didn't pay any attention to the elderly patient's comment. Jake was satisfied to see that his father was adjusting to his new situation, at least for the present, and so he said goodbye. "I will stop by later this evening to see you, Dad. Now, you co-operate with the doctor and nurses so they can do the tests they need, and you can come back home, okay?'

Doc Hartman caught Jake as he was leaving, "I think it would be a good idea if you skipped the visit this evening. It'll be best to allow your father to get settled in, and another visit might confuse him even further. Perhaps if you wait until tomorrow morning to visit again, it would be better."

Karl slept through the second night without issue but, when he woke the next morning, he didn't know where he was and was completely disoriented. Frantically he looked right, then left. He searched the room for something, anything familiar. He was used to seeing wallpaper in his bedroom and these walls were white, in fact everything was white, with no wallpaper. "This is not my own bedroom, or my own bed. This bed has iron railings on both sides, holding me in. I don't like to be held in my bed! So where the hell am I? Where?" Karl sat up in bed and grabbed the nearest thing he could throw, which happened to be a bed pan. Three nurses ran through the door as soon as they heard the bed pan hit the door.

"Mr. Kessel, Mr. Kessel, pleeeese do not throw things!" A pretty young nurse took hold of Karl's arm and murmured, "Here now, Mr. Kessel, let's just lay back and rest a bit. Your breakfast is coming soon. Would you like me to sit here with you until it comes?"

Karl took one look at the attractive nurse and decided her offer sounded like a good idea. The nurse fluffed his pillow and Karl relaxed back in his bed.

The third morning when Karl woke up, he was confused again. Then, he recalled he was in a hospital, "but WHY?" Suddenly, he had a flash of memory. *Katja died in a hospital, that's what they said. Did she die in this hospital? People always die in hospitals; they die here in this place. I DON'T want to be here!* Karl became extremely agitated. However, the nurses were aware of his morning confusion. A pert blond nurse opened the door to Karl's room and proceeded to talk to him, hoping to calm her patient before he started throwing things again.

After another day of tests, Karl's impatience grew with all of the poking and prodding, and the endless questions irritated him even further. Later that afternoon, he complained to the nurses that he was tired and wanted to take a nap. He waited a short while after they left his room, climbed out of bed; he put on his brown tweed hat, and retrieved his brown socks and shoes from the closet. He edged over to the door and, opening it a crack, peered into the hallway. Lucky for Karl, the emergency room alarm rang at that moment; all the nurses on the floor ran to the west end of the hospital to help. A sly smile spread across Karl's face; the coast was clear!

Raisa was busy in her kitchen that fall afternoon, canning dill pickles she had picked early that morning. As she was preparing to spoon the vinegar brine into the waiting mason jars, the phone rang. Raisa put down the canning ladle and reached for the telephone. "Hello," she said. The voice at the other end of the line asked if Jake Kessel was home. "Well, yes, he is, but he is sleeping; he's working the graveyard shift this week."

"Is this Mrs. Kessel?" Raisa replied that it was. "Mrs. Kessel, this is Del White down at the pool hall. I think you'd better wake up Jake. His father is down here in his hospital gown and brown hat. He wants me to give him a beer and credit to play poker. I thought I better call you first." Raisa could hear snickering in the background along with the crack of a pool queue hitting a ball.

Jake was sleeping soundly until Raisa shook his shoulder. When she told him what the owner of the Lovell Pool Hall said, Jake woke up real fast. He jumped out of bed, "Damn it to hell! How did he get out of that hospital without anybody seeing him?"

Raisa had to laugh. "I told you he was sneaky. He might wet his pants, but when he wants to do something, he still has some wits out there somewhere, that seem to kick in. He finds a way to do what he wants!"

Embarrassed, Jake Kessel walked into the Lovell Pool Hall to retrieve his father, the escapee from the Lovell Hospital. Karl was sitting at one of the tables, talking to a group of older men. He was still waiting on his beer, but instinctively knew *that* was probably not going to happen when he saw his son Jake approach his table. "Hi there, Jakob, pull up a chair, but go over there to the bar first and get me a cold beer. I have been here for hours and can't seem to get any service. After you get that beer, how about a hand or two of five-card stud?"

Jake did a quick mental survey and decided he wasn't quite sure how he was going to handle this situation. He didn't want to cause further embarrassment to his dad, who wasn't aware he had already caused embarrassment to himself when he walked into the pool hall with his hospital gown flapping in the wind! Jake looked into the faces of the older men who had been talking with Karl, men who had known him for a long time. One man nodded his head and gave a wink of his eye in acknowledgment to Jake. They all seemed to realize the situation with Karl Kessel and appeared willing to help Jake get his father back to the hospital without a fuss. But nobody had a current plan.

Del, the owner of the pool hall, walked up to the table where Karl was sitting. "Hey there, Karl, I just had a call from the hospital. They are missing you and want you back over there. I guess Doc Hartman isn't quite finished with the tests and stuff they are doing. Tell you what, my friend, when you get out of that place come on back here and you can have a beer on the house. We might even play a few hands of five-card stud. How does that sound?"

Karl's face lit up upon hearing the offer, "*Ja*, that sounds pretty good. I WILL be back!" He rose and followed Jake out of the pool hall and back to the hospital.

Karl's friends sat rooted to their chairs with their own thoughts until one of them spoke, "Damn, never thought Karl Kessel would end up like that. He was always one tough son of a gun. He did a lot of good for this town and was a darn good farmer, and a good man, too. It's a cryin' shame, just a cryin' shame!"

On the drive back, Jake reassured his father he would pick him up in a couple of days. Jake realized he could probably tell his father anything because, by tomorrow, or even in the next hour, he would forget it all anyway. Jake was more concerned about dealing with the situation at hand than he was with telling little stories to his father. As soon as he walked through the front door of the hospital, a pretty, young nurse took over from there, ushering Karl back to his room and into bed.

Doc Hartman was waiting for Jake out in the hall. "Jake, I think the next step is to get your brothers and sisters in here for a meeting. The test results have come back and they aren't good. We think your father is suffering from dementia, along with more serious mental difficulties we don't even understand completely.[5] In fact, he is going to get worse. There is no turning back or cure for this situation. I will be the first to tell you, Jake; your wife cannot be expected to care for your father any longer."

The next day, the Kessel family met at the doctor's office. Jake basically knew what the doctors were going to tell his family. Doc Hartman went over the tests in detail, then came the unexpected blow. "Doc Kraft and I agree that you should have your father committed to the Wyoming State Hospital (for the mentally ill) at Evanston. He needs to be in a lock-down facility because he's what is termed 'a runner.' It's probably the only facility that will admit him, considering all of his problems and his mobility."

Silence, dead silence. There was not a sound from the six people sitting in the doctor's office, as they tried to digest what the doctors had just told them. "Put their father in an insane asylum? Dear Lord, WHY? How could they, in all good faith and duty, do that to their father who was deteriorating before their eyes each day? This man who left his country, crossed an unknown ocean alone, traveled across the expansive American West in order to carve out a new life for himself and his young family. They were expected to commit him to an institution for the insane? Was he really insane? Or was he just old?"

Louise and Dottie began to cry openly and several brothers wiped tears from their eyes. Louise begged her older brothers, "Oh, Jake, Ralf, how can we do this? Isn't there some other way to take care of Dad? Do we have to deliver him to strangers and let them lock him up like an animal? He's harmless; he isn't going to hurt anyone."

Doctor Hartman added, "I know you might be thinking that perhaps you could put him in a nursing home. That solution is not going to work and it would only be temporary at best. Besides, chances are they won't take him because he would run away, as you well know. Unfortunately, the only solution available in the state is the institution in Evanston, which is a locked facility. Let us know what your decision is by tomorrow. Thanks for coming in today, and please know we are sure sorry we have had to deliver this kind of news."

The Kessels were shaken to the core. Never in their wildest dreams did they ever think this might happen; if they decided to take the doctor's advice; *who* would be the one to drive their father down to Evanston? When would they have to do this? There were so many questions, all with unpopular answers. The doctors explained that once he arrived at the institution, they were sure he would not come in contact with dangerous or crazed patients. Most likely, he would be in a separate ward with elderly patients just like him. He would have good days when he would participate in activities, etc., and he would have bad days when he would have to be sedated. Unfortunately, the bad days would increase in frequency as time passed. In the meantime, the doctors thought it best to try and keep Karl in the Lovell Hospital, until his transportation could be arranged.

Jake drove home in an utter daze. He sat with Raisa at their kitchen table and, over a cup of coffee; he tried to tell her what happened at the hospital, what the doctors had told them. The words seemed to stick in his throat and he had a hard time controlling his emotions. Raisa was not surprised at any of the things her husband told her. She had experienced the most direct, daily contact with Karl and she *knew* what he was capable of. She had witnessed his rapid decline firsthand.

The next few days were a blur for the Kessel family. On Sunday after church they all went over to Jake and Raisa's house to discuss their father. None of them wanted to be the one to drive their father to the state hospital. After an hour or so of talking, they still hadn't decided how they were going to get Karl down to Evanston. Jake didn't have much to say; he sat in his chair, head down with his hands clenched between his knees, listening to his brothers and sisters discuss the possibilities. Suddenly, he stood and taking a deep breath, said, "We can't ask somebody else to take care of our family problems; we need to do it ourselves. I am the oldest; it should be me. I will take Dad down to Evanston."

Several audible gasps could be heard from the family as Jake's offer registered. Raisa's head snapped up as she looked at her husband, her own eyes wide with shock and concern. Jake's face was pale and his jaw was clenched; his wife was the first to recognize the hurt and dread in his blue eyes.

After everybody left, Raisa embraced her husband. "Jake, let me go with you to Evanston. Please, Jake, I can help you. I am your wife and I want to be with you; it will make it easier if there are two of us. It will be a long drive back to Lovell, all by yourself." She had a mental list of reasons why she should be allowed to go with her husband. She knew how hard this was going to be.

"Raisa, I appreciate your offer to come with me, but I hope you understand this is something I have to do, alone. I know I'll need the quiet time to myself on the drive back to Lovell. I need time, honey, time to come to grips with this thing that I volunteered to do to my father."

In two days, Jake had made arrangements with his bosses to take a week off from work. They understood the situation and they all wished him the best, but none envied what the man was going to have to do.

The Lutheran pastor came to the Kessel house the night before Jake was scheduled to leave; he sat in their living room and talked to the two of them. "Jake and Raisa, I realize you and your whole family are suffering with the decision the doctors believe is best. I can only imagine how you must be feeling, but remember that our Lord Jesus Christ goes with you and with your father. We will ask for his guidance, for strength, and for his calming courage and peace."

Pastor Swartz reached over and took Jake's broad, work-hardened hands in his. "Jake, remember the verse in Deuteronomy, Chapter 31, Verse 6? Be strong and courageous. Do not be afraid or terrified because of them, for the Lord your God goes with you; He will never leave you nor forsake you!" The pastor continued, "God is with you, Jake, let Him help you. Allow Him to fill your heart and soul with courage and peace. Put your burden on Him; it's what He wants. God knows, Jake, we cannot face every life situation with a callous heart or conscience. He knows our every fear, our weakness, even our thoughts. You have to admit your dad to a place where none of us would ever want to be ourselves, and of course you feel responsible. But, Jake, remember this, God has given us doctors, nurses, and institutions where people are trained to take care of those who have special needs."

Jake could not control his seething emotions as the pastor's gentle and wise words loosened the hardened dam of emotions within him. Jake put his face into his hands and wept bitter tears. Raisa was also crying openly, wiping her eyes and nose with her white lace handkerchief.

Pastor Swartz spoke, "Let's join hands and pray." He bowed his own head as he began to speak, "Lord, we ask for strength and courage, for peace of mind and heart in the days ahead." He began, "Dear Lord God, hear our prayer this evening. We admit our own hopelessness and weakness especially in this our time of trial and trouble. Fill Jake and Raisa with your strength, goodness, courage, and peace as they face the days and weeks ahead. We know without you we are not capable of facing times and duties of strife and stress. It is not through our own strength and courage we are able to face this life, but only through the power of your son, Jesus Christ. May he grant us courage to endure and to overcome our trials. Lord, grant your servant, Jake, and his father, Karl Kessel, a safe journey. Fill their hearts with your love and peace. This we ask through Jesus Christ our Lord, Amen."

Jake and Raisa walked the pastor to the door. "Thank you, Pastor Swartz, for coming over tonight; both Raisa and I appreciate your prayer. Please keep us in your thoughts and prayers, especially during this coming week."

As Pastor Swartz turned to walk down the front steps, Jake asked, "Oh, and uh, Pastor, would you mind stopping by the hospital tonight and giving my father communion? It might be his last."

The pastor replied, "Of course, Jake, I think that's a good idea. Goodnight, and may God bestow upon you both, his blessings, and peace."

The next morning, as the sun came up over the Big Horn Mountains, Jake backed his sleek Mercury out of the driveway and headed over to the hospital. He parked the car out front, so Karl would see it when he walked out the front door. Jake found his father in his room, sitting in a chair already dressed, holding his brown tweed hat in his hands. He sat alone, quietly staring at the wall.

Karl looked up as Jake entered the room, but without expression or recognition. Jake thought to himself, *I just can't get used to seeing my dad act like this, even though the doctors have told me time and time again that his condition is going to get worse. This is bad enough, what is he going to be like as this illness progresses? It simply wounds my soul when he looks at me and all I see is that blank stare. Maybe it's for the best that we won't have to witness this deterioration firsthand; it might be a blessing to us that he will be far away."*

Jake stood in the doorway for a moment, looking at his father before he spoke. "Good morning, Dad, are you ready to go for a ride in my car?"

Karl's face lit up as he recognized his son's voice, then his face. "*Ja, ja,* let's get out of this place. I have been here for months and I want to get out of here. I have been sitting here for three days waiting for you to come. What took you so long? Let's go! Pick up my suitcase, Jake, come on!"

Jake stooped to pick up his father's small suitcase. When he looked up, Karl was already to the door. Jake moved quickly, taking his dad by the arm, they walked down the hall and out of the Lovell Hospital.

Karl had no clue where it was they were going; all he knew at the moment was—he was getting out of that place. He looked over at his son as they walked down the sidewalk, "*Ja, mein* Jakob came to take me out of this place. He is a good boy!"

In reality, Karl didn't remember he had lived at Jake and Raisa's house for the last five years. He had no idea it was April, or 1950, and he didn't realize he lived in America or that his wife Katja had died years before. As the two men walked slowly down the sidewalk toward the spot where Jake had parked the Mercury, his father stopped and pointed to the car. "OH, JAKOB, look at that fancy automobile! I wonder who owns that nice car."

Jake grinned; his dad said the same thing every time he saw this car, but at least he still liked nice cars. "This is MY car, Dad, do you like it?"

Karl smiled as he stroked the shiny green finish on the Mercury, "*Ja*, this is a good car. Where did you get the money to buy such an expensive car, huh?"

Jake smiled at his father, "I have a good job in the oil fields and it pays well." Jake took hold of his father's elbow to help him into the passenger's side of the car, and was shocked at how frail it felt. His father appeared to have lost weight and it was possible he had. *Probably gave those nurses a rough time about the food, bet a dollar on that one, I would!*

Jake closed the door and went around to the driver's side, opened the door and slid behind the wheel. He turned to his father and said cheerfully, "Dad, how would you like to take a trip, just the two of us?"

Surprised, Karl turned and looked at his oldest son, "Sure, Jakob, when do we leave? It isn't going to be too far, is it? I don't like going too far away anymore. He turned his head to look out the window of Jake's car; no I don't like to do that anymore!"

Jake smiled, "No, Dad, it's not too far; we can get there in a day. I've talked to Raisa and she said to tell you goodbye. How about we leave right now? Are you ready?"

Karl turned and looked blankly at him, "What do you mean by you talked to Raisa? Who *ist das Raisa*!"

Shaking his head in wonder, Jake cleared his throat and replied, "Raisa is my wife, Dad, she has taken care of you for the last few years, when you were living at my house. Do you remember her, now?"

Karl immediately became agitated, "NO, I do not know who it is you are talking about. You are not making any sense; I did not live at your house. I live in a good brick house on my fine farm. THAT is where I live!"

Jake didn't continue the conversation. He pointed the Mercury toward the highway heading south out of Lovell, past the east-end rose garden and away from the home, the family, and the dignified, respected life that had been Karl Kessels'.

Jake thought, *Dad lived the life he had dreamed about. I know he was proud of the successful life he carved out of the Wyoming dirt. It was an impressive accomplishment, realizing his lifelong dream. Now, oh dear Lord, now it is all fading into the distant horizon just like his mind.*

It was a long trip south to Thermopolis, then through the Wind River Mountains, where they hit a five-mile patch of icy road going through the canyon. Jake pulled over into a rest stop near the Boysen Dam on the south end of the canyon. "Let's get out a bit and stretch our legs, Dad. This is the dam they built down here to help get water to the area farmers, just like the Buffalo Bill Dam in the Big Horn Basin. Looks like they have plenty of water in here; it looks good!"

Karl just stood beside the car, one hand resting on the front fender. He turned his head and looked over the vast expanse of water, "What place is this you brought me to?" Taking a deep breath, Jake went through the whole explanation again, knowing full well he might have to repeat it in another five minutes.

They climbed back into the car and Jake looked at the map again before he turned onto the highway heading to Shoshoni, where they stopped for a hamburger at a little café. After lunch, they climbed back in the car; Jake turned right, heading west toward the mountains and up through Riverton and Lander.

Jake looked at the map again before they left Lander. He decided to take a cutoff road to Rawlins where they turned west again, into the afternoon sun, toward Rock Springs, Wyoming. It was getting close to suppertime when Jake pulled into a Rock Springs filling station for gas. Karl woke again sitting up in the seat; he looked around as though trying to figure out where he was.

As the attendant filled up his car, Jake came around to the passenger side and opened the door. Karl jumped, startled by the opening of the car door. "Damn it, are you trying to make me to fall out of this car? What are you doing, Jakob?"

Jake smiled, "Sorry, Dad, didn't mean to startle you; just wondered if you need to go to the bathroom?"

Karl started to move his legs. "My legs don't move so good. I don't know if I can walk. Is it far to the toilet?"

"No, Dad, it isn't far, you need to get out and stretch your legs; we gotta get them moving. Here hold on to my arm and we can just take it slow. That's right, put one foot in front of the other."

Karl looked up at his son, "You are a good boy, Jakob. *Ja*, that's right, you are a good boy to help your papa!"

Shocked by his father's statement, Jake smiled to himself and thought about how often, when he was growing up, he had wanted his father to say something like that to him. *Now, when it is so close to the end, I've finally heard those words come from my father's mouth. It feels good, it was worth waiting for, it sure was!*

They finished their business at the filling station, climbed back in the Mercury and headed west toward Green River. Karl's head fell forward in slumber again as soon as the car picked up speed. They arrived in Green River about forty minutes later and Jake pulled into a roadside diner. Turning off the engine, he turned to his sleeping father. "Dad, Dad. Wake up. Are you hungry? Would you like to get something to eat?"

Karl jerked, and his eyes opened wide as he squirmed up in the seat and looked around and yelled, "Where in the hell are we?"

He turned and faced Jake who was sitting behind the steering wheel. "Who are you? What am I doing in this car?"

Jake was never prepared for this kind of reaction. Even though he now understood the cause of it, it didn't make the acceptance any easier.

"Dad, it's me, your son, Jakob, remember? We are taking a little trip in my car. Are you hungry, Dad? Do you want to go into this diner and get some soup and maybe a piece of apple pie?"

Karl looked intently at Jake and replied, "*Ja*, sure I remember who you are, and I remember we are taking a trip. I don't want anymore to eat. We just stopped and ate, I am still full. You better not eat so much Jakob, you will get fat! When are we going to be there? I want to go to bed and sleep. I am getting tired."

Jake thought to himself as he put the car in reverse and backed out of the diner's parking lot, *I don't have the energy to argue with him. Probably be best to just keep going, it isn't much further to Evanston.*

He jerked the gear shift out of reverse and into first, pulling back onto the highway. Karl immediately fell back to sleep. *Just as well*, thought Jake, *I can't take much more of his erratic responses; it's making ME crazy!*

The closer they got to Evanston, the more anxious Jake became and could literally feel his body tensing up as each mile registered on the speedometer. EVANSTON–50 miles. EVANSTON–30 miles. EVANSTON–10 miles. *Ten more miles and I will be leaving my own father at an insane asylum.* Jake had never been inside one of those places, but he'd heard plenty of stories and it scared him to death. *How in God's name can I do this to my own father?*

Jake began to feel the panic rise in his throat, the closer they got to the small Wyoming town. Suddenly, he saw the glittering of the lights of the town in the distance. *How, dear God, how? Give me the strength and courage to do this. Why, oh why, did I ever agree to be the one to bring Dad down here?*

He could feel sweat bead up on his forehead as panic filled his throat. *I can't do it. I can't, I can't!* He considered turning around and taking his dad back to Lovell. Of course, that wasn't a realistic solution; he knew what Raisa and the doctors would say. There was no place there for him to be taken care of; that was the reality of it all.

Suddenly Jake experienced the ethereal sensation of a soft, soothing voice inside his own head, "Jake, you are doing the right thing. Do not despair, do not doubt. Do what you have to do, the Lord is with you. Remember this!"

Jake shuddered with a sigh somewhere between fear and relief, "I'm losing it, damn, now I am the one hearing voices!" Jake began to do the only thing he knew would help him at this point, he prayed, like he had never prayed before.

Soon, Jake spotted the closed, looming iron gates of the Wyoming State Hospital. He shifted down and slowed the car, rolling up to the impressive gates. He cranked the window down and heard the gravel crunch under the tires of his Mercury, as it rolled to a stop in front of the guard house.

A burly, middle-aged guard came to the window of the car. "Do you have business here, sir? Is there someone in particular you need to see?" The guard bent forward and was looking in the window as he spoke to Jake. He noticed the elderly, disheveled old man sleeping on the passenger's side.

As quietly as possible, Jake opened the car door and stepped out onto the gravel driveway. "How do you do? I am Jake Kessel. I think the doctors at the Lovell Hospital have called and made arrangements for my father, Karl Kessel, to be admitted tonight."

The guard walked back to his shack and checked his book and, returning, replied, "Yes, sir, I have you down in the log. It says here that you would be arriving this evening. Just drive on through these gates here and up to that main building up there, the one with the lights on. If you need some help getting the old fellow into the building, there will be people up there to help you. I will call now and let them know you are on the way. Have a good night, sir!"

As Jake drove through the gates, he thought, "RIGHT, have a good night! This is going to be the worst night of my life, if you want to know the truth."

Jake rolled to a stop in front of the main building and shifted into neutral then cut the engine. He reached up and turned out the headlights. Karl was still asleep in the seat beside Jake. Jake sat there a moment and turned his head to the right, letting his eyes fall on his father who was sleeping like a baby. Jake bowed his head as the bile rose in his throat and hot tears filled his blue eyes. *Well, here we are, this is the moment I have been dreading for weeks. Just get it over with Jake, get it DONE—NOW!*

He got out of the car and walked around to the passenger's side. "Dad, Dad, wake up, we are here. We are here, where you will spend the night."

Karl stirred and slowly opened his ice-blue eyes. Jake reached inside the car, easing his hand under his father's elbow. He pulled gently, but Karl sat stiff as a statue. He sat with his hands folded in his lap, staring straight ahead, not looking at his son, not looking at anything in particular. Jake tugged again and still no response. Karl sat in the car as though he was frozen to the spot. His legs were stiff, unmovable, and unresponsive.

Looking at his father, Jake thought, *It's almost like he knows! It's like he knows if he gets out of this car, that's IT!*

Jake stood for a few minutes, just looking at his father. He could almost hear what his dad would have said to him IF he were standing beside him. "Be a man, Jakob, men have to do things they don't like sometimes; that's the way it is, that's life. Quit being a child and do what you have to do. Are you capable of being a man, huh—are you, Jakob? Your family is counting on you to take care of this thing; let's see if you are strong or weak."

Jake tried to shake the thoughts from his head. *I don't want to remember how Dad used to treat me. That's not what this is all about; it isn't pay back, it isn't! I love my father, even though he treated me badly as a child, like a lot of fathers did back in those days. I still love this man and more than anything, I always wanted his love in return.*

"Dad, come on now, you can't sleep in the car; come on, Dad." Jake looked up at the building and saw people looking out of the windows. Soon, he heard footsteps coming down the sidewalk.

A male nurse affectionately patted Karl on the back, "Mr. Kessel, greetings! We have been expecting you. Your room is all ready, but before you retire for the evening, we have a nice hot slice of apple pie for you. If you would like, I think we can put a scoop of ice cream on it."

Well, Karl heard the last part about the pie and ice cream and it inspired his legs to move as he reached for Jake's arm, "*Ja, das ist gute!* I like *das* apple pie. *Wunderbar, wunderbar!*"

Jake watched in awe as his father began to speak the German words of his youth. He was like a child, a child who could be lured with the promise of something good to eat. Karl walked slowly, he was weak and tired from the long ride, but he had apple pie on his mind. He kept moving forward, putting one foot in front of the other, moving slowly toward the light in the doorway of the main building.

Nurses took Karl into the dining area, while Jake spoke with the man in charge of the institution. "We think it is best to say your goodbyes tonight. Your father is slightly disoriented and tired from the long trip. We have administered a sedative in his apple pie and he will not put up a fuss tonight. We will help him adjust with the aid of medicine for the first few days until he gets settled in. I assure you, our intent is to keep your father calm and happy. We do not want him to become agitated and anxious. It would not be good for him, or you."

"I don't know if the doctors in Lovell explained what we do for our patients here. We have daily activities for whoever is able and willing. Patients are allowed, even encouraged, to go out onto the fenced grounds on nice days to take in the sunshine and get a little exercise. We will be in touch with the doctors at the Lovell Hospital with weekly reports. If you have any questions, please contact them or call me directly. Here is my number. We don't encourage family visits for six weeks, in order to give the patient time to adjust to their new surroundings. We hope you understand and agree with these regulations."

The director led Jake into the dining area where his father sat at a table, devouring a large slice of apple pie topped with vanilla ice cream. "*Ja, Jakob, das ist gute pastete, das ist gute.* Would you like some, too?"

"Thanks anyway, Dad, I really don't have much of an appetite right now;

besides, Raisa doesn't like me to eat anybody's pie besides hers."

Karl finished his pie and stood. Jake walked up to his father, putting his arms around him he said. "Give me a hug goodnight, Dad; I will see you in the morning."

Karl appeared alarmed. "*Vhat* do you mean, say *guten nacht;* you *vill* see me in the morning. *Vhere* are you going?"

The director hurried to Jake's side and interceded, "Oh, *Herr* Kessel, your son will have his own room, he will see you soon now, say goodnight and come along and see the nice room we have prepared for you!"

Jake put his arms around the narrow shoulders of his aging father and hugged his fragile body for the last time. He held him close—this man who gave him life and took care of him when he was young. Jake needed to remember this moment for the rest of his life and so he hung onto his father until the old man pushed him away. "Okay, that is enough for the hugging, Jakob."

But it wasn't enough for Jake; he needed to spend another minute or two or three with his father. No, he wasn't ready to leave yet; when he did, it might be forever!

Jake threw his arm around his dad's thin shoulders, giving him a final little squeeze. "We had a good day didn't we, Dad? I love you, Dad, I love you very much, please remember that, please. Night, Dad, hope you have a good rest."

Karl's response was meager at best as the sedative began to take effect, he muttered, "*Ja*, Jakob, good night to you, too. Thank you for taking me to drive in your car!"

With that, his father was ushered down the long hallway to his assigned room. Jake stood there in the dining hall and watched as his father shuffled slowly after the director and nurse, much like he had followed his own mother when he was a child. The image of his father walking away from him would be etched in Jake's mind for the rest of his life.

Jake had hoped his dad would have told him he loved him, one last time. But, Karl Kessel rarely told anyone he loved them. Still, Jake knew his father did love him; he knew it in his heart. And of course, Karl Kessel didn't realize this could be the last time he would see his oldest son.

Jake turned, as if in a dream, feeling like he was outside his body, watching himself put one foot in front of the other. Watching himself as he walked out of the entrance and down the sidewalk, feeling the cool air of the Wyoming night wash over his face. Jake walked like he was automated, back to his waiting car.

Later, when he thought back on those last moments, Jake couldn't remember walking down the sidewalk or getting into his car. It was all so fuzzy, driving to the motel, checking in for the night, all like a bad dream. All he could remember of the rest of that night was that he didn't sleep. His guilt, his grief, the horror of what he had done, stayed close to him, tormenting him throughout the night, never releasing him to the sleep he so desperately needed. He wanted to escape into the oblivion of sleep, but his thoughts never left him, never gave him peace.

With a day's growth of beard, Jake rose from the tangle of bedclothes as first light seeped through the thin drapes that hung at the motel window. He stumbled into the bathroom, turned on the shower and stepped in. Jake let the hot water hit him square in the face, and he stood there for the longest time allowing, even willing the heat to relax him. Then, he purposely turned the faucet to cold. The frigid liquid slapped him in the face and shocked him into the new day. Jake finally turned the shower off and stepped out, toweled off, and threw on the same clothes he had worn the day before. "Oh, yeah, yesterday when I committed my own father to the insane asylum."

Jake was his own worst enemy. He was tormented by his conscious mind and knew he would be for a long time. Jake was quite sure his guilty conscience would remember and remind him of this day forever. He stood in front of the mirror, looking at his reflection. "Oh GOD, I've got to talk to someone; I can't get in my car and drive back home like this. I have to talk to—someone!" He grabbed a Yellow Pages phone book, turning the pages to "churches." *"Lutheran, Lutheran, the number, dial the number!"*

A man's voice answered the phone: "Peace Lutheran Church, Pastor Ralph Mercer speaking."

Jake held the phone in his hand, trying desperately to find the courage to speak to the pastor. "Ahhh, yeah ahhh, my name is Jake Kessel, I'm a member of St. John's Lutheran Church up in Lovell. I just got into Evanston last night. Last night, I, ahhh, I, last night I committed my father to the institution on the hill. I left him there." Jake couldn't go on, there didn't seem to be words to explain or justify what he had done.

Pastor Mercer recognized the man's pain and quickly responded, "Mr.

Kessel, would you," he paused, "would you like to stop by the parsonage and have a little breakfast with me? I could use your company this morning, too. My wife is away and I am all alone here. Come on over and we can have something to eat and talk for a spell."

Jake hesitated, "Sure, Pastor, I appreciate the invitation. Ah, where do you live?"

Jake got directions and drove over to Pastor Mercer's house. The pastor opened the door. He had a kind face and he extended his hand to Jake. As they shook hands, uncontrollable tears began to roll down Jake's face. Much to his horror, he completely fell apart and there was no stopping it as it spewed from his soul.

The pastor put his arm around Jake's shoulders and drew him into the warm kitchen, "Here, Jake, sit down here and have a cup of hot coffee. How do you like your eggs? I can't guarantee anything, but it will be hot and will probably fill your belly."

The pastor talked to Jake for about an hour. He read Psalm 23 to him, and that seemed to help. Jake knew he had to get back on the road, because he had a good day's drive before he was home again. Jake thanked the pastor and was assured the clergyman would look in on Karl Kessel, visiting him often and giving him communion when he could. Reassured and comforted, Jake fired up the Mercury, turned it around, and headed east out of Evanston.

Eight hours later, he pulled into Lovell. He drove the Mercury into his driveway and killed the motor, sitting silently inside the car for a few moments. The silence of the night roared in his ears and in his mind. He had spent the entire trip thinking about what both Lutheran pastors had told him, thinking about the last moments with his father. Of course his rational mind knew he had taken his father down the only road possible, there were no other choices. But that didn't stop his heart from hurting. Peace would take a long time to come to Jake Kessel and to his family; just as death would take its time claiming Karl Kessel who was alone, living in a world he didn't recognize.

Several weeks after Jake returned from Evanston, he and Raisa were sitting out on the front porch, relaxing in the cool of the summer evening breeze. Jake flipped through the daily paper while Raisa rocked steadily in her chair, working on her crocheting. Suddenly, Jake threw the newspaper in a heap onto the porch floor, got up, and walked to the porch railing. He reached over to the opposite shirt pocket and pulled out his pipe. Jake jammed the tobacco into the pipe's bowl, struck a match, and lit the pipe. Putting the pipe between his teeth, he took a long impatient draw, inhaling deeply. He blew the smoke out of his lungs with one long forceful breath and began to pace.

Raisa sat quietly in her chair, aware of her husband's discontent and, when she couldn't take it any longer, she said, "Jake, WHAT is it? Why are you so nervous tonight?"

Jake flashed a sideways glance, acknowledging her question, but electing not to answer. He wasn't ready to talk, not yet. He walked out onto the lawn and moved the hose to a dry spot, then returned to the porch. He took another pull on his pipe and sat down in the chair next to his wife. "You know, Raisa, I just can't get Dad off my mind. It's like he haunts me; I've been thinking a lot about his life and what it was like for him." Jake paused to inhale deeply from his pipe, giving his emotions a short reprieve. "All his life, Dad planned and worked, planned and worked harder. He always seemed so, so strong, so confident, so in control! He lived a hard life, but it was the life he wanted, he got the success that he came to America to find. NOW, at the end of that life, he is alone filled with humiliation and forced to endure a long, slow death, alone. I think about it all the time—his life must be without pride, without hope. All is lost to him, everything he worked for and dreamed of! He never even understood what happened to him and Ma, why she was like she was, in the end. He was totally confused by her, but he never stopped loving her, even after she rejected him." Jake walked to the edge of the porch and looked out into the yard, "It's all so damn unfair, so damn cruel!"

Raisa's eyes filled with tears as she felt her husband's grief and frustration. She rose to her feet and, closing the distance between them, drew him into her arms and they stood there on the porch, holding each other. Finally she released him and pushed, keeping her hands on his muscular upper arms. "Jake, I don't think all is lost to your father. Karl didn't lose his dreams and success. He realized them and lived them. They are his legacy. I know much of what you say is true, but we have to remember what the doctors have told us about your dad's mental condition. He doesn't realize all these things are happening to him, his mind has gone back to the past where he is happy. It's only us, his family who realizes what is happening to him now. It's God's way of protecting him, of giving him peace until his body is ready to stop living, too. Try to think of it like that and it might help, don't you think?"

The reports came often from the institution in Evanston. At first, they reported that Karl Kessel, or patient # 58473, had adjusted as well as could be expected. He had his good days when he liked to talk about his past, his home in Surtschin, Yugoslavia, and his travel to America with his friend's ticket. Often he talked about the hardships of building a new, a free life in this country. They said he talked about his wife Katja and their marriage. He was so proud of his eight children, and often spoke especially of his oldest son, Jakob. Karl spoke of his son Johnny who died such an unexpected death in World War II, and how his son's death affected his marriage and later, his life. When he was lucid, Karl told them his one regret in life, was when he was denied citizenship in the United States of America. He never became a citizen of the country he loved so much, the country that gave him freedom and opportunity to be all he could be. He was denied, because he came to this country illegally on another man's ticket.

Over the months and the next two years, several of Karl's children made the trip down to Evanston to visit him, but as the months went by, his health deteriorated to the point that he didn't know who they were. Reports from the doctors at the asylum became increasingly grave. Karl continued to run away, he hid, he lashed out at the staff, he was completely incontinent, and he was not eating. Toward the end, Karl rolled his food around in his mouth, not swallowing. He was more belligerent, forcing the staff to administer additional sedatives to calm him. The reports advised the family that Karl stopped talking, followed soon by the inability to walk.

On a bitter cold February day, just sixteen days after Jake and Raisa celebrated their thirty-fourth wedding anniversary, the phone rang at their Lovell home. Raisa answered it on the second ring. The voice on the other end asked for Jakob Kessel. Alarmed, Raisa replied, "Just a minute, please, I have to go out to the garage where he's working on the car. Just a moment, I will get him, hold on."

"Jake, you have a phone call. They didn't say who it was, but its long distance and they sound serious."

Jake brushed his greasy hands off on his work pants and hurried up the steps into the house. He picked up the phone, not knowing what to expect. "Hello, this is Jake Kessel."

The voice on the other end was sharply formal, "Mr. Kessel, this is Marshall Grant, director of the Wyoming State Hospital in Evanston." A cold chill ran down Jake's spine. "I regret to inform you that your father, Karl Kessel, passed away this morning, at five-fifteen a.m. Do you wish the body to be shipped back to Lovell, or do you wish us to perform the burial services here?"

Stunned, Jake could hardly think, after a couple moments he regained his composure and replied, "Uh, thank you, Mr. Grant, for the phone call. I think my family and I would prefer that our father be shipped back to Lovell for burial in the family plot next to his wife. Can this be done immediately?"

"Of course, of course, but the embalming will have to be done here, before shipment. I expect the deceased will be ready for shipment later this afternoon, arriving in Lovell on the train in approximately two days. We will send him directly to the local mortuary, is that satisfactory?"

Jake took a deep breath, "Yes, Mr. Grant that would be fine. I will make the necessary arrangements here in Lovell for his funeral. Thank you again for all you did for my father, Mr. Grant, thank you."

Jake hung the phone back on its cradle and turned to Raisa who was standing nearby, his face was ashen. "It's Dad, he's gone—he died this morning about five o'clock. It's finally over for him, Raisa; it's over. I need to call the others and of course the pastor to arrange the funeral."

Raisa walked over to her husband and put her arms around him, holding close to her.

"Jake, your father's at peace now, there is no more suffering. Come, come here into the kitchen, sit down and have a cup of coffee and a piece of *Yagada* to calm you down so you can think good, and we can talk about the funeral."

Later that morning Jake made the phone calls to his family, to the pastor, and to the funeral home. The funeral was scheduled for February 25, at St. John's Lutheran Church. Pastor Swartz gave a comforting sermon, talking about all the good things Karl had done for the town of Lovell and the years he had served the church. He spoke about Karl and Katja and the eight children they raised and brought to the Lord. The pastor closed the service for Karl with a passage from the Bible: "Blessed are they that mourn, for they shall be comforted." (Matthew 5:4)

It was a balmy winter day, unusual for that time of year in Lovell. After the funeral services, friends and family gathered in the basement of the church to express their sadness, to speak of Karl Kessel and to have a bite to eat. Later, the immediate family left to go to Jake and Raisa's home. The large family that Karl and Katja Kessel created—their sons, daughters, and grandchildren—were all recipients of the opportunity of freedom to live their lives as they wished. They were free, they had opportunities to succeed. They were all prosperous, and happy because of the sacrifices and the decision Karl and Katja made to immigrate to America, all because of—*the ticket!*

ACKNOWLEDGEMENTS

★ ★ ★ ★ ★

This story, this book, began to take shape in my mind years before I put pen to paper. It took a village to produce the final product. I am indebted to all who encouraged me to persevere with my dream. Primarily, I am grateful to my husband Michael, my rock, my unrelenting advocate. There were no complaints as he made numerous "reservations" for dinner. Thank you to my four sons—Mark, Todd, Brett, and Erick; as well as family and friends who read and critiqued my numerous drafts: Emily Rapp, Janie Lewis, Judy Viola, Bette Sailors, Julia Cheatham, and sisters Laura Gwinn and Linda Woods. My success is dedicated to my esteemed middle school teacher, Cleo Riley. I am eternally indebted to my mother, Beata Wamhoff, for her enduring patience with my endless questions about the "old country." A special thanks to long-time friend and author, Tom Davis, for his knowledge, guidance, and historical expertise. Lastly, to my German cousins—Siegfried and Sylvia Mell and the Jurgen Laubin family, especially daughter Karen; you enlightened and enabled this story with the priceless family history you gave me. You were instrumental in breathing credibility and substance into this novel.

My gratitude to everyone at Langdon Street Press for their guidance, patience, and encouragement—bravo! You helped to open the doors of opportunity, making it possible for me to claim my place in the sun and tell this story.

This book is dedicated to the afflicted, hope-filled, and courageous people who immigrated to this country to find a better life, a fresh beginning, and desired opportunity. Also, my heartfelt gratitude to all who wore and wear the uniform, serving this amazing country we call home, especially those who didn't return—who gave their lives that we may live in freedom.

ENDNOTES

★ ★ ★ ★ ★

1. For generations, Pryor Mountain has been home to large herds of wild Spanish mustang horses, which roam the cedar-covered slopes, wind-washed gullies, and flash flood washes. They are federally protected and a beautiful sight to behold.

2. A former Indian hunting ground described as inhospitable in 1906, the Big Horn Basin is one of the driest regions found in North America. The annual mean level of precipitation in the Basin is eight to twelve inches; winters are cold and summers hot. The Basin has a relatively cool, dry climate because of the elevation—with a mean temperature of ninety degrees in the summer months to a mean temperature of zero in January.

The grassy hills of the Big Horn Basin first attracted cattle ranchers, followed by sheepherders, and finally homesteaders. The Basin is the warmest area in the state where principal irrigated crops include sugar beets, wheat, oats, alfalfa, corn, and barley. Because of the semi-arid conditions, large dams were constructed to catch mountain snow melt and channel water through a series of canals to irrigate the farmland. Late freezes are characteristic in the spring with early freezes in the fall months, which result in a short growing season that averages 130 days. Occasional tornadoes touch down, but the most destructive summer storm comes from hail, with damage primarily to crops. During the winter months there may be a two-day blizzard followed by down slope, melting Chinook winds, and brilliant sunshine.

3. Part of the 1803 Louisiana Purchase, the land now comprising the state of Wyoming is 97,809 square miles, and ranks ninth in size. Wyoming Territory was recognized in 1869. On July 10, 1890, Wyoming entered the Union as

the 44th state; it was the first state where women won the right to vote, and became known as "The Equality State." In 1906, five percent of Wyoming's land was owned by the federal government, leaving ninety-five percent of the vast land open for settlement.

Home to Grand Teton and Yellowstone National Parks, Wyoming's numerous mountain ranges to the west and vast plains to the east are split by the Continental Divide. Wyoming contains rich grazing range for 1.5 million cattle and a large number of sheep; this state also ranks second largest in uranium deposits in the nation. The mean elevation of 6,700 feet is second only to Colorado.

The Shoshone River which originates in the Rocky Mountains to the west runs through the northern part of the Big Horn Basin and flows north to the Missouri River.

4. Kane remained a small town in Wyoming until 1966, but now rests under the collected waters of the Yellowtail Dam (built in 1966).

5. Karl most likely died of Alzheimer's disease, which had been researched and was recognized in larger, metropolitan hospital facilities. The small-town physicians who treated Karl never addressed his condition as such. Even if they had knowledge of the disease, as tragic as it was, there were no other facilities equipped to care for Karl—except where the family sent him.

ABOUT THE AUTHOR

★ ★ ★ ★ ★

Karen Wamhoff Schutte was born and raised in the Big Horn Basin of Wyoming on a farm homesteaded by her German-Lutheran grandparents. The oldest of four daughters, Karen attended a two-room school for the first eight years of her education, then traveled by school bus to attend high school in Greybull. She studied at the University of Wyoming for two years, married, and raised four sons.

After earning a correspondence degree from the New York School of Interior Design, she established *Interiors by Karen* in 1980, which she owned and operated successfully for the next twenty-five years. In 1984, Karen returned to the University of Wyoming, graduating in 1987 with a Bachelor of Science (B.S.) degree in interior design. She then applied and was accepted into the American Society of Interior Designers as an allied member.

Karen recently made the decision to reinvent her life and pursue a  longtime passion of writing. *The Ticket* is her first historical fiction novel. She remembers her own tender moments with Karl Kessel near the end of his life, and has dim memories of her diminutive great-grandmother, Katja.

Karen and her husband Mike live in Fort Collins, Colorado.